The Art of Revision in the Short Stories of V. S. Pritchett and William Trevor

Permissions

The author and publisher are grateful to the following copyright holders or their agents for authorizing extracts and quotations from copyrighted materials that appear in this book. All quotations from the unpublished and published material of V. S. Pritchett, and the author's computer-drawn transcription of the "You Make Your Own Life" typescript are reproduced here by permission of PFD (www.pfd.co.uk) on behalf of the Estate of V. S. Pritchett © V. S. Pritchett; permission to quote from the published work of William Trevor was granted by Peters, Fraser, & Dunlop on behalf of the author. The BBC copyright material appears with the permission of the BBC Written Archives Centre. Extracts from Gerald Brenan's letters are reproduced by permission of the Estate of Gerald Brenan c/o Margaret Hanbury, 27 Walcot Square, London SE11 4UB © Gerald Brenan, all rights reserved; those from the letters of John Lehmann with the permission of the John Lehmann Literary Estate; those from the letters of Roger Angell by permission of Mr. Angell. All quotations from the Pritchett-Angell *New Yorker* correspondence appear courtesy of the New Yorker/The Condé Nast Publications Inc. (www.newyorker.com). Permission was also granted by the New York Public Library for use of this material in the *New Yorker* Records, Manuscripts and Archives Division and in the Berg Collection of English and American Literature, the NYPL, Astor, Lenox and Tilden Foundations and for all quotations from the Berg Collection's Pritchett Papers. Permission was granted by the Harry Ransom Humanities Research Center, University of Texas, Austin, for quotations from Pritchett's unpublished material in its Pritchett Collection; those from John Lehmann and Gerald Brenan's letters to Pritchett; and for the publication of the author's computer-drawn transcription of Pritchett's "You Make Your Own Life" typescript. Chapter 4, "V. S. Pritchett's Ministering Angell," first appeared in a different form in the *Sewanee Review*, vol. 112, no. 2, Spring 2004 © Jonathan Bloom. Chapter 2 first appeared in a somewhat different form in the *Journal of the Short Story in English/ Les Cahiers de la Nouvelle*, no. 45, Autumn 2005.

The Art of Revision in the Short Stories of V. S. Pritchett and William Trevor

Jonathan Bloom

The Art of Revision in the Short Stories of V. S. Pritchett and William Trevor
Copyright © Jonathan Bloom, 2006.
All rights reserved. No part of this book may be used or reproduced in any manner whatsoever without written permission except in the case of brief quotations embodied in critical articles or reviews.

First published in 2006 by
PALGRAVE MACMILLAN™
175 Fifth Avenue, New York, N.Y. 10010 and
Houndmills, Basingstoke, Hampshire, England RG21 6XS.
Companies and representatives throughout the world.

PALGRAVE MACMILLAN is the global academic imprint of the Palgrave Macmillan division of St. Martin's Press, LLC and of Palgrave Macmillan Ltd. Macmillan® is a registered trademark in the United States, United Kingdom and other countries. Palgrave is a registered trademark in the European Union and other countries.

ISBN-13: 978-1-4039-7325-2
ISBN-10: 1-4039-7325-3

Library of Congress Cataloging-in-Publication Data

Bloom, Jonathan, 1960-
  The art of revision in the short stories of V.S. Pritchett and William Trevor / by Jonathan Bloom.
    p. cm.
  Includes bibliographical references and index.
  ISBN-13: 978-1-4039-7325-2 (alk. paper)
  ISBN-10: 1-4039-7325-3 (alk. paper)
  1. Pritchett, V. S. (Victor Sawdon), 1900-1997--Criticism, Textual. 2. Pritchett, V. S. (Victor Sawdon), 1900-1997--Technique. 3. Trevor, William, 1928- --Criticism, Textual. 4. Trevor, William, 1928- --Technique. 5. Short stories, English--Criticism, Textual. 6. Short stories, English--Themes, motives. 7. Short stories, English--Irish authors--Criticism, Textual. 8. Short stories, English--Irish authors--Themes, motives. I. Title.

PR6031.R7Z63 2006
823'.912--dc22   2006043419

A catalogue record for this book is available from the British Library.

Design by Macmillan India Ltd.

First edition: November 2006

10 9 8 7 6 5 4 3 2 1

Printed in the United States of America.

Contents

Preface		ix
Acknowledgments		xi
Abbreviations and References		xv
1	Fanfare for the Common Man	1
2	Revision as Transformation: The Making and Remaking of V. S. Pritchett's "You Make Your Own Life"	17
3	William Trevor's "Distillation of an Essence": From "Meeting Mrs. Faraday" to "Cocktails at Doney's"	35
4	V. S. Pritchett's Ministering Angell	65
5	Real Incursions in Fictive Worlds	93
6	Living on the Other Side of the Frontier	119
7	The Roads Taken Make All the Difference: Comic Spirit and Tragic Comedian	151
8	English Fantasy and Irish Entrapment	179
Appendix		199
Notes		211
Bibliography		235
Index		245

Preface

The modern British and Irish short story from before the outbreak of the Second World War to the present is the neglected genre of the period. This book is a close examination of two of the most important modern practitioners working in England, V. S. Pritchett, the Englishman, and William Trevor, the Anglo-Irishman, who, despite their admirable contributions as novelists and men of letters, are most likely to be remembered for their short stories.

Although separated by a generation (Pritchett was born in 1900 and Trevor in 1928), they are ideal subjects for comparison. Profoundly influenced by the instability of their peripatetic childhoods, they both see themselves as outsiders living on the periphery of society. Yet instead of distancing themselves from their subjects, their constant exposure to different schools, neighborhoods, and social situations heightened their interest in human nature at large and later helped them to write objectively yet sympathetically about the foibles, eccentricities, meanness, and heroism of ordinary human beings. Raised in unliterary families where "there was just ordinary life going on," they avoided involvement in literary groups—or groups of any kind—throughout their lives, drawn instead to the lives of locals. Inspired by such writers as James Joyce and Liam O'Flaherty, Pritchett began writing short stories in Ireland while working as a journalist for the *Christian Science Monitor*. By a curious chiasmus, the Anglo-Irish Trevor, a devotee of Pritchett's short fiction, began writing "English" short stories in England while working as a copywriter in London. Among the most prolific short-story writers of the past century with over ten collections each, they work with similar themes and characters, are astute critics of the genre, and admire each other's work. Masters at incorporating the telling colloquial phrase, they fashion stories in which, from their earliest drafts, characters take precedence and dialogue creates plot. While working within traditional narrative, both writers have incorporated subtle innovations in narrative technique and modern themes, yet they have not received the detailed scholarly attention they deserve for their enrichment of the form.

There is much to be learned from studying them together. Instead of merely executing a critical analysis of the published works, this book defines their contribution to the genre through an examination of hitherto unexplored archival materials including correspondence, notebooks, unpublished interviews, and extensive manuscript revisions. From these revisions it is possible to trace both writers' painstaking transformation of original impulses and drafts into the concentrated artistry of their finished work. And from the archival papers as well, in Pritchett's case at least, one can follow the revisions that are suggested by an editor and are often no less transformative for all that. Beyond this, there are the extraordinary, artful transmutations of experience, personal or observed, that proceed with arresting enhancement from memory, notebook, or memoir to fully realized, fully imaginatively altered, fiction.

My goal has been to demonstrate that in the hands of master practitioners, the short story, sometimes dismissed as either a principally commercial genre or the poor stepchild of the novel, requires just as much craftsmanship as the lyric poem. While there are a number of commendable books on theoretical approaches to the genre, my own uses empirical research to examine the actual living art of short-story composition. My choice of short-story manuscripts from the many I consulted in the archives has been determined more by the completeness of particular drafts and the authors' technical approach to composition, than by their themes. The craft of fiction, highly valued by both authors, guided me in my archival explorations and led me to my discoveries.

Yet these explorations are not confined to the stages of the writers' craft. Such differences as exist between Pritchett's and Trevor's published stories are examined here as well. Their contrasting approaches to shared themes—Pritchett is a predominantly comic, Trevor a predominantly elegiac writer—and their frequent concern with different themes altogether are important elements of this book too. The most regrettable difference, though, is that while Trevor is celebrated today as one of the finest short-story writers of our time, the equally distinguished work of Pritchett, the most significant English short-story writer since D. H. Lawrence, has been largely neglected, despite praise from such eminent writers as Trevor himself.

Before turning to these matters, my study begins with a chapter on the foundation for all of them: Pritchett's—and by extension Trevor's as well—pervasive and profound commitment to ordinary people as subjects for his stories.

January J.B. 2006
Paris, France.

Acknowledgments

When I began work in 1998 on what eventually became this book, I had long been a champion of the short story and believed that it had been largely overlooked as a subject worthy of sustained critical attention. At the start, I did not anticipate embarking on a long journey to such far-flung locations as Reading, England; New York City; Tulsa, Oklahoma; and Austin, Texas, for many months at a time. My early discovery, however, of significant collections of both writers' work in archives on both sides of the Atlantic dramatically altered my course and transformed my conception of a book that was originally going to be confined to published material. A. Walton Litz's and Jon Stallworthy's seminal work on revisions in giants of the more dominant genres—Joyce in the novel and Yeats in the lyric poem, respectively—helped inspire my own work on revisions in two giants of this relatively neglected one.

I am indebted to Jon Stallworthy for his wisdom, guidance, and generosity during my preparation of an early version of this book; to John Kelly for his unfailing support while I was at St. John's College, Oxford; and for their friendship ever since. I am grateful too for research and travel grants awarded by Oxford University, the Meyerstein Special Research Fund, the JC Maxwell Fund, and St. John's College that made my work possible.

My encounters outside the archives with important people in Pritchett's and Trevor's lives enriched my understanding of their work and made this a living study. I am most indebted to writers and editors whose conversations with me contributed to my own revisions: to Roger Angell, the only editor to have worked extensively with both Pritchett and Trevor, for his generosity and candor during two extensive interviews and for his considerable assistance since; to Frances Kiernan, for a long interview and for her valuable guidance and subsequent encouragement; and to Charles McGrath, for adding to his former colleagues' portrait of the *New Yorker* Fiction Department when both Pritchett and Trevor were published in that magazine's pages. William Trevor somehow made time to read a late draft of the full manuscript and gave me valuable suggestions that strengthened Chapters 3 and 5 in particular. I appreciate his seriously considering my appeal to retain the extracts from his short-story manuscripts that appeared in my late draft and regret, yet understand, his decision not to allow such passages rejected on the way to his published versions to appear in my book. I am grateful to Oliver Pritchett for his extraordinary generosity and assistance from the beginning and for his comments on a late draft; to Jeremy Treglown for his comments on an early draft of this book while he was busy finishing his fine biography of Pritchett; to Ross McKibbin for discussing matters of class and commenting on an early chapter; to George Core for his editorial suggestions; to Kurt Heinzelman for his comments on a draft; and to Michael Sissons, who on behalf of the Estate of V. S. Pritchett granted me permission to explore all of Pritchett's unpublished material and allowed me to publish the first piece on Pritchett to draw on the *New Yorker* Records. I am indebted to others who knew Pritchett and enabled me to tie together some loose ends: Claire Tomalin, for her gracious help from the beginning; Julian Barnes; Pat Kavanagh; and Lynda Pranger.

I would like to thank the staff of Palgrave Macmillan USA, especially Farideh Koohi-Kamali, Julia Cohen, and Elizabeth Sabo, and the staff of Macmillan India for their invaluable assistance.

Other help and support of various kinds came from Xavier Amandolese, Paul Burns, Martha Campbell, Wayne Furman, Catherine Hilliard, Claire Hodder, Claire Larrière, Michael Millgate, Leigh Montville, Ruth Ogden, David and Barbara Oldham, Catherine Rovera, Robert Spoo, Heath Tarbert, and Rita Wynn. I am indebted to Véronique Bandelier for her affection, belief, and support while I was writing the book and for providing me with ideal working conditions during its final stages.

I would not have been able to accomplish much, however, without the help of the librarians and staffs at the institutions I visited. I am greatly indebted to the following for information and assistance: Pat Fox, John Kirkpatrick, Cathy Henderson, Rich Oram, Director Tom Staley, Tara Wenger, Richard Workman, and former intern Alex Rogers at the Harry Ransom Humanities Research Center, University of Texas at Austin; Stephen Crook, Philip Milito, former intern Michael Schwartz, Diana Burnham, and Curator Isaac Gewirtz at the New York Public Library's Berg Collection and the staff of the Library's Manuscripts and Archives Division; the McFarlin Library, Department of Special Collections, University of Tulsa, especially Lori Curtis, then Head of Special Collections and Archives and Milissa Burkart; the staff of the BBC Written Archives Centre, especially former document researcher Mike Websell, Jackie Kavanagh, and Louise Weston; the staff of the British Library Reading Room; the National Sound Archive, British Library, especially Chris Mobbs and Ike Egbetola; the British Film Institute; the Special Collections at Reading University

Library and their archivist, Michael Bott, and the University of Sussex Library Special Collections. As the first investigator in many instances to view the Pritchett or Trevor holdings in these archives, I was the beneficiary of exemplary patience and cooperation.

Finally, to two of the most extraordinary people I have had the pleasure of knowing, my parents, Robert and Gloria, I dedicate this book with love and admiration.

Abbreviations and References

This book is intended for the general reader and scholar alike. Detailed endnotes for each chapter give the source and exact location of all unpublished and uncollected items to which they refer as well as occasionally enriching and supplementing various matters in the text.

Titles of Books by V. S. Pritchett

CCS	*Complete Collected Stories*	1990
CD	*A Cab at the Door*	1991
MO	*Midnight Oil*	1991

Note on the editions: Published simultaneously in Britain and the United States under slightly different titles, V. S. Pritchett's *Complete Collected Stories* (Random House) and his *Complete Short Stories* (Chatto & Windus) have the same contents and pagination, making all references to *CCS* herein valid for *CSS*. All references to *CD* and *MO* are to the Hogarth edition that combines the two autobiographical works, first published in 1968 and 1970 respectively, in a single volume.

Titles of Books by William Trevor

CST	*William Trevor: The Collected Stories*	1993
Excursions	*Excursions in the Real World*	1994
AR	*After Rain*	1996
HB	*The Hill Bachelors*	2000

Collections

All of the V. S. Pritchett-Gerald Brenan and Pritchett-John Lehmann correspondence is in the HRC; and, unless otherwise noted, all of the

Pritchett-Roger Angell correspondence is in the *New Yorker* Records, Manuscripts and Archives Division of the New York Public Library.

BC	Gerald Brenan Collection, Harry Ransom Center
Berg	Berg Collection, New York Public Library
BFI	British Film Institute
BL	British Library
HRC	Harry Ransom Humanities Research Center, University of Texas at Austin
JLP	John Lehmann Papers, Harry Ransom Center
NYR	*New Yorker* Records, Manuscripts and Archives Division, New York Public Library
NSA	National Sound Archive, British Library
NYPL	New York Public Library
PC	V. S. Pritchett Collection, Harry Ransom Center
PP	V. S. Pritchett Papers, Berg Collection, NYPL
WAC	BBC Written Archives Centre, Reading, England
TC	William Trevor Collection, Department of Special Collections, McFarlin Library, University of Tulsa, Tulsa, Oklahoma

Other Abbreviations Used in the Notes

Ams.	autograph (handwritten) manuscript
app.	appendix
BBC	British Broadcasting Corporation
B	Box
F	Folder
GB	Gerald Brenan
JL	John Lehmann
n.d.	no date
p.m.	postmark date
RA	Roger Angell
TF	Talks Files
VSP	Victor Sawdon Pritchett

Note on the text: Unless otherwise noted, all references are in the endnotes in order to keep the text free of clutter and dates are in day-month-year form separated by periods. Square brackets [ ] indicate any material that is not a part of the original citation, or, in certain cases, suggested words and phrases for illegible handwriting. Please note that Pritchett's sometimes idiosyncratic handwritten spelling and punctuation have been retained to avoid an insistent use of "*sic.*" All quotations have their original spelling and punctuation and, where possible the author has reproduced the physical presentation of the notebook extracts. Upper and lower case letters have been retained in all quoted material except when English syntax rules them out completely.

Chapter 1

Fanfare for the Common Man

[W]e had come to think that our talent alone was responsible for what we did. This is a very dangerous conclusion. We forgot that a writer lives at a certain time, in a certain class, that he belongs to society and, like everyone else, reacts to—what shall I call it?—he reacts to the situation of his society. In one very real sense, a writer is the voice of the time and the society in which he lives.[1]

The BBC and most writers are snobbish about the ordinary man and our snobbery takes the form of admiring his virtues and ignoring his rascalities [. . .]. The "century of the common man" is preparing some shocks for us [. . .].[2]

What later proved to be a close and fruitful relationship between V. S. Pritchett and the BBC began inauspiciously. At the suggestion of Stephen Spender, Lloyd Williams of the BBC wrote to Pritchett to enquire about his interest in English Literature broadcasts, inviting him to discuss the BBC's plans for the following year.[3] Lacking previous broadcasting experience, Pritchett was required to audition at the microphone before the English Committee of the Council could consider him as a broadcaster. After playing the recorded audition for the Sherborne School for Girls' Miss Somerville and Miss Stuart, Chairman of the Council's English Committee, Williams informed Pritchett that he would not be recommended as a broadcaster to schools. Although his voice reproduced well, "it did not possess quite the power and enthusiasm needed for a series of talks to elementary school children."[4] Of course the supposed lack of "power and enthusiasm" may simply have been a substitute for this triumvirate's real, unspoken reason.

BBC English was the voice of the elite at the time, and Pritchett's accent and speech readily betrayed his lower-middle-class beginnings. Disadvantageous as they may have been in 1935, his microphone demeanor, speech, and accent became assets during the Second World War when the BBC actively campaigned to represent the lower-middle and working classes, giving them a voice and bringing their unsung lives to the public's consciousness. And Pritchett was that much more credible in the BBC scheme as a genuine representative of the forgotten classes, having himself been in contact with them all his life.

His opportunity to become an important contributor to the BBC came about when his unsuccessful attempts to sell his short stories to the corporation brought him to the attention of Christopher Salmon, one of its most influential producers. Informed by a colleague that Pritchett was "interested in the technique of short story writing for the microphone," Salmon proposed a meeting.[5] After receiving nothing but rejections for his short-story submissions, except for his significantly altered version of "The Aristocrat,"[6] Pritchett must certainly have been "intensely interested in discovering a microphone technique."[7] Their meeting did not change his fortunes as a short-story contributor for the BBC, but it led to an invitation four years later to meet Desmond Hawkins and Edwin Muir to discuss a series of broadcasts Salmon was planning called "The Writer and His Public."[8] Salmon welcomed Pritchett to the series and entrusted him with the first draft of the scripted conversation.[9] His work as writer and broadcaster in the series led to participation in several other talk programs. When Pritchett lost his reading job with Heinemann, which had given him a substantial income, he sought Salmon's advice. Faced with a choice between either working in a government department or seeking work better suited to his experience, he enquired of Salmon about his prospects for more work at the BBC. Pritchett expressed confidence in his ability to transcend the "purely literary subjects" he was known for at the *New Statesman,* argued that most story writers were good reporters, and wished the BBC would "use people like me for descriptive things."[10] In his reply, Salmon warned Pritchett not to rely on broadcasting for a regular source of income because of its highly irregular and unpredictable nature. And, as a friend, he also spoke of ephemeral broadcasting success. Once found, a good broadcaster may enjoy immediate success and earn considerable sums, but Salmon said he and the staff would "squeeze him as dry as we can," either slowly "or even all at once," because the public would tire of him: "Unless he is one of the Senecas the public won't stand for his talking on more than his own subjects . . . and so on."[11]

Despite his discouraging words about full-time broadcasting at the BBC, Salmon believed that part-time work would be a viable supplement to

Pritchett's other income and offered him his immediate, unconditional support. He had enjoyed working with him, appreciated his flexibility, and liked the broadcasting he had done. Salmon said he would write to the Head of the Overseas Department to recommend him "as a fellow who, besides [his] known literary qualifications, could be sent here and there to do a given job of reporting."[12] In addition, he promised to bring his name forward at his departmental meeting to see if Pritchett could be used more often. Salmon's description of Pritchett in his letter to the Overseas Head indicates the obvious change in the BBC's broadcasting policy during the war. He promoted Pritchett as an experienced journalist with "a quick pen" whose versatility would enable him to venture beyond the literary side: "He also has a sincere and sensible voice and manner—not too cultivated."[13] The man whose voice several years earlier "did not quite possess the power and enthusiasm for a series of talks" was now endowed with a "sincere and sensible voice and manner"—one that, fortunately for the BBC, was not "too cultivated."

Judging from the increased workload that followed Salmon's promotional efforts, the BBC found in Pritchett a writer and broadcaster ideal for their propaganda machine during the Second World War. He served as a regular book reviewer on countless programs such as "Book Talk," but his more active, immediate, creative contribution came during the middle of the war. And of all of the BBC's producers, it was Christopher Salmon who made the most judicious use of Pritchett's talents, enlisting him in a series of programs that capitalized on his equal ease with the working class and the most sophisticated intellectuals. Erudite but unpretentious, knowledgeable but modest, well educated but self-educated, Pritchett was the ideal broadcaster for a government-run radio network bent on boosting British morale through the exploits of the common man. The BBC, however, was not the sole beneficiary of this relationship. The role Pritchett believed in and played so effectively served his purpose as well. And his accomplishments as a self-made man from the lower-middle class facilitated his relationships with working-class people.

His sincere interest in the common man was nourished even further through his collaboration with Salmon. In a letter of 12 August 1941, Salmon introduced plans for three series in which Pritchett would play an integral part: "Strength of Mind," concerning philosophical issues; "Living Image," on the relation between life and art; and "Living Opinion," a forum for working-class discussions. Eager to include Pritchett in the planning stage of "Strength of Mind," he invited him to come to a preparatory meeting[14] with "a good deal" to say, especially about "the whole problem of the relation between ideas and reality."[15] Salmon was prepared to "dive in and leave the shore behind" but asked Pritchett to "refer to the disposition of philosophy" at the end of the discussion and "where it may be found—namely those sections of the community where life has proved disappointing." He believed he had already found the right working man to share the microphone with Pritchett in the second broadcast.[16] It is evident that, even before this particular series aired, Salmon relied on Pritchett to prepare comfortable ground for the working man in the second "Strength of Mind" program, a discussion entitled "Who Is Disposed to Think?"[17] Pritchett not only prepared the ground as planned, he took sides with Salmon's working man, Mr. Higgins, during the evening's discussion, interrupting Mrs. Helen Bentwich, the Chairman of the London Country Council Higher Education Sub-Committee, to extol the virtues of working-class values and confronting the distinguished John Mabbott with their superiority. He argued that the qualities upon which working-class values are based—"generosity and kindness"—are more important than those upon which middle-class values are founded—"refinement and respectability."[18] The following year, Pritchett said he would prefer his wife to go to the cowman's wife at the back of the house if there were an invasion in his neighborhood rather than to one of the middle-class people, like himself, who "on the whole choose friends purely for interest," never considering the question of necessity.[19] While Salmon changed the "Strength of Mind" discussion panel for each program, he made Pritchett and Mabbott its mainstays, guaranteeing the audience a compelling duo, a contrast in class and education: the distinguished, classically trained philosophy tutor at St. John's, Oxford, and the distinguished man of letters, an endearing autodidact with an intuitive understanding of people and literature. Pritchett and Mabbott worked with many eminent guests throughout the series, including Margery Fry and Arthur Koestler. Salmon used Pritchett as a speaker in all six programs of "The Living Image" as well, confident that he had the versatility to discuss painting and theater in addition to literature with some of Britain's most distinguished artists, actors, and writers.

Of the three Salmon series to which Pritchett contributed, "Living Opinion" was undoubtedly the most valuable to him because it brought him closest to the British working class, giving him material for his fictional world. Though neither Pritchett nor Salmon were participants in the broadcasts themselves, their exhaustive preparation required traveling together to locations throughout Britain in search of representatives of the working class articulate enough to express their ideas and attitudes about a variety of topics. Once they found appropriate participants, Pritchett performed the dual roles of secretary and scriptwriter. Ordinarily, he attended two meetings of speakers on the given topic and wrote the broadcast script from his notes.

To honor the integrity of the worker speakers—instead of using them as BBC puppets—and to ensure the script's fidelity to the meetings, copies were submitted to the participants for alteration so that changes could be incorporated into the broadcast drafts.[20] Salmon and Pritchett's journeys took them as far as Wales and Yorkshire and brought them into contact with quarrymen, millers, miners, railroad men, and clerks. The discussion groups considered such issues as the availability of culture and education to the working class, the importance of principles, nationalism, morality, class differences, materialism, and spirituality.[21]

The two men searched constantly for suitable working men in order to authenticate their portrait of the working man's world. They were often obliged to coordinate their efforts and on one occasion composed a panel of neighborhood people. Salmon found some promising participants through his colleague Miss Rowntree, who lived in Pritchett's neighborhood and knew some working people,[22] and Pritchett found a Welsh miner and "got hold of 4 chaps from a local arms factory evacuated from Southampton," confident that three "may be useful."[23] At one point, Pritchett was such an important contributor to "Living Opinion" that he contacted the men, arranged the meetings, prepared the script, and even escorted the workers to London on the day of the broadcast.[24]

He used these opportunities to mingle with working men, attentive to the odd phrase or cliché that might give him greater insight into their lives, provide the basis for a short story, or reveal the essence of a fictional character. His notebooks, journals, and letters are sprinkled with overheard conversations, descriptions of passing encounters, and subtle, quixotic moments that define the lives he observes. While Christopher Salmon was "wrestling with all sorts of problems about the Empire, trying in particular to relate the interests of working men here to Empire problems,"[25] Pritchett simply immersed himself in their world. His commitment to their realistic portrayal, their "living opinion," made him an ideal champion. Forever interested in viewing the common man through the uncommon lens of his wartime trade, he found new angles from which to study skills he felt privileged to witness firsthand. In declining an offer to work with Salmon years later, Pritchett said, "Living Opinion was the best thing on the Radio, and enormously instructive and valuable to me."[26] Although he did not serve during the war, his travel for the BBC, the Ministry of Transport, and the Ministry of Information, for which, among other things, he researched and wrote *Build the Ships*,[27] nevertheless afforded him close contact with his countrymen, many of whom were more isolated than he, blind to the larger picture while performing as cogs within the war machine. His two years of wartime journeys gave him a better understanding of his country and the chance "to see what [?] its life & name is based on, to wonder at what people accept and endure. A factory woman said to me at her bench this morning 'I'm fed up with this. I wish I were at the docks where I could see what I was doing, what it was for.'"[28] Throughout his travels, he was always sympathetic to working-class aspirations and dreams and prized spontaneous observations, often noting them verbatim for future reference.

* * *

Pritchett was committed to portraying the common man from the beginning of his literary career, convinced that the lives of ordinary people were rich in material for fiction. He made a conscious decision not to be part of any formal literary movement. Although widely read in English, Russian, and European literature, he was determined to find his own voice and subject. A product of a struggling lower-middle-class family with working-class relatives, he unhesitatingly adopted shopkeepers, salesmen, clerks, hairdressers, and antique dealers as subjects for many of his stories and validated their inclusion in serious literature by making readers acknowledge the universality of their experience. Like Gissing, Wells, and Bennett, Pritchett proves that the lives of ordinary people contain extraordinary material for fiction. Yet he employs a different aesthetic, substitutes empathy for Wells's condescension, effaces himself from the narrative, and, unlike Bennett and Gissing, fashions lively social comedy from the most dour circumstances.

What distinguishes him from the English short-story writers of his generation, however, is his heightened critical sense. After all, he spent most of his time reviewing and analyzing other authors' work. And though he was frustrated about having little time for his own fiction, feeling he squandered it on literary criticism, his highly developed critical acumen and grasp of literary technique, like James's and Woolf's, made him an equally discerning judge of his own creations. Unlike many critics, whose powers of reflection and observation stifle their creative abilities, Pritchett was able to use them to articulate his goals and develop his own aesthetic.

At the heart of this aesthetic is his belief in the importance of common things, simple things, that, uncorrupted by "literary style," would have universal truth. An early notebook passage shows him giving himself valuable guidance:

> ~~Write~~ How to Write
> Write about feelings with the rein free not intellectually
> tightened. Put down the carelessness of living & moving life.
> Not your thoughts, but put the life down. Not catalogues of

doing things, but put the life down. Each act alive. Common things. Not literary style. Simple things. No distance from characters. Near them. No microscope. Write with the blood as well as the brain.[29]

Several years later, his identification with the "ordinary people" is central to a sketch he believed could be the foundation of a short story:

> People
> People & people & people. Ordinary people in coats, women with bits of fur on collars, silk legged girls. They are in a good humour [?] a strike is on. An adventure, the usual has occurred. Good for those strikes. The air is clear of [his?] fumes. An air of prosperity in the streets & ease instead of those blocks of [?]. A feeling that everyone has: we don't want money, but we want more leisure & good health, less news & more rest.
> A girl steps off the moving staircase after having got on. "She ought not to do that"[.] Ordinary human beings. The people. The rain as numerous as the people in its drops falling upon them. The common rain on the ordinary people. A story could begin[:]
>   The common rain was falling on the ordinary people.
> I feel <u>with</u> these people in the tube.[30]

Pritchett not only chooses common or ordinary people as his subject, he empathizes with them and includes himself among them in the scene. The proposed first line of the "story" above is a lower-middle-class version of the final line of Joyce's "The Dead," a story Pritchett mentioned on several occasions, most notably in an extensive debate with George Orwell on the air and in print that helped articulate Pritchett's divergent conception of the modern short story.[31]

His subjects are linked to his self-conception and self-reliance. Initially unaware of the Bloomsbury intellectuals, even though he was unwittingly living amid them as a young writer, and distanced from the Auden-Spender circle, he was proud of his unliterary beginnings. As a true Londoner who had lived and worked in the city all his life, beginning in the leather trade at Bermondsey, he had a fundamental claim to the capital and was "so to speak, indigenous."[32] His "real London life" working in a trade outside literary circles even determined his approach to the act of writing. The Protestant ethic fortified by the leather trade compelled him to approach his new craft in the same way and precluded "the free life" other writers prized.

He allied himself with the working man in his dependence on a steady job—often working seven days a week—and spoke of his "real 9 to 6 treadmill sense" that came from his early workhouse experience: "I get fed up with liberty after a bit and I'm not a Garbo for solitude."[33] Pritchett was conscious of his distance from other writers and, like William Trevor, never felt comfortable with or a part of any particular school of writing or group—especially those composed of university-educated intellectuals, such as the "Auden-Spender family circle,[. . .] wracked by its inner ecstasies and storms." Among its members, Pritchett told John Lehmann, he felt "like some coarse taxi-driver who has picked up with a lot of eccentric fares who are all going to different places."[34]

He found his own inspiration in the work of a small group of pioneers who dared to make the lives of ordinary men their central concern, chiefly Gissing, Bennett, Wells, and Hardy, and the Russians Turgenev and Chekhov. His study of the strengths and weaknesses of their respective approaches helped him to fashion his own portrait of the English common man. He applauded Gissing's crusade to represent the unclassed: "This discovery that in all character there sits a mind, and that the mind of the dullest is not dull because at its very lowest, it will at least reflect the social dilemma into which it was born, is arresting."[35] Like Gissing, he envisioned creating meaningful portraits of the forgotten, believing such people to be as worthy of attention as any other. One might note, however, that the onus is on the writer to find a substitute for the language appropriate to more erudite subjects capable of self-expression. Though critical of Arnold Bennett, Pritchett felt "he has something universal to say [. . .] about the depressed lower middle class in England" and "an extraordinary, unassuming fidelity to life."[36] But he recognized that more modern writers had surpassed Bennett to achieve a more realistic presentation of ordinary urban life without "worshipping the mere fact of the ordinariness of ordinary life, as Bennett did."[37] He also saw Hardy mine the rural and regional life of England, transforming common provincial life with his "poetic imagination and his Elizabethan eye for the extraordinary scene." Arresting images such as the blood coming through the ceiling in *Tess of the D'Urbervilles*, or Henchard's sighting his effigy floating in the millstream in *The Mayor of Casterbridge*, brought to Pritchett's attention the value of elements "taken out of the common provincial life of the people, which elegant writers have so often despised."[38] Hardy merely corroborated his conviction that there was a rich vein of uncommon, unmined material in ordinary lives and inspired him by using the stories of Wessex village people as the basis for his fiction. Pritchett explained that the stories one hears village people tell about each other in cottages and pubs now were the "stuff of literature" for Hardy: "He magnified them, transposed them, gave them dignity of a high imagination. He caught from the common people their belief in Fate and he enlarged it to the tragic and universal dimension."[39] Like Hardy, Pritchett was determined to focus on the classes and milieu he knew from his own experience and avoid Hardy's unsuccessful portrayal of the upper class. More importantly, he was encouraged to find Hardy's "little people [. . .] dwarfed by the magnitude of historical time, and yet magnified to the proportions of Greek tragedy by Hardy's sense of the universe."[40] The choice of the ordinary man as a subject was therefore not an inherent limitation. It offered an infinite amount of material for the imaginative writer.

As encouraged as he was by Hardy's world, Pritchett had even greater admiration for Turgenev's portrayal of Russian peasants "as feeling people," endowing "even the humblest" with "a self-preserving genius," and he eventually learned to bring his English lower-middle-class characters to life in similar ways. So "incurably human" and tangible are they that "it is a shock to remember 'These are slaves.' The silent power of Turgenev's sketches comes from the fact that his art is liberating the people he describes; each one is more alive and human than his 'situation' as part of the problem of serfdom. [. . .] Turgenev reveals people living in their natures."[41] Turgenev's work was instrumental in arming Pritchett with another technique. The Russian writer worked as an outsider or "scrutinising spectator," unearthing his truth by penetrating the inside from the outside with his images and sentences.[42]

Gerald Brenan, Pritchett's closest friend—and arguably his most perceptive critic—had condemned him prematurely as a mere "victim" of the "proletarian romanticism" of their time when they first met in 1936 at the Savile Club, convinced of the absurdity of Pritchett's choosing for the subjects of his stories "the very class which, in England, is least able to express itself." Reflecting on his initial skepticism in a letter four years later, Brenan understood how Pritchett's choice of and innovative approach to an unlikely subject eventually won him over. Handicapped by his subjects' inability to express themselves articulately at length, Pritchett developed his "fauna of images" in his stories that relied on his keen auditory and visual sense, avoiding the pitfall of most modern novelists.[43] Brenan's insight into Pritchett's accomplishment elicited a response five days later akin to a career-long manifesto. Though avowedly apolitical, Pritchett acknowledged his extra-ideological debt to the "proletarian or Marxist or popular movement"—a movement that made him understand himself better, validated and invigorated his commitment to the common man, and spurred him to express the lives of "ordinary" people through literature. Naturally sympathetic to the class from which he came, he was "struck by the pathos of their expression. Lives so deeply self-absorbed, words, thoughts, ideas so struggling, accidental, half baked and silly." Pritchett enjoyed the challenge, as an artist, of choosing "people hard to accept," because an artist "must <u>accept</u> people." The very difficulty of capturing the ordinary man's self-expression was precisely what he found most compelling and stimulating. Unlike Proust, he "found the unprotected lives of 'ordinary' people much more extraordinary" than the lives of educated and highly civilized people, "covered with a veneer of some conventional or even real perfection. Their fantasies, their extraordinary stories are the subject of constant attention by their more or less expert minds. They are the beauty specialists who can hide age or wrinkles. A writer like Proust can get at the maggot in them or the lovely insect." The political movement reminded him that he had a life of his own.[44]

In an earlier letter to Brenan the same year, Pritchett distilled the essence of his burgeoning "theory" in an epigram worthy of Oscar Wilde: "The meaning of life is on the surface and profundity is the alibi of those too impatient to see"[45]—a fitting statement for an author who strives to explore characters from the outside, using their language, gestures, and expressions, instead of working from within their minds, like Joyce, James, or Woolf. In a lecture about the importance of dialogue, he recalled being liberated by "the delights of the vernacular" and becoming "a member of the human race":

> My education, my sensibility went out of the window. [. . .] There was talk as you heard it, there was talk inside the mind. One lived sensationally by eye and ear. [. . .] I noticed, with suspicion, that it was getting difficult to write about the educated—they had so little "savage poetry".[46]

Convinced of the importance of his subject, aware of previous attempts to capture ordinary lives, whether rural, urban, or suburban, Pritchett devoted himself to their portrayal through "the poetry of ordinary speech":

> I mean [. . .] the speech of the ordinary man which is not poetical at all. But there is a kind of poetry in the gulf between the emotion that is <u>felt</u> and the words that try, altogether inadequately to <u>express it</u>. And yet which nevertheless <u>do</u> express this emotion, by repetitions and by their very inconsequence.[47]

The "gulf" he perceived and reproduced helped infuse his fiction with heroic but comic pathos. In "The Scapegoat," for instance, the Terence Street residents, in their bid to outdo rival Earl Street's, put their trust in the widower Art Edwards, "made serious by death," as the keeper of their collection box, convinced they "had chosen the right man." Speaking sympathetically about Harry Law and his wife and Harry's underlying problem of drink and spousal abuse, Art proclaims, "They've had their ups and downs. [. . .] We've all got our faults. He's had his ups and downs." Pritchett invests this common colloquial expression with poignance and macabre significance when Harry Law himself reiterates it at the end of the story as the neighborhood comes to terms with and excuses Art Edwards's shocking gambling loss and suicide by hanging: "Every man [. . .] has his ups and downs." The title story from *You Make Your Own Life* involves all the elements of true melodrama—passionate love, tragic illness, rival lovers, attempted murder, and attempted suicide—but achieves the poetic "gulf" between the emotions such dramatic events would seem to inspire, and the words that, while comically inadequate and irrelevant, paradoxically "do express this emotion": "'You make your own life.'" At the beginning of the Second World War, Pritchett noticed that the behavior and "real life" of the poor has little relation to the clichés they employ:

> All the poor round here are better off since the war, the middle class people poorer. Yet they talk gloomily about the war:
> "We must keep a stiff upper lip."
> "We've got to expect it."
> "We must see it through."
> The war is to[o] big for their ordinary language. They have to talk in clichés. Their behaviour, their real life, has only the faintest relation to those big phrases, though they are a kind of mythology & morality for them.[48]

Pritchett's figurative language is consistent with that of his subjects. In "The Landlord," Mrs. Seugar's voice "went like a lawn-mower running over the same strip of grass, up and down, up and down, catching Mr. Seugar like a stone in the cutters every now and then, and then running on again." The working-class narrator of "The Scapegoat" also utters a working-class simile: "For some of us had to admit we'd go mad at times with temptation tingling in our fingers and *hissing like gas in coal in our hearts*" (my italics). Pritchett matches language to class in "Blind Love," representing Mrs. Johnson's lower-middle-class world with a lower-middle-class simile and comparisons upon her husband's discovery of her birthmark, her human stain: "this ugly blob—dark as blood, like a ragged liver on a butcher's window, or some obscene island with ragged edges. It was as if a bucket of paint had been thrown over her." The liver simile evolves into a metaphor and a lower-middle class symbol later in the story when Mrs. Johnson, exasperated by blind Armitage's jealousy, rubs the enormous birthmark on her breast—"'the whole plate of liver'"—against his face.

Convinced of the overriding importance of speech to a writer, since "[w]ords are the signs of things spoken," he downplays the significance of sight, feeling that "it doesn't matter if he hardly sees at all—if he's frightfully unobservant."[49] While other writers are nonetheless equally impressed with his keen eye for detail, Pritchett has an exceptional ear for dialogue and believes that "we really learn more [. . .] about human beings by listening to them than by seeing them."[50] He was struck with the realization "that speech of itself is a pathos—a touching evidence of incapacity."[51] And it is that very incapacity that he found most intriguing in the dialogue he overheard. Furthermore, he recognized the creative use of slang and swear words—even expressions such as "browned off" and the "looney bin"—by people trying to describe the way they feel.[52] Many of his early short-story titles, such as "You Make Your Own Life," "Handsome Is As Handsome Does," and "The Fly in the Ointment," as well as later ones such as "The Key to My Heart," "Blind Love," "A Family Man," and "On the Edge of the Cliff," come from popular colloquial expressions, clichés, or aphorisms around which he constructs the narrative.[53] Pritchett may have based a story on "a simple moral idea" such as "'good people aren't as good as they look' or 'goodness isn't as good as it looks' or 'badness isn't as bad as it looks'. [. . .] I think I'm really writing little parables, or allegories or poems or interpretations in which people are necessary, but they aren't the main thing."[54] While this is perhaps an accurate description of his earlier, more anecdotal stories and sketches—fiction with a Maughamish flavor—it is not indicative of his more mature character-based fiction such as "The Wheelbarrow," "Blind Love," "The Camberwell Beauty," "On the Edge of the Cliff," or "A Careless Widow."

Pritchett's empathy for people enables him to understand their plight and convey that understanding to the reader. During a "Strength of Mind" discussion, he said that people should neither think of themselves as isolated from the outside physical world nor "as individuals who must oppose the encroachment of other people." Instead, he felt, "We must try [. . .] to enlarge our sympathies, refusing to be limited only to the appreciation of those characters and personalities to which our own temperaments incline us."[55] Pritchett's identification with his subjects, whether he describes a tree or reviews another writer, is the foundation of his Whitmanesque approach to all forms of writing.[56] Of course, he was well aware of other artists who subscribed to such an approach. In his biography of Balzac, he admired Balzac's infiltration of the French lower-middle class and his empathy and compassion: "His observation, he said, 'penetrated the soul'. He said he simply 'became them.'"[57] Years of living as a foreigner in Roman Catholic countries that at the time were hostile to Anglo-Saxon thought and custom merely strengthened Pritchett's resolve to efface himself in order to understand the natives.[58]

Cultivated while abroad, Pritchett's ability to efface himself, to empathize wholly with his subjects, enabled him to penetrate the contemporary British scene with the curious, objective eye of a foreigner. While the publication of *You Make Your Own Life* (1938) signaled his arrival as an accomplished British short-story writer, the more virtuosic *It May Never Happen* (1945) persuaded Walter Allen that Pritchett wrote about English life with "a directness and immediacy that [were] new," that his "mastery of dialogue as a means of revealing character" was "unsurpassed by any of his contemporaries."[59] And it was to John Lehmann's *New Writing* that Pritchett owed much of his triumph. Many of the best stories eventually collected in *It May Never Happen* first appeared in Lehmann's leftist publication and might never have been published at all had the visionary editor not recognized their worth. Shortly after meeting Lehmann at a party, and before the appearance of the introductory volume of *New Writing*, Pritchett enquired of him about submitting an unsolicited manuscript. He was probably aware of the intentions and requirements outlined in the *New Writing* "Manifesto" that would eventually appear in print. It aimed "at providing an outlet for those prose writers [. . .] whose work is too unorthodox in length or style to be suitable for the established monthly and quarterly magazines."[60] Not only was this new publication purportedly "first and foremost interested in literature" and "independent of any political party," it asked for paid contributions of up to 15,000 words, a length that would normally exclude a submission from publication in the British reviews of 1936.[61] Encouraged by such unusual criteria, Pritchett contacted Lehmann, whom he had recently met at a *New Statesman* party, about submitting a 7,000-word story, wondering if Lehmann would consider unsolicited manuscripts.[62] Though pessimistic about the story's suitability for other publications, Pritchett hoped Lehmann would overlook its apolitical nature: "It is a very laconic and realistic story but not political. I mean it has no political moral. On the other hand, I think it is really contemporary. You will see, however."[63] Lehmann was pleased to accept the story for publication in volume 2, only regretting that its appearance precluded Pritchett from reviewing the volume. Initially titled "The Commercial Traveller," Pritchett changed it to "Sense of Humour" at Lehmann's request to avoid its appearing in the same issue with a similarly titled translation. Although he was paid a pittance for it, the story was widely read and praised. (In both his autobiography and an interview, Pritchett credits his two early stories, "Sense of Humour" and "The Sailor"—for which he was paid £3 and £7 respectively—for making his name.[64]) Pittance or no, he was nevertheless pleased to have "Sense of Humour" in *New Writing*, knowing the magazines that paid handsomely would not publish it.[65]

In addition to having an objective sense about the suitability of particular stories for publication, Pritchett may also have been aware of the importance of establishing and maintaining his reputation as a short-story writer in his own country. However little he was paid—in this case a paltry £3— he was eager to make regular contributions to the leading publications. *New Writing* had just emerged, but it was a promising outlet for a writer like Pritchett. Even though he had been successful placing stories in a variety of British publications, his fiction was evolving and he needed an editor like Lehmann who would be receptive to longer, more unconventional stories. On a number of occasions, Lehmann accepted Pritchett stories that had been rejected by other editors—stories that then became famous and were widely anthologized. For instance, Pritchett submitted "Many Are Disappointed," praised by Valentine Cunningham as one of the finest stories to appear in *New Writing*,[66] to Lehmann after the *Fortnightly* rejected it, "upset by its 'un-literaryness.'"[67] Lehmann gave the story his highest compliment by informing Pritchett he had already sent it off to the printer and could not understand the *Fortnightly*'s comment: "It gave me a headache trying to think."[68] He accepted Pritchett's "The Fruit Robbery," a short allegory atypical of Pritchett that would be retitled "The Ape Who Lost His Tail" and immediately appealed to him for one of his longer stories on the order of "Sense of Humour" or the "brilliant" "You Make Your Own Life" for the next issue.[69] Clearly he had found a writer ideally suited to the pages of his publication. Ever apologetic, but far from prolific in the early years of their relationship, Pritchett was encouraged by Lehmann's endorsement, promising to "try and become a reformed character and produce some stories."[70] A Pritchett notebook entry shows that Lehmann often asked him to contribute to *New Writing*, as a critic, essayist, short-story writer, and novelist—sometimes simultaneously.[71]

He paid tribute to Lehmann's effectiveness as an editor, seeing him as "a sort of Simon Legree of letters, the slave master, whip in hand, who drives us all to work with an air both flattering and threatening"[72] and likened himself to "a negro slave under the lash" in finishing his office story "The Chestnut Tree"[73] for *New Writing*: "He rings me up and says I promised him a story and where is it? I mumble, he puts on an air of editorial indulgence with a faint edge of threat. So I then enter a period of frenzy, despair, headaches, indigestion, boredom, exhaustion. The thing is done."[74] His playful account of the relationship suggests that had Lehmann failed in his task, Pritchett might have lost the impetus to produce short fiction altogether. As it was, his slow trickle of choice contributions to *New Writing*—in all of its permutations—was perhaps his most significant early work: it included "Sense of Humour," "Many Are Disappointed," "The Ape Who Lost His Tail," "The Sailor," "The Chestnut Tree," and "Aunt Gertrude," and was complemented by an assortment of articles and essays and personal accounts of Second World War experiences. Lehmann believed in Pritchett's talent, immune to the prejudice that might have resulted from the insecurities and self-deprecating remarks the writer expressed about his submissions. And Pritchett was always appreciative of Lehmann's perspicacity. He was beholden to Lehmann for publishing a story "that but for New Writing I would probably have torn up [. . .] as it had been rejected by every paper in the USA & England!"[75] While eventually proud to have been outside a "school" or "generation" of writing, Pritchett "was quite homeless and isolated as a writer" and did desire to belong to one early on. Excluded from both world wars because of his age and thus a member of a generation apart, he was grateful for the shelter of *New Writing* and its validation of his identity as an artist at a time when no one else would publish him consistently. "Something" had indeed "crystallised in New Writing."[76] Twenty years later, Pritchett recalled his debt to Lehmann once again, expressing pride in and gratitude for having been published in *New Writing* and *London Magazine*, "for my work is not always everyones' cup of tea."[77]

When in 1946 Lehman solicited Pritchett's comments for a talk he was preparing on his colleague, Pritchett gave his views on his characterization of the lower-middle class and his identity as a writer that reaffirm his devotion to the extraordinariness of ordinary life:

> [C]ritics frequently say my people are bizarre in the sense of not being normal people. My impression [. . .] is that my people are not bizarre. That all "normal" people of the lower middle class—which is my country—have the characteristics I describe. My sailor is odd, but his oddity is true of all sailors![78] I'm pretty well a documentary writer, but I don't subscribe to "the love to mother" outlook of the documentary school. Frank O'Connor made a brilliant crack about me. He said I wrote about English people anthropologically as if they were South American tribes being interpreted to educated Russians! Yes, I am an anthropologist. [. . .] I think I'm a <u>comic</u> writer.[79]

Though he was convinced of the validity of the documentary writers' subject matter, Pritchett distanced himself from their ranks. Documentary writing, however interesting in the late 1930s and at the beginning of the war, became mundane and repetitive once the reading public was routinely exposed to ordinary civilians' wartime experiences. In reviewing *New Writing* for the BBC, he described the limitations of this movement—its focus on "entertaining and informative" personal adventure to the exclusion of "literature [. . .] about human beings, their passions, their spiritual conflicts, their adventures, the comical things they do and the tragic things that happen to them." Documentary writers failed to "see inside the mind and heart." In the end, he concluded, "literary questions sooner or later come down to questions of words and style."[80] Pritchett believed that the important effect of the documentary movement was "its introduction of precision, exactitude, the clean image and the clean, direct line in writing."[81] A writer, however, is no more than a journalist if he cannot suggest meaning beyond mere documentation. The artist must transform life into art; he "must not leave life where he found it."[82] When Pritchett chose to portray the ordinary man, he certainly did not have the documentary school's approach in mind.

* * *

While assessing English writing during the war—"New Writing and New other things"—Brenan commented on Pritchett's unsung accomplishments, praising his friend for his vision and his successful, compelling treatment of the common man and *la vie quotidienne*. He thought that all English writers under forty were attempting to do what Pritchett was doing: "penetrate deeper into the actual sordid, dramaless daily scene—and yet failing, failing boringly and totally, to do so." Joyce and Woolf had begun working "under the star of Impressionism," he continued, and Pritchett was continuing it, "but <u>with eyes</u>."[83] Pritchett's ambition was to convey the inner world of the ordinary man through judicious selection of talk—as convincingly as Proust does for his world: "Proust analysed the sensations of a sensitive, educated and civilised society; would it be possible to do [. . .] its equivalent [. . .] for the servant's hall?"[84]

In the chapters that follow, we shall see how Pritchett, and his successor, Trevor, as well, pursue this exploration of the humanity of ordinary people by transforming them into extraordinary fictional presences.

Chapter 2

Revision as Transformation: The Making and Remaking of V. S. Pritchett's "You Make Your Own Life"

I have an impatient character; for every page I write there are half a dozen thrown away. The survivors are criss-crossed with deletions. [. . .] There is the fascination of packing a great deal into very little space. The fact that form is decisive concentrates an impulse that is essentially poetic.[1]

V. S. Pritchett has been lauded as the finest English short-story writer of his time and one of the most important practitioners and ambassadors of the genre in the world. Major critics and writers throughout the English-speaking world are unanimous in their praise of his unusual gift for the short form. Walter Allen considered him to be the most outstanding English short-story writer since D. H. Lawrence.[2] Paul Theroux judged him "Our best short story writer."[3] In his review of Pritchett's *Collected Stories,* Valentine Cunningham called him "the best living English short story writer,"[4] and Frank Kermode believed him to be by far "the finest English writer alive."[5] Other internationally acclaimed practitioners of the art are equally enthusiastic about Pritchett's accomplishments. William Trevor feels Pritchett "has done more for the short story in his lifetime than anyone since Joyce or Chekhov"—high praise from perhaps the finest living short-story writer:

> The more parochial and domestic these stories appear to be on the surface the deeper the depths they acquire when considered in retrospect. Pritchett writes of the universal by way of a narrow particular, allowing humor and the variations in human relationships to create his patterns of truth.[6]

Eudora Welty claims "that any Pritchett story is all of it alight and busy at once, like a well-going fire. Wasteless and at the same time well fed [. . .]. He is one of the great pleasure givers in our language."[7]

Although he has established an enviable reputation, he has proved a conundrum for critics and scholars alike, a number of whom claim that his short stories are simply too elusive to be studied. While some criticize their lack of plots, others complain about their inconsistent structure. One reviewer who was clearly frustrated with the complexity of "When My Girl Comes Home," for instance, recognized Pritchett's technical prowess, but managed to turn it against him: "The story needs to be read twice for its flavour to be appreciated, and even then one may perhaps feel that its obliquities and lacunae are as much the result of the temptations of a teasing technique as of artistic necessity."[8] The only critic to write a full-length study in English of Pritchett's short fiction believes "the essential Pritchett" to be "elusive of all critics." He feels that the stories' dearth of "clear interpretive clues" and the "dim or ambiguous" causality of their plots make them resistant to New Critical analysis: "Most Pritchett stories seem to be wafted away in the wind as heavy critical machinery is driven up."[9] Another reviewer feels that "in Pritchett's stories nothing is ever quite resolved; indeed, having come full circle, his situations seem to dissolve at the very place where they began."[10]

Even those genuinely interested in his craft—who believe it worth study—have not managed to come to terms with it. The lavish praise some critics have given Pritchett—praise intended to give him the recognition he so richly deserves—has somehow discouraged detailed critical appraisal, giving his achievement the power of the old man's magic trick at the end of Pritchett's "The Aristocrat." He seems to be viewed as either too fine a craftsman by his admirers or too unorthodox a practitioner by his detractors to warrant further critical attention. As long ago as 1982, Douglas Hughes made an impassioned plea in a guest editorial, chastising the academic community for its shameful neglect of Pritchett's substantial body of work.[11] Except for a handful of brief articles, one book-length study, a chapter of another, and a special journal issue in 1986, there has been little response to Hughes's call to arms over twenty years later. Some reviews of Pritchett's short-story collections come closer to understanding his art, but the promising ideas necessarily lack development, bound as they are by space limitations. Unfortunately, without further study, Pritchett may indeed be relegated to the list of forgotten short-story artists whose work seems too slight to merit serious scholarly attention. Until as recently as 2005, all of his books published in his lifetime were out of print, and despite Jeremy Treglown's new Pritchett biography, which should help revive interest in him, his publishers have reissued only *Mr. Beluncle* and a short selection of his short stories.

Pritchett fashioned his stories through an elaborate process in order to achieve his intended effect, rewriting each one four or five times while "boiling down" one hundred pages to short-story length.[12] He knew that one had "to cut down, cut down, cut down": "It always seems [. . .] that every event has equal importance, that every bit of it ought to have three sentences to it; when sometimes three words is quite enough."[13] His seemingly effortless style and construction are therefore dearly achieved. A tireless reviser obsessed with his "protest against the discursive,"[14] he never "just dashed off a short story."[15] Throughout his childhood, Pritchett's son, Oliver, now a journalist in his own right, observed his father's labyrinthine revisions during visits to his study: "The handwritten pages, covered in revisions, crossings out, second and third thoughts, and sideways writing in the margins, were given to my mother [Dorothy] to type. They would be revised and typed again and again."[16] He was amazed by his mother's "brilliant telepathy" in deciphering VSP's scrawl because it would take him a couple of days to decode one of his father's five-line postcards.[17] Pritchett's lifelong correspondent, Gerald Brenan, believed Dorothy's powers to be just as magical.[18]

From an examination of his papers at the Harry Ransom Center in Texas and the Berg Collection in New York, it is evident that the English language was precious to him, but the physical presentation of that language was not. On the backs of many short-story drafts are rough drafts of book reviews he wrote for the *New Statesman,* or essays he composed for other publications—writings that sometimes interfere with the chronology of a short-story draft. Pritchett delegated all of the typing to his wife and handwrote all of his revisions. And while there is no formula for the revisions, the extensive deletions, additions, interleaving of rewritten pages, and roadmaps for Dorothy, they are in evidence throughout his career.

The extensive collection of short-story manuscripts has preserved the evolution of Pritchett's art, not only throughout his career, but between the drafts of each story. This chapter focuses on one short story to permit a comprehensive analysis of the additions and deletions, from autograph manuscript to final typescript. The discussion of Pritchett's revisions shows this exceptional artist at work, sculpting one of the most compact and successful stories of his career, "You Make Your Own Life."

The simplicity of plot, structure, and language belie the complexity of the story's scope. Instead of relying on well-wrought psychological portraits or an elaborate plot and setting, Pritchett makes the telling of the story its essence. Impeccable timing, diction, mastery of the vernacular, and narrative technique make "You Make Your Own Life" quintessentially Pritchettian. Like most of his short stories, it has few characters—the nameless narrator, Fred the barber, and Albert, the other customer in the barber shop—yet like a Chekhov story, it has far-reaching implications.

* * *

While it is tempting to compare Ring Lardner's "The Haircut" with "You Make Your Own Life," the two stories are far more remarkable for their differences than for their superficial similarities. Lardner creates suspense through his narrator's folksy, ungrammatical, small-town vernacular—copied from *Huckleberry Finn*—and the barber's tantalizing digressions, tangents, non sequiturs and repetitions, which cover for Lardner's lack of plot. While both stories are set in barbershops, the American author's achieves its comic effects through a relentless monologue—a barrage of language that becomes comical, if tedious. Lardner's 4,500-word tale suffers from its length, and once finished, the suspense diffused, it fails to provoke further thought. Contrary to one critic's observation, "The Haircut" narrator does not engage in a conversation with his out-of-town customer, an omission that necessarily limits its scope.[19] The customer's passive role precludes closer examination of the barber's character and the veracity of his story. Pritchett's barbershop story, on the other hand, is a spare 2,200 words, devoid of the inessential, in which subtle verbal and situational irony depend upon a deftly chosen word or phrase. Most importantly, Pritchett's story involves a tale placed within a crucial if unobtrusive frame—a profound technical difference that enables the writer to transform a mere yarn into the complexity of a truly modern short story.

If V. S. Pritchett had not made extensive revisions in the typescript draft of "You Make Your Own Life," it would almost certainly not have become one of his most celebrated stories. One can argue that the act of selection—self-editing—that all short story artists must undertake is just as creative and important as the initial writing. Excising the inessential is an art, and few can have done it better than Pritchett. On the way to the published version, he removes many of the frame-narrator's speculative remarks about the barber, based on intermittent interpretations of his facial gestures, and judgments about his character. Wishing to leave interpretation to his reader, Pritchett creates subtle ambiguities.

The title story from the collection *You Make Your Own Life* exemplifies the breakthrough Pritchett made in the early part of his career as he established his inimitable elliptical style perfectly suited to comic irony. Unlike some writers, whose numerous drafts of particular stories undergo subtle, usually minor changes from one to the next, Pritchett often made substantial alterations between his autograph manuscript, first typescript with autograph revisions, and final typescript, the most significant of them usually appearing in the first typescript.[20]

Our discussion will begin with a brief comparison between the openings of the autograph manuscript and the heavily revised first typescript. Although the former has a few autograph emendations, it is most interesting for the way in which its opening was restructured. And except for the opening, a few line corrections, and a handful of rewritten lines, the surviving first version is reflected in the first typescript. As well preserved as the drafts are, however, the first page of the typescript was replaced by one page of autograph manuscript, probably because Pritchett chose to transform the original opening completely. For the purpose of witnessing the evolution of a Pritchett story, the corrected first typescript is most revealing. For that reason—and to facilitate the reading of Pritchett's nearly illegible handwriting—I have supplied a transcription of this telling draft as an appendix to which I will refer parenthetically during the course of my comparative analysis. To differentiate between the typewritten and handwritten words in the transcription, Pritchett's penned emendations are italicized and his handwritten deletions are represented by a single line through the words. Except for a few emendations, the third version—the typescript carbon copy—is a faithful transcription of the emended first typescript.

* * *

Entitled "The Barber" in the top left-hand corner of the autograph manuscript, the story begins with a visitor's description of a town rather than its barbershop. Instead of intriguing the reader with the inviting, veiled sentence of the second version, "Upstairs from the street a sign in electric light said 'Gent's Saloon'," Pritchett allows the visitor to state his purpose plainly, ending the undistinguished three-sentence paragraph with two unremarkable sentences. The personal pronouns that begin those sentences make the narrator's position more important than the story he is about to tell. Here is the opening page of the first draft:

> It was a small town in a valley with a slow mud-coloured river running through it, one long main street and only two good trains in the day. I had an hour to wait. I thought I would get my haircut.
>
> Genevieve's was the name of the place. Permanent nursery 12/6, chiropodist in attendance; it looked like a women's place. But upstairs an electric sign said "Gent's Saloon". It was a small hot back room full of sunlight with newspapers on the chairs. "Take a seat. I won't be long", said the barber. He was finishing a ~~man's~~ shave ~~hair.~~
>
> "~~I haven't got too long~~", I said.
>
> The barber took no notice. He was a young man with fair hair receding & brushed up into the air from his forehead. ~~He clipped away in silence with the sun on his back. He did not say anything to his customer and his customer said nothing to him. There was only the sound of the step of his foot in the room on the floor and the, his grunt and grunts of absorption as he cut and the tedious movement of~~ He said nothing to his customer and his customer said nothing to him. There was only the harsh sound of the razor over the skin, the rattle of the brush in the jar, the step of the barber on the floor and his absorbed breathing.
>
> I read all the murders in the papers. I read the abductions. There were mothers clamouring for lost babies, a clergyman's wife was caught stealing, a man's ~~wife~~ met his wife on Folkstone pier three days after he had identified her as a drowned body at an inquest, a girl was drowned trying to save a dog. The skeletons of five men killed in the battle of Hastings had been dug up in the Downs. There it was in black & white, very black, very white and big letters. I put the papers down ~~& looked up~~. I didn't believe it.[21]

And here is the opening page of the second draft:

> Upstairs an ~~electric s~~ from the street ~~an electric light sign~~ a sign in electric light said "Gent's Saloon". I went up. There was a small hot back room full of sunlight, with hair clippings on the floor, towels hanging from a peg and newspapers on the chairs. "Take a seat. Just finishing", said the barber. It was a lie. He wasn't anywhere near finishing. He had in fact just begun a shave and the customer was having ~~any~~ everything.
>
> In a dead place like this town you had to wait for everything. I was waiting for a train, now I had to wait for a haircut. It was a small town in a valley with one long street, ~~one cinema on Thursdays and Saturdays~~ and a slow mud-coloured river moving between willows and the backs of houses.
>
> I picked up ~~the~~ a newspaper. A man had murdered an old woman, a clergyman's ~~wife~~ sister was caught stealing gloves in a shop, a man who had

identified the body of his wife at an inquest on a drowning fatility met her ~~the foll~~ three days later in Folkestone pier. ~~Ten An~~ Four thousand Japanese had been killed in an earthquake, an Indian had walked ~~on a bed of~~ barefoot on a bed of fire. Ten miles from this town the skeletons of men killed in a battle eight centuries ago had been dug up in the Downs. That was nearer. Still, I put the paper down. I looked at the two men in the room.[22]

Pritchett not only transforms the opening, deleting such extraneous, misleading details as "Genevieve's," the nursery, and the chiropodist, with their incongruous feminine overtones, but finds his true first line embedded in the second paragraph. The second draft begins more appropriately with the barbershop and, ingeniously, incorporates all the central elements of the story—the setting, speech from the barber, the rivals upon whom the barber's story will be based, and the narrator's keen eye for detail and human behavior—in the first six lines. The narrative sequence in the first draft makes little sense as we move from town to shop to description of the barber and his work to newspaper headlines. The restructured second draft, however, immerses the reader in the central setting of the story before moving to the larger world of the town, and finally to the outside world, through the newspaper headlines.

To make the opening more suspenseful, Pritchett moves the description of the barber and his work that appears in the third paragraph of the first draft to the fifth paragraph of the second draft, albeit with substantial alterations—changes that will be examined later in the analysis. This shift slows down the pacing of the story by delaying the introduction of the main characters, and allows for the completion of the more natural progression described earlier. Furthermore, while the paragraph devoted to news stories separates the portraits of the two main characters in the first draft, its repositioning in the second inextricably links Albert, the customer, and Fred, the barber, "best friends" and rivals, in the narrator's opening, in the barbershop, and in the forthcoming barber's tale.

Finally, the editing of the newspaper contents reveals Pritchett's intentions as well. The news items in the first draft are clearly more numerous and sensational than they are in the third. Without specifying the publication, the frame-narrator, in three sentences, refers to "all the murders," "the abductions," and the "mothers clamouring for lost babies." The first draft also includes a "girl [. . .] drowned trying to save a dog." This combination of the tragic and absurd is typical eye-catching tabloid fare, emphasizing the incredible, not the credible. In both drafts, a clergyman's relative is caught stealing, but her identity changes from wife to sister; the object of her theft, unspecified in the first draft, is identified as a pair of gloves. While the isolated incidents appear similar, the addition of four thousand Japanese killed in an earthquake and an Indian's barefoot fire walk serve to enlarge the dimensions of the events while making them both more distant and abstract. Ultimately, however, they are weeded out in the third draft, or final typescript. Even "the skeletons of five men killed in the battle of Hastings" that had been dug up ten miles from town become simply "the skeletons of men killed in a battle eight centuries ago"—the unspecified number of skeletons and nameless battle reinforcing the extent, distance, and anonymity of the human tragedy. Evidently, Pritchett was not satisfied with the second version, because he later excised the Japanese earthquake and the Indian fire walk, probably to render the series of events less exotic and more credible. In addition, he probably wished to accentuate melodramatic incidents involving two people, not hundreds or thousands, in order to foreshadow the barber's own sparsely populated tabloid tale. The sarcastic description of the tabloid itself—"There it was in black & white, very black, very white and big letters"—with its mock plea for the veracity of the written word, has the opposite effect. This phrase is replaced by the subtler "That was nearer," a sarcastic appraisal of the more personal battle's comparative proximity. Ironically, the narrator himself believes the "battle of eight centuries ago" to be "nearer" than the incidents mentioned earlier. But as soon as he lowers the paper, he looks at the two men whose story involves all the elements of true melodrama—passionate love, tragic illness, rival lovers, attempted murder, and attempted suicide. The barber's story is no less sensational than what he has just read. His matter-of-fact telling in such a common setting only heightens the irony. After all, barbershops are full of forgettable banter, not passionate tales of woe. Even the artful addition of the word "Still" in the second draft, expressing the frame-narrator's ironic (tongue-in-cheek) feigned interest in the final news item, adds to the comic irony in the passage in a way that the more heavy handed phrase, "I didn't believe it," does not.

* * *

From the very opening of the published version of "You Make Your Own Life," Pritchett puts the reader in the nameless narrator's shoes. Attracted by an "electric light" advertising the "'Gent's Saloon'," the narrator climbs "Upstairs from the street" and into the small-town barbershop where he is invited to wait his turn. His succinct description of the shop is followed by his obvious impatience with the slow pace of provincial life. Instead of accepting the inevitable wait patiently, the narrator reveals his unspoken thoughts to the reader in an accusatory tone, frustrated with the barber's unrealistic estimation and unconscious dishonesty:

> "Take a seat. Just finishing," said the barber. It was a lie. He wasn't anywhere near finishing. He had in fact just begun a shave. The customer was having everything.
>
> In a dead place like this town you always had to wait. I was waiting for a train, now I had to wait for a haircut. It was a small town in a valley with one long street, and a slow mud-coloured river moving between willows and backs of houses.[23]

Paradoxically, Pritchett creates suspense through inaction at this early stage in the narrative, and uses the narrator's contempt for small-town life to accentuate its dislocation from the outside world. Stranded in this "dead place," where "you always had to *wait*," he must "*wait* for a haircut" while "*wait*ing for a train" (my italics). The telescoped view of the "small" valley town with one "long" street, and a "slow" mud-coloured river "moving between willows" recalls the bucolic frieze on Keats's Grecian urn. The willows that have been planted in the second draft are not mere incidental ornaments by the side of the river but a symbol of grief for unrequited love or the loss of a mate. Later in the analysis we will see that even Pritchett's choice of tree is consistent with the story's themes.

After establishing the dislocated, seemingly uneventful identity of the town, the bored narrator picks up a newspaper and shifts his and the reader's attention to the predictably sensational stories—distant stories of murder, shoplifting, unsolved mysteries, and exhumed war graves that, ironically, have become banal through the frequency of their appearance. Only in retrospect will the reader understand Pritchett's abrupt transition from peaceful town to distant troubles involving barbarous acts, the last of which confirms their great distance from the slow time of the town:

> Ten miles from this town skeletons of men killed in a battle eight centuries ago had been dug up at the Downs. *That was nearer.* Still, I put the paper down. I looked at the two men in the room.[24] (my italics)

Like a camera, the narrator's eye refocuses on the scene before him. The short, declarative, objective sentences beginning with subjects and verbs force the reader to see the scene distinctly, each sentence establishing a separate image or physical detail. The full stops enforce the languid rhythm experienced by nameless narrator and reader alike. Herein lies one of the pacing techniques more closely associated with verse than with prose—a hallmark of the modern short story that is rarely used in the novel: "I could see the man in the mirror. He was in his thirties. He had a swarthy skin and brilliant long black eyes. The lashes were long too and the lids when he blinked were pale."²⁵ In this section of the revised typescript, Pritchett has crossed out a number of the frame-narrator's subjective, interpretive remarks about both customer and barber that judge, compare, and evaluate. He must have realized that the effectiveness of "You Make Your Own Life" would depend, in part, on the relative discretion of the frame-narrator, especially in that narrator's opening descriptions of the main characters. With this objective in mind, many of the passages have been excised throughout the second draft while others have been completely rewritten (see appendix). In his description of Albert, for instance, we see Pritchett has deleted "a well-made man" from "He was a well-made man in his thirties." The phrase "bright long black eyes like a gypsy's" sheds the comparison and trades "bright" for "brilliant" to become simply "brilliant long black eyes" (app. ll.4–6). Yet almost imperceptibly, Pritchett's frame-narrator begins to describe the customer in more subjective terms, unable to report everything wholly without a "suggestion" of interpretation or figurative language. He adds "just that suggestion of weakness" to the customer's eyes, and where once there was "a glister to his skin like a Hindu's," there is now "a sallow glister" (app. ll.7–8) as he sits "engrossed in his reflection, half smiling at himself and very deeply pleased." Ever careful to monitor his narrator's assessment of the main characters, Pritchett restricts his interpretive remarks to their facial gestures. Fortunately, the incongruous "bright violet socks" that were probably intended to complement the customer's "very dandyish" dress, described before his exit, but that merely detract from the portrait at this stage, have been removed as well (app. l.11).

Initially content to present the barber as "a careful man," Pritchett deletes his frame-narrator's direct, unequivocal statement about character in the typescript, preferring to restrict his narrator's description to the barber's actions. The rewritten description of the barber as "careful and responsible in his movements but nonchalant and detached" assigns human qualities to "movements" in a way that differs from the earlier, more objective reporting of the story's opening (see app. ll.12–13). Ever careful to preserve his narrator's objective tone, Pritchett has pruned away the likening of his barber's regard for the customer to a painter's regard for a "picture in a frame" (app. ll.13–15). This comparison has been replaced by a simple physical description of the barber, lifted from the third paragraph of the autograph manuscript, that balances the description of his customer in the previous paragraph. At the end of the same typescript paragraph we find a similar deletion. Although Pritchett has added "A peculiar look of amused affection [. . .] on his face," as he looks at the black-haired man, for the purpose of enticing the reader, he has crossed out the more extensive interpretation of the "look" that seems to compare the customer's "soaped head" to "a piece of putty"(see app. ll.19–21). Clearly, Pritchett wishes to arouse curiosity about both characters without giving away too many interpretive clues. Yet even from these early revisions, whether deletions or additions, whether in the autograph manuscript or the corrected typescript, we can see that the barber is the focus.

At this stage in the narrative, in fewer than 400 words, Pritchett has not only established the story's setting, situation, tone, and characters, but has begun a subtle, intentional comparison between the barber and his customer. Both men are in their thirties, but the customer has curly "glossy black hair" to contrast with the barber's "fair, receding hair." Pritchett's redundant insistence on this comparison in the first draft has been removed from the second draft: "They were youngish men, both of them, the fair and the dark, much the same age" (app. ll.54–55). Their notable lack of conversation indicates that they are either perfect strangers or know each other well. We are left to wonder whether their mutual silence is a result of familiarity or intimacy. The barber, though silent, is in control of all the action and movement in the story. The narrator's active verbs, multiplied through revision, and longer sentences reinforce the sense of speed with which the barber works as he is "rattling his brush," "wiping the razor," "pushing" the chair, and "soaping the head" (app. ll.16–19). Clearly, the barber is in the dominant position as he prepares his customer for the final treatment, and the narrator's humorous description of his "machine," replete with war imagery, suggests an instrument of torture in a laboratory or an electric chair:

> He wheeled a machine on a tripod to the back of the man. A curved black thing like a helmet enclosed the head. The machine was plugged to the wall. There were phials with coloured liquids in them and soon steam was rushing out under the helmet. I don't know what happened to the man or what the barber did. [. . .] [T]hat customer had everything.[26]

To reinforce the implied reference to war, the narrator describes the customer as "dressed in a square-shouldered grey suit" and likens him to "a guardsman" (app. ll.42–43), a comparison the author has added to the second draft. Interestingly enough, the long sentence that has been deleted on page three is even more revealing. Just as he has been editing out some of the visitor's interpretations of the barber's facial expressions, Pritchett has deleted several of the visitor's interpretations of the customer's expressions: His "eyes closed into long slits with satisfaction like a cat's", and "he smiled slightly at himself in the mirror and then, with the idle luxurious step of a

~~cat, he went to the door.~~" (app. ll.39–40, ll.46–48). Always sensitive to language, Pritchett has removed both cat comparisons along with their hackneyed associations and has exchanged Albert's parting "wide smile" for a faint one. The "unmistakable" "look of dandified derision" (app. l.49) that has been penned into the second draft has been crossed out in the third and final draft. The barber's parting good-bye is accompanied by "a small, hardly perceptible smile too" (app. l.51).

* * *

At this point, approximately a third of the way through the story, the frame-narrator becomes more of a participant as he succeeds Albert in the barber's chair. Pritchett continues to permit him to interpret the barber's behavior, piquing the reader's curiosity, but he has deliberately repressed explicit comparisons that may either anticipate the content of the barber's story or undermine the balance of the narrative. The following passage is a good example of this judicious deletion:

> The barber put the sheet round me. The barber was smiling to himself like a man remembering a tune. He was not thinking about me. ~~The small sardonic smile like the abstracted smile of a man who remembers a story he has been told and is getting another unsuspected flavour from it~~. (app. ll.57–62)

Similarly, the "stronger and more sardonic" smile (app. ll.95–96) has been changed to a "faint," "sardonic" smile in the second draft and deleted altogether in the final typescript. One of the salient differences between the drafts is effected through changes in the narrator's perception as Pritchett attempts to make him more of an observer than an interpreter.

We learn much more about Albert in his absence, not through the action perceived by the narrator, but through the barber's own story within the story. Even though Albert leaves the shop, the barber remains eerily preoccupied, smiling to himself as he "glanced at the door where this man had gone," long after his departure. While making reference to Albert, the barber is described as having "nodded to the door" (app. l.82) in acknowledgment of Albert's weekly visits. This too has been written into the second draft. Although they have been crossed out in the corrected typescript, the descriptions of the barber's reaction to Albert's exit and the barber's altered "state [. . .] as if he were still with that man who had just gone out of the door"(app. ll.78–79) show that Pritchett wished Albert to haunt the shop. Even at the end of his story, the barber is said to have "glanced sardonically at the door as if expecting to see the man standing there" (app. ll.191–192).

Of course the most profound changes in the second draft are those involving the central character, the barber himself, as he is transformed from a crude, sinister, sardonic, vengeful, scheming villain, into a more mysterious, illusive figure—a transformation that necessarily alters the relationships between the characters and has far-reaching implications for the story as a whole. Through a close examination of the extensive revisions, we can see Pritchett altering the very conception of the barber through his frame-narrator's evolving portrait. Many of the changes involve the deletion of expressive smiles that punctuate the barber's dialogue. One of the added smiles, however, demonstrates the subtlety of the revisions. In the first draft, the barber is portrayed as "a dull young man with pale blue eyes and a look of ironical stubbornness in him" (app. ll.72–73). Conscious of the rigidity of such a statement, Pritchett has inserted one of his panoply of smiles through a simile that complicates the reader's conception and builds suspense: "The small dry smile was still like claw marks at the corners of his lips" (app. l.74). Later on, the barber makes an observation with a veiled but sadistic "grim sort of pleasure," in reference to a local girl, that Pritchett has crossed out (app. ll.136–137). At the point at which the barber divulges the identity of Albert's love interest, Pritchett has cut away another, more sinister expression conveyed through the barber's eyes and mouth: "His small pale eyes glared a little but the dry smile was still on his lips" (app. ll.148–149). Furthermore, throughout the first draft version of the barber's tale are numerous telling remarks that Pritchett has excised because they portray the barber as overtly vengeful and threatening. The following passage demonstrates just how pervasive is the first draft's more marked characterization:

> ~~The barber stared me hard in the face.~~
> "In front of me", he said. ~~He grinned with quiet assurance.~~ "What did you say?"
> *"I told him to keep quiet or he'd*
> ~~"Keep quiet", I said. "Or you'll~~ be a corpse".
> ~~"And so he would if he didn't keep quiet", he said, relaxing his stare.~~
> "Consumptives want it, they want it worse than others, but it kills them", he said.
> "I thought you meant *you'd* kill him", I said.
> ~~The young barber gave a short, dry laugh. He chuckled~~
> ~~looked at me scornfully.~~
> (app. ll.197–207).

This passage is indicative of the original barber's more pronounced malevolence in the first draft before he was metamorphosed through Pritchett's artful excision. Presumably, Pritchett recognized that by diminishing the role of the frame-narrator, and simultaneously modifying the barber's character, he could create the ambiguity necessary for more evocative, impressionistic literary possibilities. The revisions in the second draft show Pritchett creating a more subtle portrait through the implied but unsaid. And as we shall see through a close examination of the story's most important section, he knows just how to engineer such a transformation, pruning dialogue, creating silences, manipulating the plot, and restructuring the sequence of events so that the barber's story haunts us long after the final sentence.

Appropriately enough, Fred the barber's story begins with a brief comment about Albert's receding hairline. Curiously, it is the barber who has the receding hairline, not Albert, who has a full head of "glossy black hair" (app. l.2). From the outset then, the reader must wonder about the veracity of the details that follow. A second unsolicited comment from the barber, an observation about Albert's throat, indicates his desire to engage the narrator in conversation. Pritchett has revised this exchange extensively in order to draw both narrator and reader into the drama. In the first draft, without the narrator's participation, the barber appears overzealous, indiscreet, and loquacious. Pritchett has changed the passage dramatically, however, by enlisting his narrator as discreet participant and commentator, adding simple actions that retard the pace and create suspense between the lines (see app. ll.116–120). Gone are his earlier, subjective asides, replaced by the eerie revelation of an attempted suicide, spoken in the barber's hushed tones close to the neck with a "small firm friendly grin" and scissors in hand. A surprisingly modern aural flashback has been penned in as well. The narrator suddenly hears the echo of Albert and Fred's earlier good-bye: "So long, Fred. Cheero, Albert." (app. ll.119–120).

In the corrected typescript, Fred recounts his story about Albert's tuberculosis and suicide attempt with subtle, unobtrusive interpretive commentary from the narrator. Except for the narrator's five brief phrases, this melodrama is uninterrupted for two pages. One has the illusion of a dialogue, but this is a monologue that continues until the end of the story, with a handful of the frame-narrator's comments describing the barber's gestures and actions. Nevertheless, the narrator's involvement evinces important responses, misunderstandings, ironies, and clarifications.

Instead of allowing the barber to spill the contents of his story prematurely in the succeeding paragraph and dissipate the suspense, Pritchett has cut fifteen sentences of background information from the second draft, the important details of which have been condensed, refined, and relocated in the conclusion of the final typescript. This substantial deletion helps to maintain the reader's interest in a character that might otherwise be rendered a loquacious bore (see app. ll.122–134). Already a mature writer when he crafted "You Make Your Own Life," Pritchett understood that silences are often more suspenseful than conversation. Dialogue should not be a verbatim record of what has been said, especially not in a short story where every word counts. It must advance action, and wherever it has not, Pritchett has pruned it. This simple principle is the foundation for his elliptical style, and one can see merely by glancing through the appendix just how exhaustively it has been applied.

The barber's speech itself becomes increasingly elliptical as he nonchalantly tells his tale of woe. Speaking in half sentences, "absently," accompanied by the sound of his scissors, he tells a disturbing story in the vernacular that is, ironically, anything but "usual." We can see that Pritchett has weeded out the narrator's perfunctory questions designed to further the conversation, preferring the barber's unfiltered monologue. The reliability of the barber's narration is most in question once the frame-narrator becomes the listener. In short, clipped phrases lacking proper quotations and subjects, relayed indirectly by the frame-narrator, the barber begins his seemingly dispassionate account of the suicidal Albert: "He fell in love with a local girl who took pity on him when he was ill, when he was in bed. Nursed him. Usual story. Took pity on him but wasn't interested in him in that way" (app. ll.138–141). Despite his denial, the barber's insistence on the local girl's pity suggests, especially in a story full of irony, that she may have had romantic interest in Albert. After all, the barber describes her as "A very attractive girl." He suddenly reveals her identity after a pregnant pause: "'Matter of fact,' said the barber *stepping over for the clippers and shooting a hard sideways stare at me*. 'It was my wife'" (app. ll.146–147; my italics for autograph addition). To further complicate the situation, we learn that Albert, the consumptive, "'got it badly'" and must have been passionate about and full of desire for the girl who became the barber's wife. Furthermore, while we know from the first draft that Albert and Fred have known each other since childhood, Pritchett has added "Used to be his best friend. Still was" to Fred's account of Albert, a comment full of irony (app. l.154). Even the characters' backgrounds change from one version to the next. The following passage from the first draft, which has been crossed out in the second draft, shows that the girl was first Albert's, not Fred's: "~~She knew him before she knew me. But she went away for a couple of years to look after a lady and when she got fed up she came back. Then I took up with her~~'" (app. ll.156–159). Pritchett has removed this background from the story in order to make our conception of the barber more ambiguous. While the original version makes him more villainous—an unscrupulous man who steals women away from sick friends, chuckling about his success—the revised draft creates the kind of ambiguity for which Pritchett is famous. Similarly, he has deleted the barber's mention of Albert's visits to the girl's shop—a passage that betrays obvious jealousy "in the same tone of amused scorn" (app. ll.168–170). Yet Pritchett has salvaged an idea from the too obvious expression of jealousy: "I didn't mind. I knew my mind. She knew hers" (app. l.172). To preserve the potential irony of the barber's supposed confidence in the couple, he has also deleted the more insecure line, "I was glad someone was looking after her" (app. ll.172–173). All the while that the barber expresses and reiterates his confidence in the harmlessness of the river excursions, we cannot discern the reality of the situation. His insistence on purportedly knowing the minds of the other players could be a sign of complete confidence or utter insecurity. Likewise, his seemingly permissive attitude about the river excursions could be interpreted variously. Yet even if we are willing to accept the barber's self-proclaimed confidence in his wife and "best friend," we soon realize that the sanctioning of their outings may be part of a more sinister scheme. The barber's description of the river's unhealthy humidity in the first draft is utterly factual, but the few words Pritchett has added to the second and third drafts belie the barber's subtle competitiveness. In the second draft the barber speaks "reflectively"(app. l.178), and makes an ambiguous reference with the indeterminate subject "It" to either the origin of Albert's illness, or the complex triangle relationship (see app. l.179). And in the final typescript, Pritchett has written in an even more telling phrase that hints at Albert's tactical mistake in his and the barber's fight for the girl: "That's when he made his mistake." Consistent with this competitive tone is a more piquant two-sentence addition to the second draft: "'He couldn't get away with it.' he said. He was smiling at the past" (app. l.184). Though the first of these sentences betrays the possibility of a malicious barber full of pent up jealousy and ill will, the description of the barber's smile has been excised from the third draft because it portrays him as pleased with his rival's misfortune, gloating about his demise.

Other revisions contribute to the ambiguity of the final version. The barber's account of his and his wife's visits to the convalescing Albert is modified as well. Pritchett has crossed out his frame-narrator's detailed assessment of the barber's character, replacing it with a comment about his "cocksure irony" (see app. ll.192–193). In the first draft, in mentioning his and his wife's visits to Albert's before they were married, the barber explains that "'Both of us used to go'" (app. l.188). This sentence has been deleted in the second draft, leaving the reader to wonder about Albert and the girl's relationship during the day, before the barber would "'turn up in the evenings'" after closing (app. ll.188–189). We cannot determine whether Albert's lurid bedside invitation to the girl in the barber's presence is a provocative joke or merely a pathetic plea, because the barber's "short laugh" punctuating his retelling could be interpreted variously in our mind's ear (app. ll.194–196). Pritchett allows the barber to react with fervor during his telling of the attempted murder, but he has removed the barber's defensive explanation, which the reader might associate with a possessive, jealous man—a figure whose demeanor would be inconsistent with the self-assurance Pritchett has fashioned for him in the second draft (see app. ll.211–213). The barber's unsolicited remark "I rumbled him" (app. l.247), which means that he uncovered Albert's plan, uttered while singeing the narrator's hair, has been crossed out of the second draft to preserve the ambiguity of the rivalry. Yet these three words and the deleted sentences that follow suggest that the barber may have been uncertain about his own relationship with the girl and sought a way to defuse the threat his friend posed. Once again, Pritchett has made deletions consistent with his subtler portrait of the barber.

After finishing "You Make Your Own Life," we cannot be sure that the girl loved the barber more than Albert, or if Fred simply destroys his rival by allowing his "best friend" Albert to endanger his health on the river. The autograph manuscript confirms a more pronounced vengefulness and malevolence in the barber while the deletion of numerous lines, facial gestures, and vindictive phrases makes the barber more sympathetic, still allowing for the possibility of his retaliatory scheme in the end. There is no "black and white" (see transcription of p.1, first draft) for the mysterious relationships between the three main players in the final version of this understated drama. And it is our inability to explain the relationships beyond a doubt that enhances this most thought-provoking fiction.

The critics who have written about "You Make Your Own Life" believe the barber implicitly, but the role he plays in the trio makes his account necessarily subjective. If he is indeed an unreliable narrator, to what extent is he telling the truth? In an overtly ironic story, which lines mean the opposite of what they say? Why does Albert's brief appearance at the beginning of the story completely contradict the barber's portrait of him? And what is the explanation for the trio's continuation? What, after all, is the complex nature of their continued association?

* * *

An examination of numerous short-story drafts reveals Pritchett's expert fashioning of the unspoken or the unsaid. There are two kinds of unsaid—what has been deleted from the story and the far more subtle, illusive unsaid that remains in silences. Yet the two work in concert; the first must be excised to create the second. Distilling the essence from a tangible whole creates the desired effect. And, like impressionist paintings, Pritchett's stories permit his readers to interpret them variously on different readings. One may wonder why he felt it necessary to work in such a laborious, meticulous manner. But the answer becomes clear once we have consulted his revisions. His initial drafts often contain explicit descriptions of his characters' appearances, inner thoughts, and motivations that, through extensive revision, deletion, and rewriting, make for subtle narratives that give the reader a more active role in the interpretation of the stories. Instead of writing to measure, Pritchett prefers to exceed it and then to cut out unnecessary material in successive drafts. The mere writing of the overexplicit passages gives him a more tangible sense of the characters he has created—a keen sense that enables their elliptical yet convincing presentation. Pritchett's stories, like Chekhov's, continually disclose the complexities of human nature through subtle evocation.

Pritchett is a maximalist, not a minimalist, whose well-wrought, concentrated stories owe their uncommon intensity to their creator's meticulous revisions. Dismissed by some readers as a merely traditional writer, he is actually a deft innovator whose genius for making and remaking will occupy us yet again in the chapters that follow our examination of Trevor's curiously similar approach to short-story writing.

Chapter 3

William Trevor's "Distillation of an Essence": From "Meeting Mrs. Faraday" to "Cocktails at Doney's"

You have to know all sorts of things about the characters that the reader is not going to be bothered with—that he's not even going to be told. I don't mind writing an awful lot of stuff about people and then letting it end up in the wastepaper basket—or sometimes getting rid of the character completely.[1]

A short story is like an impressionist painting. You cut down everything enormously and you get the effects from one big splash or explosion. You have to cut to the very edge. What excites me is to go as far as I can.[2]

Like V. S. Pritchett, William Trevor has been heralded as one of the greatest short-story writers of the modern period, and, like Pritchett, his stories typically evolve through a process of extensive and elaborate revision. Though an accomplished novelist as well, Trevor has been candid about his preference for the short form, believing that it is the one to master. For him, everything begins as a short story.

The drafts for over one hundred short stories in various stages of completeness in the William Trevor Collection at the Special Collections Department of the University of Tulsa's McFarlin Library consist of autograph, typescript, and carbon copy typescript manuscripts with extensive handwritten and typewritten revisions. Trevor's creative process is as elaborate as Pritchett's and his method is similar, but his technique is completely different. In contrast to Pritchett's consistent use of multiple separate drafts, Trevor sometimes condenses several drafts worth of revisions into one. In many instances he begins stories on the typewriter, using the initial double-spaced blue paper typescripts as a point of departure and reworking them extensively between the lines as well as in margins and on the backs of pages with numerous autograph revisions, deletions, and additions. His composition process in some of these composite drafts, however, obscures the sequence of revisions. Pasted over many of the heavily revised typescript pages are typescript additions of a couple of lines to half a page in length that mask earlier versions and revisions underneath. Trevor once likened this process to film editing.[3] When he realizes that a particular passage is out of place, he simply cuts it out and pastes it in where it belongs. He occasionally types corrections between lines or even cuts his typescript between lines and splices the separated pieces of typescript together with autograph inserts that often considerably lengthen the original page. Although there is no formula for the revisions, the multilayered approach is prevalent. The cutting and pasting technique anticipates computer editing and, unfortunately for the genetic or textual critic, often leaves as few clues as a computer draft. To make matters even more difficult for the scholar, Trevor has blackened with magic marker the once discernable revisions in many of these particular short-story drafts, including those for his last submission to the Library, *After Rain*.

Fortunately the extensive William Trevor Collection includes some heavily edited short-story drafts free of the multilayered technique—be they autograph manuscripts or typescripts—that enable us to follow Trevor's artful revisions through to their respective published versions. As we saw in the previous chapter, revising a short story is as important as the initial writing, and Trevor does it as well as Pritchett. This chapter, like the last, analyzes the growth of a well-known short story that, like Pritchett's "You Make Your Own Life," eventually became the title story of a collection.

Published in Trevor's sixth collection of short stories, *The News from Ireland* (1986), "Cocktails at Doney's" is set in Florence amid its legacy of Italian Renaissance art and architecture. True to Trevor's intentions, this character study is without an elaborate plot, focusing instead on the mysteries of human nature. The story is based on the chance meeting of a married American woman, a fashion-shop proprietor, and a middle-aged British guidebook writer preparing a new guide on Florence. A tall, attractive woman in her mid- to late thirties, Mrs. Faraday makes an annual February excursion to Florence for the Pitti Donna. She claims to recognize the guidebook writer one evening after dinner in the bar, joins him the following day after lunch, and invites him to dine at a restaurant of his choice the same evening. In order to thank him for graciously treating her to the meal, she persuades him to join her for cocktails the following evening at Doney's, but, inexplicably, does not appear. Puzzled by her behavior, he inquires of the hotel receptionist and finds out that Mrs. Faraday has departed mysteriously from the hotel without paying, left all of her belongings in her room, and taken her passport. He makes a fruitless search for her, including a visit to the flats she coveted in their conversations, before informing an official at the American consulate of her disappearance. Finally, he is interrogated by the Florentine police in the course of their investigation, but neither they nor her husband's private detectives solve the mystery.

Originally published in the 8 April 1985 issue of the *New Yorker*, "Cocktails at Doney's" exists in earlier versions in the William Trevor Collection. The only complete draft in the McFarlin Library, however, is a thirty-eight-page autograph manuscript written on 8 ¼" x 11" white graph paper with light-blue graph lines. The perforation marks at the top of each page indicate that the pages were from a tablet. With the exception of the first two pages in pencil, this manuscript is written entirely in royal blue ink with royal blue autograph deletions and additions, but some pages are written in a blue/black ink with a combination of royal blue and blue/black emendations. Appearing at the top of the first page, the working title, "Meeting Mrs. Faraday," is deleted and replaced by "Cocktails at Doney's." Designated "an early version" on the back of its last page, the manuscript draft with its extensive revisions reveals much about Trevor's work as a writer. Another autograph manuscript, obviously incomplete, consists of four miscellaneous pages (25B, 29, 30, 32) all in pencil on light-green 11 ¾" x 8 ¼" typing paper. They may have served as inserts. Finally, there is an incomplete typescript consisting of six pages (1, 26, 29, 29b, 31, 32) on 10" x 8" "Croxley Script" watermark paper, which has a number of minor autograph emendations in pencil. At the top of the first page, the "Meeting" of "Meeting Mrs. Faraday" is deleted and replaced in Trevor's hand by "Losing."

This chapter is principally concerned with a comparison of the complete autograph manuscript version with the most recent version published in *William Trevor: The Collected Stories* (1993). Reference is made, where appropriate, to particularly illuminating deviations in the four-page autograph manuscript and the *New Yorker* version. The few minute differences between the *News from Ireland* and *Collected Stories* versions are inconsequential. Unless otherwise specified, the complete autograph manuscript,

(Ams.), will be referred to as "the manuscript" or "the manuscript version" and the *Collected Stories* version will be termed "the published version." In this chapter page references to *Collected Stories* and the manuscript are in parentheses in the text. In instances where the manuscript and published versions are identical, both page references appear in parentheses.

* * *

"Cocktails at Doney's" depends upon achieving a balance between its characters. The portrayals of the unnamed Englishman—named "Curtis" in the *New Yorker* version—Mrs. Faraday, and their relationship are interdependent. One cannot be altered without affecting the other, and any substantial changes to one necessitate the readjustment of the whole. By means of a number of cumulative changes in the autograph manuscript, Trevor reduces the guidebook writer's overt interest in Mrs. Faraday while increasing her interest in him. From the outset of the published version of the story, their relationship is shrouded in mystery. While Mrs. Faraday behaves as if she has met him on a previous visit, he cannot recall her. A few deleted but visible lines in the manuscript, entitled "Meeting Mrs. Faraday," suggest the possibility of a prior meeting, but although they may heighten the reader's curiosity, even they do not confirm Mrs. Faraday's recollection. She reminds him of the circumstances, though he only pretends to remember her name. Crossed out as well is her recollection of him as a guidebook writer that confirms their earlier meeting (Ams. 2).

Curiously enough, the Englishman's own reflection, added to the published version, achieves the same effect: "Before their conversation ended he was certain they had not ever met before" (980). Instead of eliminating the possibility of a prior encounter, his reflection paradoxically arouses our curiosity further. We wait for him to recall the meeting he denies having had. In the manuscript version, after lunch the following day, he asks himself again if they have actually met when Mrs. Faraday sits down at his table (Ams. 7). The cutting of both passages creates even more suspense by enlisting the reader's participation early in the narrative. Instead of following the Englishman's genuine attempts to recall Mrs. Faraday's identity in the manuscript, we are stimulated by what is unsaid in the published version, inherently more suspicious of his outright denial, and intrigued by the possibility of a hidden prior relationship.

In the manuscript, the Englishman furthers the conversation by responding to Mrs. Faraday's questions, whereas in the published version he deflects most of them in order to maintain his distance from her. When queried about his marital status in the opening page of the published version, for instance, he says he is not married and succeeds in avoiding the subject altogether for the remainder of the story: "'And your wife? Is she here with you?' 'I'm actually not married'" (979). In contrast to his reticence in the published version, however, he is forthcoming when asked the same question in the manuscript's genial but banal exchange, admitting to being married twice with three grown children (Ams. 7). Careful to preserve his protagonist's ambiguousness however, even in the manuscript, Trevor calls the Englishman's supposed honesty about his family into question. Immediately following the exchange in which he claims he is still happily married, we learn that the Englishman is not married, happily or otherwise (Ams. 7). Mrs. Faraday succeeds in evincing intimate responses from him in the manuscript version. Even his lies to her provoke an outpouring of feeling confined to his consciousness but available to the reader. His excised bald reflections about his failed life demonstrate the self-pity and self-recrimination that consume him in the manuscript version and merely preoccupy him in the published version. Unsuccessful at marriage or in any relationships with women, he considers his life a failure. In a deleted but legible passage, he decides he will live vicariously through his sons, whom he hopes will make amends for all his shortcomings (Ams. 7).

His attitude toward Mrs. Faraday undergoes a gradual transformation during the course of the manuscript as he explores his conflicting feelings about her. Initially disdainful, he thinks of her as a philistine, overwhelmed by but poorly informed about the magnificence and grandeur of Florentine art. Yet, although he finds it difficult to admit to himself, he is attracted to her beauty and femininity. In the published version, instead of using his expertise to dazzle and entice the willing student, however, he avoids her as much as possible, behavior that, ironically, only intensifies Mrs. Faraday's interest. The crippling impotence that the narrator alludes to early in the published story—the condition supposedly responsible for his two failed marriages—is the obvious explanation for his unnatural, inhibited response to her overtures.

In the manuscript, they both participate as Mrs. Faraday succeeds in engaging the Englishman in conversation, but in the published version, where he initiates nothing, speaking as little as possible, she does most of the talking. Trevor makes several attempts in the manuscript to establish the conversation about marriage—conversations that reveal the Englishman lying about his marital troubles. But even if he lies, he also divulges personal details that are concealed from Mrs. Faraday in the published version or are altogether eliminated. She complains in the manuscript about her disappointing life, wishes to escape her husband, has lost her only child, and cannot conceive. Trevor explores her identity as well in his manuscript portrait of her. Some passages suggest that she is unhappy with her husband, while she praises him in others as generous and well meaning (Ams. 11). At one point she smiles while speaking tenderly and affectionately of him in a husky voice (Ams. 13). Her brief explanation for his absence in the published version makes her sound accepting of her husband who "was not a man for Europe, preferring local race-tracks" (979). Mrs. Faraday's account in the manuscript, however, while containing similar information, indicates that their relationship is unsuccessful. Their tastes are incompatible, and she laughs at the thought of her husband accompanying her to Europe. For instance, not only does he prefer racetracks to culture, but they sometimes had to spend time apart (Ams. 2). With hindsight, she says that her marriage had been insignificant (Ams. 8). At one point, where Trevor emphasizes her adoration of Florence, she even mentions wishing to leave her husband. If this alteration emphasizes Mrs. Faraday's love of Florence, it also communicates her indifference to her husband and, more subtly, her availability. Both characters are more talkative in the manuscript as Trevor experiments with their interaction, seeking the meaning in their encounter. In addition to their dialogue about marriage and children, they discuss the idea of settling down, the Neri di Bicci Annunciation in Santa Trinita, Savonarola, Florentine art and history, and the idea of living in Florence. These conversations establish the Englishman's underlying self-pity and self-recrimination as well as Mrs. Faraday's melodramatic situation.

Not surprisingly, all of this was excised. The Englishman simply reveals too much to Mrs. Faraday. And though he imparts his dread of tourist relationships to the reader, he encourages her interest, reciprocating politely, unable to control himself. Through his thoughts, the reader learns all that Mrs. Faraday would like to know. In the published version, however, his reticence creates the necessary tension. There, instead of being liberated in the company of a woman so forthright about her disappointments, he guards his own even more vigilantly.

Difficult as it is to admit to himself, he is attracted to her. In both the manuscript and the published version, he notices that "She was a beautiful woman" (Ams. 2, 979), while in the published version alone she has "classic features" (979). Interestingly enough, there is similar divergence in his otherwise identical description of her dress and makeup as he observes them after lunch. In both the manuscript and published version "Her nails were shaped and painted, her face [...] meticulously made up," but his overall impression of her allure—deleted in the manuscript (Ams. 7)—is left out of the published version. In their last moments together, immediately after she persuades him to meet her again the following evening for cocktails at "Doney's," he applauds—figuratively and inaudibly, of course—her commanding beauty and style (Ams. 16, verso). This too is kept out of the published version.

Trevor prunes most of the Englishman's direct statements of interest in her to preserve the uncertainty of his sentiments—uncertainty that creates suspense in the published version. In a surprising, suspicious departure from all versions—the manuscript, *The News from Ireland*, and *The Collected Stories*—the *New Yorker* edition undermines the Englishman's otherwise guarded response to Mrs. Faraday's appearance by comparing her to the mythical beauty who launched a thousand ships: "In his looking glass he examined the faint smear of lipstick and didn't wipe it off. He woke in the night, *thinking that Helen of Troy might have looked like Mrs. Faraday* and wondering if her lipstick was still on his cheek" (my italics).[4]

There are numerous contradictions within the manuscript, including blatant inconsistencies in characterization and behavior. At one point the Englishman is annoyed with Mrs. Faraday, impatient with her casual speculation about the Italian masterworks he reveres. And though he tolerates her conversation, he dismisses her predilection for Annunciations, not wishing to entertain her preferences or exchange views on Florentine art (Ams. 9). (Ironically, while his ex-wives had no interest in his work, Mrs. Faraday finds it fascinating—yet instead of welcoming her interest, he dismisses it.) Furthermore, he resents her seating herself at his table after lunch (Ams. 7).

In the manuscript, at the end of their coffee together, she thanks him for his directions to San Spirito and calls him a kind person. Unable to suppress a natural reaction to such a soothing compliment, he experiences a fleeting "pleasant sensation" but, seemingly haunted by his disastrous relationships with women, takes refuge in his inhibited self, stifles his need for affection, and convinces himself not to become involved in any way with Mrs. Faraday (Ams. 10). Although too explicit in the manuscript, his conflicting emotions are consistent with his characterization in the published version. So emphatic is the self-denial, so calculated the response, that through his own dialectic we witness the Englishman's conflict between his fear of and desire for a relationship. Similarly, later in the manuscript, his expressed fear of not merely a travelers' relationship but of a love affair as well (Ams. 11) may simultaneously betray his wish to have one. Even his reaction to her dinner invitation in the earlier version portrays a more sympathetic, divided man who, when invited, cannot think of an excuse to avoid dining with her and fears being caught in a lie. In the published version her insistent plea to dine—"I'd really appreciate it if you'd accept" (983)—replaces the option for him to decline (Ams. 11), making him even more determined to reject her: "He wanted to reply that he would prefer to be left alone [. . .] that he had never met her in the past, that she had no claims on him" (983).

Though the Englishman denies himself a relationship with Mrs. Faraday in the manuscript, he does not altogether conceal his regret. Consistent with the numerous passages mourning his lost youth—also excised before publication—are those that justify his inaction. For instance, he tells himself that as few as three years earlier, he would have reached out while at the table to make physical contact and praised her as the most beautiful American he had ever met (Ams. 15). Flattered by her attention, the incredulous, self-effacing man of the manuscript even entertains her idea about not merely a love affair, but about starting a new life together in Florence before concluding that while he might have shared her optimism a decade earlier, it is now too late (Ams. 15–16). Neither the mere contemplation of such a romantic union nor any intimation of stifled optimism can be found in the published version.

The Englishman is clearly obsessed with Mrs. Faraday in the manuscript version. As he strolls through the cloisters at Santa Maria Novella, he imagines her speculating about fashion trends, worried that she would be changed from the previous night in his company, "preoccupied with her business, no time for silliness" (Ams. 16, 986). (In the published version, he imagines her exhibiting this behavioral change "after her love-making" with "some man she picked up.") Inserted afterward, in a finer pen and boxed, this emendation shows the Englishman to be, ironically, wistful about and suddenly appreciative of the frivolity for which he earlier showed disdain. Despite his contempt for her and resolve to maintain his distance, he is drawn to her, preoccupied with her, and haunted by her when he is alone (Ams. 16). Her sudden, mysterious disappearance provokes an even stronger emotional response in him during his conversation with the hotel receptionist. The notable difference in the manuscript version is that he is "worried now" (Ams. 19) because she has neither paid her bill nor taken her belongings. Once again, Trevor excises any overt indication of the Englishman's interest in Mrs. Faraday.

Surprisingly, when Mrs. Faraday's character is scrutinized by the consulate's Mr. Humber and the carabinieri, the formerly disinterested protagonist defends her reputation from insinuation and slander. Instead of merely stating that "'She's a respectable proprietor of a fashion shop'"(987)—a response taken verbatim from the manuscript version (Ams. 20)—in order to counter the carabinieri's suggestion that "maybe she ran up her hotel bill and slipped it" (987), he vouches for her character. While his defense of Mrs. Faraday's professional competence is maintained in the published text, his more subjective, personal defence of her is discarded. Further evidence of his real interest in her is eliminated as well. In the manuscript, desperate to locate the American woman, he withholds information about her from the police, not out of concern for himself, but because he is afraid that with more detailed, intimate disclosures, such as her wish to rent a flat and be devoured by Florence, they will stop looking for her (Ams. 21). In the midst of this speculation, in response to Mr. Humber's unflattering description of Mrs. Faraday as a "gallivanting lady" (Ams. 21, 988), he recalls lipstick on his cheek, regrets not complimenting the American woman on her beauty, and questions the impression he gave the police.

Anxious about her welfare, he defends her reputation during his conversation with the detached Mr. Humber, as if elevating her image in his and the carabinieri's eyes will give them more incentive to find her. In a pronounced attempt to shield her from Humber's suspicion, the Englishman of the manuscript distinguishes between the woman and her profession, arguing that "she only seemed to be" vulgar by association with her "vulgar business," a "rubbishy" shop, admits that he too is in a vulgar business, and claims that he and Mrs. Faraday are the same kind of people (Ams. 22). The subtler published version is consistent with the Englishman's more detached view of Mrs. Faraday:

> "She's not a vulgar woman. From what I said to the police they may imagine she is. Of course she's in a vulgar business. They may have jumped too easily to conclusions."
> Mr. Humber said he did not understand. "Vulgar?" he repeated.
> "Like me she deals in surface dross." (988)

An overall comparison of the manuscript draft with the published version reveals just how comprehensive Trevor's revisions are—dramatic excisions that narrow the detailed panoramic view befitting a novel to the smaller scope of the short story. In the manuscript, Trevor overwrites, including details that blur the focus of the story. Extensive background information, biographical details, and exhaustive characterization of the Englishman detract from the story's impact.

Furthermore, the manuscript of "Cocktails at Doney's" divulges too much too early. Material from this version is either cut altogether or displaced. The first page reveals the protagonist's incredulity about losing Mrs. Faraday, foreshadowing elements are insistent, and ideas best parceled out during the course of the story are introduced prematurely. Instead of beginning with Mrs. Faraday's recognition of the Englishman, as in the published version, the first page of the manuscript, cut before publication, opens with a Dutch boy enquiring where he can dine with his girlfriend. The focus shifts to the man who has responded to the question (Ams. 1). Using a minor character to introduce a protagonist is legitimate in a novel, but misleading in a short story, especially since we never encounter the Dutch boy again. Narrated in the present tense in limited third person from the Englishman's consciousness, the story begins at the end, encased in a contrived, clichéd frame, its suspense undermined. The Englishman continues his stroll in the present, posing questions about Mrs. Faraday, puzzled about his preoccupation with a woman he claims he does not love and hardly knows. He remembers her unflattering reputation and mourns her disappearance. Naturally, all these elements are more effective in the definitive version where they are developed over the course of the story. Trevor finds the true beginning on the second page of the manuscript with Mrs. Faraday's sudden appearance and exclamation that the Englishman has forgotten her (Ams. 1a). Uninfluenced by the man's remembrance of things past in the manuscript, the reader witnesses the enigmatic relationship from the beginning, the story's suspense preserved by the chronological telling through the Englishman's consciousness.

The manuscript suffers from the accumulation of foreshadowing elements that would increase suspense in a novel but merely foretell Mrs. Faraday's disappearance in this short story. The manuscript includes, for instance, her unwittingly portentous wish, expressed during her after-lunch conversation with the Englishman, to be devoured by the city of Florence and it is reinforced several lines later with her speculation about what would happen if she were (Ams. 8). Not only does her insistence spoil the suspense of a subtle, tragically ironic foreshadowing line, it is further belabored by the Englishman's subsequent laughter and their overly explicit exchange about the fuss that might ensue (Ams. 8). Conscious of telegraphing her fate, Trevor preserved almost verbatim in the text her initial wish to be devoured, but eliminated the subsequent dialogue. Later in the manuscript, during a deleted exchange about settling in Florence, she utters another ironic, portentous line about disappearing that is accentuated by her smile and the Englishman's foreboding silence (Ams. 14). During the same conversation, she expresses interest in vanishing into the Palazzo Ricasoli as if into the netherworld (Ams. 15). Finally, as he sits outside Gilli's after her disappearance, overhearing Italians comparing the murder of a janitor to the highly publicized murder of "innocent Gabriella," an Italian school girl, the protagonist draws further attention to Mrs. Faraday's unnatural absence as he recalls her coincidental talk of disappearance that telegraphs the ending (Ams. 20). Once again, Trevor's judicious excision of such insistent foreshadowing elements maintains the story's tension.

Most of the Englishman's personal history is excluded from the published story—his frustrations, scenes from his failed marriages, memories of his childhood, and his crippling impotence. Presumably to portray him convincingly and make his adult behavior realistic and comprehensible, Trevor returns to the Englishman's childhood early in the manuscript, chronicling the development through his consciousness. There is, for instance, a long passage about a Brother's praise of his schoolboy writing, his unrealized ambition, and subsequent recognition of his shortcomings. In a page-length deleted passage, he recognizes his limitations as a writer (Ams. 3). The genesis of his writing career is given a disproportionate amount of attention as he recalls his inspiration while in post–Second World War Dublin to write a vernacular guidebook about the city's public houses and attractions. He even recalls a passage from it—the first of many such passages sprinkled liberally throughout the manuscript and designed to anchor Trevor's limited third-person point of view in his protagonist's consciousness. More importantly, his reflection on guidebook writing reveals his inquisitiveness and enthusiasm for every aspect of the process (Ams. 3). His reminiscences continue when, unable to sleep, he sees himself as a child playing next to a whitewashed wall in the back garden of his parents' provincial house—an image developed in novelistic detail within the ensuing dream. He dreams of himself with a full head of hair and a face free of wrinkles; he sees himself in Istanbul, Marseilles, Antwerp, and the Copenhagen Botanical Gardens, where he strolls with his first wife and belittles his ephemeral guides. The dream shifts to the garden of his youth where his father has a surreal premonition that his infant son would marry twice and travel to foreign countries. His mother, convinced that writing "rubbish" about cities is no way to spend a life, reveals that she has requested a different future for her child: that he remain in the town, become a post office clerk, marry the auctioneer's daughter, and work in the auction rooms. His dream expresses professional regrets and a fear of family rejection altogether absent from the published version. Developed in minute detail, the fantasy demands the frame of a novel, whereas its expansiveness would strain the delicate architecture of the short story (Ams. 4–5). Once again, the manuscript is overly discursive. At the outset, the narrative is mired in the completed action of the past instead of the continuing action of the story's present. Designed for the purpose of acquainting the reader with the main character, the detailed portrait arrests the story at its fledgling stage and impedes dramatization.

The expansiveness of Trevor's manuscript is determined, in part, by a loquacious protagonist unable to stifle his responses to Mrs. Faraday's personal enquiries. His lack of control emphasizes her disarming kindness as much as his psychological conflict and need for companionship (Ams. 9–10). While supposedly dreading the creation of a "travellers' friendship" and Mrs. Faraday's prolonged stay, he entertains her notion about settling down. Furthermore, in response to her demand to know more about him, the Englishman, instead of telling her "superficial things [. . .] about the Italian cities for which he'd written guidebooks" (984)—as he does in the published version (while being increasingly irritated by her voice)—here invites further involvement, willingly divulging details about his children: his son is a university professor; one daughter is married to an English eye specialist; and the other is a professional cellist (Ams. 12A). Trevor explores the relationship further still, making his protagonist as forthcoming in the manuscript as he is closed-mouthed in the published version. In contrast to his tacit dismissal of her enquiry in the latter, for instance, he is surprisingly unguarded in the manuscript, candid about personal matters, and open to Mrs. Faraday's questions about his family situation (Ams. 13).

Responsive as he is in such exchanges, we learn far more about him from his ruminations: he imparts self-pitying regrets about his life and unflattering personal details to the reader, yet withholds them from Mrs. Faraday. Perhaps afraid to lose her interest, he keeps his sense of loss and failure to himself. Life seems to have passed him by; he was no more than a father; his second wife did not wish to see him again; he had failed in all his relationships with women and often wished he could start over in the small town where he spent his childhood, and remain there (Ams. 14).

During his final encounter with Mr. Humber, he acknowledges to himself the crippling self-absorption responsible for his failed relationships with women. The passage includes ideas that undermine the story because they concentrate on biographical details rather than on the Englishman's speculation about Mrs. Faraday, his possible relationship with her, her suitability for him, and his reaction to his admitted "lameness" (990) or impotence. His insistent solipsism is as detrimental to the success of "Cocktails at Doney's" as it is to his relationships with women. Once more, the novelistic character-background and speculation in the manuscript is inappropriate in a short story. Trevor removes this kind of melodrama as the dross is shed. In an equally unbecoming, sentimental, almost identical companion passage, also excised before publication, the Englishman meditates on all that he regrets not having told Mrs. Faraday in his fifty-eighth year: the "surface dross" he had become; the accusations of Rosie (a woman with whom he had had a failed relationship); the recriminations of his daughters and his son; his admission that he was consumed by work; attempts to share his past with his first wife, Dora (including his memory of the whitewashed wall);

the confession about his wasted life; and Dora's reproach about his selfish introspection (Ams. 24).

The Englishman is not the only character in the manuscript, however, who indulges in melodramatic thoughts. Clearly at ease with her tourist companion, Mrs. Faraday does not merely reflect on intimate details of her own life; she discloses them. In addition to revelations that are maintained in the final version, such as the death of her baby and her poor relationship with her sister, are the later expurgated sentimental details reminiscent of Victorian melodrama: her small-town life, her convent schooling, her mother's early death, and her father's devotion to his work to the exclusion of his family (Ams. 15). And in a number of other places Trevor wisely cuts superfluous details and inconsequential minor characters that populate the manuscript. In an imagined or recollected passage from his tourist guide, for example, the Englishman gives advice about finding a cinema showing undubbed films. This idea is mentioned in an earlier deleted tourist-guide passage (see Ams. 13), but here it is developed further and includes an imagined encounter with the Tourist Information woman. Other characters failing to make the final cast include a baby-faced young man singing and strumming a guitar and an anonymous French girl overheard expressing her surprise in English upon discovering her father's relationship with a twenty-four-year-old girl (see Ams. 20). The novelistic description of Mrs. Faraday's walk across the dining room with her coat is reduced to a few lines in the published text (see Ams. 7). Trevor also eliminates a detailed, page-length conversation between the Englishman and the hotel receptionist concerning Mrs. Faraday's disappearance through the judicious use of a gap between paragraphs in the text (see 986 middle) and replaces the receptionist's broken English with the guidebook writer's paraphrase from his point of view:

> In the morning he asked again at the reception desk. The hotel bill wasn't important, a different receptionist generously allowed. If someone had to leave Italy in a hurry, because maybe there was a sickness, even a deathbed, then a hotel bill might be overlooked for just a little while. (986–987)

* * *

Trevor's protagonist contributes to the writing of the story through his necessarily speculative interpretation of Mrs. Faraday's and Mr. Humber's feelings and behavior. It is often difficult, for instance, for the reader to distinguish faithfully reported speech from the Englishman's imaginative rendering. The Englishman may make an imperceptible transition from reported speech to his own thoughts, thereby blurring such a delineation. Ultimately Trevor succeeds in fashioning a subtle, hybrid narrative by embedding the guise of omniscience in an essentially limited third-person point of view. This indeterminate point of consciousness invests a traditional narrative with enlivening modernist ambiguity.

Located early in the manuscript, Mrs. Faraday's account of her marriage and loss of her daughter is clearly reported speech from her point of view. A nearly identical version relocated to the Englishman's ruminations during the course of his Cascine Park walk in the published version, however, could be either reported speech or his own judgment of her situation. The passage in the text is more ambiguous, mixed in as it is with the Englishman's ruminations, and could be construed as his speculation or interpretation:

> [. . .] in order to rid himself of a contemplation of his failed relationship with Rosie he allowed the beauty of Mrs. Faraday again to invade his mind. Her beauty would have delighted him if her lipstick stained cigarettes and her silly repetitious chattering didn't endlessly disfigure it. Her husband was a good man, she had explained, *but a good man was not always what a woman wanted. And it had come to seem all of a piece that her daughter had lived for only a week, and all of a piece also that no other children had been born, since her marriage was not worthy of children.* (983, my italics)

So subtle are the shifts that the reader cannot be sure of where one consciousness ends and another begins. Mrs. Faraday is said to judge the death of her daughter, her marriage, and her husband in the manuscript version, whereas the italicized portion of the published version might be transferring the same judgments to the Englishman's consciousness. In other words, they could be his judgments, not hers—judgments motivated by his romantic wish to save her. If readers are not careful, they will unwittingly give tacit credibility to an unreliable protagonist.

In the manuscript, Mrs. Faraday even speculates about the consequences of remaining in Florence: her husband would notice her absence; the girl she employed would lose her job; and the fashion shop her husband bought for her to keep her "occupied" she supposes—or to keep her quiet, she adds—would close down and not be missed (Ams. 14). The final words of this explanation suggest that her marriage may be far from satisfactory. Moreover, in the significantly different published version, Mrs. Faraday's account is altered by the Englishman as it is told secondhand, filtered through his consciousness as her speech:

> In the restaurant she ate pasta without ceasing to talk, explaining to him that her boutique had been bought for her by her husband to keep her occupied and

happy. It hadn't worked, she said, *implying* that although her fashion shop had kept her busy it hadn't brought her contentment. Her face, drained of all expression, was lovelier than he had so far seen it, so sad and fragile that it seemed not to belong to the voice that rattled on. (983, my italics)

The reader cannot be certain of the veracity of all that immediately follows the Englishman's subjective word "implying." The published version departs from any of the similar manuscript passages (Ams. 11b, 13b, 14b) in its questionable interpretation of Mrs. Faraday's words through the Englishman's consciousness. Employing indirect or reported speech invests the narrative with thought-provoking ambiguity. We cannot be certain about Mrs. Faraday's dissatisfaction, yet we can see that the Englishman is attracted to her. Furthermore, the conversion of direct speech to reported speech enables him to internalize his conception of her, making the reader dependent on him for an understanding of Mrs. Faraday.

The Englishman's account of Mr. Humber's feelings about tourists, added in the published version, is equally ambiguous:

> Mr. Humber's bland face twitched with simulated interest. Tourists were a nuisance to him. They lost their passports, they locked their ignition keys into hired cars, they were stolen from and made a fuss. The city lived off them, but resented them as well. *These thoughts were for a moment openly reflected in Mr. Humber's pale brown eyes and then were gone.* (989, my italics)

This last sentence indicates that the preceding account of Humber's outlook might be based entirely on the guidebook writer's interpretation of a fleeting glance. Yet the reader has perhaps already accepted the series of suppositions as indirectly reported but factual speech before encountering the subtle qualification of their accuracy. The guidebook writer's interpretation of Humber's facial expression may betray his own contempt for tourists. After all, he makes his living from them and profits from their naïveté. His comment about another of Humber's facial expressions further compromises his portrayal of the bureaucrat. Mr. Humber reports the police's reaction to Mrs. Faraday's disappearance objectively, yet Trevor's subtle insertion in the manuscript draft (Ams. 20)—italicized below—that was retained verbatim in the published version makes the protagonist's conception of Humber more sinister. Replacing the police's banal reassurance in the manuscript about Mrs. Faraday's whereabouts with their suspicion of "some kind of jaunt," underlined below, casts further aspersions on Mrs. Faraday's reputation:

> "They suggest she's gone somewhere," he said. "<u>On some kind of a jaunt.</u>" *He paused in order to allow a flicker of amusement to develop in his lean features.*

"They think maybe she ran up her hotel bill and skipped it." (987, my italics, my underlining)

Seen through the Englishman's eyes, Humber's supposed pause and "flicker of amusement" tell us more about his consciousness than about Mr. Humber. Such subtle description and interpretation of facial gestures recall Pritchett's in "You Make Your Own Life."

More subtle still is the difference between the manuscript and the published versions of an exchange between the two men. At the end of a conversation composed of direct speech, the Englishman recalls Mrs. Faraday's description of her husband. His impression of her account, which was inserted in the manuscript, whether accurate or not, at least invokes her own complimentary judgment about her husband: "She made her husband sound considerate, the kind who would be troubled and confused" (Ams. 23). By contrast, the published version, by excluding her as a source, empowers the Englishman's editorializing with the force of omniscience as he speculates about her marriage, the circumstances that formed her character, and his fleeting relationship with her. The italics indicate the more developed insertion in the published version:

> "Faraday is naturally confused. And, of course, troubled."
> "Of course." He nodded to emphasize his agreement. *Her husband was the kind who would be troubled and confused, even though unhappiness had developed in the marriage. Clearly she'd given up on the marriage; more than anything, it was desperation that made her forthright. Without it, she might have been a different woman—and in that case, of course, there would not have been this passing relationship between them: her tiresomeness had cultivated that.* "Tell me about yourself," her voice echoed huskily, hungry for friendship. He had told her nothing—nothing of the shattered, destroyed relationships, and the regret and sham; nothing of the pathetic hope in hired rooms, or the anguish turning into bitterness. (989–990, my italics)

There are subtle but important differences between the two passages. A difference in point of consciousness, for instance, is immediately apparent in the comparison of the similar sentences. In the manuscript, the Englishman hears Mrs. Faraday's description of her husband, while the published version does not mention her as author of any statement, making the source of his comments ambiguous. Ultimately we do not know whether this is her reported speech or simply the Englishman's unreliable assessment. Ambiguity of this nature seems intentional, designed to invite the reader's participation. (The idea that circumstances would have made a different woman of Mrs. Faraday is borrowed from an earlier passage. See Ams. 22 verso.) Consistent with this emendation is the alteration of her echoed request. She wants to know "more" about the guidebook writer in both versions. Echoing "dimly" in the manuscript, her voice echoes "huskily" in the published version, and instead of remaining pleasant in his memory (Ams. 23), is "hungry for friendship" (989–990). Once again, we experience the story through the guidebook writer's consciousness. Instead of witnessing the more conventional unreliable narrator speaking in the first person—the kind of narrator we find in Conrad—we experience the unreliable element through the Englishman's consciousness in this way.

Trevor extends a limited third-person point of view into a false omniscience through the guidebook writer's imaginative speculation about Mrs. Faraday's thoughts. His protagonist's projections deceive the reader. The use of the conditional tense helps to create the illusion. In this way, the guidebook writer contributes to the writing of the story through his subjective interpretation of Mrs. Faraday's feelings and behavior. Detached himself, he invests her with the feelings he himself cannot express. Although the reader can mistake this for remarkable empathy—as a kind of empathic wondering—the Englishman's purported understanding of her—a self-flattering projection—tells us far more about him and his fantasies, as his wishes underlie hers. Employing the past perfect tense, he chronicles her evening, describing her thoughts as if writing about her in limited third person: she had gone to bed full of admiration for him, imagining them in a Florentine apartment, not wanting to return to her life in America, believing she had found someone with whom to share the city (Ams. 30). But he concludes that he must disillusion her.

* * *

At the heart of "Cocktails at Doney's" is the guidebook writer's quest for Mrs. Faraday and his simultaneous, unwitting search for meaning in his own life. His reluctance to seize the opportunity to be reborn or awakened sexually and spiritually is more pronounced in the manuscript, where it is accompanied by the Annunciation as a leitmotif. He denies himself a relationship that will save him from his life as a mere observer. Living outside society, he has ceased to participate, his only occupation consisting of giving dubious advice to naïve tourists. (In fact at one point, he even admits to enjoying publishing unproven statistics in an absurd defiance of his reading public.)

The Annunciation figures more prominently in the manuscript than in the published version, where it gives an unlikely character, Mrs. Faraday, great inspiration. While the guidebook writer's knowledge of and interest in the Annunciation is limited to the aesthetic, Mrs. Faraday's appreciation is, in contrast to her materialistic fashion world, surprisingly, purely spiritual. Their shared appreciation, however, for a particular rendering unites them for the reader early in the manuscript. In an imagined, daydreamed passage on Annunciations from his guide in progress—dreamed up while supposedly listening to Mrs. Faraday's observations about marriage—the Englishman writes while hearing the American woman's voice proclaim that Neri di Bicci's Annunciation in Santa Trinita is the finest of them all (Ams. 8). Later in the same conversation, in response to her query, he dismisses the content of his Florentine guidebook as "further banalities" about Transfigurations and Annunciations, the cynical remark eliciting her naïve exclamation that she loves Annunciations (Ams. 9). More exposed in the manuscript as direct speech iterated by Mrs. Faraday, it is reported by him in the published version: "It was the Annunciations in Santo Spirito she wanted to see, she explained, because she loved Annunciations" (983). This apparently inconsequential emendation is consistent with changes noted earlier. In expressing the thought himself, the Englishman makes her more a part of his consciousness in the published version. It turns out that the Neri di Bicci Annunciation in Santa Trinita is her favorite as well (Ams. 9). She voices her interest in it yet again in a passage that confirms the mystery of the Annunciation as a thematic device in the story—especially the deleted yet still visible di Bicci version (Ams. 12). Her obsession with the Annunciation reaches its climax in her intriguing interpretation of the di Bicci rendering. Although the manuscript and published versions are similar, a comparison reveals some notable differences. Her speculation about the di Bicci Annunciation is cut down and modified. Most notable in the manuscript version is her inclusion of Adam and Eve in the background and her insistence on the Virgin's complete fabrication of the "plush surroundings," the Annunciation, the angel, and Adam and Eve. She says it all makes sense to her when she thinks of it as the Madonna's dream (Ams. 12A). She speaks of a second angel's visit, and although this sighting is maintained in the printed version, her final line imagining the Madonna's sense of resignation upon awakening is not. Instead of condemning her as hopelessly naïve and irreverent, her interpretation, however misguided, demonstrates her preoccupation with a momentous biblical event—the Virgin's understanding that she is carrying God's child. Clearly indifferent to Mrs. Faraday's fixation, the guidebook writer ignores her for several minutes. When he listens again, she is still talking about God, seeing Him in humankind's timeless creation of art, music, and literature (Ams. 12A). While Trevor pruned much of this material to avoid detracting attention from his protagonist, he was careful to preserve Mrs. Faraday's interest in the Annunciation—an interest that will have a profound effect on the Englishman.

Her disappearance changes the guidebook writer's behavior. As he waits for her to arrive for cocktails at Doney's, listening to the taped music, he overhears someone other than Judy Garland singing "Over the Rainbow" (Ams. 17). Because Trevor's references to popular songs and their lyrics strengthen the thematic content of his stories, we can be sure in this instance that the famous words, although not printed in either the manuscript or published versions of the story itself, are meaningful, meant to resound in the reader's ear. The lyrics of "Over the Rainbow" transport the now ethereal, dream-like Mrs. Faraday faraway. The Englishman has not dared to dream the dreams that "Really do come true." Mrs. Faraday, linked with the murdered virgin Gabriella at several points throughout the story, has perhaps already ascended "Beyond the rainbow" to the afterlife. It is as if the anonymous voice simultaneously sings Mrs. Faraday's last words and expresses the Englishman's repressed dream as well, mocking him from the next world for his inability to act on suppressed desires in this one.

In the manuscript, after his consultation with Mr. Humber, a suddenly despondent Englishman regrets that Mrs. Faraday did not see San Spirito. He realizes that her appreciation of Annunciations, her theory of dreams, and the dreams of the Virgin Mary are of no interest or use to either the police or Mr. Humber, not being technically part of her identity. Yet at the end of his inner dialectic about Mrs. Faraday, he believes that they are paramount. His impression of her changes dramatically as he comes to an understanding of her interest in the Annunciation. Suddenly, in her absence, he believes her to be better identified by her love of Annunciations and dreams—her spirituality—than by her appearance. He tells Mr. Humber that he may have misled the police (Ams. 22). Following from the previous ruminations, this admission only reaffirms his futile desire to acquaint the police with Mrs. Faraday's character rather than with her appearance. Despite Humber's reassurance that the police have photographs and her husband's explicit description, for example, the Englishman says he believes they have been seeking a different woman (Ams. 22). He is now desperate to keep others from focusing exclusively on her appearance, even if that is the only practical way of locating her, and yet, ironically, he himself was heretofore unconcerned with her spiritual being. Premature at this stage in the narrative, his reconsideration of Mrs. Faraday will be relocated to the story's end.

The guidebook writer's newfound appreciation of Mrs. Faraday is evident in yet another discarded but revealing passage in which he speaks of her true identity and the vicissitudes of life. The long paragraph includes his wistful, sympathetic description of her experience and his speculation about his own fate as well. There is a Hardyesque emphasis on circumstance as he realizes that her desire to be devoured by Florence was more profound than he had imagined. Ultimately, this passage confirms his understanding of and heightened interest in her as well as a maudlin, retroactive optimism for what their lives might have been. As he listens to her speak, he observes the effects of both her dull, childless marriage and her husband's effort to fill the void with the boutique "jangling" in her "obtrusive nerviness." Both he and she would be different, he surmises, if they had been either more or less extreme about their lives (Ams. 22 verso).

The Englishman's fantasies and dreams play a more significant role in the manuscript than in the final text, especially toward the end of the story. Remarkably, there is even an imagined seduction scene, narrated in the regretful conditional tense, in which he "would have" closed the bedroom door; "would have" removed Mrs. Faraday's necklace and rings; and "would have" undressed her. Until that point, the reader learns, he "had believed" that such a moment "would never" come again; that he would renounce any attempt to love again because of its complications and his failures (Ams. 22). Inspired by Mrs. Faraday, his interest in love revived, he wishes to vindicate her once again in Mr. Humber's disdainful eyes. So precious is she in retrospect that the Englishman vows she "*would have* seemed different in the morning," her formerly incessant chattering "*would have* [. . .] been silenced by San Spirito and Ognissanto" (Ams. 22, my italics). The explicitness of this fantasy, while appropriate for a novel, is relinquished for the more subtle suggestiveness of the published version. In a related passage, also confined to the manuscript, shortly after his departure from Humber's office, he champions her in the conditional tense, once again his thoughts betraying his conditional wishes, transcending reality. He imagines that exposure to Florentine life and culture will magically transform Mrs. Faraday while eliminating her most unattractive habit; San Spirito and the bus to Maiano "would" silence her; she "would" fall in love with other Annunciations; and people searching for a loquacious, bothersome woman "might" not notice her (Ams. 24).

Pursued by disturbing memories of his unsuccessful marriages in this version, rejected by his children, and dogged by their hurtful accusations that replay in his mind, the Englishman leaves the American consulate for the last time and walks along the quay. He gazes into the Arno wondering if its murky green waters have claimed Mrs. Faraday (Ams. 25). Faced with the likelihood of her death, and oppressed by self-pity and shame, he seeks refuge not in his own childhood memories, as he did extensively at the outset of the manuscript, but in Mrs. Faraday's. Apparently, he informs the reader, his consciousness registered some of what she said, even though he had not been listening to her "chattering conversation." Yet the dreamlike quality of his recollection makes it difficult for the reader to distinguish her reported facts from his embellishments, making the protagonist's adopted memory unreliable. Using the simple past tense, Trevor has the Englishman see Mrs. Faraday as a child with the same remarkable features. She plays with dolls in a yard with an old black-and-white terrier asleep beside her— a scene that parallels his own childhood backyard experience. He then pictures her sister, with whom she did not get along, in a garden chair when both are considerably older (Ams. 25). At the end of the manuscript, haunted by Mrs. Faraday, the guidebook writer even hears the echo of her voice— an echo he hears in the final text as well. Her consciousness lives on in his mind's ear as he retrieves details of her background he ignored from their earlier conversation but claims to have retained in his auditory memory— miscellaneous reminiscences about her dog, a striped dress, a cocktail bar, her husband, and a blue convertible. Deprived of her presence, he resorts to recalling her past life. Haunted by her voice, he haunts the sites that unite them in their mutual appreciation. He walks about Florence, frequenting her favorite places, such as the Boboli Gardens, the rooms of the Uffizi, and the cloisters of Maria Novella, and pictures Pietro Perugino's *Agony in the Garden* in his mind's eye, an ironic title in the light of Mrs. Faraday's likely fate.

In a passage from the manuscript's epilogue, most of which does not appear in the final text, the Englishman restores Mrs. Faraday's reputation in his own mind after having cast aspersions on her fidelity, convincing himself in his ruminations that she was ultimately a faithful wife and would have said otherwise if she had not been. He pictures her with Mr. Faraday when she cries at the death of her child, and again when told she cannot have another, reviewing her life as if he has witnessed it. Indeed, there is an imposition of his point of view as he perpetuates her life through his melodramatic account. Finally, in his Prufrockian quiet desperation, as he speculates about the past, obsessed with the potentiality of a relationship that might have offered him happiness, he recognizes, albeit reluctantly, the forgiveness and salvation that might have been his—the salvation that was Mrs. Faraday had he been willing to admit to his crippling impotence. Once again, Trevor employs the speculative conditional tense as the Englishman wonders if she would have cried to discover the truth about him, been motivated by the problem itself, and have declared her love for him despite his impotence. But he concludes that he would have disparaged her, spurned her, and rejected her salvation. And despite this treatment he imagines her, still full of admiration for him, kissing his cheek.

* * *

Trevor's substantial amount of manuscript material, although indispensable to the initial formation of the characters, their motivations, and their relationship, is either stripped away altogether or reduced to its essence. But his deletions work in concert with several substantial additions in the published version that invigorate the story by endowing it with a climax and a discernable theme. Most importantly, he creates other missed opportunities for his protagonist by expanding on minor details in the manuscript. Mrs. Faraday's deleted thought about "disappearing" into the Palazzo Ricasoli for a week, for instance, is the basis for a guileless confession in the published version meant to test the Englishman's attraction to her. Important as their mutual appreciation for the di Bicci Annunciation is to the story in symbolic and practical terms, Trevor replaces it here with Mrs. Faraday's gauche admission of a previous tryst that is mutually embarrassing. At first she teases him with "'a secret about the Palazzo Ricasoli,'" and despite his obvious wish to change the subject, she reveals that she "'spent a naughty week there once'" (982) with a countryman of the Englishman's from Horsham whom she met at the Pitti Donna. So anxious is he to distance himself from this unwelcome revelation that he denies ever having been to Horsham. Her sincere apology for embarrassing him and his gentlemanly refusal to admit it characterize them perfectly. Her recognition of her faux pas and earnest pursuit of forgiveness demonstrate her openness. In a comment appearing in all versions except the *New Yorker*, she chastises herself as "an awful shady lady," and, as if to console the protagonist in his solitude, admits the "naughty week" "was a flop"(982). Furthermore, undaunted by the awkward dialogue, she even attempts to restore goodwill with "a nicer kind of secret," when she compliments him on his appearance. Faced with Mrs. Faraday's self-confessed failure, protected by his anonymity, and reassured by a beautiful woman's interest in him, he would seem to have the perfect opportunity to reciprocate. "Still," we are told, "he did not respond" (982). During their dinner later in the story, a guilt-ridden Mrs. Faraday makes herself more vulnerable by returning briefly to the Palazzo Ricasoli episode, disparaging the anonymous man and admitting to poor judgment in an attempt to encourage the Englishman's interest in her: "The guy I shacked up with in the Palazzo Ricasoli was no better than a gigolo. I guess I don't know why

I did that" (984). Finally, obviously preoccupied, she seeks reassurance once again with a sudden reintroduction of the topic, fearful her indiscretion has forever precluded the possibility of a romance with the guidebook writer: "'I've ruined it, haven't I, telling you about the Palazzo Ricasoli?' 'Ruined what, Mrs. Faraday?' 'Oh, I don't know'" (984). Of course, he behaves as if he is oblivious to her intentions.

Trevor procures another opportunity for his protagonist to awaken in a pivotal addition to the text, an insert immediately following Ams. 16 line 12 and beginning with the invitation to Maiano. First expressed in a single line of the autograph manuscript, Mrs. Faraday's wish to take the bus to Maiano—a trip on which she hopes to be accompanied by the Englishman—is transformed in the published text into an explicit invitation to him during their last scene together. In contrast to his reluctance to act on his suppressed desire, she risks rejection repeatedly in her open pursuit of him as she seeks to prolong their relationship. For many reasons this serves as the climax of the story, although the Englishman and the reader alike can acknowledge this only in retrospect. The additions in the published version are designated in italics:

"*Will you come with me to Maiano one day?*"
"*Maiano?*"
"*It isn't far. They say it's lovely to walk at Maiano.*"
"*I'm really rather occupied, you know.*"
  "*Oh God, I'm bothering you! I'm being a nuisance! Forget Maiano. I'm sorry.*"
  "*I'm just trying to say, Mrs. Faraday, that I don't think I can be much use to you.*"
  He was aware to his embarrassment, that she was holding his hand. *Her arm was entwined with his and the palms of their hands had somehow come together. Her fingers, playing with his now, kept time with her flattery.*
  "You've got the politest voice I ever heard! Say you'll meet me just once again? Just once? Cocktails tomorrow? Please."
  "Look, Mrs. Faraday –"
  "Say Doney's at six. I'll promise to say nothing if you like. We'll listen to the music."
  Her palm was cool. A finger made a circular motion on one of his. Rosie had said he limped through life. In the end Jeremy had been sorry for him. Both of them were right; others had said worse. He was a crippled object of pity.
  "Well, all right."
  She thanked him in the Albergo San Lorenzo for listening to her, and for the dinner and the wine. "Every year I hope to meet someone nice in Florence," she said on the landing outside her bedroom, seeming to mean it. "This is the first time it has happened."

> She leaned forward and kissed him on the cheek, then closed her door. In his looking-glass he examined the faint smear of lipstick and didn't wipe it off. He woke in the night and lay there thinking about her, wondering if her lipstick was still on his cheek. (985)

Such additions make Mrs. Faraday more actively seductive and accentuate the guidebook writer's repressed interest in an eventual relationship. So "crippled," he cannot seize the opportunity, even though he shows signs of recognizing it. The addition includes elements central to the story's characterization and conflict: Mrs. Faraday's gregarious nature and interest in the protagonist; the protagonist's frigidity and impotence; the haunting characters Jeremy, a homosexual friend, and Rosie, with whom he was unable to have sexual relations; his veiled allusion to his impotence; her perpetual, seductive hand play; her insistence, despite his outward lack of interest, on meeting again; her desperate plea to meet for cocktails—a final request that overlaps with the same invitation in the manuscript. And, curiously, in an example of art controlling life, Trevor himself accedes to Mrs. Faraday's request, a concession that prolongs the story. At the end of the unlikely couple's dinner meeting in the manuscript, he emended the dialogue in another ink with a finer pen nib, changing his protagonist's response from a decisive "no" to a reluctant "yes". At her insistence, the Englishman agrees to meet her for cocktails at Doney's.

Trevor's artful revisions at the close of the story culminate in an ending that is itself an amalgam of earlier ideas. In the final paragraphs of the text, he employs the narrative technique and characterization he established in the manuscript. Three paragraphs from the end, the description of the Englishman's walk along the quay and his speculation about Mrs. Faraday's death in the Arno is actually a synthesis of two manuscript passages. And the subsequent passage, a tour of the Uffizi Annunciations, is a reprisal of his day-dreamed tour of the Uffizi. Even the ensuing description of his sighting of Mrs. Faraday in Santa Trinita and her call to him is appropriated from the manuscript. But Trevor does not simply combine and reiterate these descriptions in the published text. Instead, he makes the museum visit ambiguous by conducting it in the conditional instead of the simple past; and he changes the Englishman's encounter with Mrs. Faraday from the present tense to the conditional:

> In the galleries of the Uffizi he *would* move from Annunciation to Annunciation, Simone Marini's, Baldovinetti's, Lorenzo di Credi's, and the others. He *would* catch a glimpse of her red coat in Santa Trinità, but the face *would* again be someone else's. She *would* call out from a gelateria, but the voice would be an echo in his memory. (990–991, my italics)

Trevor's subtle tense change makes the passage marvellously ambiguous. Indeed, it has become as difficult for the reader to distinguish between the imagined and the real as it is for the Englishman. Trevor ingeniously obscures point of view while dislocating his protagonist's sense of place and time. Used in this singular manner, the conditional tense obscures the Englishman's very notion of time. In a subtle reflection of his own emotional state, he becomes detached from himself as limited third-person point of view masquerades as omniscient. Are the reported events recollections of repeated actions in the past, or merely the Englishman's desperate, hopeful, conditional promise to himself that he will experience them in the future?

* * *

As important as the substantial additions that have been mentioned are to the final text—especially the Piazza Ricasoli "secret," the Maiano invitation, and the use of the conditional tense—they are made even more meaningful as they resonate in harmony in the penultimate paragraph, itself a textual addition with a manuscript precursor. In order to fully appreciate the virtuosity of the published version, however, we must compare it with its obvious forerunner found on the last of the four miscellaneous pages of the incomplete, perhaps later, autograph manuscript draft on light-green typing paper (Ams. 32). Here is the published version:

> He sat outside a café in the Piazza della Repubblica, imagining her thoughts as she had lain in bed on that last night, smoking her cigarettes in the darkness. She had arrived at the happiest moment of love, when nothing was yet destroyed, when anticipation was a richness in itself. She'd thought about their walk in Maiano, how she'd bring the subject up again, how this time he'd say he'd be delighted. She'd thought about their being together in an apartment in the Palazzo Ricasoli, how this time it would be different. Already she had made up her mind: she would not ever return to the town where her husband managed a business. "I have never loved anyone like this," she whispered in the darkness. (991)

Although the respective versions begin similarly, there is an immediate difference. In the four-page manuscript version, the guidebook writer imagines Mrs. Faraday's thoughts as she had undressed on the last night, whereas in the more detailed published version he imagines them "as she had lain in bed on the last night, smoking her cigarettes in the darkness." However inconsequential this alteration may appear to be, it too recalls the paragraph preceding the Palazzo Ricasoli insert in the published version that anticipates the writer's projected thoughts about Mrs. Faraday:

> He did not comment, not knowing what she meant. But without wishing to he couldn't help thinking of this beautiful woman lying awake in her bedroom in the Albergo San Lorenzo. He imagined her staring into the darkness, the glow of her cigarette, the sound of her inhaling. She was looking for an affair, he supposed, and hoped she realized he wasn't the man for that. (982)

This earlier passage in the published version establishes his preoccupation with and interest in Mrs. Faraday as a sexual being. Even more developed than the eventual refrain in the penultimate paragraph of the published version, this passage contains the same image of her in bed, smoking in the darkness of her hotel room, while including the more intimate "sound of her inhaling." Furthermore, his supposition that "she was looking for an affair" and his immediate self-disqualification from consideration belie his desire to have one.

In the manuscript version, the simple past is used to describe the Englishman's thoughts and actions while he speculates about Mrs. Faraday's thoughts in the past perfect. He "*sat* outside Gilli's," "*knew* she was dead," "*glanced* through the windows," "*went* to Doney's," and "*watched* Americans"(my italics). Observations about Mrs. Faraday's thoughts through his consciousness, however, employ the past perfect to create a perfectly romantic conception of her feelings. He imagines "her thoughts as *she had undressed* on that night" when "*She had arrived* at the happiest moment of love." And, in a sentimental touch deleted before the published version, he passes the "suitably empty" table where they sat when "*she'd thought* the world of him" (my italics). Although the Englishman pays tribute to her, "He knew she was dead," and Trevor's deletion in the final sentence of the manuscript version removes any vestige of his protagonist's hope that Mrs. Faraday will reappear.

Trevor's use of tense is more daring in the published version where, added to the simple past and past perfect, the conditional intensifies the illusion of an omniscient point of view. Here, the guidebook writer seems to look even more deeply into the recesses of Mrs. Faraday's consciousness in an effort to retrieve her, rescue her from oblivion, and thus resuscitate their relationship. So detailed is his account of her thoughts that it seems factual. Of course, without his ever having known her intimately or, more importantly, spoken with her after their evening together, his description of her thoughts is necessarily imagined. Yet we certainly learn much more about him through his speculation about Mrs. Faraday than we do about her. In fact, oddly enough, the repressed Englishman's most telling expression of feeling is hidden in his falsely empathic wondering about her own thoughts and feelings. He simply projects his consciousness onto hers. Her purported determination to reintroduce her invitation to Maiano betrays his wish to retrieve the opportunity, and likewise her vow that "this time he'd say he'd be delighted" reveals his determination to accept. Her thought about sharing an apartment in the Palazzo Ricasoli, and her promise that "this time it would be different," convey his promise to succeed in his relationship with her, erase her unpleasant "naughty week" with a pleasant stay, and seize the opportunity to awaken sexually and spiritually. Expressed in the conditional tense, these plans give the illusion of procuring a future. Her resolve never to return to her life in America expresses his wish to keep her in Italy. And finally, she haunts him in her own words when her declaration of love, "whispered in the darkness," romanticizes her love for him and his love for her: "'I have never loved anyone like this.'" Trevor succeeds in suspending the reader's certainty about point of view by camouflaging the Englishman's consciousness in the fabricated consciousness of Mrs. Faraday.

Ultimately, the penultimate paragraph of the published version is not so much an elegy for her as a sotto voce dirge for the relationship he never had. His muted epiphany, a quiet, self-conscious, painfully reluctant revelation, is in keeping with his repressed character. And in contrast to the tone of the last manuscript lines, the Englishman of the published version's final paragraph remains tragically hopeful for Mrs. Faraday's return until the very end:

> In his hotel bedroom he shaved and had a bath and put on a suit that had just been pressed. In a way that had become a ceremony for him since the evening he had first waited for her there, he went at six o'clock to Doney's. He watched the Americans drinking cocktails, knowing it was safe to be there because she would not suddenly arrive. He listened to the music she'd said she liked, and mourned her as a lover might. (991)

The constancy of his meticulous nightly preparation and faithful "ceremony" at Doney's almost recalls the unrealized, undisturbed wedding-day expectations of Dickens's Miss Havisham. He does not merely watch the Americans drinking cocktails, he expresses a kind of optimistic pessimism, his hopefulness couched in optimistically pessimistic uncertain terms, "knowing it was safe to be there because she would not suddenly arrive," yet hoping nevertheless that she would. His skepticism betrays his wish for her arrival. Incapable of assuming the role of "lover" in her life, he imagines playing it in her death.

Whether through intuition or conscious design, Trevor demonstrates once again that the short story is closely related to the lyric poem, recasting the pedestrian last sentence of the manuscript as two four-stress lines ending in assonance:

> He listened to the music she'd said she liked,
> and mourned her as a lover might. (991)

Furthermore, the assonance—"liked, might"—itself is unfulfilled, much like the Englishman's tardy epiphany and unfulfilled opportunity for love. Even the last word is pregnant with meaning, pathos, and the uncertainty of his intentions. The final conditional verb "might" captures the essence of his retrospective insight and his mourning conditionally for the relationship he never had.

There are a number of parallels between "Cocktails at Doney's" and Henry James's long short story "The Beast in the Jungle," which is also about a man's missed opportunity to awaken. Like John Marcher, Trevor's middle-aged writer does not embrace the opportunity to love a woman. Both men yearn for their women when it is too late. But instead of prostrating himself on a grave, crying more for the lost relationship than for the woman herself, as John Marcher does at May Bartram's tomb in James's melodramatic ending, Trevor's anaesthetized, Eliotic guide-book writer muffles his own epiphany discreetly while sitting in a Florentine cocktail bar. Trevor's story exceeds James's in its ambiguity.

"Cocktails at Doney's" certainly qualifies as a story with an open end. The reader is left with many questions. Did the Englishman meet Mrs. Faraday in the past? Does she use her opening line with other men? Ultimately, we cannot determine whether she is seeking an extramarital affair, is particularly attracted to the guide-book writer, or is merely a "gallivanting," disenchanted wife on a habitual "sexual excursion" or "jaunt" in Italy. Is she as innocent as she seems, or a highly sexed, seductive, enticing temptress? Her crass revelation about her pick up in the Pitti Donna, her "naughty week," and her subsequent admission that the relationship with the "gigolo" "was a flop," cannot be verified. Is she telling the truth, or merely attempting to entice the reluctant writer? (The manuscript epilogue includes the Englishman's conviction that Mrs. Faraday was faithful to her husband despite their poorly matched interests.) Like the Englishman's former wives, she may be sexually frustrated. This unspoken parallel forces him to confront his impotence in the face of yet another unsatisfied woman who is unaware, as his female companions were initially, of his inability to consummate a relationship. Is she sincere when she flatters him in remarking,

"You have the cleverest face I've seen in years!" and "You're a kind person" (982–983)? Has she met the same fate as the murdered virgin Gabriella or merely escaped a loveless marriage? Are the regretful questions he asks himself not the same as those the reader asks?

> Had she simply forgotten? Or had someone better materialized? Some younger man she again hadn't been able to resist, some guy who didn't know any more about Masaccio than her good husband did? She was a woman who was always falling in love, which was what she called it, confusing love with sensuality. Was she, he wondered, what people referred to as a nymphomaniac? Was that what made her unhappy? (986)

* * * *

> Would her tiresomeness have dropped from her at once, like the shedding of a garment she had thought to be attractive, if he'd told her in the restaurant with the modern paintings? Would she, too, have angrily said he'd led her up the garden path? (990)

* * *

As novelists explore the dimensions of their central characters—their personal histories, relationships, and dreams—during the course of a novel, Trevor, in order to achieve a similar depth, explores the lives of his short-story characters through extensive short-story drafts, forging tangible identities and psychological profiles for them that give their behavior novelistic depth and resounding verisimilitude within the heavily edited draft. While it would be wrong to say that his short stories are condensed novels, it would be fair to credit his characters with novelistic density. And it is just such depth and verisimilitude that the lengthy revision process enables Trevor to achieve. He constructs the comprehensive psychological portraits to understand how his characters would perform in any given situation, whether within the manuscripts or the published versions. Clearly, he understands the underlying motivation for his characters' behavior, having worked it out in the manuscripts. That is precisely why the unsaid element in "Cocktails at Doney's" is credible. It has been expressed in the manuscript draft. And as we have seen in the earlier chapter on Pritchett's "You Make Your Own Life," there are two kinds of unsaid: the details that the author has stripped away and the resulting ambiguities that enlist the reader's interpretive powers. The two work in tandem. Instead of being impoverished by the deletions, Trevor's story, like Pritchett's, is enriched by them.

The removal of the explicit material and the addition of selected passages creates the calculated, controlled, artful ambiguity that solicits the reader's participation. Trevor once said that "It's like a lot of jigsaw pieces, and the reader has got some of them and you've got some of them."[5] From the manuscript draft we can see that Trevor writes spontaneously. Originally, there was not going to be a planned meeting for cocktails at Doney's, yet his reworking of the dialogue gives birth to a meaningful prolongation—the search for Mrs. Faraday that provokes the protagonist's epiphany. The emendations and subsequent rewriting of this passage show the way in which Trevor, with his penchant for expansion, explores the subject he writes about while writing, reins himself in, and finally distills the essence of his material.[6]

Let us turn now to a different aspect of the story writer's craft: the response to alterations proposed by an editor. Such intervention tests the writer's resolve, flexibility, diplomacy, and very conception of his art during a delicate but necessary collaborative process.

Chapter 4

V. S. Pritchett's Ministering Angell

In spite of the fact that almost all the reviews were filled with praise, I don't think that one of them has come very close to describing the real nature of your short fiction. My only reason for ever wishing I were not your editor here is the fact that I am disqualified from trying to write a review of your book.[1]

—Roger Angell 1961

I wish indeed that someone like yourself who has the gift of following a text, would address himself to my work for it would reveal a lot to me who am too blinded by the pen to know what I have written.[2]

—Victor Pritchett 1961

Most successful short-story writers have subjected their work to the scrutiny of magazine editors entrusted with selecting and preparing fiction for publication. Not even Guy de Maupassant and Anton Chekhov, both of whom began by writing newspaper sketches, were exempt from editorial control. And although his reputation is now secure as the undisputed father of the modern short story, Chekhov was a commercial artist from the beginning, selling weekly made-to-order whimsical sketches purely for money to popular Russian newspapers such as *Oskolki* and *Peterburgskaya Gazeta* until Alexei Suvorin recognized his genius, published him in *Novoye Vrema*, and encouraged him to become a more profound artist.[3]

Like Maupassant and Chekhov, V. S. Pritchett began as a freelance journalist, peddling sketches and vignettes to newspapers, tailoring his work to the space limitations and ethos of such publications as the *Christian Science Monitor*, his main employer for the first few years of his career. Given freedom to write more substantial short stories once he had established himself, Pritchett became one of England's leading practitioners, appearing with some regularity in Britain's finest periodicals. Yet just as he had begun to achieve notoriety as a fiction writer in his native country on the strength of his Second World War magazine publications and his postwar collection of stories, *It May Never Happen* (1945), the British little magazines, literary reviews, and journals on which all British short-story writers had relied from the 1930s began to disappear, leaving him without an audience. Pritchett once observed that by the early 1950s they had almost all vanished, driven out by printing costs, the advent of television, and the diversions of a leisured society.[4] Although he earned his living as a literary journalist, he derived the most pleasure from the writing and publishing of his short stories—a craft he saw as his art.

* * *

Pritchett's association with the *New Yorker* began inauspiciously. And although the magazine expressed interest in him through a series of rejections, it did not publish him until 1949. Perhaps bolstered by his success with *You Make Your Own Life*, he made his first short-story submission with "The Oedipus Complex" in 1938. Almost two years later, his second submission, sent by his agent, Harold Matson, was rejected as well; but Gus Lobrano, a *New Yorker* fiction editor, claimed the magazine was interested in Pritchett and wished to see more of his stories.[5] Five years later, William Maxwell, his distinguished colleague, turned down "The Gift Horse." In 1946, however, Katharine White, then a senior editor, wrote to Pritchett expressing her admiration for his acclaimed comic tale "The Saint," which she and her colleagues had read in the American edition of *Horizon Stories* and found "delightful." She noted the scarcity of humorous pieces and hoped he would send some equally amusing stories or reminiscent pieces to the magazine.[6]

After running into a seemingly impenetrable wall at the *New Yorker*, Matson succeeded in placing "The Saint" in *Harper's* the next December, much to Katharine White's astonishment.[7] Although the *New Yorker* allowed material published in its own pages to be reprinted elsewhere, it never published anything that had previously appeared in England or any other country.[8] This iron-clad policy succeeded in guaranteeing original fiction for the magazine, but it also precluded from consideration acclaimed stories by such writers as Pritchett who sought to maintain their reputations on both sides of the Atlantic while maximizing their meager profits. Even though she was aware that many American magazines followed this practice, White was nevertheless surprised *Harper's* would publish a story that had been available to American readers in book form for many months. Having received no Pritchett submissions for five months, she was eager to know if the two Pritchett stories *Harper's* promised would follow had, like "The Saint," already been published in England.[9] Once again she expressed the wish to see some new stories. A year later, in a conciliatory letter about "Double Divan," the second of two more rejections since her previous solicitation, White recognized the "touches of Mr. Pritchett's fine humor all through" but expressed the staff's opinion that it was "so confused as to be really unsuccessful, and with the author in England, we feel it would be almost impossible to work out with him a revised and more coherent version—even if he cared to want to try one, which seems doubtful."[10] White was wrong on all counts, but she remained hopeful nonetheless, assuring Matson of the magazine's unflagging interest, convinced that "when he is at his humorous best, he certainly <u>seems</u> to belong in the *New Yorker*."[11] Knowing that Pritchett was not writing new stories, yet remaining eager to place some of his fiction in the *New Yorker*, White even consulted the magazine's editor, Harold Ross, to see whether prior book publication in England would eliminate from consideration two Pritchett stories that had never appeared in the United States in either magazine or book form. Ross was faithful to the magazine's code. "The Aristocrat" and "The Two Brothers" "would not work" because of the magazine's large circulation in England.[12] There would be no special dispensation for Pritchett. The fiction department rejected his next submission five months later, despite its strong appeal, citing its too British flavor and a "mannered and self-conscious tone" resulting from the author's unconventional use of the present tense. Robert Henderson, the editor involved, apologized for the disappointment and reiterated the magazine's interest in publishing Pritchett.[13]

Finally, Katharine White's steadfast belief in Pritchett was rewarded. In August the *New Yorker* accepted "The Landlord." In his letter to Don Congdon, Pritchett's agent at Harold Matson, Gus Lobrano enclosed notes on the story that he wished to be forwarded to Pritchett for his consideration, apologetic about their seemingly "finicky" nature, wary of the new writer's reaction to queries that might undermine the triumph of his first acceptance. Lobrano also wanted Pritchett to know that the editors were ready to discard any of the mostly "suggestive" notes that Pritchett could prove were inappropriate.[14]

Pritchett's first accepted story would not be his first to appear in the magazine. "The Landlord" would not be published until 2 September 1950.[15] Shortly after Congdon returned the draft reflecting Pritchett's response to the suggested alterations, he telephoned Robert Henderson about the imminent publication of "The Ladder" in *Nash's Annual*, sent the story to Henderson on 6 October 1949, and announced 10 November as the British magazine's publication date. This clever maneuver forced the *New Yorker*'s immediate purchase of the new story so that it could anticipate *Nash's* date, honor its own strict code, and lay claim to Pritchett's latest story. The Fiction Department would not always be apprised of such Pritchett sales; nor would it have the flexibility to rush a submission into publication as it had done in scooping *Nash's*.

Katharine White, acting on behalf of the indisposed Lobrano, sent Congdon the paperwork for a solution to their quandary that would be beneficial to Pritchett as well. Only five days after its publication of "The Ladder," the magazine offered Pritchett the arrangement it had long tendered to some of the finest writers on both sides of the Atlantic—the *New Yorker*'s First Reading Agreement (FRA)—and made it retroactive to include its last purchase.[16] Pritchett had already informed Congdon of the offer. The document only lacked his signature. White enclosed two checks: one for $100 to validate the contractual obligation and make the agreement legally binding on the magazine, and a second of $240 for what the magazine owed Pritchett under the agreement for "The Ladder"—a premium on his original payment of $960.[17] This cost-effective measure gave the magazine a monopoly on the best stories by its finest writers and eliminated bidding wars with other magazines. The arrangement was advantageous for both parties. The Fiction Department had the right of first refusal for all those writers' short fiction, and the writers were given a yearly payment for submitting all their fiction to the magazine. Stories that were deemed unsuitable were simply released to the writers' agents so that they could be sold to rival publications. Therefore, all stories by FRA writers appearing in other magazines were necessarily *New Yorker* rejects, but the confidential arrangement eliminated the possibility of prejudice in the market. Exempt from the arrangement were all of the critical essays and reviews that Pritchett wrote for the *New Statesman* and other periodicals.[18]

The *New Yorker* did not see immediate returns, however, on its investment in the English writer. Shortly after signing his initial FRA at the end of 1949, Pritchett ceased writing short stories in order to finish what would be his last novel, *Mr. Beluncle* (1951), a veiled fictionalized biography of his father, which was heavily subsidized by his close friend Gerald Brenan. A year later the magazine chose to renew the agreement with Pritchett, even though it had not received any stories. Perhaps, as an inexpensive form of insurance against a sudden period of productivity, it continued to speculate, renewing its established writers' FRAs, never knowing when those in its stable might produce attractive work. It rejected a lone submission in August 1951, but Lobrano was encouraged enough to renew Pritchett's FRA two months later. Finally, nearly two years after the initial agreement, Lobrano expressed qualified interest in "Two Roast Beefs." He explained the staff's reservations, its specific suggestions for revision, and its judgment that the story would "be sharpened by a fair amount of cutting."[19] Pritchett cut over 1,000 words of the 7,000 and, with a few additional cuts by the staff, the story was published in the 12 July 1952 issue.[20] Lobrano was much more enthusiastic about "Passing the Ball" and wished to publish the story if Pritchett would consent to making one line more explicit. The story—only his fourth to appear in the magazine—was published with the minor alteration, but it would be Pritchett's last for several years. Serious marital problems dominated his life in the 1950s; and, though he continued working as a literary journalist and contributing book reviews to the magazine, he stopped producing stories.

* * *

Pritchett returned to short-story writing in the late 1950s and reemerged as a *New Yorker* contributor. By then Lobrano had retired and Roger Angell, a younger editor, was in charge of Pritchett's fiction submissions. Although relatively new to the *New Yorker* fiction department, Angell was neither a newcomer to magazine editing nor a stranger to Pritchett. Born in 1920, he had earned his BA from Harvard in 1942, served in the military from 1942 to 1946, and began what would be a nine-year tenure with *Holiday* magazine in 1947. The two men started their writer-editor relationship working with nonfiction at *Holiday*, for which Pritchett "wrote vigorous, impeccable travel essays,"[21] and continued with the short story when Angell went to the *New Yorker* in 1957. Their nearly fifty-year relationship, from the late 1940s to Pritchett's death in 1996, is one of the longest relationships of its kind. Of the twenty-seven Pritchett stories the *New Yorker* published from 1949–1989, Angell served as editor on all but the initial four. His eclectic interests and enthusiasm for different genres made him an ideal editor for Pritchett, a realist with a passion for social comedy and comic irony. A writer himself, Angell published a collection of stories in 1960, *The Stone Arbor and Other Stories*, all of which had originally appeared in the *New Yorker*. In addition, his humorous essays for the magazine in his early years also appeared in book form.

Eventually, however, he traded humor for sport. His elegant, contemplative *New Yorker* essays every year punctuate the eight-month baseball season at regular intervals, from spring training to the World Series. His passion for the nuances of the game, his penetrating characterization of its diverse cast, and his sensitivity to the seemingly inconsequential incidents, have made him the dean of American baseball writers.

Pritchett's FRA guaranteed Angell's rare privilege of being the first professional to read them for the first time. Pritchett's second wife, Dorothy, whom Angell generously credits with being Pritchett's "most trusted editor,"[22] typed and retyped all of his work, making her the true first reader. Angell accompanied Pritchett into the pages of the magazine, occasionally troubleshooting for him as a go-between with William Shawn, negotiating compromises between his writer's wishes and his editor's known preferences. A discerning reader, Angell was rewarding for the skilled writer. He was undoubtedly the most discriminating reader—except, perhaps, for Gerald Brenan—that Pritchett would ever have.

While it is not unusual for writers and editors to develop relationships beyond the strictly professional, Angell and Pritchett became unusually close and sympathetic early on and remained so throughout their five decades together. Of course Angell has had longstanding, close relationships with such *New Yorker* contributors as Donald Barthelme, Ann Beattie, and John Updike, but they were all Americans based in the United States. He has strong feelings about his special relationship with Pritchett: "I think there was a profound understanding between me and Victor; there's no doubt about it. We enjoyed each other, and going back and re-reading the stories [. . .]—some of them—brought back an immense sense of pleasure and closeness to him."[23] Their voluminous correspondence attests to Angell's recollection that they "wrote each other ceaselessly back and forth, and talked about everything—well, maybe not his neckties."[24] In addition to postal correspondence there were occasional telegrams and telephone calls bringing either headline good news from Angell or editorial queries and responses from both men. At a time when transatlantic calls were still a novelty, Angell discovered that "Victor liked to be called on [. . .] now and then and speak—get the news first hand."[25]

Their relationship was stimulated by personal meetings on both sides of the Atlantic. Pritchett, who trekked through Appalachia as a young man, knew America well, and made a habit of passing through New York during or after his visiting appointments at Princeton, Berkeley, Columbia, Smith, and Brandeis in 1953, 1962, 1965, 1967, and 1969, respectively. The last three of these visits enabled him and Dorothy to see Angell and his wife, Carol, in America. In turn the Angells reciprocated, dining with Victor and

Dorothy on more than one occasion in London at their Regent's Park Terrace home in Camden Town. And they were never closer than when, during a sweltering summer in the mid-1960s, by the kind of eerie coincidence that would lack credibility in a short story, the Pritchetts ended up subletting the walkup apartment directly over the Angells' on New York's East Ninety-fourth Street. The Angells even became familiar with their summer neighbors' eccentricities: "the odd, bumping footsteps we kept hearing overhead were finally explained when they told us that they stayed cool up there by going naked all day."[26]

* * *

The *New Yorker* employed an elaborate editorial system established by founder Harold Ross that ensured the scrupulous preparation of all articles for publication—including fiction. An entire department was devoted to establishing the accuracy of all facts in both nonfiction and fiction contributions. All material that appeared in the magazine passed through the legendary Fact Checking Department and editors were responsible for conveying any queries it had about submissions to their writers. While such a procedure would seem standard for nonfiction pieces, it was *New Yorker* practice to be equally discriminating with fiction. The fact checkers verified short-story details as seemingly inconsequential as the color of a Venetian hotel, the existence of a particular cinema in Ireland in 1939,[27] and the name of an 1880s Jubilee Stakes winner.[28] Whenever a fictional setting was based on an existing place, the magazine sought to anchor the fiction with authenticated factual elements. This commitment to accuracy necessarily influenced and complemented the Fiction Department editors' approach, especially those who were indoctrinated early in their careers. They corresponded with writers using Ross's traditional numbered lists of queries and suggestions. Such a procedure helped clarify stylistic, contextual, and thematic ambiguities that might confuse a reader's understanding of a published story. Realistic fiction was scrutinized for its credibility throughout all stages of the editorial process, from the initial typescript submission to working proofs, author's proofs, and galleys. While the Fiction Department made exceptions, occasionally publishing stories with pronounced fantasy elements like Sylvia Townsend Warner's fairy stories, its allegiance was to realistic fiction. Awareness of the central role that realism played in *New Yorker* fiction informed all its editors' choices and editorial suggestions.

As successful as Pritchett was in placing his stories in the *New Yorker*, over time Angell nevertheless rejected half his submissions. In several instances, Angell simply did not appreciate Pritchett's sense of humor. In turning down

"The Educated Girl" in 1959, for instance, he communicated the staff's feeling that the "wonderful dialogue" was not enough to compensate for the "terribly familiar" "basic humour"—"the business of a talkative untrained waitress giving advice and back talk to the patrons of a restaurant."[29] Angell speculated that what he and his colleagues felt to be hackneyed in their country was perhaps "not such a well-known phenomenon" in England and that "The Educated Girl" was "simply an example of the kind of story that does not travel well."[30] In 1969 Angell also disqualified "The Editor Regrets," finding it forced and exaggerated: "We only have one reservation about the story, but it is crucial; it didn't strike anyone here as being funny."[31] He was disappointed to see Pritchett "pushing for wilder events and astonishments" instead of relying on his always "vivid and surprising" fictional characters.[32]

Angell had a marked preference for surprises and revelations that made predictable, hackneyed situations anathema to him. "The Honeymoon" was deemed too broad and predictable all the way through and condemned for "its familiar mold of the high-strung bride on her wedding night."[33] In addition, the raid on the hotel was seen as a predictable plot device. Angell surmised that Pritchett's design was inherently flawed: "I suppose that Victor meant this to be funny, but it is neither funny nor sad—or so it seems to us."[34] Despite a "wonderfully promising fictional situation," Angell rejected one of Pritchett's more successful late stories, "Tea with Mrs. Bittell," because he was able to anticipate the victimization of the central character and felt that the perpetrator's eventual comeuppance lacked the surprise to compensate for it.[35] Though read and reconsidered by all of Angell's colleagues, including William Shawn, and highly praised for its masterful execution, "Things" was let go as well, despite Angell's admission that he could hardly find a line or a sentence he would question. He felt Rhoda's eccentricities and inventions, while charming and believable, made her an all-too-predictable caricature of the "colorful" relative found in many families. The other characters' preoccupation with Rhoda made them less interesting by association.[36] Angell dismissed Rhoda as a Dickensian figure unworthy of Pritchett's attention. Angell's preference for Trollope illustrates his predilection for unpredictable characters: "I like Trollope better because Trollope's characters always astound you and Dickens's never do."[37] Unfortunately, on one notable occasion, Angell's usually reliable litmus test was partially responsible for the rejection of one of Pritchett's finest stories—"Blind Love." Angell reluctantly turned down the story, despite finding the first half promising: "Once I learned that Mrs. Johnson couldn't swim," he wrote to Pritchett, "I knew that she had to fall into the swimming pool."[38]

To the *New Yorker*'s fiction editors "The Educated Girl" was not the only story "that does not travel well."[39] Angell rejected several others because he felt they were too British for an American publication. The major objection, for instance, to Pritchett's own favorite, "When My Girl Comes Home," was its overly British flavor: "What bothered us most here [. . .] is the fact that this seems to be a totally British story. The reactions of the entire family to someone like Hilda seem strange to us."[40] Although he found the characters convincing and realistic, in returning the submission to Pritchett's New York agent, Angell expressed his opinion that "American readers simply would not be interested in learning about a lower-middle-class family in such detail; this is one British story that does not export."[41] "The Speech" was rejected on similar grounds for its unfamiliar political content. Angell believed the radical movement in England had been so different from his compatriots' that "there may be many overtones and meanings that entirely escape American readers [. . .]."[42] Even some of the British slang, expressions, and idioms Pritchett used posed problems for American readers. He was, for instance, obliged to find an alternative for the incomprehensible "Watcha cock,"[43] "the commonest low London greeting of the merry kind."[44] After offering several possible substitutions to Angell, he changed it to "Evening guv."[45]

There were other, less pervasive explanations for Angell's rejection of other Pritchett stories—criticisms that occasionally resurfaced in his commentaries on the stories he did accept. He turned down "The Last Throw," despite praising it for its "remarkable energy" and "many splendid comical moments," because the "rambling, indirect form" of what he termed a "dialogue story" made it too difficult to follow.[46] Angell had an identical reaction to Pritchett's comedy "The Worshippers." He told Matson that the time shifts and seemingly random dialogue "full of names and puzzling references" required too much attention for the story's worth."[47] Less than a month after rejecting "The Worshippers," he sent back "The Accompanist." He was clearly frustrated with Pritchett's emphasis on dialogue: "[O]nce again V.S.P. is mostly interested in presenting the reader with the kind of discontinuous, scrappy bits of dialogue that he loves so well, and that none of us can follow or make ourselves care about."[48]

Angell did not appreciate Pritchett's penchant for "scrappy bits of dialogue," which was Pritchett's way of capturing the "savage poetry" of the common man, as he explained in his lecture on dialogue.[49] Pritchett always believed dialogue was more important than plot. Angell found one particular story—"Did you Invite Me?"—"done in an intentionally elliptical fashion" to be "unduly difficult and puzzling," and it left him convinced that he had missed or misunderstood something.[50] Even a writer's standard of excellence could sometimes be a liability. Although Angell admitted "The Cage Birds" was undoubtedly much better than some stories that had been and would be published in the magazine, he rejected it nevertheless, believing it was not up to Pritchett's own "very high standard."[51] This seemingly capricious decision was consistent with the *New Yorker* policy of protecting established writers' reputations.[52]

Angell's acceptance of two early Pritchett stories, "Citizen" and "The Wheelbarrow," depended upon Pritchett's initial willingness to comply with the editor's directives for alteration. Angell was insistent about the changes. The aggressive tone he employed in his provisional acceptance of "Citizen," a resubmission of a story rejected by Gus Lobrano in 1953,[53] was, however, an aberration. Known for his discretion, sensitivity, and tact, he perhaps then lacked experience as a young fiction editor. He said that when he edited "The Wheelbarrow," he "didn't really know what [he] was doing."[54] Angell made it clear from the outset of his letter that the acceptance was conditional:

> Citizen is basically successful, and [. . .] will be entirely successful if you will agree with us about a few changes. This time, I think that the changes are absolutely essential, and I so hope that you will be willing to consider them and to go along with us on what we feel needs to be done.[55]

Two months later, he reminded Pritchett about the importance of agreeing about the ending of the story: "I strongly hope you will see our point and will be willing to go along with it."[56] Initially, he was equally aggressive in his demands for changes to "The Wheelbarrow," stating in his telegram of conditional acceptance that the story would require changes,[57] and reaffirming and elaborating on such demands in his subsequent letter full of queries about the typescript.[58] Angell was certain the story would "work out to be a really fine and original piece of work" but believed it would "require considerable clarification."[59] "Noisy in the Doghouse" had even more difficulty meeting with the *New Yorker*'s approval. Angell had so many "distressing observations" about and criticisms of the manuscript that he could only offer Pritchett the possibility of a full-scale revision and resubmission, without even a conditional offer of eventual publication. Revise the story according to his instructions, he said, or the *New Yorker* would "sadly have to let it go."[60] To compound the rejection, he informed Pritchett that if he attempted to sell the story to another magazine, the *New Yorker* would be unable to publish any future stories featuring the character Noisy Brackett. The magazine had a policy that kept it from accepting parts of a series that had appeared in other magazines. Pritchett revised

"Noisy in the Doghouse" according to the editor's directives, but Angell found Pritchett's refashioned pub scene in the author's proof more, not less, confusing.[61] Under pressure from deadlines, overwhelmed with work, and anxious about a reader's comprehension of the story, Angell overstepped his role as editor and became a collaborator. Instead of consulting Pritchett about additional revisions and allowing the writer to make the changes himself, he restored the original scene, stating it in "simpler, more direct terms"; and he made a number of small revisions to clarify a few characters' actions and motivations. He mailed the corrected galley page to London and asked Pritchett to cable his approval—which Pritchett did. Although Angell gave Pritchett permission to change some of the details in the cable, or voice dissatisfaction with the revisions altogether and postpone the story for a later issue, he presented them as a fait accompli. Ultimately, Angell's emendations were "ADMIRINGLY APPROVED,"[62] but he never again employed such tactics with Pritchett.

Angell seemed to feel that the achievement of clarity precluded narrative indirection and multiple effects within the same story. This legitimate concern for clarity was in the best interest of the magazine's readership. His own comprehension became the barometer for the reader's. If the perceptive *New Yorker* editors could not understand a story, how could they publish it? Opposed to indirection and unconventional uses of point of view, Angell sought to harness the ambiguous and elliptical passages in Pritchett's stories—as he did with other writers throughout his career. As an editor Angell has remained interested in the magazine form of a story, whereas, in writing it, Pritchett must have considered the more permanent book form that would reward multiple readings. An unusually close, perceptive reader, Angell had a heightened sense of details that could be misconstrued, but his emphasis on clarity was far more pronounced in their early association, especially in their discussions about "Citizen," "The Wheelbarrow," and "Noisy in the Doghouse."

Overbearing as Angell was in his letters about these early stories, however, most of the changes he suggested sharpened them. And although the detailed correspondence seems at first glance to reveal a series of major, story-transforming alterations, the changes themselves, however helpful, were seldom intricate or difficult to accomplish. The only changes Pritchett made to "Citizen," except for its ending, were to revise the date of a statue, a few phrases, and a comment that may have been misconstrued as one character's confession of homosexuality. In the case of "The Wheelbarrow" Pritchett acceded to his editor's initial requests to give Miss Freshwater's niece a name (Miss Wantage), specify the ages of the two characters, add a few words, and make the text of an old letter more explicit. Even Pritchett's most significant alterations—the subtle clarification of the main characters' motivations at the climax of the story and their ambiguous interaction—were accomplished with few revisions. Elicited by Angell's detailed queries, Pritchett's lengthy explication of the initial typescript proves not only that he had thought about every aspect and phrase of the story, but that his changes for the *New Yorker* version did not compromise his intended meaning, destroy the story's intriguing ambiguities, or undercut its subtleties.[63]

Pritchett's revelation about his working methods early in his relationship with Angell may have invited editorial intrusions. Early on, he apprised his editor of his penchant for endless revision: "I usually write at least half a dozen drafts of a story and until the last one, when the whole thing is transformed, it cant be said to be anything but wooden and pointless. [. . .] [T]he fact is that I am the kind of writer who does endless re-writing."[64] This self-effacing description perhaps corroborated Angell's sense that Pritchett revered the editing process and would be a willing collaborator in redrafting his short-story offerings. Even at the peak of his powers, Pritchett spoke of his endless quest and authorized Angell's exhaustive scrutiny of his submissions: "There is almost no limit to the amount of attention to detail one can give to a story."[65] Angell himself mentioned this in his tribute to Pritchett: "I came to understand that the amiable attention he gave to even the smallest suggested cut or rephrasing in his text was not a sign of politeness or modesty but came from the intense, almost sensual pleasure he took in every part of the writing business."[66]

More than anything else, the early correspondence enabled Pritchett and Angell to forge a stimulating, productive, and healthy working alliance. Angell learned that there was nothing haphazard or careless about his writer's creations, and Pritchett, though he did not always agree with him, came to trust in and appreciate his editor's sensitivity to fiction. The opportunity of lunching together in New York during the summer of 1962 gave Angell "great pleasure," and though it was not their first meeting, it confirmed for him the "feeling of understanding" that had developed between them by letter over their first five years together.[67] In recognition of this "understanding," and for the first time in their correspondence, Angell greeted Pritchett by his first name. Pritchett reciprocated with "Dear Roger" in his reply, and the formal address was abandoned for the duration of their correspondence. The more intimate greeting signified a subtle but important change in their relationship.

Angell became more deferential as the relationship evolved, increasingly confident of Pritchett's ability to fashion effective "fixes" in response to his usual list of queries. Instead of telling Pritchett what needed to be done and insisting on particular solutions to the problems he found, as he had early in their correspondence, Angell identified problematic aspects of a story in his queries, suggested possible solutions, but deferred to Pritchett for the final decision. Their collaboration in the revisions was rich and multifaceted. Pritchett accepted many of Angell's suggestions for revision in preparing stories for the magazine. In some instances he retained the revisions when the story was published in book form, but in others he returned to the original version. In some cases, Pritchett was indebted to Angell for a particularly valuable change, while in others he solved a problem that baffled his editor. Occasionally Angell merely grafted a phrase from Pritchett's revision onto Pritchett's original.

Many of their exchanges focused on the clarification of details. In discussing the author's proof of "Chatty," Angell raised William Shawn's objection to the following simile in the midst of others: "her noble breasts were like a pair of grenades with the pins out."[68] Shawn thought that the "noble" made the woman's breasts seem large but that comparing them to a pair of grenades made them seem small. Angell advised Pritchett, if he agreed, to "change the 'noble', not the simile." Although he removed "noble" as suggested, Pritchett explained that his "idea about 'noble' breasts was that they were one moment large and noble and the next like grenades, —a subjective fantasy [. . .] that Nature does not allow."[69]

Except for its altered title, all of the changes to "Our Wife" that Angell requested Pritchett make for the *New Yorker* were retained for his *Collected Stories*. Angell praised the story as "absolutely delightful," was pleased to send him "some good news for a change," and was "very happy" to have Pritchett "back aboard." His tone in the letter of acceptance is remarkably different from that of a decade earlier. Instead of demanding changes from his writer, he is deferential:

> I wonder if you would consider adding some brief amplifying passages about Molly. She is the central figure, of course, and yet she is given very little to say except those highly enigmatic staccato remarks, and one longs to know her a little better. I realize that she is meant to be a mysterious figure, but we all feel that she could be somewhat more fully rounded. Please tell me what you think about this, and don't hesitate to disagree if you feel strongly about this matter. I will hold off any editing until I hear from you.[70]

Initially, although he broached a change of Pritchett's ingenious title, he considered it a minor matter.[71] But, two months later, he argued for a new title and renewed his appeal to Pritchett to supply some alternatives: "OUR WIFE seems a little too tricky, and it also gives away a central point in the story, which the reader should perhaps be allowed to discover."[72] Pritchett explained that "the story was an explanation of the title and not a surprise; indeed the title was, in this sense, part of the story."[73] Although he disagreed with Angell, Pritchett offered the Pushkinesque compromise of "The Captain's Daughter"; but he informed Angell that he would restore the original title when it was published in book form.[74] All of Angell's other suggestions, however, were adopted permanently. Pritchett was not at all against filling out Molly's character and, in addition to making some minor alterations of a few words and phrases, enclosed a page-long insert for the draft already in Angell's possession that amplified her character without making it banal.[75] Finally, in the author's proof of "The Captain's Daughter," Pritchett made further emendations at his editor's request. Angell was troubled by the conceit in the opening of the story—"Even her little eyes are noisy"—because it "is such a startling and unlikely notion."[76] Pritchett explained that it was a Dickensian conceit on the principle of Pecksniff's throat ("Even his throat was moral").[77] He changed "Even her little eyes are noisy"[78] to "Even her little eyes long for trouble."[79] Angell felt an additional line was needed to clarify the idea that the wife was too much for any one man,[80] and Pritchett added a sentence to remind the reader: "Hadn't he said she was a woman who needed two husbands?"[81]

Pritchett appreciated Angell as a critic, and though he did not always act on them, Angell's numerous queries and suggestions helped him refine his stories, correct inaccuracies, clarify ambiguous references, or test the strength of, and his resolve to maintain, the original presentation of their most significant elements. One crucial issue was the protection of the "unsaid" element. Angell respected his writer's wish to avoid the overly explicit in his stories—a wish that was clear early in their correspondence. In response to Angell's query about "The Key to My Heart,"[82] for instance, Pritchett sent him a two-page alternative ending that he hoped Angell would "think rather stronger and sharper for the end of the story,"[83] but expressed his interest in preserving the original ending's suggestive ambiguity—"the feeling of rather dull doubt in the narrator's mind and the sense of innuendo for the reader."[84]

In their discussions about "The Fall,"[85] Angell urged Pritchett to protect the unsaid and trust the reader's interpretive powers: "And finally, at (I), it seemed to me that the statement that Peacock had become Shel is really unnecessary. If the reader doesn't realize this by this time, he simply hasn't understood the story at all. I think the point is entirely clear without actually saying it."[86] In proposing the excision of some of the repetitive lines, the detailing of the central character's confusion, his last fall to the floor, and the shortening of a speech, Angell sought to accelerate the story's ending and protect the unsaid element. So, in contrast to his insistence on clarity, Angell argued for being less, not more, explicit in this instance. Yet, uninhibited by an interpretive formula, and committed to considering each story separately, he also cautioned Pritchett about being overly elliptical and burning through scenes too rapidly, as in the working proof for "The Nest Builder":

> This entire section, in which Ernest is trapped by Miss Staples, is very important to the story, and it certainly should not be over-explained. I do think, though, that you have made it a little too fast and off-hand, and I'm sure that small revisions can bring out exactly the right tone.[87]

Delighted as he was with one of Pritchett's late stories, "Neighbors," and as much as he admired its final paragraph, Angell pointed out that "the story also ends very neatly and effectively if it's omitted."[88] Given permission to do as he wished, Pritchett removed the paragraph for the *New Yorker* version. When Angell received the final proofs, and transferred Pritchett's "fixes," he was especially pleased to effect Pritchett's deletion of the last few lines: "They were lovely, but the story is even better without them, I think; it's odd how often that seems to be true about endings."[89] Angell liked inconclusive, Chekhovian endings, but Pritchett, who was usually a champion of the understated and unsaid, reinstated the ending in the story's book form, perhaps seduced by the high quality of his own writing.

Pritchett did not always reject the alterations he made for the *New Yorker* version at Angell's suggestion in the final versions of his stories in book form. There are important examples where he retained them permanently. The editorial collaboration on what is perhaps Pritchett's most famous story, "On the Edge of the Cliff," is a significant variation on this characteristic interplay of suggestion, rejection, and acceptance. It became the title story of one of Pritchett's most successful collections and was later selected by A. S. Byatt for *The Oxford Book of English Short Stories*, in part, she said, to show Pritchett's mastery of the genre, a "sense of how much and how little could be contained in its space."[90] Some of Angell's editorial recommendations may have contributed to Byatt's impression. The story is about old friends—Harry, a widower, and Daisy, a widow—both engaged in May–December romances. Their awkward meeting at a fair with their young lovers in tow forces them to realize that their respective relationships, as blissful as they are, are necessarily ephemeral. In a private conversation with each other toward the end of the story, Daisy suggests that she and Harry avoid any further meetings that might suggest the more appropriate coupling of their young lovers, Stephen and Rowena.

As fond as he was of the initial draft, Angell decided to put the story into "working proof," an intermediate stage, in order to solve various problems before scheduling the story. He believed it was "a little too long and talky in its latter stages," especially the entire scene between Daisy and the old man toward the end. Angell compared it to an old-fashioned play that Pritchett had allowed to go on too long and advised the excision of up to two dozen lines.[91] More important he alerted Pritchett to what he perceived as a flaw in the story's last turn of event: the revelation that the two young people have already crossed paths in the village and will probably undermine the older pair's plans by becoming a couple themselves.[92] He surmised that this was the central idea around which Pritchett wrote the story, but felt the meeting had the neatness of "a Maugham story or play." He suggested cutting the paragraph revealing the meeting, believing that it was clear without it that the old man and Daisy would not be able to isolate their lovers from each other or from other young people for long. Once again Angell wished to make an ending understated and suggestive, protective of the unsaid element:

> I only suggest this, Victor, because this is such a beautiful and moving story that I hate to see it concluded with any kind of a trick or surprise. It is entirely convincing and moving without that, and the reader must know somehow what will happen to these people, even if it isn't allowed to happen onstage, so to speak. You have made it all inevitable, and so it doesn't have to happen before our eyes.[93]

Not wanting to be "Maughamish," Pritchett thought Angell and Shawn might be right about cutting the paragraph in question—the "surf-board meeting."[94] Ten days later, when he had had the chance to make a more detailed examination of the proofs, he agreed "entirely with [Angell] about deleting the idea of a meeting [. . .]. It's much better without it."[95] Pritchett found the cutting of the long final scene between Daisy and Harry more problematic. Yet he was obviously sympathetic to Angell's philosophy, having himself made preliminary cuts amounting to twenty lines throughout the scene and having removed the "surf-board" meeting in the carbon of his final typescript.[96] He pruned an additional thirty lines between the scene and the rest of the story, but was restricted from even more radical surgery by his own particular use of dialogue:

> The cutting of the long final scene was difficult. I've cut quite a bit to make it sharper, though I didn't want to spoil Daisy's slow deviousness. I may have

cut more out of the commentary [. . .] and not enough of the talk, but what I've left in—given the love of sly repetitiveness in human conversation—seems to be necessary.[97]

Angell was delighted with the corrected proofs for "On the Edge of the Cliff," told Pritchett that his alterations had "solved everything brilliantly," and was "filled with admiration for [his] willingness to cut as much as [he] did and where [he] did." And Angell may have been justified in claiming that the once "marvellous" story had been made "even better."[98] Ultimately they arrived at a compromise. When the *New Yorker* version appeared, it was free of the "long and talky" passages to which Angell had objected when he first read the story—although he may have wished to cut even more—and it was also free of the gratuitous "surf-board" meeting between Stephen and Rowena. When Pritchett published the story in his collection of the same title, however, he reinstated most of the lines that he had excised for the magazine with one exception: the "Maughamish" ending, an example of Angell's enduring contribution to the importance of the unsaid.

* * *

Even when he was at a loss to give Pritchett specific indications for improvement, Angell's dissatisfaction and high standards prodded the writer into producing some of his best work. The making of "The Fig Tree" is the most dramatic example of this. Pritchett's initial submission was rejected, but Angell and his colleagues, including William Shawn, praised "more than half" of the story as "perfectly splendid" and hoped Pritchett would respond to their enthusiastic invitation to rewrite it.[99] Angell expressed his reservations about the story, speculated about its unsuccessful ending, and offered suggestions for improvement. This was a story he wanted in the magazine: "It disappoints me not to be able to respond instantly with an acceptance. The best of this is absolutely top-level Pritchett, and we all want to see it in the magazine if possible." Even Shawn was adamant about persuading Pritchett to save "The Fig Tree."[100] Six weeks later, Pritchett submitted a revised version, saying he was indebted to Angell for his "very helpful suggestions" that he believed "greatly improved the story."[101] Despite incorporating his editor's suggestions for revision, however, Pritchett's revised version of "The Fig Tree" met with the same result. Angell's attempt to help Pritchett with the story was well intentioned, but, by his own admission, misguided. And although he could appreciate

Pritchett's significant alterations, he could neither understand nor explain why the rearrangement did not achieve "the clarification and resolution that seemed so nearly attainable in the first version":[102]

> I blame myself for this. I wish I could now urge you to take back the manuscript and attempt a few specific further alterations, but I have no idea now what these should be and no confidence that they would produce the brilliant story that we all have glimpsed at different times and places in these pages.[103]

Clearly distressed about failing to respond favorably to alterations he himself had suggested, and embarrassed at his inability to help with the manuscript, Angell returned both versions to Pritchett's agent. Pritchett then agreed with Angell's assessment and, as was his way with stories that went awry, decided to give "The Fig Tree" "a few months rest on the compost heap."[104] Six weeks later, Angell responded to Pritchett's second revision, applauding it as "an absolute triumph."[105] Angell recalled this amazing metamorphosis during our recent interview,[106] and he also reminisced about it in his *New Yorker* tribute:

> The third version, which came in almost a year after the first, was a major restructuring, front to back, and required nothing from this end except gratitude: he had got it right, and there was almost more pleasure in that than there would have been in a perfect first manuscript—of which he was also capable, of course.[107]

In accepting the story for publication, Angell thanked Pritchett for somehow solving all the problems that he and his colleagues sensed but could not elucidate. After praising the specific alterations in detail, he saluted Pritchett for engineering a transformation of which he himself had not been able to conceive: "I <u>never</u> would have guessed that this was what was needed."[108] Pritchett himself was aware of his debt to Angell, and in his reply paid tribute to him, grateful for his editor's significant contribution to the extraordinary growth of "The Fig Tree":

> I hasten to thank you for giving me this thrill; but even more for your having shown, all along, your prolonged and helpful interest in the story. It did stir me to get the puzzling thing right. [. . .] [E]verything depends on working and re-working—a tiresome but ultimately rewarding process; your generous concern encouraged me to keep at it.[109]

Although Pritchett himself was responsible for this most radical transformation, Angell played an important role. Without him, Pritchett would not have arrived at his masterly final version, and the story would not be regarded as one of his finest.

* * *

Angell was not merely Pritchett's editor. He also served as a go-between with William Shawn, effecting compromises between his writer's wishes and his editor's known preferences. On numerous occasions he argued on Pritchett's behalf about problems of clarity, grammar, locution, idiom, usage, and content. Angell often assured Pritchett in his notes that accompanied galleys and proofs of Pritchett's stories that he would mollify Shawn. Of course Shawn's surveillance extended to more important issues of theme, language, and content. An example of this came in his objection to phrases that were "perhaps too vulgar for us." Although he asked Pritchett for an alternative phrase in case Shawn remained adamant about its removal, Angell promised to do his "utmost to urge him to let this stand."[110] In "On the Edge of the Cliff," Shawn objected to Daisy's euphemism for performing oral sex on her young lover:[111] "'I'd go down on my knees to him. In fact', (she gave one of her old coarse laughs), 'I often do'."[112] Angell explained that Shawn was uneasy about the passage and thought it should be removed. But he gave Pritchett a choice and promised to fight for him: "If you strongly feel that it belongs in the story, then I will certainly do my utmost to keep it in. Shawn often backs down on these issues under a serious challenge, but I don't like to force this sort of crisis unless the author involved cares deeply about the matter."[113] Ultimately, Pritchett agreed with Shawn's objection to the passage on the grounds that "it is too strong in the context, though the girl is coarse."[114] He deleted the second of the two sentences definitively: "'In fact', (she gave one of her old coarse laughs) 'I often do'." Nevertheless, he was aware of Angell's support—support that had been instrumental in achieving a breakthrough at the *New Yorker* in 1970.

Without Angell's delicate negotiations, it is unlikely that "The Fall"—the second of two identically titled stories published ten years apart in the magazine and retitled "The Diver" thereafter—would have been published at all. A comic tale of a young man's first sexual experience, it includes an encounter between him (the narrator) and a married woman. Pritchett believed it was one of his best stories but feared that its provocative content and explicit bedroom scene would go "altogether too far for The New Yorker."[115] Angell informed Pritchett that his fears about the "'naughtiness'" of the tale and the magazine's "old tight-lipped reactions to the sexual realities" had been somewhat justified.[116] But he succeeded in his delicate negotiation. With the modification of a few phrases in the bedroom scene—in particular the insistent comic description about the young man's erection—the story was cleared for publication. The compromise accomplished, Angell hoped Pritchett would sanction the suggested changes and help him bring down the magazine's rigid policy: "Actually, running the story in this new form would still be precedent-breaking for us—a small revolution that I, for one, am anxious to bring about. For all these reasons, I await your reply with the sharpest interest."[117] Pritchett praised Angell's efforts on his behalf:

> I see that [. . .] you have obviously put up a fight for it and this I greatly appreciate, for I know there must be strong differences of opinion. [...] In short I am delighted to be in the mag., specially if this, as you suggest, helps the break through.[118]

Despite arguing with great conviction for changes to Pritchett's stories, Angell always insisted that any alterations he made during the collaborative editorial process would be subject to Pritchett's approval. Even in his most demanding early years, he constantly reminded Pritchett of his right to veto any revision: "As you know, all these changes are subject to your approval, and if you disapprove of anything I have done here, be sure to say so."[119] Later in their association, during one of Pritchett's more prolific periods, Angell was even more deferential. In asking him to attempt a new ending for "Chatty," for example, he allowed Pritchett to ignore all of his suggestions: "All this is entirely up to you, of course, and we will take the story just as it stands, if you want it that way."[120] In this instance Pritchett had complete freedom to do as he wished, even though Angell wanted the story altered. His tone is far different from the intrusive, almost dictatorial tone of their earlier correspondence, where Angell strong-armed Pritchett into changing aspects of his early stories. Still later in their association, in a list of queries about "The Rescue," Angell once again reminded Pritchett of his editorial liberty: "This is up to you, of course—as is everything else here."[121] This confirms how much the relationship had evolved since the late 1950s, and how far Pritchett had come since his first few years with Angell. The *New Yorker* initially conferred prestige on Pritchett but, by the 1970s, having established himself as the leading English short-story writer of his time Pritchett was also conferring prestige on the magazine.

Cooperative as he was in responding to Angell's editorial requests, Pritchett did not undertake alterations or rewrite stories merely to satisfy his editor and place them in the *New Yorker*, seductive as that option must have been professionally and financially. In many instances he held his ground, defending elements in some stories that he was unwilling to change on principle and refusing to rewrite others. Angell's late colleague, William Maxwell, in explaining the magazine's considerable leverage with writers, once told Frances Kiernan, then a young editor, "We hold the cards."[122] And though many short-story writers acquiesced routinely to the editorial demands made of them, Pritchett sometimes refused to play the game. Angell turned down some of his finest stories, including the eventual title stories to three collections, but those rejections did not undermine Pritchett's belief in them.

One of Pritchett's first opportunities to overhaul a story came in Angell's response to "On the Scent."[123] Its "admirable and tantalizing qualities" intrigued Angell and four of his colleagues, but the story baffled them in the end. Although they professed to like the "basic idea," no two of them could agree on Pritchett's "basic intention"; and, after serious consideration, they reluctantly turned it down. Angell did not reject the story outright, however, believing it could be salvaged. He offered Pritchett the chance to revise it "in such a way as to make us reconsider our decision," but stated that the reworking would "have to be a major enterprise—almost a complete re-telling of the tale."[124] Angell understood Pritchett's intermingling of "two very difficult, submerged themes"—Maningtree's secret life of the imagination, and the spy life he shared with the German—but felt that Pritchett's indirect method of telling the story led to "too many questions, revelations, and doubts as to what is fact and what is fancy."[125] He advised him to simplify the story, omit the spy business altogether, and make it merely an encounter between two failures who lead fascinating lives. He hoped Pritchett would have some doubts about the story, but was convinced his writer would reject the "gamble of a major revision." Pritchett was drawn to portraying such people, after all, and sometimes indulged in indirect narration that Angell often found objectionable. Although he offered to make a few minor adjustments, Pritchett rejected his editor's offer, confident of the story's success:

> I am sorry my beautiful little contrivance baffled you. I might alter a couple of lines on page 2 and add one line before the end, but I'm afraid I cant rewrite and the espionage is essential. Such are spies—blatant, consumed by fantasy. Never mind. It is kind of you to write. I'll be interested to hear what you make of the very long, long tale.[126]

The "very long, long tale" to which Pritchett referred—"When My Girl Comes Home"—was rejected as well, ostensibly because it was "too British" and "dated,"[127] but also because the telling of this most impressive long short story relied too heavily on the very technique of indirection that Angell and his colleagues spurned. Pritchett was silent about this particular rejection for many years, but he would refer to it again in the course of their correspondence. Another story, "The Speech," was also disqualified on technical grounds. Angell found the "various devices—stream of consciousness, the impressionistic switches, the inner voice"—"intrusive and confusing," rather than absorbing, and the woman "hard to believe in."[128] Its difficult foreign political subject was held against it as well. In this instance Pritchett had anticipated his editor's reaction, but, proud of his creation, vouched for its success: "I didn't for one moment think The New Yorker would like The Speech. Its whole background would be incomprehensible to an American reader. However, it seems to be a success in England and is certainly thought to come off."[129] (Pritchett had only submitted "The Speech" to honor his longstanding FRA with the magazine.)

Pritchett asserted his independence as an artist in his refusal to refashion "The Skeleton." Angell called it a "marvelous story" that was "almost impossible to turn down." Yet even though he praised it as a "comic masterpiece," he complained that it was too long—"not just in words, but in the manner of telling."[130] He surmised that Pritchett had been swept away by the characters and his manner of telling—unable to limit himself in writing about them—and likened the story to a "slice of a novel." Furthermore, despite enjoying the ending, he criticized it as inconsistent with the story. As he had previously done, Angell asked for a rewrite and resubmission, emphasizing the need for considerable cutting that might benefit the story's loose structure. Though convinced the results "could be quite spectacular," and full of praise for Pritchett's inimitable blending of comedy and pathos, Angell was nevertheless unwilling to commit himself or the magazine to a provisional acceptance. Instead, he offered Pritchett a "speculative" chance for revision.[131]

Pritchett's unwavering rejection of the invitation to rework the story was a resounding affirmation of his artistic integrity. Always willing to entertain Angell's suggestions, he did not always agree. In this case, Pritchett was convinced that "The Skeleton" was as good as anything he had ever done— "the fruit of a large number of re-writings and polishings"—and although he offered a few minor changes, he was unwilling to make any significant alterations: "The Skeleton is a story, but it is even more a portrait or an account of a way of life, an investigation of old age with the terms of comedy and while I think it can be improved in detail I am sure it cannot be shortened."[132] He admitted to having already sharpened a few pages in the middle and several details in the beginning, but surmised that such minor changes would not satisfy an editor eager for major alterations. The conclusion of the same letter suggests a role reversal, with Pritchett, not Angell, giving the ultimatum for a story he knew Angell could not pass up: "This is, as I understand your letter, not what you really thought necessary, but in case you have second thoughts I am sending it to you. If you remain of your opinion will you hand it over to Matson? Naturally I hope you will take it."[133] Eight days later, by telegram, Pritchett received the result of this ultimatum: YES WE SHALL TAKE THE SKELETON WITH ALL BONES INTACT. LETTER FOLLOWS. CONGRATULATIONS. ROGER.[134] Angell admitted in the letter that "The Skeleton" was simply "too good for us to miss."[135] He agreed to buy the story at its original length, "without reluctance or hesitation, but with joy."

Angell regretted his rapid dismissal of one of Pritchett's most imaginative stories, "Blind Love," shortly after its publication in the collection of the same title—an inscribed copy of which Pritchett mailed to Angell and his wife, Carol. Mystified about the weeks of silence that followed his gesture, Pritchett enquired about its safe arrival. Angell explained that they had indeed received the copy weeks earlier, had devoured it, discussed it, and "loved it," but had forgotten to acknowledge it.[136] But Angell was also disturbed to read the "perfectly lovely collection of stories" that he believed was Pritchett's best, confronted as he was by his rejection of some of its stories for the *New Yorker*:

> You will still probably conclude that the book made only the smallest impression on me, but I know that isn't true. In fact, the only other explanation I can come up with for my gaffe is the fact that I had so much difficulty, after rereading those stories, in understanding why we (I) had turned down so many of them. "The Skeleton" is my favorite in the collection, but the title story ["Blind Love"] is so fine that I can only conclude that I was the blind one for letting it escape us. Maybe I am in need of a sabbatical.[137]

Angell recently explained that all editors can question their decisions not to run particular stories, adding that "this isn't a science, you just do the best you can."[138] The length of "Blind Love" may have been against it as well. Four years later, Pritchett spoke out again, disappointed, yet not surprised, to receive another invitation to rewrite the last of his long stories,

"The Camberwell Beauty." Once again he refused to consider the radical alteration of a story he valued just as he had written it:

> I think your criticisms miss the point—as they have done in stories like <u>Blind Love</u> and one or two others. I am told by those who have read the story that it is among the best I have recently written and [. . .] I am therefore disinclined to revise and re-submit it. It will be the making of the completed volume as it stands.[139]

* * *

Katherine Anne Porter submitted her own "Fig Tree" story to the *New Yorker* in 1960. In her reply to William Maxwell's letter intimating that the story would require revision, she responded vehemently: "I have never changed a story in any way at all at any one's suggestion but my own. [. . .] If you do not agree with me—You Plural, the New Yorker editors—I am sorry. And there I expect it must end."[140] There can be no greater contrast to Porter's position than Raymond Carver's during the years when Gordon Lish edited him at *Esquire*. Lish's intervention appears to have had significant influence on the final versions.[141] The relationship between V. S. Pritchett and Roger Angell—in its intricacy, fullness, and extraordinary outcome—lies between these polar opposites and, as we have seen, offers an unusual example of editorial interaction. Theirs was a special association that deepened to intimacy and persisted for over forty years. Neither man dominated, neither surrendered to the other; and their mutual respect, admiration, and consideration—all elements of their enduring friendship—enabled them to come to an informed consensus about Pritchett's short fiction and together forge twenty-three stories for the *New Yorker* that would constitute fully one-third of the pages in Pritchett's *Complete Collected Stories* (1990). The prestige conferred upon Pritchett fortified his reputation as England's finest practitioner of the genre, and the *New Yorker*'s handsome remuneration may have enabled him to continue rather than abandon writing stories.

* * *

William Trevor's "love affair with *The New Yorker*" began in 1946 when he was seduced by James Thurber's eccentric world in which "the mayhem of the Marx brothers was a millimetre beneath the most mundane of human surfaces."[142] Five years later he was hooked for good while perusing its twenty-fifth-anniversary album of cartoons. Initially attracted to its humor, Trevor began reading such writers as John Updike and John Cheever at a time when Dorothy Parker's "fingerprints were everywhere" in the "bright, smart pages" of the magazine. Years later, as a young writer, however, Trevor's professional interest was unrequited. In fact, his start at the magazine was far less promising than Pritchett's inauspicious beginning. Although already an established novelist and short story writer when his agent began submitting work, Trevor was not published in the *New Yorker*'s pages until eleven years after his first submission. And had it not been for the perspicacity and determination of one of the magazine's most dynamic editors, Veronica Geng, he might not have been recognized by it until much later, if at all.

Had Trevor's first offerings been inferior, his initial lack of success would have been understandable, but this was clearly not the case. The *New Yorker* rejected two accomplished early stories, "The Table" and "The Penthouse Apartment," claiming there was "a streak of gratuitous cruelty in them that doesn't seem justified either by character or situation," and later dismissed one of Trevor's most moving stories, "Access to the Children," without justification.[143] Amazingly, even such masterpieces as "The Ballroom of Romance" failed to achieve the breakthrough.[144] While these rejections seem baffling today, they are easier to understand in retrospect. Frances Kiernan, Trevor's second editor at the magazine, who "inherited" him in August 1981 with Geng's departure, believes his agent's practice at the time of sending three or four stories simultaneously diminished their chance of success. The strategy was inherently flawed because the magazine would never take them all together. Faced with such a choice, the fiction editors would perhaps select one or two at the most, naturally taking "the best, or the most usable" of the group.[145] Submitting stories separately gave each one more of a chance.

Both Frances Kiernan and Charles McGrath, colleagues for many years in the Fiction Department, credit Veronica Geng for reintroducing Trevor to the department and convincing all her colleagues to reconsider his work. She was a passionate, highly respected editor who "was willing to fight if it came to getting her way." Unlike most of her colleagues, who had been raised and trained within the system, she came "full-blown" as an experienced editor from outside and that may have given her the autonomy to question it.[146] Kiernan believes that the more senior editors, including William Maxwell, Roger Angell, Rachel MacKenzie, and Robert Henderson, may not even have seen Trevor's early submissions when he was first trying to break into the magazine because they were rejected early in the selection process.[147] Read quickly, Trevor's fiction appeared too traditional and obvious "with that leisured [...] old-fashioned voice" that may have been the main obstacle during the late 1960s and early 70s. It seemed a throwback to another era at a time when the magazine was conscious of pushing its boundaries, publishing Donald Barthelme and Ann Beattie. Yet with their underlying twists, his stories were not quite what they appeared to be:[148]

> I think some people didn't notice that they were subversive. It took Veronica to point it out. And so they never got past whoever was reading them. And they just thought "Oh this looks like an old fashioned this or an old fashioned that" or "I've seen this story before. It's very well done but why should we be doing that?" Because we were all looking for new writers, young writers. [. . .] And that's not what Trevor was doing. And I think [. . .] once it became apparent to all of us what he *was* doing, it was fine. He just needed an advocate to explain him to everybody else [. . .].[149]

Kiernan recalls that Geng, hired with the mandate of bringing in new writers, made a strong case for Trevor with Shawn. And because she had eclectic tastes, and had brought in European writers like Milan Kundera, Shawn may have valued her opinion all the more. Trevor was not the kind of writer she would have normally argued for. The times had changed as well. An approach that seemed unfashionable when editors were searching for more experimental fiction during the previous decade was finally given a chance.[150] Charles McGrath was not convinced at first, but when Geng's enthusiasm persuaded him "to take a longer harder look" at Trevor's stories he "was completely sold [...]" and now admits that "Trevor should have been at the *New Yorker* for a decade, at least, before he was."[151] Just shy of fifty, and with considerable support from Geng, Trevor broke through in 1977 with the publication of his first story, "Torridge."[152] And although the magazine did not take another story for five months, it showed sincere long-term interest by offering the coveted FRA in December that it has renewed with him yearly ever since. Despite his newfound status and staunch advocate, however, Trevor experienced his share of rejection as well. His agents continued to make the mistake of sending in several stories at once, with four going in together at one point.[153] In correspondence, Geng was candid about her lost battles, disappointed the magazine rejected such stories as "The Teddy Bears' Picnic" and "Mulvihill's Memorial." But she was responsible for turning the tide. The *New Yorker* accepted five more of his stories during Geng's tenure in the next four years, including such important contributions as "Death in Jerusalem," "Attracta," "Autumn Sunshine," and "Beyond the Pale."

Ironically, the very approach for which he was once ignored now fit the magazine *sur mesure*. In time, Trevor became the heir apparent to his countryman Frank O'Connor, who contributed over thirty stories during his career. A late starter like Pritchett, also forty-nine when he placed his first story, Trevor has contributed forty-two stories at this point, already exceeding the Englishman's output by fifteen.[154] But in stark contrast to Angell's extensive collaboration with Pritchett, Trevor's *New Yorker* editors, including Angell, who has been editing him since Frances Kiernan's departure in 1987, have published many of Trevor's submissions with exceedingly few changes.

We return in the next two chapters to the idea of revision culminating in new vision. This time, though, the focus is on autobiographical or observed experience, the transmutation of life into art. We begin with Trevor in Chapter 5 and turn to Pritchett in Chapter 6.

Chapter 5

Real Incursions in Fictive Worlds

Writing is a professional activity, yet when fiction is the end product it must necessarily also be a personal one. As you engage in it, you cannot escape the person you are, even if you are not inquisitive about yourself and even though you instinctively know that the less your fingerprints blur your novels and stories the better. All fiction has its autobiographical roots in the sense that as a person you are your characters' litmus paper, their single link with reality. They taste as you taste, they hear as you hear. The blue they see is your blue, the pain they experience is your pain, their physical pleasure is what you know yourself. And the workings of memory you cull from yourself also.[1]

The American poet Wallace Stevens was so conscious of the necessary interdependence of the real and the fictive that it became his major subject. His imagination-reality dialectic is, after all, at the heart of his oeuvre. Similarly, Marianne Moore acknowledged the existence of "real toads" in "imaginary gardens."[2] While Stevens confronted the relationship directly, other authors have a more ambiguous mixture in their work. Some confess to basing entire works on their experiences while others claim that their novel, play, poem, or short story in question is a complete fabrication. But more often than not, works of fiction, however imaginative and inventive, are, to some extent, kindled by material from their author's world. Although both Pritchett and Trevor claim their short stories are imagined, Pritchett acknowledges basing some of them on experiences and people in his life. And while Trevor ostensibly excludes direct autobiographical material from his fiction on principle, finding it more stimulating to explore other lives, he too uses elements from the real world. Details gleaned from essays, interviews, correspondence, and notebooks link some of their experiences to specific short stories. Tracing their geneses reveals the way in which both writers transform actual incidents or people into fiction.

If William Trevor is not a born writer, he was born into an unusual constellation of circumstances that determined the writer he became. He himself feels fortunate that his accident of birth placed him on "the edge of things," and the outsider's role he assumed from childhood helped him cultivate the objectivity that informs his approach to writing fiction. He believes the writer "has to stand back—so far that he finds himself beyond the pale, outside the society he comments upon in order to get a better view of it."[3] The process of becoming a writer began for him in the provincial Ireland of his youth. Trevor was born in 1928 into a Protestant family in County Cork and has always spoken and written positively about living on the periphery. As lace-curtain Protestants, his family belonged to a four percent minority "caught between the distant glories of the Protestant Ascendancy and the new Catholic Ireland."[4] The son of a bank manager, he followed his family from town to town, moving thirteen times during his peripatetic youth—the perennial outsider, forever the new boy, always set apart by religion. But he believes his very identity as a displaced person—"which is what a writer should be"—enabled him to see things more clearly than he would have had he belonged to either of those worlds.[5] And though he "never suffered any real problems" as a Protestant in a predominantly Catholic milieu, he was always conscious of the difference: "It was about like being Jewish."[6]

Trevor has spoken of his nomadic childhood as "very gypsylike." Both his and his parents' friendships were broken easily and frequently.[7] Consequently, although deeply attached to Ireland, where much of his work is set, he has "no home town in Ireland, no particular town I can call my own. Every town in Ireland feels like mine."[8] Consistent with this greater sense of nationhood is his refusal to be pigeonholed as a member of a particular group. Contrary to a widely held belief, Trevor's own background is "not Anglo-Irish—whatever that misused term means."[9] His ancestors were Irish Catholics from County Roscommon, of the same derivation as the McQuillans, and in the practice of the Penal Times in the late eighteenth century, one of the boys became a Protestant to avoid the penal laws in force against Catholics, taking the English name of Cox, which is Trevor's actual surname—a name he abandoned with his sculpting career. While not belonging to the Ascendancy, they were, Trevor surmises, "an adjunct to Big

House society."[10] Indeed, he imagines that had he been born earlier in Mitchelstown, he may have been a tennis ballboy at Bowen's Court[11]—once again on the outside looking in. He is attracted by the "shrunken, withered little" Protestant Church of Ireland yet feels more drawn to Catholicism when in England.[12]

Born into exile, he has always felt most at home when he is away. Initially, as a foreigner in England fascinated by its strangeness, he had sufficient distance to write convincingly about the English, and then, after many years away from his homeland, he was "able to see Ireland from the right end of the telescope" and began writing stories about it.[13] He believes remaining in County Cork would not have given him the proper perspective. More recently, his increased presence in both England and Ireland has made it difficult for him to write about either, necessitating prolonged stays in Italy, a neutral country away from the English language and the true subjects of his interest. Paradoxically, he now feels more at home there than anywhere else, *not* speaking, *not* knowing what the Italians are saying. Though he manages to get along in restaurants and shops, his poor comprehension relaxes him because he is not tempted to eavesdrop in public places, never participates in a "reasonable conversation," and yet is soothed by the mellifluous sound of the language.[14]

Trevor's identity as an outsider has determined his approach to writing fiction. Though convinced that "Real life is the raw material of the fiction writer," he is determined to exclude his own, opting instead to scrutinize others "with a beady eye."[15] His out-of-print first novel, *A Standard of Behaviour* (1958), "served the useful function of draining a lot of autobiographical material out of the system"[16]; and since returning to writing in his midthirties he explores what he does *not* know, believing it "very dull to write only about personal experience."[17] As a young man he portrayed a group of elderly men in his award-winning novel *The Old Boys* (1964), and many of his early short stories, such as "The General's Day," "The Penthouse Apartment," "Broken Homes," and "Matilda's England," are populated by the elderly, grappling with struggles outside Trevor's own experience. At that stage, he wanted "to know what it's like to be old, what it's like to cross a room when your limbs are all seized up."[18] He writes about women because he is not a woman and about girls because he is not a girl. The relationship between a boy and his father, however, does not fascinate him because he has experienced it from both sides himself and knows "too much about it."[19] In general, his heightened curiosity about women makes them preferred subjects, and in the early 1980s he recognized that they were far more prevalent in his fiction than his men.[20]

Driven by his insatiable curiosity about other people's worlds, Trevor sees fiction writing primarily as a process of discovery. Consequently, as he ages, he tends to write more about children because he is out of touch with the experience, having "forgotten what it's like to be a child."[21] He would classify himself as a non-autobiographical practitioner, working from the outside in, like Pritchett, instead of employing the egoist's method. But this approach does not preclude an intimate understanding of characters. On the contrary, his self-effacement—to the point of invisibility—enables him, as a sympathetic, empathic "sort of predator, an invader of people," to achieve a profound understanding of others: "By the end you should be inside your character, actually operating within somebody else, and knowing him [...] as that person knows himself or herself."[22] He is fiercely attentive to his subjects, passionate about understanding the motives of even the most loathsome creatures:

> It is true that some people in certain circumstances can do evil things even though they are not truly evil. If a terrorist plants a bomb and kills people, you have to assume that he is "evil," but I'm curious about what makes this person evil. I'm curious about why someone would plant a bomb knowing that innocent people will be harmed. I write in order to try to find out.[23]

As successful as he is at effacing himself and invading people, however, Trevor concedes that "all fiction is rooted in autobiographical experience: the fiction writer is like a piece of litmus paper. He or she experiences pain, or distress, and that personal experience is his yardstick."[24] Furthermore, such experience necessarily involves the physical world. Trevor's surroundings impinge on him, and when memories of things in the real world are vivid and insistent enough—even inconsequential details, such as the color of his Aga cooker—he puts them in his fiction. Although he claims not to tell anything about himself, he admits being an autobiographical writer in his use of "these little backdrops."[25] But it seems he uses much more than mere backdrops. More meaningfully, childhood memories impinge on him as well—and find their way into his fiction, imperceptibly fortifying the fictive with the real. In his introduction to *Excursions in the Real World*, for instance, Trevor quotes from the opening of his short story "Memories of Youghal" without identifying it by title, to demonstrate how he culls the workings of memory from himself, investing a character with his personal souvenirs:

> His first memory was of a black iron gate, of his own hands upon it, and of his uncle driving through the gateway in a model-T Ford. These images, and

that of his uncle's bespectacled face perspiring, were all in sunshine . . . He remembered also, at some later time, eating tinned tomato soup in a house that was not the house of his aunt and uncle; he remembered a tap near a greenhouse; he remembered eating an ice-cream outside Horgan's Picture House while his aunt engaged another woman in conversation.[26]

"They are my memories too," he continues, "but I am not the character in the story." He justifies the "projection" as "natural" because the town, incidents, and period coalesce, as they undoubtedly did in his own childhood in Youghal. After all, "no point in rejecting reality just for the sake of it."[27] In the most profound way, though, fiction reveals its author's life, paradoxically perhaps more truthfully than biographical details. Anything of importance will necessarily filter through. Reviewing a biography of one of his favorite writers, George Eliot, Trevor criticizes its author's attempt to capture Eliot's essence through biographical facts, believing the method to be inherently flawed. All authors, he believes, are necessarily present in their fictional worlds where, even without conscious self-projection, "the ego cannot fail to make itself felt," where "people who appear to be no reflection whatsoever of their author [. . .], of course, are. Their author is there in the style, in the selection and rejection of detail, in voices speaking, in the places where he lets comedy in and where he keeps it out, in his demands for pity, in his pouring of scorn."[28] Trevor reiterated this idea on other occasions. In reviewing a study of Somerset Maugham, he stated that all fiction is necessarily autobiographical, reflecting the mind and imagination of its author.[29] And in his review of a BBC film on Francis Bacon he agreed with the painter's observation that "you are painting not only the subject, you're painting yourself as well [. . .]."[30]

* * *

Trevor has always been circumspect about disclosing the relationship between his life and work. In presenting his collected nonfiction "sketches" of "real people" who "have remained snagged" in his memory, he admits that in any such personal record, "the recorder cannot remain entirely in the shadows, much as he might wish to do."[31] Ultimately, as determined as he is to separate his life from his art, they inevitably overlap. At the end of his introduction to *Excursions in the Real World*, he notes that when he became a writer of fiction, he began "to refashion the real world, to pick over bits and pieces of experience and use anything that was useful." The essays that follow it are supposedly "a small part of what has been left behind after all that."[32] Yet in several instances, the essays include episodes that he transformed into fiction—proof that the "real toads" hiding in the shadowlands inevitably encroach on his fiction. He has often proclaimed childhood his richest source, so it is not surprising that one of his most disturbing childhood relationships would seem to be the basis for one of his most disturbing short stories. Sequestered in the essay chronicling his earliest memories in County Cork, this experience marked him, inspiring one of the stories in his first collection *The Day We Got Drunk on Cake and Other Stories* (1967) several years before the essay "In County Cork" itself appeared in print.[33]

While a small boy in Skibereen, Trevor had a severe Methodist teacher who humiliated him and undermined his self-confidence. On several occasions, he was ridiculed. More than thirty years later, revisiting the small church standing behind high iron railings and gates in the West Cork town, he recalls her unforgettable lessons:

> Beyond the door that used to be green is the dank passage that leads to Miss Willoughby's schoolroom, where first I learnt that the world is not an easygoing place. Miss Willoughby was stern and young, in love with the cashier from the Provincial Bank. Like the church beside her schoolroom, she was Methodist and there burnt in her breast an evangelical spirit which stated that we, her pupils, except for her chosen few, must somehow be made less wicked than we were. Her chosen few were angels of a kind, their handwriting blessed, their compositions a gift from God. I was not among them.
>
> On the gravel in front of the red-brick church I vividly recall Miss Willoughby. Terribly, she appears. Severe and beautiful, she pedals against the wind on her huge black bicycle. "Someone laughed during prayers," her stern voice accuses, and you feel at once that it was you, although you know it wasn't. *V. poor* she writes in your headline book when you've done your best to reproduce, four times, perfectly, *Pride goeth before destruction*.
>
> As I stand on the gravel, her evangelical eyes seem again to dart over me without pleasure. Once I took the valves out of the tyres of her bicycle. Once I looked in her answer book. "Typical," her spectre says. "Typical, to come prying." I am late, I am stupid. I cannot write twenty sentences on A Day in the Life of an Old Shoe, I cannot do simple arithmetic or geography, I am always fighting with Jasper Swanton. I move swiftly on the gravel, out on to the street and into the bar of the Eldon Hotel: in spectral form or otherwise, Miss Willoughby will not be there.[34]

Trevor's Hawthornesque reminiscence of Miss Willoughby contrasts sharply with his complimentary portrait of the talented, enigmatic Miss Quirke, a young tutor who subsequently enchanted him and his brother during a gap in their formal schooling, and the subject of a later essay.[35] In Miss Willoughby's classroom, he recalls learning that the world is "not an easy-going place," unless one is among the "chosen few." In her religious zeal, she apparently gave preferential treatment to her "angels" while treating the others as original sinners. And as one of the "wicked," Trevor was not only excluded from her Methodist world, but ostracized as well, condemned as a hopeless delinquent—an attitude that, not surprisingly, provoked delinquency. A daunting study in contrasts, "stern and young," "Severe and beautiful," Miss Willoughby emphasizes failure not success, and inspires fear, not admiration. Yet seen through a child's eyes, Trevor's recollection is necessarily one-sided. By itself, his experience alone is inadequate for a short story because it lacks development and a point—proof that even the most compelling, seminal autobiographical episodes must be refashioned if they are to become meaningful fiction. Perhaps to exorcise the spectre of Miss Willoughby, or simply to understand her, Trevor made the relationship between a homely young boy, James Machen, and Miss Smith, his severe, disapproving schoolteacher, the subject of his first Irish story. His usual reluctance to divulge the real incursions in his fiction makes this transmutation of raw material precious. Although only one manuscript of the story exists, it is surprisingly complete, incorporating as it does both the penultimate and final versions, replete with the substantial inserts and deletions responsible for the metamorphosis. A close examination of these significant alterations illuminates Trevor's method of fictionalizing an actual experience. He once praised a book "for the insight it allows into its author's writing technique, his skilful control of nostalgia, his distancing of himself from his own experience before cautiously using it as the raw material for his drama."[36] The same comments apply to the genesis and composition of "Miss Smith," first collected in *The Day We Got Drunk on Cake and Other Stories* and reprinted unchanged in the *Collected Stories*.

* * *

Initially, the story reflects Trevor's autobiographical account by focusing predominantly on James Machen's point of view. Except for a brief passage on the fourth page and the two-page shift into Miss Smith's consciousness in its last two pages, the penultimate draft is limited to the boy's point of view. So strong and constant is the identification with James that this earlier draft seems to have been conceived in limited third person. (Trevor often uses this technique, camouflaging omniscience by remaining within the consciousness of individual characters for prolonged periods, a practice originating in the nineteenth-century novel—e.g., *Emma* or *The Portrait of a Lady*—that is somewhat exceptional in the brevity of the short story.)

The opening paragraph of this draft begins with a description of Miss Smith from the eight-and-a-half-year-old James's point of view. Like Trevor's Miss Willoughby, she is "severe" in her approach and mercilessly demanding.[37] And, like young William Trevor Cox, James Machen is troubled by his teacher's mysterious, unrelenting persecution of him. There is even a direct parallel between young Trevor Cox's failure to write a series of sentences on "A Day in the Life of an Old Shoe" for Miss Willoughby and James Machen's inability to write six sentences about dogs for Miss Smith—a detail excised from the final version of "Miss Smith."[38] Furthermore, both boys have pet terriers—Trevor's family dog "Dano," a smooth-haired fox terrier,[39] becomes James's large, old Sealyham, whom he loves.[40] As Trevor said of using his own memories of Youghal for the story of the same title, there is "no point in rejecting reality for the sake of it."[41]

Instead of merely replicating his own experience, however, Trevor initially exaggerates Miss Smith's persecution of his surrogate, James, through a series of embarrassing incidents that ostracize the boy. As soon as his peers have forgotten about James's embarrassing reply of "pony" instead of "foal" in response to the teacher's query about the name for a baby horse, Miss Smith invites their ridicule once again. She demands to know what James is scribbling on the back of his exercise book, summons him to the front of the class, insists on being shown the childishly replicated "Walt Disney" logo, and cruelly embarrasses him once again by berating him in front of his peers. When James admits not knowing the response to her subsequent query, in a passage deleted from the typescript, she laughs, accuses him of ignorance, and calls him a "dopey" child. In turn, all of his classmates laugh, and James scrunches his toes in embarrassment before returning to his seat.[42]

The penultimate draft includes other episodes left out of the final version that further polarize James and Miss Smith. For instance, the boy cannot escape her wrath, even when she gets married and leaves the school. Instead of being inexplicably courteous as he expects her to be when inadvertently meeting her in town, she is as direct and damning as before, hurting James all the more because he feels she has given up the right to insult along with her teaching position.[43] Her reaction upon finally catching him putting flowers cut from others' gardens on her window-sill is more aggressive and threatening as well. She asks him rhetorically if he knows the fate of horrid "underhand" little boys, telling him at once in her response that they go to prison for stealing, asks if he had thought of that, and calls him a delinquent.[44] (In the published version, she exclaims, "Flowers from the creature, if you please!"[45], accuses him of trying to get her and her husband into trouble by leaving the stolen flowers outside their home, and calls him an "underhand child.")

The repercussions of this misguided play for Miss Smith's approval are also more pronounced in this draft. His peers laugh at him in school for many weeks following the disclosure of the flower incident, and Miss Smith glowers at him and looks away when she meets him in town.[46]

In addition, Trevor makes James more outwardly emotional and eccentric in the penultimate draft than he is in his final incarnation and conveys his thoughts more explicitly. At one point, enraged about Miss Smith, James runs to his room to cry, pounding the wall until his arms are battered.[47] This initial, exaggerated portrait includes the child's compulsive avoidance of every third step of stairs, his twice-daily friendly address to his right shoe—for fear that it will discover his arbitrary dislike of it—and regular prayer, because he is convinced that forgetting even one person will endanger that person's life or work. Included in this earlier portrait is James's desperate faith that talking to God will enlighten him about Miss Smith, enable him to conform to her expectations, and make his life her focus.[48] In distilling James's compulsion about Miss Smith from the detailed obsessive-compulsive portrait, Trevor emphasizes his surrogate's need for her approval instead of making him merely clinically compulsive:

> Almost without knowing it James developed a compulsion about Miss Smith. At first it was quite a simple compulsion: just that James had to talk to God every night about Miss Smith, and try to find out from God what it was about him that Miss Smith so despised. Every night he lay in bed and had his conversation, and if once he forgot it James knew that the next time he met Miss Smith she would probably say something that might make him drop down dead.[49]

Trevor eliminated other details that add depth to characterization and motive in a novel, but that are detrimental to the impressionistic suggestiveness of the short story. Convinced that Miss Smith simply does not like him after the flower incident, and frustrated by his powerlessness to change her mind, James accepts her rejection of him but remains obsessed with her. He discovers what it means to dislike someone merely by thinking about her.[50] This explicit disclosure of his innermost feelings further undermined the story by anticipating James's eventual retribution. Mindful of the precept that dialogue dispenses with description, Trevor excised the passage to accentuate the ensuing exchange between James and the man who cuts the grass. Formerly the homework ghostwriter of six sentences about James's dog in a deleted paragraph earlier in the draft,[51] he resurfaces as the unwitting mastermind of the boy's eventual crime. Miss Smith's cruelty indirectly brings about a lesson in cruelty from another adult whose hypothetical example involving himself and his daughter inspires James's exploitation of the parallel relationship between Miss Smith and her son. Here, in place of an explicit disclosure of James's innermost thoughts, Trevor subtly dramatizes the boy's pain, frustration, and desire for retaliation. Except for a phrase indicating that the gardener is accustomed to James's queries—and is the only one who responds to them—the following published passage came verbatim from the manuscript version.

> "When somebody hurts you," James said to the man who came to cut the grass, "what do you do about it?"
> "Well," said the man, "I suppose you hurt them back."
> "Suppose you can't," James argued.
> "Oh but you always can. It's easy to hurt people."
> "It's not really," James said.
> "Look," said the man, "all I've got to do is to reach out and give you a clip on the ear. That'd hurt you."
> "But I couldn't do that to you. Because you're too big.
> How d'you hurt someone who's bigger than you?"
> "It's easier to hurt people who are weaker. People who are weaker are always the ones who get hurt."
> "Can't you hurt someone who is stronger?"
> The grass-cutter thought for a time. "You have to be cunning to do that. You've got to find the weak spot. Everyone has a weak spot."
> "Have you got a weak spot?"
> "I suppose so."
> "Could I hurt you on your weak spot?"
> "You don't want to hurt me, James."
> "No, but just could I?"
> "Yes, I suppose you could."
> "Well then?"
> "My little daughter's smaller than you. If you hurt her, you see, you'd be hurting me. It'd be the same, you see."
> "I see," said James.[52]

Once again, pruning a story's explicit elements creates suspense by causing the reader to suspend judgment and take on an active interpretive role. Excised as well is Trevor's habitual novelistic speculation that helps him understand his characters at earlier draft stages but obscures the glimpse upon which the genre depends in the final version. In one such passage, James escapes Miss Smith but she haunts him nonetheless. When asked questions by subsequent masters, he often imagines they are Miss Smith and, consequently, cannot respond, even though he knows the answers. As a result of this impediment, he never distinguishes himself in school, although he does once come to the attention of a young, unseasoned geography master whose idea that hidden within the boy is a "streak of brilliance" provokes such boisterous laughter from his colleagues that he immediately changes his mind. At the end of this excised passage we learn that James's father finds him a shipping office job when he leaves school.[53]

* * *

Had Trevor's story remained focused primarily on James Machen's sense of oppression, it would have been little more than an inflated version of his autobiographical reminiscence. By distancing himself from his limited childhood perspective, however, Trevor transcends his experience, widens the scope, and achieves a meaningful, ultimately moral, fiction. Instead of merely seeing himself at an objective distance, he uses his "interested point of view" to fashion the Miss Willoughby surrogate, Miss Smith, from the outside in and, driven by his "enormous sense of curiosity," constructs a character to complement James. His hallmark compassion enables him to empathize with all his creations—including those apparently based on disturbing figures from his past, such as Miss Willoughby. Ultimately, once both characters are well defined, the story is less about James or Miss Smith than about the consequences of her behavior for both of them—the horrifying result of their intertwined fate. The substantial inserts chronicling Miss Smith's life outside the classroom make her—not the boy—the story's principal character, while James's resultant prolonged absence creates necessary tension.

The first insert divides consecutive scenes in the penultimate draft questioning Miss Smith's performance as both pedagogue and mother: James's portentous discussion with the grass cutter, quoted above, and Miss Smith's initial dialogue with her husband about her mistakes with their infant. This one-and-a-half-page handwritten insert—a search for understanding emanating from her consciousness, arousing the reader's sympathy by revealing her sense of vulnerability, uncertainty, and isolation—distances Miss Smith from the domineering, self-possessed model on which she is based. Trevor later pruned her speculation that her life with the baby had been initially too good, that the novelty of motherhood was perhaps waning, as well as her uncertainty about the reason for her depression. Discarded as well is Miss Smith's reminiscence about the late afternoon silence in the empty school and her appreciation for the quiet life she enjoyed and had been prepared to continue indefinitely until she married. Otherwise, the insert is the same as the published version below:

> All was not well with Miss Smith. Life, which had been so happy when her baby was born, seemed now to be directed against her. Perhaps it was that the child was becoming difficult, going through a teething phase that was pleasant for no one; or perhaps it was that Miss Smith recognized in him some trait she disliked and knew that she would be obliged to watch it develop, powerless to intervene. Whatever the reason, she felt depressed. She often thought of her teaching days, of the big square schoolroom with the children's models on the shelves and the pictures of kings on the walls. Nostalgically, she recalled the feel of frosty air on her face as she rode her bicycle through the town, her mind already practising the first lesson of the day. She had loved those winter days: the children stamping their feet in the playground, the stove groaning and crackling, so red and so fierce that it had to be penned off for safety's sake. It had been good to feel tired, good to bicycle home, shopping a bit on the way, home to tea and the wireless and an evening of reading by the fire. It wasn't that she regretted anything; it was just that now and again, for a day or two, she felt she would like to return to the past.[54]

In addition to capturing Miss Smith's depression, doubts, and insecurities while raising her first child, this insert exposes her more disturbing evangelical notion—reflecting Miss Willoughby's belief in original sin that dictated her classroom behavior—that she "recognised in [her child] some trait she disliked and knew that she would be obliged to watch it develop, powerless to intervene."[55] Of course the same attitude manifests itself in the classroom and is responsible for her condemnation of pupils like James Machen. This feeling highlights her loss of control and her acknowledgment of the indomitable in human beings.

This first insert, profiling Miss Smith's psychological struggle, prepares the reader for her decline in the penultimate draft's succeeding section, where she gradually begins to lose control. Here, in contrast to her classroom dominance, she seems increasingly unable to manage her own affairs. Most alarmingly, she endangers her child, her seemingly unconscious mistakes putting his life in jeopardy: "Yet somehow she felt that they weren't her mistakes. It was as though some other person occasionally possessed her: a negligent, worthless kind of person who was cruel, almost criminal in her carelessness."[56] The self-doubt and fear in her introspection arouses curiosity about—and sympathy for—the formerly one-dimensional taskmaster as well as a certain mystery consistent with Trevor's passion for detective fiction.[57] At first she alone is aware of her errors. In one instance, when the child escapes from his pram, she notices that she had forgotten to attach his harness to the pram hooks. Subsequently, a woman draws her attention to the danger of hundreds of small red glass beads in the pram, "regarding curiously the supplier of so unsuitable a plaything."[58] Though the former teacher cannot fathom how the child had got them, the beads are indeed hers. Similar incidents abound in the penultimate draft, most taking place in the child's nursery when he is only months old. For instance, Miss Smith finds an angry cat scratching at the child's body because she apparently forgot to close the window. In an even more serious incident, the child burns himself badly because it seems she had forgotten to erect the fire-guard. She questions her health, wondering whether she is afflicted by absentmindedness or blackouts, but the doctor's inconclusive diagnosis convinces her that she is simply a bad mother. Her carelessness continues, but the overabundance of incidents—not the incidents themselves—lacks verisimilitude in this draft: she finds him eating a turnip; packets of needles are found in the child's cot; a standard lamp is knocked down and the bulb removed. (In addition to removing the latter two, Trevor excised the previously mentioned burn incident and made the child's bedding, not its body, the object of the cat's attack.) Nevertheless, not surprisingly, disturbed by such negligence, her husband suggests they employ someone to look after the child—a proposal that threatens her very identity and their marriage:

> "Someone *else*? Am I then incapable? Am I so wretched and stupid that I cannot look after my own child? You speak to me as though I were half crazy." She felt confused and sick and miserable. The marriage teetered beneath the tension, and there was no question of further children.[59]

At this juncture in the penultimate draft, the story was 500 words from its end. In the premature conclusion that was eventually postponed, the child disappears on his second birthday after Miss Smith leaves him to play alone in the garden, apparently escaping through the open back gate that leads to the fields. She believes he must have managed to release the catch himself, an act her husband deems impossible because of the height and stiffness of the catch. Furthermore, he is convinced she wishes to do away with their child.[60] Their unsuccessful search through the field with the police until the early hours of the morning leaves Miss Smith hoping the child has been kidnapped. But without demands for ransom, her hope of his survival fades and she is left to brood about the thought her husband kept to himself: she opened the gate to rid herself of the child. The dénouement that follows the child's disappearance in this draft, to be discussed later, suffers because of the story's lack of development.

Instead of concluding the story in this way, Trevor expanded it with a lengthy typed insert, two-thirds of which was incorporated almost verbatim in the final version.[61] This development and recapitulation enriches the story by involving the nameless husband, depicting a family life, and building suspense through the dramatization of the couple's conflict. In the insert, two months pass without incident following the husband's threat of child care. Miss Smith gains control of her daily life during the reprieve, the parents experience the joy of raising a child, and the child himself flourishes, amazing his "unathletic" parents with his inexplicable athleticism. (Once again, this time in a more positive vein, Trevor reminds us that human nature is irrepressible.) The child's well-being unites his parents, "the little monster" behaving "like gold," and, like many proud parents, they revel in Miss Smith's daily reports of his "sayings and doings" saved up from the day.[62] And in the absence of the mysterious mishaps, Trevor complicates the husband's portrait, making him as concerned about his wife's welfare as his son's. Although Miss Smith remains the principal character, the reader begins to see through her husband's eyes as Trevor subtly shifts point of view in this pivotal insert to create as much empathy for him as he did for the once-beleaguered Miss Smith:

> He sighed with relief as he climbed the stairs, thankful that all was once again well in the house. He was still sighing when he opened the nursery door and smelt gas. It hissed insidiously from the unlit fire. The room was sweet with it. The child, sleeping, sucked it into his lungs. The child's face was blue.[63]

They remove the child from the room, summon the doctor, and wait helplessly while he revives. The child survives, but the doctor makes them aware that he was close to death. The husband's shocking last-minute discovery of this most dramatic, nearly fatal event destroys his dearly achieved, revived confidence in his wife and signals an abrupt end to their short-lived stability and happiness. Once again, her domestic carelessness has threatened the child's existence. Instead of protecting their son, she constantly puts him in danger. He vows to make a change because the strain on him is unbearable, and her inability to explain the incident merely strengthens his mounting case against her. Except for the replacement of two pronouns with nouns and another minor change, the published version is identical:

> Every precaution had been taken with the gas-fire in the nursery. The knob that controlled the gas pressure was a key and the key was removable. Certainly, the control point was within the child's reach but one turned it on

or off, slipped the key out of its socket and placed it on the mantlepiece. That was the simple rule.

"You forgot to take out the key," Miss Smith's husband said. In his mind an idea took on a shape that frightened him. He shied away, watching it advance, knowing that he possessed neither the emotional nor mental equipment to fight it.[64]

During the course of their argument, in order to explain the incident, her husband suggests that after turning off the fire, she "idly turned it on again." His suspicion of Miss Smith's motives becomes uncontrollable, and he supplies his own chilling hypothesis for the reader while suppressing it from his wife:

> Miss Smith's husband didn't know. His imagination, like a pair of calipers, grasped the ugly thought and held it before him. The facts were on its side, he could not ignore them: his wife was deranged in her mind. Consciously or otherwise, she was trying to kill their child.
>
> "The window," Miss Smith said. "It was open when I left it. It always is for air. Yet you found it closed."
>
> "The child could certainly not have done that. I cannot see what you are suggesting."[65]

At the outset of the story, James Machen is the victim, but toward the end there has been a dramatic reversal: Miss Smith is on trial, her sanity in question. Like James, she is humiliated and punished, treated like a delinquent child during this thoroughly dramatized exchange in the penultimate draft. Despite her pleas for another chance, her husband ultimately decides they must find a woman to care for their child.

In addition to employing a shifting point of view to empathize successively with James, Miss Smith, and Miss Smith's husband, Trevor refined the story by reshaping the scene that follows the child's disappearance.[66] The account of the search is more ominous than in the penultimate draft: "it was a search without hope, and the hopelessness in time turned into the fear of what discovery would reveal."[67] Here, instead of abandoning the quest after searching through the fields with her husband and the police, the despondent Miss Smith continues alone as she "dragged her legs over the wide countryside, seeking a miracle."[68] The reader reenters her consciousness, and her isolation permits Trevor to give the story haunting symmetry by putting her in contact with a young boy whom she barely recognizes while passing a sawmill on the edge of town:

> He spoke some shy salutation, and when she blinked her eyes at his face she saw that he was James Machen. She passed him by, thinking only that she

envied him his life, that for him to live and her child to die was proof indeed of a mocking Providence. She prayed to this Providence, promising a score of resolutions if only all would be well.[69]

James's brief appearance in this search insert makes his reemergence at the very end of the story—preserved intact from the penultimate draft, and absorbed with minor alterations in the published version—all the more disturbing, haunting, and meaningful. In place of the search insert's anonymous ransom note, written in sprawling capital letters, is James's more dramatic sudden appearance at her kitchen door where he utters the same question in person: "Would you like to see your baby?"[70] The question recalls his earlier request when he meets her in town with her baby ("Miss Smith, may I see the baby?") that is met with her laughter and rapid escape, as though her child might be affected "by the proximity of the other"—a seemingly irrational fear that is justified in the end. Here she perceives him differently. Trevor's subtle details seem to transform him in her eyes from the homely classroom outcast into an almost mock satanic figure, staring at her in judgment. The sun "is mirrored [. . .] in the child's glasses" and he smiles at her "more confidently than she remembered."[71] Miss Smith's listlessness in this scene contrasts markedly with her classroom demeanor at the story's outset. Her child's disappearance has destroyed her life. Beside herself with grief and self-recrimination, she does not sleep because she is afraid of nightmares. Her pitiable psychological state is manifest in her appearance and her automaton-like behavior:

> Her hair hung lank about her shoulders, her eyes were dead and seemed to have fallen back deeper into her skull. She stood listening to this child, nodding her head up and down, very slowly, in a mechanical way. Her left hand moved gently back and forth on the smooth surface of her kitchen table.[72]

The coda reverberates with the refrain of earlier details. Miss Smith is infantilized as James takes her hand and leads her on a familiar route from the house to the fields by way of the garden and the gate. The harmonious image of them walking hand in hand "across the warm, ripe meadows" contrasts disturbingly with the true underlying nature of their relationship. Finally in the ascendant position, empowered with his secret, James picks beautiful flowers for her from the meadows—a gesture that looks back to his clandestine window-sill offerings. Desperate as he is—and always has been—for her approval, he explains innocently that "You give people flowers [. . .] because you like them and you want them to like you."[73] It is interesting to note that this scene derived from the discarded "Insert A"[74] in which James fantasizes about picnicking with Miss Smith, becoming good friends, having tea every day in her house, and moving in with her. And it is the residue of fantasy that gives their very real journey an eerie, even surreal, flavor. As she carries the flowers and he skips and dances beside her, hurrying her along, Miss Smith becomes increasingly aware of his ghoulish presence. The reader is very much in her consciousness once again as she hears James laughing and sees "his small weasel face twisted into a merriment that frightened her."[75] This impression echoes her earlier description of his appearance—"like a weasel wearing glasses"—while in conversation with her husband, during which she admits the boy gives her "the creeps."[76]

Trevor's empathy extends beyond the psychological to the corporeal in his description of Miss Smith's sensations in the "fierce" sun. Ominously, in contrast to her overheated, sweaty body, "the child's hand was cool, and beneath her fingers she assessed its strength, wondering about its history."[77] James's laugh punctuates this silent reflection before modulating into blood-curdling variations—a reply to the earlier humiliating laughter at his expense—that anticipate the horror of which his depraved heart has proven capable:

> On the heavy air his laughter rose and fell; it quivered through his body and twitched lightly in his hand. It came as a giggle, then a breathless spasm; it rose like a storm from him; it rippled to gentleness; and it pounded again like the firing of guns in her ear. It would not stop. She knew it would not stop. As they walked together on this summer's day the laughter would continue until they arrived at the horror, until the horror was complete.[78]

Although the reader senses an invisible presence in Miss Smith's home throughout the story, its ending reveals that she was erroneously held accountable for James's sinister household mischief. At one point Miss Smith asks for forgiveness, convinced herself that she released the gate. The truth makes this forced admission all the more disturbing. Possessed with revenge, consumed with jealousy, James haunted Miss Smith in the street, entered her household, destroyed her confidence in herself, embarrassed her in the community, weakened her marriage, and murdered her only child. "Miss Smith" ends similarly to other Trevor stories such as "Mr. MacNamara," "In Love with Ariadne," and "August Saturday." Trevor maintains suspense by withholding crucial information that when ultimately revealed simultaneously solves the mystery and gives meaning to the narrative. Guy de Maupassant popularized such an ending in stories such as "Les Tombales" and "The Necklace," and his English disciple, Somerset Maugham, carried on in the same tradition. But while their ultimate revelations often achieve complete closure at the expense of character development, Trevor's more deeply imagined, complex people survive such disclosures, fortified as they are by intriguing mysteries of character that inspire reflection long after the story ends. Trevor believes that no twentieth-century short-story anthology makes much sense without Maugham. While he was "fifth-rate at his worst," at his best he achieved greatness: "Seeing himself as the fearless prober into hearts and minds, he did not probe often enough, or ruthlessly enough."[79] As a truly fearless explorer, Trevor cannot be accused of such a shortcoming. His uncommon empathy for diverse people, regardless of their behavior, circumstances, or morals, enables him to fashion a blameless tragedy from the relationship between a discouraging teacher and an unbalanced child desperate for her approval.

* * *

Miss Willoughby is not the only person from Trevor's childhood who "remained snagged" in his memory and became the basis for one of his fictional characters. The Cox family maid, who figures so prominently in "Jigsaws," and about whom Trevor later wrote his more developed portrait, "Kitty,"[80] seems to have been the inspiration for her counterpart, Kathleen, in one of his most celebrated Irish stories, "Kathleen's Field."[81] In his autobiographical accounts, with his familiar "interested point of view" and retrospective empathy, Trevor reconsiders the young woman who cared for him—but for whom he had little appreciation—during his formative years. He and his brother became "unruly" pyromaniacs during their time in Skibbereen, lighting fires on the kitchen floor, and, when their parents were out, "marching about the house with pieces of flaring wood held high above their heads" or rolling and smoking damp paper when they could not buy woodbines. "Most of this behaviour," Trevor admits, "was a continuing act of defiance directed against Kitty." Although she was a "joky, friendly person, devoted to the family" they "couldn't resist treating her appallingly." She would return to the kitchen after changing into her afternoon black and white to find it full of smoke and flames or stand terrified in the hall while the boys rampaged about with their flaring wood, often dressed up in some of her clothes. Severe punishment did nothing to discourage this behavior.[82] Kitty went back to her own family in Ballycotton, but years later, when the Cox family was living in Enniscorthy, Trevor's mother—unable to find a maid to her liking—asked her to consider returning. As an adult, reflecting on meeting her at the Enniscorthy railway station with his brother and graciously escorting her to their new home, Trevor wrote that

"Guilt had managed to grow in us."[83] Eleven years later, and more than fifty years after Kitty first became the Cox's maid, Trevor's experience blossomed into his sympathetic portrayal of the central character in "Kathleen's Field."

In the story, a struggling farmer, Mr. Hagerty, already heavily in debt to the bank, goes to town in the hopes of securing a further loan so that he can purchase a lush pasture more profitable than all of his other land combined. While consoling himself for the bank agent's refusal with a bottle of stout in the bar next door, he learns that the proprietor's wife, Mrs. Shaughnessy, the barmaid, is looking for a country girl to serve as their maid. Mrs. Shaughnessy enquires about the possibility of Mr. Hagerty's sixteen-year-old daughter, Kathleen, filling the position. He remembers that her husband is "a considerable businessman" who, in addition to the bar, owns a barber's shop and is an agent for the Property & Life Insurance Company; "he had funds to spare." More importantly, Hagerty has heard of people mortgaging an area of their land with Mr. Shaughnessy, who arrives at this propitious moment, in time to hear about Mr. Hagerty's dilemma. Buoyed by Mrs. Shaughnessy's strong interest in securing Kathleen, and aware that her husband also "liked to have a maid about the house," he angles for financial aid in exchange for filling the Shaughnessys' domestic needs. In the end, they make a mutually beneficial arrangement. He promises to send them Kathleen, and Mrs. Shaughnessy says they will "do business." From the beginning, Kathleen suffers her mistress's demeaning treatment and, after seven weeks, her master begins sexually harassing her when they are alone together. Kathleen accepts her miserable existence, unable to reveal Mr. Shaughnessy's disturbing behavior to her parents during her brief Sunday visits home, conscious that her sacrifice is saving her immediate family from ruin.[84] "Kathleen's Field," as Mr. Hagerty calls the pasture in honor of his daughter, makes the eldest son, Con, a more attractive husband, giving him a more promising inheritance and incentive to stay and perpetuate the Hagerty farm.

Trevor appropriates aspects of Kitty's appearance and situation for her fictional counterpart, in much the same way—albeit less extensively—that he used aspects of Miss Willoughby's character and situation as a foundation for Miss Smith. In addition to people, places and objects are snagged in Trevor's memory. Situated in the attic, Kitty's room contains a "chipped, white-painted wash stand, with a narrow cupboard and dressing table to match, a single discarded hearthrug on the boards of the floor." Kathleen's "small bedroom at the top of the house" is similarly furnished with a white-painted wash stand, a cupboard and a "rug stretched on the boards by the bed." They lead solitary lives, "as the life of any general maid tended to be at that time"; lend social status to their respective families; change from the blue to black uniform in the middle of the day, as was the custom; and sit alone in the kitchen by the range every evening. They are both awakened at six-thirty by an alarm clock that summons them to the same initial task: the lighting of the range, and making eggs for the master of the house before being sent back to the kitchen to make their own breakfast. They even share the same name. Mrs. Shaughnessy immediately renames Kathleen "Kitty" for her convenience because two of her previous maids were named Kitty.

Much of Mrs. Shaughnessy's approach to and attitude about procuring maids appears to come from Trevor's recollection of his mother's. When she was without a maid, Mrs. Cox would search randomly in the countryside "to see what the cottages had to offer." Following Kitty's initial departure, the Coxes had a "long procession of unsatisfactory maids." In announcing her own protracted search for a country girl to Mr. Hagerty, Mrs. Shaughnessy complains that "If they're any good they're like gold dust these days." Furthermore, the standard criteria for selection mentioned in "Kitty"—"Is she clean?" and "Is she honest"—are Mrs. Shaughnessy's as well: "You get in a country girl and you wouldn't know was she clean or maybe would she take things." Trevor claimed his mother had "the sharpest tongue of any woman I've ever known," and Mrs. Shaughnessy mirrors her in this respect as well: "'Haven't they brains like turnips?' she said, even though Kathleen was in the room. [. . .] 'Try and speak a bit more clearly, Kitty [. . .]. It's not everyone can understand a country accent.'" At one point Mrs. Shaughnessy calls Kathleen "mad" when her maid suggests throwing paraffin on the range fire to accelerate it. Curiously enough, while living in Terenure as a university student, Trevor accidentally set the chimney of his room on fire: "as I listened to it roaring I recalled how Kitty, our maid, used to throw paraffin up a chimney and light it to burn off the soot. Cheaper than a chimney sweep, Kitty used to say. I imagined the blaze would stop, as Kitty's always did, but in fact it didn't."[85]

Kitty and Kathleen are both unattractive. Kitty has "never been pretty," with "eyes that were always blinking" and "a mouthful of enormous white crags." Kathleen's glimpse of her nakedness in the Shaughnessy's tarnished looking-glass reveals her "plumply rounded thighs and knees, the dimple in her stomach." Kitty is isolated from men her own age, seemingly destined for spinsterhood: "No man ever took Kitty out: she didn't have the looks for dancehalls, or for courting in hedges; the housepainter who tried something on was a married man in his fifties, father of nine." Similarly, Kathleen's appearance makes marriage unlikely and restricts her to "the attentions of a grey-haired man," the sinister Mr. Shaughnessy:

> "Did you hear that, Kitty? Enid Kenny's getting married. Don't go taking ideas from her." He laughed, and Mrs. Shaughnessy laughed, and the son smiled.

There wasn't much chance of that, Kathleen thought. "Are you going dancing tonight?" Mr. Crawley [the butcher] often asked her on a Friday, and she would reply that she might, but she never did because it wasn't easy to go alone. In the shops and at Mass no one displayed any interest in her whatsoever, no one eyed her the way Mary Florence had been eyed, and she supposed it was because her looks weren't up to much. But they were good enough for Mr. Shaughnessy, with his quivering breath and his face in her hair.[86]

As Kitty must have been herself, Kathleen is starved for attention from boys her age—and always has been. She reminisces about one who tried to kiss other convent schoolgirls but never pursued Kathleen even though she often went home alone. And unlike her more socially successful sisters, she thought it "nice" that the "Pests" they complained about wanted to kiss girls while dancing with them. Cut off from her peers, her feeling of isolation is intensified by the secret she keeps from her family about Mr. Shaughnessy's behavior.

Here again, as in "Miss Smith," Trevor's reconsideration of someone from his childhood inspires his sympathetic portrayal of a fictional counterpart. But even though Kathleen is based on actual details from the Cox family maid's life, her character and plight are invented, and it is Trevor's realistic but wholly imagined world informed by Irish history that makes "Kathleen's Field" such an evocative Irish story.[87] The class schism between the prosperous Shaughnessys and the struggling Hagertys creates the opportunity for their "bargain" in the first place. Seven of the ten Hagerty children have emigrated leaving Con, who will inherit the farm, mentally handicapped Biddy, who cannot take care of herself, and Kitty, who is the only expendable child. Mr. Hagerty tells himself he wants to keep Kathleen from going to England, but in truth he merely justifies trading his daughter for a mortgage, selling her into indentured servitude through a deal made in a bar. In a chilling irony, Mr. Hagerty names the field "Kathleen's field," his daughter literally giving her life for its acquisition, in effect replacing the bullocks he cannot sell at the beginning of the story. Mrs. Shaughnessy's replacement of Kathleen's name with the generic "Kitty" usurps the young girl's identity, and her expectation that she will "have to train every inch of her," as well as Mr. Hagerty's promise that "Kathleen wouldn't go running off," makes her sound more like an auctioned animal than a human being. He himself is under the Shaughnessys' scrutiny. Concerned about the return on his investment, Mr. Shaughnessy asks Kathleen if her father is "fit," knowing that the success of the bargain and the payment of the mortgage depend, in large part, on Hagerty's ability to work the lush field.

In "Kitty," Trevor observed that "it is hardly an exaggeration to say that [Kitty] gave the greater part of her being" in return for modest wages.[88]

In "Kathleen's Field," her counterpart yields much more than that, losing her pride and dignity in the process. And there are indications throughout the story that a subtle, unspoken, sinister complicity exists between the Shaughnessys in their sharing of Kathleen. In her initial discussion with Hagerty, for instance, Mrs. Shaughnessy winks at him while revealing that her husband, despite his denial, "liked the style" of having a maid around the house. Kathleen both relieves Mrs. Shaughnessy's housework, leaving her mistress free to enjoy the social side of working in her shop, and becomes the object of Mr. Shaughnessy's fantasies as well. His wife seems to procure young maids for his sexual needs that she is perhaps no longer interested in satisfying herself. And there are indications that she knows about and encourages her husband's deviant behavior. She dresses Kathleen in maids' uniforms sizes too small that are so tight they are embarrassingly revealing, and allows her husband to attend an earlier mass service so that he is home alone with the maid while she is in church with her son. Kathleen cannot escape her master's humiliating degradation of her and becomes an isolated prisoner forced to keep her disturbing secret. Formerly honest, she must deceive everyone. Consistent with Trevor's intermittent religious focus, Kathleen is a virgin, yet she is symbolically treated as if she were a whore, Mr. Shaughnessy's frequent masturbation in her presence effecting a mock rape. And she even begins to feel guilty for her submission, wondering if her silence about the disturbing encounters is a sin. Ultimately, she accepts this sublimation, and her parents' ignorant refrain that "a bargain was a bargain." Although the story is inspired by elements in the real world, it is at the same time a product of Trevor's imagination.

* * *

Excursions in the Real World offers further insight into the real world's role in Trevor's work. In "Assia,"[89] against the colorful backdrop of 1960s London that "had the flavour of a dream," Trevor reminisces about the enigmatic polyglot Assia for whom he became a sympathetic confidant. Not surprisingly, several of his female characters seem to have been infused with her mysteriousness, most notably Mrs. Faraday in "Cocktails at Doney's" and Iris Smith in "In Isfahan"—both enigmatic, unhappily married women alone on holiday who meet, and are ultimately rebuffed by, inhibited, perhaps impotent, Englishmen.[90] This prose elegy for the striking woman of "muddled nationality" who was once David Wevill's wife, and briefly Ted Hughes's mistress, is also permeated with a sense of inevitable loss found in many of Trevor's short stories. From her fairytale encounter with the

Canadian poet, to blissful marriage, presumed adultery, separation, divorce, and suicide, the sketch, like Trevor's stories, captures tragedy on a novelistic scale—this time within a few pages. Assia's account of her teatime rendezvous with Ted Hughes may indeed have been "tinted with a personal emphasis." Nevertheless, her convincing concoction of fact and fiction that is the storyteller's art wins Trevor's approval. Her approach to storytelling is one with his:

> Liars lie in order to obscure; Assia exaggerated only in the interests of what she saw as a greater veracity and, as her voice continued, doubts slipped away. Clearly, some part of this was not invented, but how the truth and the liberties taken with it were arranged I did not then know.[91]

In addition, he seems to have found the kernel for one of his finest early stories, "The Table," within Assia's fascinating but often unreliable account of her own life:

> She reported that she and her husband, advertising in the *Evening Standard* a table for sale, met—through their efforts to sell it—David Wevill's fellow-poets Ted Hughes and Sylvia Plath, who were at that time man and wife. According to one at least of Sylvia Plath's biographers, what was advertised was a flat. But a table formed a more interesting heart to the story Assia told, the fingers of the poets passing lightly over its surface as value and age were assessed.[92]

In "The Table," a solitary Jewish antique dealer, Mr. Jeffs, becomes personally involved in a series of transactions that begins with the sale of an antique table. He is ordinarily detached from other people and their concerns, except when his "attention to such nagging details" helps make him money.[93] He purchases the table from Mrs. Hammond, sells it to Mr. Hammond—who may be purchasing it for his mistress—and makes an unsuccessful yet profitable attempt to reacquire the table for a sentimental, distraught Mrs. Hammond, who ultimately regrets the original sale of her family heirloom. The parasitical, mercenary furniture dealer and his conscience, not his customers, are at the heart of the story, and the events surrounding the transactions simultaneously arouse Mr. Jeffs's and the reader's curiosity. Eventually, motivated by a latent, misguided sense of moral responsibility, Mr. Jeffs intervenes, but his irresponsible intervention is based on an uncorroborated, imaginative interpretation of the events he has witnessed. Trevor's extensive, successful cultivation of Assia's table incident testifies to his own fertile imaginative powers and proves that the stories based on incidents or situations outside his own experience—even those he does not witness himself—are as convincing, rich, and meaningful as those based on autobiographical material.

* * *

Trevor begins his short stories in a variety of ways. When asked about the genesis of some of them, he routinely offers the kernel he says was the inspiration for his widely anthologized "Going Home"—a story V. S. Pritchett also selected to represent its author in *The Oxford Book of Short Stories*:

> [T]here's a story which I wrote called "Going Home" which concerns a young matron and a little boy from a prep school and the journey on the train becomes very dramatic as the boy bullies her—and then she bullies the boy. And that came simply out of sitting on a rather empty train one day and noticing a couple like that and wondering about them. There was a certain melancholy about the woman, there was a certain sort of harshness about the boy and I just made up the rest. Now, I think that's how stories do begin. You see a tiny little bit, or you overhear a tiny little bit—the way somebody moves a hand, or the way someone says a certain word—and it triggers something off. This applies very much to short stories, not to novels.[94]

Already a well-known practitioner of the short story by 1970, Trevor contributed a piece to the *London Magazine* for its then ongoing feature, "Some Notes on Writing Stories," that shows how he generates a piece of fiction from a completely imagined situation.[95] While many of the famous short-story-writing contributors to this feature make astute comments about the genre, he dispenses with theorizing in an attempt to apprehend the creative act itself. True to his penchant for working telescopically, he imagines a dramatic situation about which he has never written: "two strangers on a long, non-stop journey find themselves in a railway compartment with the door jammed." He knows that ninety-nine times out of a hundred nothing would happen, but, as a short-story writer, is drawn to the hundredth occasion, the stimulating exception: "in this vacuum, one character might gradually proceed to involve the other: a surface peels away, an encounter begins."[96] Presumably, the encounter is purely imagined, without any connection to Trevor's experience. Like Henry James, he has the facility to fashion convincing motives, dialogue, and inner conflict. In no more than 700 words, he establishes the principal characters, the woman's anterior life, a mysterious stranger—about whom the reader knows nothing except for his accent and appearance—and two conflicts, one psychological and one situational.

The woman is alone in her compartment, preoccupied with thoughts of her absent husband while reading a magazine romance. Suddenly, an ungainly, unkempt Irishman in a stained suit and soiled mackintosh enters her compartment and closes the door violently. While conducting a conversation with the Irishman, who makes tiny harps in bog-oak, Mrs. Merriott considers what she should do about her marriage, haunted by the disturbing scene she witnessed through a broken window involving her husband and his part-time assistant. Trevor teases readers with this fragment in order to explain that "encounters such as this—between strangers, or people who have known each other a long time, or old enemies, or acquaintances—have been the starting points of many of [his] short stories, offering a spring-board from which to work."[97] He writes stories simply to discover what will happen with particular characters in a given situation.

Most of Trevor's work, however, takes its inspiration from "something that somebody says. Or something that you remember from a long time ago, from childhood, or from some experience, or from some person."[98] Characters "may have been tipped into existence by some passing face, some remark, or observed encounter."[99] "The Mark-2 Wife"—along with its title—came out of *Woman's Hour*. While a guest on the same program, Trevor recalled hearing an interviewee years earlier talking about how successful male executives, after having become board members, buy new cars and houses in Kingston and new wives as well. He was struck by the sadness of the situation and wrote about what became of one of the abandoned wives.[100] The Protestant schoolroom in Skibbereen where Trevor "spent a couple of inattentive years," described in great detail in his famous story "Attracta," "is in fact precisely the schoolroom where the Attracta of that story teaches."[101] In "O Fat White Woman," the embarrassing geometry tutorial in Digby-Hunter's study during which the student, Marshalsea, demonstrates complete ignorance of what he was supposed to learn, came from Trevor's own experience as a schoolmaster.[102] He acknowledges having once met someone like Millie, the narrator of "Beyond the Pale," in passing, but adds that his Millie is merely how he imagined the woman to be.[103] He discovered the spinster Bridie of "The Ballroom of Romance" in his childhood in Ireland, but while he noticed many of them, it was only in retrospect that he empathized with their plight. And the very place where he once lingered—The Great Western Royal at Paddington—on the way home from the "riches" of the London streets and parks, became the setting for "Lovers of Their Time." He brought two lovers there once, "to conduct their illicit affair in a second floor bathroom that nobody used very much. They just walked in, out of the crowds of the station [. . .] again, and again, week after week."[104] Remnants of Trevor's advertising days are recalled in apparently only two of his stories, "Office Romances" and "Mulvihill's Memorial," in whose title character there is "certainly a glimpse of a man" Trevor once knew.[105] In the latter, a nondescript designer of labels for soup tins and confectionery packets becomes an office pornographer after hours, secretly filming an in-house affair. Yet Trevor believes that the reality of stories does not usually lie in background detail taken from the real world, but in their more significant imagined parts. In "O Fat White Woman" it is Digby-Hunter's relationship with his wife, while in "Mulvihill's Memorial," it is the nature of Mulvihill's relationship with the organization that employs him.[106]

Whether the geneses of Trevor's short stories are autobiographical, observed, or synthesized, their successful development depends wholly on their creator's imaginative transmutation.

Chapter 6

Living on the Other Side of the Frontier

And when I read some of my stories I very often can remember from what particular real instant in life—or something like it—any sentence came from. And I've often thought—supposing I lost my memory—I could always go back to my stories and find the whole geography of my life, the travelling, friendships, goodness knows, in random detail, going back even into childhood. They don't belong to the period of the story necessarily. They sometimes go right back to childhood. I think childhood is an enormous source, the real well from which literature really comes.[1]

I became a foreigner. For myself that is what a writer is—a man living on the other side of a frontier.[2]

There is an eerie resemblance between William Trevor's and V. S. Pritchett's early lives and approaches to fiction—almost as if the earlier writer were Trevor's progenitor. Curiously, much of Trevor's experience—and his use of it—had been anticipated by Pritchett a generation earlier in England and echoes the Englishman's more extreme version. Pritchett's own peripatetic childhood, for instance, was even more disruptive than Trevor's, his family moving eighteen times before he was twelve.[3] Born in Ipswich, he spent his youth in and around London, where he attended a variety of schools. But his father's unstable professional situation often necessitated prolonged stays for Pritchett with relatives in Yorkshire while Micawberish Walter Pritchett reinvented and reestablished himself. Instead of uniting during these routine transitions, however, the immediate family dispersed. Victor's parents often went to different destinations. The siblings usually separated as well—sometimes for weeks or months, Victor going north to his grandfather's in Repton or to Sedbergh, his brother Cyril to stay in Ipswich with Aunt Ada; and his sister, Kathleen, and youngest brother, Gordon, to the new residence with their mother. Walter's frequent, abrupt displacement of his family from district to district in Greater London was not, however, as James Cox's regular displacement of his family in provincial Ireland had been, the result of his professional advancement, but to evade creditors pursuing him for his succession of failed business ventures. As in Trevor's case, instead of affecting him adversely, these events began Pritchett's "love of change, journeys and new places"[4] that eventually inspired his flight from England and very much determined the writer he became. On the eve of moving his own family as an adult, Pritchett, looking back, confessed to having always enjoyed it. And even when the family resettled, the interiors were in constant motion: "We did it every year when I was a child and, in between, my mother was forever moving furniture round from one room to the other. The [?] I have lifted, the tables I've taken to pieces!"[5]

The family itself was equally unsettled. Pritchett's parents were irreconcilable, like Trevor's, not merely because of divergent temperaments, however, but because their backgrounds were incompatible in every respect. The Yorkshireman and the Cockney woman from Kentish town came from vastly different worlds—a situation that "created [. . .] fascinating clashes within family life. [. . .] It was like a marriage between the moors and the streets."[6] Fraught with jealousy and deceit, it produced constant conflict. According to Pritchett, there was almost a class division within his immediate family because his father considered his lineage, religion, and accent superior to his mother's.[7] From the beginning of their marriage, "The battle between North and South was on."[8] And throughout their childhood, Pritchett and his siblings suffered the consequences of this contentious union.[9] The love once responsible for such an unlikely pairing was no longer in evidence:

> One knows little about the inner lives of one's parents. [. . .] The appalling things they said about each other expressed the fascination of their knowledge of each other and of the undoubted passion that had, at some time, entangled two temperaments so disastrously different.[10]

Pritchett believed that the violent quarrels in his childhood home had the effect of closing his heart for a long time.[11] Years later, in discussing the situation with Margery Fry, he agreed with her observation that children raised "in an atmosphere of violent discussion are likely to have more difficulty with their own opinions later on—they may arrive at more valuable opinions, but they have more difficulty in doing so." Raised by "passionately quarrelsome people" himself, Pritchett readily agreed: "I myself found great difficulty for that very reason. I even find it difficult talking to you. Every thought splits up into two quarrelling halves."[12] His nearly four year stint in the leather trade, during which he commuted from home, was punctuated by a sudden collapse attributed to the postwar flu epidemic, but that Pritchett—likening himself to "a kipper being cut in half"—believes was the culmination of years of domestic tension.[13]

After a lengthy convalescence, he decided to pursue his dream of living abroad instead of returning to the leather trade. He intended to become French and live in a foreign country—an experience he believed essential for the professional writer—and promised himself he would never return once on the other side of the frontier. Unlike his younger brother Cyril, however, whose relocation to France and apprenticeship in the Lyon silk trade was unexpected, Victor was primed for his defection. Though there were certainly gaps in his formal education, he excelled in languages, profiting from daily foreign language instruction while in school before his father consigned him to the leather trade.

Pritchett's fluency in French and Spanish, and lengthy stays living and working in France, Ireland, and Spain, gave him a more profound understanding of their respective cultures—experiences that made him a foreigner in a more complete sense than Trevor. Initially an outsider, he learned to see through natives' eyes. Although he thought the British Empire "the most beneficent thing in the world," he did not want to belong to it, feeling compelled instead to "unself" himself and become a foreigner—a principle he adhered to throughout his life.[14] Effacing himself in order to understand others seemed "to be almost a religious matter."[15] Like Trevor, Pritchett made this identification his governing aesthetic—an aesthetic he saw in the work of Turgenev, whom they both admire—that informs Trevor's work as well: "He observes and listens so that they appear to us clearly, untrammelled and living, as human beings do, in their own effortless justification."[16] Living abroad enabled Pritchett to learn English history from a foreigner's perspective, as an outsider looking in. Consistent with Trevor's telescopic approach, he believed he would never understand England's history and its people until he "went to the Continent and saw history upside down from the point of view of the people outside ourselves."[17] Contradicting the imperialist's approach, he learned about European and world history while in Spain, not "from the confident feeling which we had in England, but from the unconfident feeling which existed abroad."[18] Pritchett admired George Meredith for his depiction of foreigners and the way "he looks at England with a foreign eye and has no mid-Victorian model [. . .] in him."[19]

His exposure to other countries and cultures during his self-imposed seven-year exile fortified Pritchett's English identity as well as giving him a more objective view of his countrymen upon his return. According to Pritchett, Turgenev discovered that "Westerner though he was, he carried an ineffaceable Russia inside him; the Russia of his boyhood and young manhood became all the clearer in detail and stronger in meaning for being distant."[20] In much the same way, and in subsequent international travels, Pritchett carried an ineffaceable England inside him. Unlike Trevor, however, who maintains the exile he began over fifty years ago, and who continues to do his writing in England and Italy, Pritchett, though widely traveled, spent most of his life within his native country. In commiserating with Gerald Brenan about the imminent death of his wife, the poet Gamel Woolsey, in Spain in 1968, for instance, he was troubled by the thought of dying in a foreign country: "Perhaps Gamel doesn't feel this but it must be hard to die outside one's own country—at any rate I think I would feel this."[21] And in passing through Paris from Ireland on the way to Madrid in 1924, he was "as English as [he] could possibly make himself," ashamed of his "silly notion of 'becoming French!'"[22] "I feel deeply attached [to England]," he said when asked to contemplate permanent exile. "[I]t's the only country which really [. . .] feeds my mind [. . .], or feeds my imagination or makes me feel real. [. . .] My life, my real roots and [. . .] all the juices [. . .] flow into one's arms in this country."[23] And for this quintessentially English writer, it is only fitting that he discovered the aesthetic that informed his fiction, and that was further developed through his experiences on the other side of the frontier, in his English childhood during the First World War.

* * *

Pritchett became a writer and discovered his aesthetic in executing his Alleyn's School master's in-class assignment to write about the previous night's air raid. Initially Victor did not know what to write, but found upon further reflection that his experience as the surrogate man of the house, huddling with his siblings and hysterical mother, had moved him. The story was a resounding success—read aloud for faculty and students alike at his school—and Victor was celebrated. He thinks they were right to be impressed because he had become someone else: "And I think that is a sign of a writer—becoming something else."[24] His extensive account of this seminal episode in his autobiography excludes details of the actual composition; and when interviewed in 1985, he had forgotten exactly what he wrote and claimed it had vanished.[25] But over forty years earlier, Pritchett included a thinly disguised autobiographical account of the experience in a radio play for the BBC that captures both his childhood and adult relationships.[26] "The Novelist" and his typist "Wife" in the play are blatant surrogates for Victor and Dorothy, respectively, in 1944, and the childhood air-raid scenario is populated by surrogates for Pritchett's childhood family. His beliefs about the writing process are sprinkled throughout the play, his air-raid episode account is more revealing than it is in his autobiography, and it contains the lost words of his childhood composition. Inspired to express his mother's experience, he was "bathed in shame and pride"—as if he had undressed in front of the class—because he had taken on his mother's life, feelings, and nature: "'Why do we have these wicked raids,' I wrote. [. . .] 'We had one last night. My husband was away and I was alone with my children. I ran upstairs and clawed my children out of bed . . .' That's what I wrote. You see, I had become my mother. I pretended to be her. I had become a novelist. Because a novelist is a person who takes the lives of human beings into himself like a burden."[27]

Although uncharacteristically speaking through the "Novelist" in this radio play, in his short stories, Pritchett, like Trevor, believes in empathizing with his characters instead of projecting his own thoughts onto them. He too explores their idiosyncrasies by becoming them. But whereas Trevor achieves this objective primarily through omniscient or limited third-person point of view—rarely through first person—Pritchett succeeds by employing the first-person point of view in over three-quarters of his *Complete Collected Stories*. But readers must beware of associating Pritchett with his narrators. His preferred point of view enables him to discard his own self, assume other identities, and write "especially about people who can't express themselves. [. . .] You have to justify people so to speak."[28] And in another radio interview seven years later, Pritchett echoed Trevor's observation during a 1980 interview:[29] "It was rather fun becoming a woman, too. It's rather nice if you're a male to become a woman, or I suppose if you're a woman [. . .] to become a man in your imagination."[30] In 1970, he remarked that the younger English short-story writers were working from the inside to the outside of their characters while he himself subscribed to the opposite approach: "I find I work from the outside, making raids upon my people."[31]

* * *

Like Turgenev, and by his own admission, Pritchett is a deeply autobiographical writer, especially in the work he did during the end of the 1930s and the 1940s. And for that reason it is illuminating to "explore the interplay of what is known about his life with his art,"[32] as he himself did with the Russian, in order to appreciate the way in which they are fused and enlarge our understanding of his short stories. As Pritchett shows in *The Gentle Barbarian*, Turgenev's mother, Varvara Petrovna, dominated his early life, determining the man and writer he became. Similarly, albeit less dramatically and absolutely, Walter Pritchett was so powerful an influence on his son that, directly or indirectly, he inspired much of his early work.

While most of Pritchett's novels are autobiographical to some extent, *Mr. Beluncle* (1951),[33] his last and perhaps most successful, simply "is a transformed autobiography."[34] So lifelike is it that, in 1966, he believed producing an actual autobiography might prove redundant: "I am hovering on the edge of writing [. . .] one framed one to 23 [years old]. It would naturally interest me, but a lot of it has gone into Mr Beluncle."[35] This admission confirms the novel as both a thinly disguised autobiographical work and a biographical study of Walter Pritchett. After finishing the first volume of his life's story, he compared it to his novel, all too conscious of his life literally imitating his art: "I've called it A Cab at the Door and it stops at twenty when I leave for France. It is an account of Beluncle—dour and, I think, amusing."[36] In fact, at one point in his autobiography, he refers the reader to a particular comic scene in the novel involving deaf Grandmamma Beluncle that is merely hinted at in *A Cab at the Door*—leading his reader to believe the two works are complementary if not interchangeable.[37] Walter was not only the heart of Pritchett's first volume of autobiography and the protagonist of his last, perhaps finest, novel, but he gave him ample grist for his mill, becoming the inspiration for several characters in his son's short stories as well. After the funeral service for the real Mr. Beluncle, his son confirmed this:

> My brothers and I returned to discuss his misdeeds. What hit us and stupefied us was not grief, but the knowledge that we were the children of a monster of such dimensions. His death leaves a huge hole and I have felt since that it will take some time for ordinary life to fill it up. He was such a fleshy, pervasive, greedy man, totally egotistical who ate people up.[38]

Pritchett's characters, however eccentric or idiosyncratic, could not have seemed more grotesque to Pritchett than his father was. Understandably, much of his earlier fiction either derives from his father's character or satirizes his ways.

In contrast to Trevor's father, Pritchett's was both domineering and religious. The son of a Congregationalist minister, Walter rejected his own father's religion. The minister teased him about his "God of the moment" because Walter in turn rejected the Baptists, the Wesleyans, and the Methodists as well, "being less and less of a Jehovah man and pushing his way [. . .] towards the infinite."[39] In fact, he had sampled a number of denominations before embracing the beliefs and practices of the Church of Christ Scientist or Christian Science.[40] He was uncharacteristically discreet about his faith, and though he introduced it to his wife, Beatrice, he refrained from proselytizing when she rejected it or from indoctrinating his children until Victor's sprained ankle in school elicited Walter's explanation of Christian Science doctrine. Victor's injury was an illusion because an omnipotent God who would make his children in his image and likeness would not let one of his children sprain an ankle. There were "'no accidents in God's kingdom.'"[41] Walter had remained silent about his religion because he had no desire to force it on his son, but in light of the circumstance, he offered it as an alternative, adding that Christian Science would heal his son's ankle because "'nothing has happened to it. That is a simple mistake.'"[42] Pritchett recalls his father's explanation of the doctrine: "If I agreed that God was Good and Infinite and Omnipotent and had created Man in his image and likeness then there was no place where evil could possibly exist. Evil was illusion generated by the five senses. They were unreliable."[43]

Initially, Victor had nothing but positive impressions of the sect. He saw Christian Scientists "as living in a dramatic and liberating illumination" and, having heretofore rarely been to church, found the sect's idealism and novelty particularly appealing, especially because he had been raised in a home with "religious echoes and disputes" and only a vague notion of Christianity. It seemed "nothing but words" in contrast to the new religion in which he received formal instruction.[44] But his unhesitating devotion was short-lived, his natural skepticism provoking yet another internal schism:

> I was soon leading a double life. I believed, yet did not believe, very comfortably, at the same time. The believing part of me was the simple idealist; also the insubordinate youth was vain of belonging to a sect that was often ridiculed. It appealed to my vanity to belong to a peculiar minority and I did not notice that we [. . .] had cut off our noses to spite our faces.[45]

The concept of "Divine Mind" that is satirized at length in *Mr. Beluncle*, and is treated comically in his autobiography, marked Pritchett's childhood experience. Initially, Victor and Cyril took pride in their father's participation in the service when he was called upon to take the collection. Nattily dressed and scrupulously groomed for these special occasions after elaborate preparation, he "so outshone the other sidesmen that they backed away [. . .]. [I]f anyone of that crowd appeared to be the image and likeness of the Divine Mind, we felt, that man was our father. We kept our eye on him, our excess of glory [. . .]."⁴⁶ But this central tenet of Christian Science, and their father's allegiance to it, was soon ridiculed:

> Before Father got into the driver's seat, he did "his work" and "knew the Divine Mind of Love" was "the only driver." We soon saw that the gifts of the Divine Mind were purely metaphysical; the Divine Mind was the most dangerous driver I have ever known. It hit banks, tore off the sides of hedges, chased pedestrians, scattered people about to get on buses.⁴⁷

During all his dangerous excursions, Walter told his passengers not to look at the destruction in his wake when he drove. In a nearly fatal outing, Walter drove the expensive car to London with Cyril and a draper as passengers. As Walter carelessly crossed a dangerous intersection, they were hit by a steam traction-engine and rammed into a fence. Although the Divine Mind saved the passengers from harm, the car itself was destroyed. And in this case, he lied to Beatrice upon returning home, claiming that he sent the car back because there was something wrong with the engine.⁴⁸ Victor came to see that self-deception and deception were inextricably linked to a sect that reversed illusion and reality.

Finally, his questions about the origin of evil undermining his belief became a problem for his congregation and for himself as well. He too was obliged to deceive:

> I had a bad month with the origin of evil, because, to my dismay, I defeated several older members of our church in my inquiries and arguments. There was alarm about my doubts: I was handed on from eminence to eminence, and eventually to a visiting Christian Science lecturer. The young are surprisingly decent and tactful; I agreed with what was said, but I did not believe a word of it. Any fool could see this error and I was a worse fool than most, but I let the matter slide. There were more important things than the question of evil on my mind.⁴⁹

Pritchett saw that the sect renounced art, music, literature, conflict, and sex—everything, it seemed, except business—and he was concerned about his coreligionaries' abstention from these. Art "prolonged the errors of the senses, the greater the art, the greater the error." In fact, they quite literally sacrificed their lives for their faith. One congregation member gave up music, despite his passion for Beethoven, unable to perceive which parts of the works came from Divine Mind and which from Mortal Mind; a lawyer gave up reading Russian novels because "there was something fleshy in Tolstoy"; one woman gave up the National Gallery, renouncing the works of genius because it was a "waste of time now to consider anything but the images of God."[50] Christian Scientists replaced the word death with "passed on" because one never died—that too was an illusion.

Pritchett objected to "the impoverishment of the mind, the fear of knowledge and living that Christian Science continually insinuates," saw it operating "like a leucotomy that puts the patient into an amiable stupor," and understood it, as William James did, as "an enfeebled form of Emersonian metaphysics."[51] Yet it appealed to those members of the ambitious lower-middle class and those of the "blander uppers" who sought refuge from late-Victorian doubts in the combination of religion and "science" that mitigated the difficulties Darwin and Huxley had introduced.[52]

* * *

"The Saint" is an ingenious distillation of Pritchett's Christian Science experience, his satirical indictment of a "sect" that renounces earthly pleasures. His indoctrination into, involvement with, and ultimate rejection of his father's religion is encapsulated and recast in this piquant comic satire. The story is not simply a replication of the incidents described in his autobiography. Instead, it is a recasting that captures their essence with the touch of magnification befitting satire.

The story is permeated with autobiographical detail. Pritchett, however, consciously masked the identities of his models; but their camouflage is transparent. Given the striking number of similarities between the couples, it is not surprising that in an earlier draft of the story the narrator's aunt and uncle are instead his mother and father.[53] The uncle is involved, as Walter was, in the furniture-making business, and, like Walter, "was always in difficulties about money, but he was convinced that in some way God would help him."[54] Like Pritchett, his surrogate is obliged to stay for long periods with relatives. As it is in the later *Mr. Beluncle*, the Christian Science counterpart is "Church of the Last Purification," and the real sect's city of origin, Boston, becomes Toronto, Canada. (Mrs. Parkinson, the surrogate for Christian Science's founder, Mary Baker Eddy, is mentioned only in *Beluncle*.) The seventeen-year-old narrator's family is "converted" into its town's first "Purifiers" when an unidentified practitioner passing through pays some capital into the uncle's business to prove that "a good and omnipotent God" would not allow "his children" to be short of money. The conversion seems more financial than spiritual, the Church of the Last Purification linked strongly, as is Christian Science in Walter's life, to business. Furthermore, the uncle's predilection for trade terms echoes Walter's. In his autobiography, Pritchett observes that "All sects have their jargon and Father, eager as an advertising man is for slogans, had picked them all up and lived by them."[55] Similarly, the narrator observes that "All dogmas have their jargon; my uncle as a business man loved the trade terms of the Purification. 'Don't let Error in,' was a favourite one."[56] Echoing the young Pritchett's initial sentiments, the young narrator takes pride in his family's isolation from the "unconverted"[57] and parrots Christian Science doctrine Pritchett first heard from Walter:

> The success of our prayers had a simple foundation. We regarded it as "Error"—our name for Evil—to believe the evidence of our senses and if we had influenza or consumption, or had lost our money or were unemployed, we denied the reality of these things, saying that since God could not have made them they therefore did not exist."[58]

Comically, the naïve narrator is proud of the "routine" "miracles" "performed [. . .] every day" by the converted—the handicaps, diseases, and illnesses "constantly vanishing before the prayers of the more advanced Purifiers."[59] But curiously enough, these "miracles" always transpire elsewhere—in London and Toronto, for instance, rather than in his own community.

His unhesitating belief in the Church of the Last Purification, however, is short-lived. Like young Victor Pritchett, he too is dogged by doubt:

> Without warning and as if I had gone into my bedroom at night and had found a gross ape seated in my bed and thereafter following me about with his grunts and his fleas and a look, relentless and ancient, scored on his brown face, I was faced with the problem which prowls at the centre of all religious faith. I was faced by the difficulty of the origin of evil. Evil was an illusion, we were taught. But even illusions have an origin. The Purifiers denied this.[60]

Although it comes early in the story, this apparition is at its heart, representative of Pritchett's own enduring quandary about Original Sin. Contrary to his supposed adolescent renunciation of the doctrine as nothing more than "an intellectual convenience," he was divided about this essential tenet of Christianity as late as four years after "The Saint" appeared in print:

> The business of writers, I think, it is to record the conflicts and the silences in the soul. Damn it, we arrive in this world committed. I do not believe in the Fall; but I think I believe in Original Sin. Can you tell me if this is theologically possible. I just see the Ape in every one.[61]

The embodiment of religious doubt, evil, bestiality, and Original Sin, the ape reappears at the end of the narrative, is used similarly in "The Chestnut Tree," and also stars in one of Pritchett's rare story-length allegories, appropriately titled "The Ape." An unlikely but devout Symbolist, he believed his stories contained several levels of experience at once, usually with "some image or symbol [. . .] that holds them together or interprets the experience,"[62] and the ape is "The Saint"'s manifold symbol. But the integration of such a powerful symbol works with, not against, Pritchett's employment of his very real experience.

Blind allegiance to Purification edict makes the uncle vulnerable to his nephew's queries. For the uncle, the "scientific and therefore exact" nature of Purification makes the mere entertainment of discussion "sheer weakness," "[i]ndeed, betrayal,"[63] and the narrator must "submit or change the subject"[64] as Pritchett may have been forced to do by his father while entertaining his own religious doubts. "Faith and doubt pulled like strings round [the narrator's] throat"[65] as his arguments defeat his uncle, his dilemma paralleling Pritchett's aforementioned religious crisis. Unable to resolve it, he walks to the river. The life that "was a dream" is now "a nightmare" because the ape is beside the narrator.[66] And he remains in this unresolved, divided state, "half sulking and half exalted," when forty-one-year-old Hubert Timberlake, an eminent leader from church headquarters in Toronto, the sect's Mecca, visits his family home the afternoon of his Sunday morning town speaking engagement.[67] Like young Pritchett, whose troubling enquiries and arguments concerning the origin of evil defeated distinguished church members and a succession of eminences alike, necessitating the intervention of a visiting Christian Science lecturer, his surrogate's similarly baffling queries necessitate venerable Timberlake's visit. Just as the ape embodies religious doubt, Timberlake embodies the Church of Purification, the two figures, fictive and real, offering tangible representations of the narrator's inner conflict.

Pritchett's transformation and development of the actual visiting Christian Science lecturer upon whom the Purification leader is based results in one of his most compelling characters by transmuting life experience into powerful comic fiction. He accomplishes much of this through indirection, building up his primary character through the eyes of others. Upon Timberlake's arrival, the narrator describes him in saint-like terms, awed that such an eminent man would dine in their company, use their utensils, and eat their food. Not only had he been to Toronto, "where the great and revolutionary revelation had first been given," but Timberlake had purportedly "performed many miracles—even [. . .] having twice raised the dead."[68] The uncle builds him up further still, praising him to his nephew for his supposedly selfless renunciation of a lucrative insurance business position to take up work for the sect—a decision from which he just happened to reap financial rewards.

As it is for Walter Pritchett, wealth is evidently next to godliness for the uncle, a perverse sign of religious well-being. Invoking one of Walter's own favorite pronouncements, "the way was shown,"[69] he praises Timberlake's honorable, lucrative path and practice. He reproaches his wife with Walter's refrain, "Don't let Error in!"[70]—as Walter reproached Beatrice—for her blasphemous suggestion that Timberlake may be tired. But the uncle shares his role as Walter's surrogate with his eminent guest, who supposedly heals the sick by prayer according to the tenets of the Church of the Last Purification—a practice Walter dabbled in as a Christian Scientist, although he was not an official "Practitioner."[71] This will not be their only common ground.

Timberlake is a unique creation, his unexpected sense of humor making him a sympathetic, unpredictable, compelling character from his first appearance, and a departure from the stereotypical, one-dimensional, proselytizing evangelist. In response to the uncle's unflattering introduction of his nephew, for instance, he immediately impresses both narrator and reader with surprisingly witty, irreverent repartee that wins over the narrator:

> "This is my nephew," my uncle said, introducing me. "He lives with us. He thinks he thinks, Mr Timberlake, but I tell him he only thinks he does."[72]
> [. . .]
> "What say we tell your uncle it's funny he thinks he's funny."[73]

The nephew is convinced that whatever Mr. Timberlake believes must be true and as he listens to him at lunch thinks "there could be no finer life than his."[74] Yet despite his admiration, the boy nevertheless sees through the visitor's patronizing invitation to go punting together after lunch, teach him how to punt, and "'get water on the brain,'" punctuated by the man's affectedly hip vernacular insistence, "'Waal, what say?'"[75] The perceptive narrator discerns the underlying motive in Timberlake's enthusiastic, condescending endorsement of the excursion: "Mr Timberlake, I saw to my disappointment, was out to show he understood the young. I saw he was planning a 'quiet talk' with me about my problems."[76]

The narrator claims he is already converted before he and the sect leader go out "to settle the question of the origin of evil," thus rendering Timberlake's mission unnecessary: "I would have to pretend politely that he was converting me when, already, at the first sight of him I had believed."[77] In addition, "'always on the river,'" he would seem to have little use for Timberlake's punting lesson. He is proud to be with the eminent leader, though, thrilled to get a boating ticket "for *the* Mr. Timberlake." Yet at the riverside, before embarking on their excursion, Mr. Timberlake is suddenly transformed, clearly out of his element, unwittingly exposing another side of himself hidden behind his "vivid and unanswerable" smile: "He was standing at the edge of the water looking at it with an expression of empty incomprehension. [. . .] He looked middle-aged, out of place and insignificant. But the smile switched on when he saw me."[78] Everything about Timberlake seems "unreal" to the narrator, making the man's interaction with "commonplace material things" "incredible," especially his incongruous presence in the punt and his offer to pole them up the river. Not surprisingly, the narrator's fears are pregnant with irony foretold: "That he should propose to pole us up the river was terrifying. Suppose he fell into the river? At once I checked the thought. A leader of our Church under the direct guidance of God could not possibly fall into the river."[79]

Timberlake is full of hubris as well, insisting on taking the pole shortly after their departure, bragging about skill he last demonstrated eighteen years earlier. Symbolically, he has difficulty steering the punt upriver, and the boy discreetly corrects its course. Familiarity with the river enables him to anticipate difficulties and offer his guest expert, practical guidance. Despite being warned about the trees, however, prideful Timberlake not only fails to make the necessary maneuver as they head for the willows, but he stubbornly rejects the narrator's last-minute offer to help paddle them out of trouble. And as they glide inevitably toward the low canopy of willow branches under which he cannot possibly pass standing upright, he even ignores the narrator's repeated advice to duck. Up until the very moment of his mishap, Timberlake continues to exhibit ignorance of the natural world with which he will be in conflict throughout their journey:

> "What makes the trees lean over the water like this?" asked Mr Timberlake. "Weeping willows—I'll give you a thought there. How Error likes to make us dwell on sorrow. Why not call them laughing willows?" discoursed Timberlake as the branch passed over my head.

The laugh, or joke, of course, is on him. These very "sorrow"ful trees soon bring about his comic literal and figurative undoing. The bow in which the narrator sits is already underneath the branches when Timberlake's forward progress is stopped as he attempts to lift a willow branch out of his way. The boat moves on, his boots leave the stern, and he finds himself caught in the tree, the immortal subject of one of Pritchett's most celebrated images rich in mock biblical allusions: the fruit simile (forbidden?), the anticipated fall, and salvation:

> He made a last minute grasp at a stronger and higher branch, and then, there he hung a yard above the water, round as a blue damson that is ripe and

ready, waiting only for a touch to make it fall. Too late with the paddle and shot ahead by the force of his thrust, I could not save him.

From this point on, Pritchett's comic ironies multiply as the story itself comes to fruition while continuing to draw from Pritchett's autobiographical experiences. Timberlake's suspension a yard above the water suggests the narrator's—and the young Pritchett's—suspended judgment of the sect. As Timberlake clings helplessly to the tree, the boy reminds himself of the Purification's precept: never believe what you see. "Unbelieving," he cannot move in the punt, stunned that the "impossible" has occurred. "Only a miracle" can save the man:

> So unperturbed and genteel he seemed that as the tips of his shoes came nearer and nearer to the water, I became alarmed. He could perform what are called miracles. He would be thinking at this moment that only in an erroneous and illusory sense was he hanging from the branch of the tree over six feet of water.[80]

Illusion takes precedence over reality as the incredulous boy feigns denying the reality that Mr. Timberlake will not permit himself to recognize. Illusion can save the sect leader from an unpleasant reality only if the boy is willing to play along. But the boy cannot dismiss the very real sight before his eyes—the double chin that forms as the hanging man's head is squeezed between his shoulders and arms, his eyelids "pale like a chicken's." In yet another irony, in a story full of them, he prays against, not for, a miracle: "I prayed with all my will that Mr Timberlake would not walk upon the water. It was my prayer and not his that was answered." Not surprisingly, gravity triumphs over divine intervention. And the comic mock tragedy becomes ever more pronounced in the pastoral theater. With Timberlake's shoes and ankles already submerged, his unsuccessful attempt to move to a higher willow branch results in his figurative and literal undoing. An unlikely comparison of Timberlake to a Greek god emerges—one having antithetical associations with poetic inspiration and pastoral life. The human statue compared to a god evolves into a human being, its "fatal flaw" its very flesh:

> [I]n making this effort his coat and waistcoat rose and parted from his trousers. One seam of shirt with its pant-loops and brace-tabs broke like a crack across the middle of Mr Timberlake. It was like a fatal flaw in a statue, an earthquake crack which made the monumental mortal. The last Greeks must have felt as I felt then, when they saw a crack across the middle of some statue of Apollo. It was at this moment I realised that the final revelation about

man and society on earth had come to nobody and that Mr Timberlake knew nothing at all about the origin of evil.[81]

The boy paddles over to him but must let Timberlake sink until his hands are at punt level and he can be paddled ashore. The image of a sinking statue signals the sect leader's mock-heroic demise but very real theological death. A quintessential Pritchettian moment, perhaps the technical climax of the story, the incident is sprinkled with mock religious allusions: baptism (of Timberlake); the Fall; John the Baptist; and sainthood:

> Amputated by the water, first a torso, then a bust, then a mere head and shoulders, Mr Timberlake, I noticed, looked sad and lonely as he sank. He was a declining dogma. As the water lapped his collar [. . .] I saw a small triangle of deprecation and pathos between his nose and the corners of his mouth. The head resting on the platter of water had the sneer of calamity on it, such as one sees in the pictures of a beheaded saint.[82]

There has been a visible change in Timberlake's expression. In place of the habitual broad smile followed by the "long depressed sarcastic curve" of his lips, he sports "a small triangle of deprecation and pathos." Once ashore, his dripping wet suit making a puddle, Timberlake is forced to acknowledge the consequence of his accident. His admission, "'we let some Error in that time,'" is a delayed reply to Walter's and the uncle's refrain, "'Don't let Error in.'" Ironically, water becomes "Error" instead of life's essence, yet the man, despite his denial, is literally drenched in reality. And after offering to wring out the sect leader's wet coat and waistcoat, the boy cuts himself off in mid-sentence, having "nearly blasphemed," having almost suggested that Timberlake had actually fallen into the river! Of course Timberlake continues to spout Purification dogma, denying the effects of the physical world: "If God made water it would be ridiculous to suggest He made it capable of harming his creatures." This comic denial continues when Timberlake insists that they continue up the river, despite being soaked to the skin. Later still, he rejects the concerned narrator's renewed offer. Although Timberlake continues pretending nothing has happened, the "glaze" that members of the sect had "on their faces and persons, their minds and manners" is no longer on his.

All is changed after the fall. Ironically, the boy has been truly enlightened by this secular experience. Appropriately enough, and in opposition to his first impression at the house, he now sees that Timberlake, after his very real, not mythological or biblical, fall, is neither a saint nor a god, but a mere mortal, "a stoutish man" with "veined empurpled skin" and "a poor heart." He recognizes "something flaccid, passive and slack" about the once-ebullient chief Purifier after the punting mishap. Timberlake's apparent boredom with everything around him—water, boats, and countryside—reveals his complete lack of interest in the outing itself and proves he considered it a mere obligation, and that his initial enthusiasm had been insincere. Timberlake is out of place on earth—out of touch with the natural world that Pritchett and his boyhood surrogate celebrate.

> By his questions [. . .] I understood that [he] was formally acknowledging a world he did not live in. It was too interesting, too eventful a world. His spirit, inert and preoccupied, was elsewhere in an eventless and immaterial habitation. He was a dull man, duller than any man I have ever known; but his dullness was a sort of earthly deposit left by a being whose diluted mind was far away in the effervescence of metaphysical matters.[83]

The narrator's once sincerely reverential tone has become mock reverential, his analysis of the proud but floundering sect leader laced with subtle irony and sarcasm, most notably in excusing his secular dullness as a consequence of lofty metaphysical preoccupation. (The "diluted mind" refers to the uncle's early joke about the boy having "water on the brain" and Timberlake's subsequent, condescending aping of the phrase.) Preoccupation with the myriad symptoms of his "Error" makes Timberlake almost mute as he continues his pathetic but heroic self-deception. He periodically squeezes water out of his drenched sleeve, shivers, and watches steam rising from his body—all, of course, illusions. Taking pity on the man, who is indeed, just as his uncle had said, "So human," burdened by the responsibility for him, the boy makes the final destination a nearby meadow of buttercups. As he was when seen unawares at the outset of their journey, Timberlake is visibly "lost, stupefied, uncomprehending" at the edge of the meadow. Mute and "uncomprehending," the sect leader is animal-like and begins to ape the narrator's movements. Without speaking, he follows him into the deep sea of flowers and sits down beside him, continuing to demonstrate his ignorance about the natural world when he cannot identify a buttercup—just as he could not identify a willow—even though he is surrounded by them.

In place of the long-awaited heart-to-heart talk that was supposed to take place between them, the boy tries in vain to wring out Timberlake's coat and trousers but the man insists on remaining as he is. But in yet another comic turn, Timberlake will be transformed willy-nilly. He literally apes the boy, who lies down in the sun, in an attempt perhaps to ingratiate himself: "He had come out with me, I saw, to show me that he was only human." As soon as the narrator sits up, anxious to return Timberlake to town, the sect leader sits up as well, aping him a second time, copying him yet again when the narrator stands up. Instead of transforming the narrator's doubts about religion through discussion, Timberlake himself is transfigured by his visit to the field: his blue suit is yellow, completely covered in golden buttercup pollen that has adhered to the wet suit. Although he survived his humiliating encounter with the willow and the river water, the flowers would seem to have delivered the coup de grâce to the sect's doctrine. Though he does literally raise his eyebrows at the sight of himself, in keeping with his heroic fidelity he sees no "Error" and no evil, and remains silent, once again subscribing to the religion's mistrust of the five senses. The pollen, after all, like the water, is an illusion. Walter Pritchett also harbored his illusions until the end, like all of the self-deceiving members of the sect. Unusual for comedy, the story achieves pathos here as well, for the boy understands that Timberlake's intentions are honorable even if his enthusiasm for the outing was obviously insincere. And ultimately the man is only human—far from the stock buffoon he might be in the hands of a less sensitive writer. The reader feels compassion for this pathetic man because, all too human, he is one of us.

Finally, gilded Timberlake is a saint—a mock saint who remains "Golden" until he boards his train. Of course he is only a saint in appearance, not in deed, "as saintly as any of those gold-figures in the churches of Sicily." Even at the boy's home, before setting out for the station, he refuses to change his clothes, sit by the fire, or acknowledge the events of the afternoon—"the disasters and beauties of the world," the coexistence of good and evil that necessarily defines human experience—preferring complete denial. Yet to the boy he seems no more than a "husk," deprived of the illusions that sustained him before the fall. The boy nevertheless owes a great debt to the shattered man after all. Timberlake delivers him from his quandary, his mock saint-like sacrifice helping the boy embrace the secular world. Long before writing "The Saint," Pritchett made such an embrace in Castile, Spain when "for the first time in [his] life [he] understood what a human being is, how his pain, his love, his hate, his hunger, his luxury, his passion and his indifference, are a treasure to which he clings. And that man is <u>really</u> flesh and that his spirit is flesh, too."[84] It was at that moment that Pritchett believes he was cured of the transcendentalist dream in which he had lived up to that point.[85] The writings of Miguel de Unamuno, in particular *Del sentimiento tragica de la vida*, gave Pritchett an approach to life consistent with his Castillian revelation and totally contrary to that of Christian Science.[86]

There are perhaps enough clues to piece together Pritchett's inspiration for "The Saint." All at once, his experiences and observations upon which the story is based converge: his involvement with Christian Science; the sight of the man falling in the river at Marlow; the description of Walter's car accident; and Beatrice's jocular comparison of portly Walter to a balloon. Pritchett once saw an evangelist fall into the water in Marlow.[87] The punting sequence strikes one as an elaborate transmutation of Walter's automobile accident replete with the driver's identical refusal to acknowledge the very real physical consequences of his actions. The image of Timberlake as a large blue damson dangling helplessly over the river recalls Beatrice's own image of enormous Walter as a prospective naval balloon officer: "'Two balloons in the air.'"[88] In replying to Gerald Brenan's reactions to the first draft of "The Saint," Pritchett more than suggests that even the story's crowning image came from direct personal experience: "But the picture of *me*, Mr. Timberlake, the sign of evil among the buttercups pleases me [my italics]. I cant help feeling that my fellow Russian geniuses among whom you so kindly place me, didn't just have strokes of luck and did go for the major subjects."[89] In a subsequent letter, before revising the story and sending it back to Brenan, he explains that it is "a much more difficult kind of thing to bring off [than "The Sailor"], for it is very hard to make the ridiculous sublime."[90]

"The Saint," however, is not composed of autobiographical elements alone. Between drafts, Pritchett found a literary inspiration for fortifying his principal character and the story's climactic scene: "I must look at Don Quixote again and hope that will improve the effect of Mr. Timberlake's pant loops. [He] could be a very great character."[91] Timberlake is an anti-Don Quixote, and if Cervantes' novel is, as Pritchett wrote, the supreme fairy tale, then "The Saint" is a comic farce. Apprised of this source of inspiration, one can see the very strong connection between one of literature's most famous heroes and Mr. Timberlake. Both characters delude themselves—one by transforming reality, the other by pretending it is an illusion. For Pritchett, for Cervantes, and for Trevor as well, satire does not preclude compassion.

"The Saint"'s epilogue reveals the reason for its telling. News of Timberlake's sudden death at the age of fifty-seven makes the narrator relive the river mishap sixteen years earlier, implicate himself ("I dropped Mr Timberlake in the river"), and identify the sight of the man's pant loops as responsible for destroying his faith. He never sees Timberlake again after their punting excursion, but learns that he had lived alone with his mother all his life, slept in a single bed, and was found by her lying on his bedroom floor half-dressed while preparing for church. Seemingly inconsequential details of Timberlake's appearance in death in the penultimate paragraph prepare for and strengthen the final lines by suggesting the animal within him: the "heavy body" "wide rather than stout," the "extraordinarily box-like thick-jawed face," and the "heavy liver-coloured cheeks [...] like the chaps of a hound." And in death the face is "coarse and *degenerate*" (my italics). As it was when he hung from the willow, Timberlake's flesh is exposed in death. Most importantly, the narrator learns the cause of death: heart disease.

And it is in telling the tale and reviewing the dramatic images on the river and in the meadow that the thirty-three-year-old narrator retrospectively comprehends the reason for Timberlake's ludicrous pretenses:

> I understood why he had made for himself a protective, sedentary blandness, an automatic smile, a collection of phrases. He kept them on like the coat after his ducking. And I understood why—though I had feared it all the time we were on the river—I understood why he did not talk to me about the origin of evil. He was honest. The ape was with us. The ape that merely followed me was already inside Mr Timberlake eating out his heart.[92]

Interestingly enough, the last line of the original *Horizon* version has the ape eating "at" instead of "out" his heart.[93] Pritchett's alteration leaves no doubt that the completion of the ape's sixteen-year meal was Timberlake's real cause of death. Both Pritchett and his surrogate understood that man cannot "Move upward, working out the beast" because "the ape and tiger" will never die. He must accept that he too is an animal.[94]

* * *

In his preface to *Collected Stories*, Pritchett claims that only once in his career—when he was twenty-three and beginning—did he take down the scene, character and conversation for a short story straight from life: "Since that lucky moment—never repeated—I have had to dig my stories out of myself and out of random events, re-imagined."[95] A number of his stories, however, particularly those written in the first half of his career, seem to contradict this assertion, including "The Oedipus Complex," "The Fly in the Ointment," and "The Lion's Den." Not only do they come "straight from life," but they include Pritchett's persona as well. Nevertheless, instead of condemning him as an artist limited to his own experience, these intensely autobiographical stories attest to their author's uncanny ability to recognize ready-made fiction in everyday life and use his acute aural and visual sense to record it through image and sound.

"The Oedipus Complex" recalls "You Make Your Own Life" in situation, design, and structure.[96] Both involve established professionals who, standing while providing their service, nonchalantly tell the seated narrators dramatic stories that contrast with their own unromantic, routine work.

Yet while there is no apparent autobiographical element in the earlier story, "The Oedipus Complex" is purportedly "straight from life." In place of the barber is a dentist whose potted autobiography could be, as it was in the barber's case, the outline of a melodramatic novel. The stories differ profoundly, however, in their mix of action and storytelling, and while the barber's autobiographical tale of jealousy dominates "You Make Your Own Life," the dentist's relatively succinct life story, though dramatic, follows the potpourri of songs, jokes, and stories with which he entertains his patients. In contrast to the narrator in the barbershop, whose consistent participation effects a dialogue that advances the barber's story, his counterpart in "The Oedipus Complex" is incapacitated, rendered mute—except for an occasional, incomprehensible (and thereby comical) guttural "'Blah'"—by the invasive dental procedure. This imbalance puts the loquacious dentist, Mr. Pollfax, center stage for his story-length comic dramatic monologue that concludes, as Browning's "My Last Duchess" does, with a surprising personal revelation. Like the Duke, Pollfax gives a virtuoso performance, but consistent with Pritchett's comic tone, in place of the Duke's arrogance and self-righteousness, is Pollfax's playfulness and mock self-importance. In his inimitable shorthand, Pritchett once again ascribes a character's disposition to a particular body part. The dentist is not only "jaunty," he has "jaunty buttocks and a sway to his walk," an idiosyncratic detail comparable to his character Trevor's slapping of his "eager knees" in "Our Wife." Pritchett's "word for Mr Pollfax," "Dogged, with its slight suggestion of doggish," not only underlines the story's central extended metaphor (to carry on doggedly is to "soldier on"), it anticipates Molly's canine behavior in the later story.

Although less than 200 words, Pritchett's pre-story notebook entry entitled "The Dentist" contains the essence of this encounter: the dentist's eccentric, theatrical behavior, idiosyncratic commands, singing, "potted biography," struggle with the patient's tooth, relentless determination, and alarming warning to the narrator, making it the story in miniature. Except for the question about Yeats, all of the elements are used in the story, most appearing once, some nearly verbatim, others transformed, while the dentist's commands to spit and rinse recur throughout:

> The Dentist
> Says 'Spit my lord' or "Rinse my lord", and has the slightly
> protruding buttocks which appeal to women. Do you like
> Yeats? Sings Tyneside songs while he has your mouth
> jacked up and gives a short potted biography of himself:
> Ruined my father, left my wife for another woman, lived
> with her 3 years till she died of t.b., not satisfied with that

would of took my brother's fiancée and and now we're married have 3 children are ideally happy. "Mr Catchside with his back against a wall."
"Mr Catchside is never defeated. Well I've got your posterior nerve but now for the anterior. For God sake don't move. If it breaks off you'll be in a nursing home having & we'll be sending a search party down for it. The deal with these bits is they move a bit further into the system every time you swallow. Thank God, touch wood – nothing that has never happened to me yet. Damn that piece would break off. I'll have to saw it through. Its wearing out my drill. Never mind old man, I wont be beaten.["]97

Paradoxically, though Mr. P., Pritchett's deputy in the published story, is silent during the procedure, as Pollfax's portraitist and interpreter of his behavior, his storytelling surpasses his subject's. It is, after all, Mr. P.—and by extension Mr. Pritchett—who fashions Mr. Pollfax from Mr. Catchside, and expands the notebook shorthand into a 2000-word short story. However faithfully Pritchett captured his experience, there is a marked difference between the notebook entry and the story. A comparison of them reveals modification and elaboration that demonstrate Pritchett's artistry, once again, much in the same way that the revision process does.

As if to announce the idea of doubling, dentist and patient share the first letter of their surnames: Mr. Pollfax and Mr. P., respectively. The author invites association with his narrator, making him a pipe smoker as well. But from the moment the patient takes the chair, both men assume other identities: Pollfax grants Mr. P. "a peerage" while Mr. P. transforms the dentist into an "English Tommy." The dentist addresses the narrator exclusively as "my lord" twelve times during their encounter, while ironically ordering around and literally manhandling the subservient Mr. P. throughout the appointment. Intelligent and entertaining, he enjoys mixing the familiar with the formal, not hesitating to make a moral judgment about the state of his patient's tell-tale mouth: "Let's see what sort of life his lordship has been leading. Still smoking that filthy pipe, I see. I shall have to do some cleaning up." At the bottom of his bills he admonishes his patients with "Be good," and in his white coat he appears priestlike. In another comic touch, instead of consulting records, Pollfax ascertains the date of his patient's previous visit by verifying the last joke he told them.

The story is a carnival of colloquial figurative language with contributions from both parties. The dentist's speech and Mr. P.'s narration work in concert to produce Pritchett's poetry of the common man. Through imaginative similes, Mr. P. periodically and fleetingly transforms Pollfax's occupation: from dentist to gardener to fisherman to signal man to wrestler. The instrument of extraction is "like a gardener's secateurs in his hand"; the drill makes "a whistling noise like a fishing line"; while working on the tooth "he levered like a signal man changing points"; at the story's climax he is "like a wrestler putting on a headlock." And in describing a dental tool as a crowbar, Mr. P. even invokes the handyman. But it is his opening observation about Pollfax that prepares the extended military metaphor central to the story: "There was something innocent, heroic and determined about Mr. Pollfax, something of the English Tommy in tin hat and full pack going up the line. He suggested in a quiet way—war." And war it is. In the confines of his office, Pollfax dramatizes a mere tooth extraction, impersonating a British private soldier involved in a military offensive that comically parallels his very real battle with the tooth. Although the story lacks a conventional plot, his constant interweaving of jokes, stories, and songs throughout the delicate procedure creates suspense for narrator and reader alike. At various points, Mr. P.'s descriptions contribute to the dentist's fantasy. For example, his mouth is "jacked up" while the dentist is "taking another weapon" from the tray for the "operation" as if mounting an offensive. But it is Pollfax who creates and sustains the story-long battle metaphor that actualizes his fantasy. "'Dug himself in, has he?'" he surmises when his initial attempt to extract the root fails, as if his enemy is safely entrenched, the metaphor extending below the gum line to trench warfare. And Pollfax is appropriately "in mid-air" with an airman's bird's eye view of the enemy when he addresses the root directly, muttering "'It's no good you thinking you're going to stay in.'" "'So that's the game is it?'" he exclaims, "withdrawing" as his "weapon" slips and a piece of tooth breaks off. "'Good rinse, my lord,'" he commands, breathing hard, while he "'considers the position,'" the Tommy momentarily a general. Suspense continues to build to the end of the story for patient, dentist, and reader, as fragments of the tooth break off in the struggle and Pollfax cannot dislodge the root. There is even an approximation of hand-to-hand combat suggested by this hand-to-mouth struggle:

> Mr Pollfax's knuckles were on my nose. [. . .] He came at me with something like a button-hook. He got it in. [. . .] Another piece of tooth broke off. [. . .] Down came the drill again. There were beads of sweat on his brow. His breath was shorter. [. . .] "Sorry, my lord, I've got to bash you about, but time's against me."[98]

At a critical moment, in the heat of battle, he is indeed "fighting against time," not for his life, but for his next appointment. Unable to vanquish the root, he dramatizes his dilemma further by narrating his heroic struggle in the third person: "Mr. Pollfax *is* up against it." There is even Owenesque diction in Mr. P.'s description of the red-faced dentist "gasping," "his eyes [. . .] glittering."

Pritchett draws from the notebook fragment at this critical point in the narrative. Acting like a soldier in a life-threatening moment against insurmountable odds, Pollfax reveals his dramatic, personal story, having saved it for this crisis. Here, at the published story's end, Pritchett uses Mr. Catchside's potted autobiography from near the beginning of the notebook fragment so that it coincides with the climax of Pollfax's dental procedure, expanding and embellishing the original significantly, exaggerating it in almost every way. In this way he fashions comically overblown but riveting melodrama from the original, already melodramatic, Catchside life.

Here is the notebook version:	Here is the published version:
Ruined my father, left my wife for another woman, lived with her 3 years till she died of t.b., not satisfied with that ~~would of~~ took my brother's fiancée ~~and~~ and now we're married have 3 children are ideally happy.	"I started well by ruining my father. I took every penny he had. That's a good start, isn't it?" he said, speaking very rapidly. "Then I got married. Perfectly happy marriage, but I went and bust it up. I went off with a French girl and her husband shot at us out in the car one day. I was with that girl eighteen months and she broke her back in a railway accident and I sat with her six months watching her die. Six ruddy months. I've been through it. Then my mother died and my father was going to marry again, a girl young enough to be his daughter. I went up and took that girl off him, ran off to Hungary with her, married her and we've got seven children. Perfect happiness at last. I've been through the mill," said Mr Pollfax, [. . .] "but I've come out in the end."⁹⁹

Most importantly, however, instead of marrying his brother's fiancée, as Catchside did, Pollfax steals his father's intended, escapes with her to a foreign country, marries her, and has seven children instead of three. This substantial alteration justifies the story's title. Pollfax mentions Freud's Oedipus complex earlier, but interrupted by his procedure, waits until the end to reintroduce it, illustrating it with his own story within the story. And the storytelling dentist's disclosure is expertly timed. Concluding with a happy ending after describing his protracted unpleasantness and tribulations is a way of reassuring the narrator that despite problems, the dental procedure will be successful in the end.

In the story's concluding lines, Pritchett makes use of his linguistic arsenal: implied metaphor, simile, cliché, and wordplay, not to mention a proverb immediately preceding the passage:[100]

> "Mr Pollfax with his back against the wall," he said, between his teeth.
> "Mr Pollfax making a last-minute stand," he hissed.
> "On the burning deck!" he gasped.
> "Whence," he added, "all but he had fled."
> "Spit," he said. "And now let's have another look." He wiped his brow. "Don't say anything. Keep dead still. For God's sake don't let it hear you. My lords, ladies and gentlemen, pray silence for Mr Pollfax. It's coming, it isn't. No, it isn't. It is. It is. There," he cried, holding a fragment in his fingers.
> He stood gravely to attention.
> "And his chief beside,
> Smiling the boy fell dead,"
> said Mr Pollfax. "A good and final spit, my lord and prince."[101]

Here, in military clichés without verbs, Pollfax once again speaks of himself in the third person while battling with the enemy root. He does not, however, restrict himself to colloquial expressions, but incorporates popular verse as well, reinforcing his own self-imagined heroic identity by quoting the opening couplet from Felicia Hemans's "Casabianca" and the concluding line from Browning's "Incident of the French Camp." "The Oedipus Complex" is imbued with Englishness and decorated with English poetic forms. Both poems are in the most common English meter—ballad meter—and "Casabianca"'s ballad stanza, though a variant, is the most popular English strophic form. Pollfax selects war poems about boys demonstrating remarkable heroism expressly to make himself a hero by association with the immortal young men. Young Casabianca, son to the Admiral of the Orient, remained at his post in the Battle of the Nile after the ship caught fire and perished with the explosion of the vessel. Reference to Hemans's poem further implies that Pollfax too, like Casabianca in the third line of the poem's second quatrain, is "A creature of heroic blood," reinforcing his self-imagined identity. These famous lines have special significance for the dentist. There is subtle self-justification on his part in alluding to a poem in which the father does not come to his heroic, steadfast son's rescue. Pollfax's allusion reveals the dentist's justification of his Oedipal behavior. And the concluding lines of Browning's dramatic monologue as spoken by Pollfax ("And his chief beside, / Smiling the boy fell dead") subtly underline Pollfax's playful sense of heroic sacrifice for his patient before he ends the session with his unique command and address.

The actual dentist upon whom Mr. Pollfax is based may have supplied much of the material distilled in the notebook fragment, but it is Pritchett's shrewd selectivity, extensive development, and deft craftsmanship that transform it into a lively piece of social comedy.[102]

* * *

As adept as he was at transmuting autobiography into fiction, Pritchett's short stories were not limited to this rich source. Many of them—especially those written in the latter half of his career—are, like Trevor's, inspired by or based on observations of actual people and incidents outside his life. One of his most famous early stories, "Many Are Disappointed," is part of this group. Although a simple sketch, like many of Chekhov's finest stories, it is full of implication and demonstrates Pritchett's ability to establish distinctly different personalities within a small space through dramatization and a judicious selection of telling detail. Four men, Bert, Harry, Sid, and Ted, cycling through the English countryside anticipate quenching their thirst with a beer at a roadside bar as a reward for their efforts. The youngest, Bert, fantasizes about being served by a comely, sensual girl without children. But in this story of expectations and desires unfulfilled, both he and his three friends, only one of whom is married, will be disappointed. They expect to find the pub marked on Harry's map where the old Roman road crosses theirs to land's end. The remote, small house marked "Tavern" where they stop, however, is not what it purports to be. Giving an indication of the sense of loss to come, they see last year's empty swallow nests under the eaves of an open barn. Instead of the comely girl Bert imagined, they are greeted by a timid, frail, drab woman in her early thirties with a small child and are "dumbfounded" and "angry" to learn that, despite the sign, her establishment is neither bar nor public house and does not sell beer. She acknowledges that "'Many are disappointed,'" and can only offer them tea, bread, butter, and tomatoes. Even her own small expectations have not been met because she has failed to receive her morning delivery. While they wait to be served, Ted's lighter does not work, Bert finds the biscuit tin empty, and Harry is disappointed upon seeing the eagerly anticipated Roman road: "It's just grass." Although she is visibly pleased when the men stay for tea—the only one not disappointed—she appears ill:

> [H]er smile was vacant and faint like the smile fading on an old photograph. Her hair was short, an impure yellow, and the pale skin of her face and her neck and her breast seemed to be moist as if she had just got out of bed. The high strong light of this place drank all colour from her.[103]

But in her case, appearances do not deceive. Sid, the frontrunner on the road, and the one who convinces the others to stay, despite the meager fare, comes to understand why when he goes to the kitchen to pay their bill.

Shy, yet eager to tell her story, amidst the unwashed dishes and the unwashed clothes, the nameless hostess reveals that her grave illness was responsible for the family's move. Her husband, whose only sign of existence in the story is the man's waistcoat Sid sees in the kitchen, was forced to give up his job for their relocation. Much is left unsaid and unknown in the story, however, including the husband's whereabouts. Pritchett's metaphorical description of her as she wonders if she should speak further about her tribulations to Sid, suggests the loneliness and pathos of her existence: "She seemed to be standing on the edge of another country. The pale blue eyes seemed to be the pale sky of a faraway place where she had been living."[104] Though in better health, she too is disappointed. Isolated with her child in such a remote location, and struggling financially, she seems to regret sacrificing company for her health. Her solitude contrasts with the delightful unselfconscious comradeship the four men share. But at the end of the story, when they depart, she and her child remain holding hands in the middle of the road, waving good-bye enthusiastically until the men are nearly out of sight, their spirits obviously buoyed by their encounter with the men. And though Bert is once again dreaming of his beautiful girl, and his companions of their beers, they have made the best of their tea. "Many Are Disappointed" demonstrates the consolation of making the most of whatever life offers, especially when it fails to meet expectations or falls short of one's dreams. As Harry, the navigator, says, when Sid defers to him about staying: "If you can't have beer, you'd better take what you can get [...]." But the story also reaffirms the precious gift of human companionship—between friends and strangers alike, and parents and children.

Pritchett recalled its genesis in an interview. Once, while in Cornwall, he was either bicycling or walking along and wanted a drink. He was disappointed to encounter the same kind of woman serving tea in the same kind of establishment depicted in the story. Afterward, however, he imagined "how splendid it would be to have four men going along, each with his own particular fantasy or expectation, arriving at such a place. And that's how it grew."[105] He suddenly realized how four men on such a cycling tour would speak to one another. Not surprisingly, the quartet's dialogue in "Many Are Disappointed" is natural and realistic. What seems to be the preliminary sketch of the story appears in an early notebook:

> Four men between thirty[-]five & forty went away on a cycling tour together. They were all fair-haired & had blue eyes, were wind-reddened & wore CTC badges and when one said "A Gold Flake, Mr Blank" & the other replied, "Try my lighter, Mr White" it was considered a good joke. They

didn't laugh, but smiled full of happiness at their amusement
with each other. They studied maps, took an interest in
places & the lankiest wore a wedding ring. They had zip-up
jackets to keep out the wind & the urgent question was
"Will they be open at London Bridge. This trains late." They
were coming back. The East wind had been blowing all the
weekend. The sky larks sounded chill.
In Novel
Mr Blank Side Car Blimey I see there up Everest. Must 'ave
felt like one on the last lap in the ruddy headwind.
The girl came in. Mr J looked up but the others lowered
their eyes shyly.[106]

Once again, a number of details in Pritchett's story derive from the notebook fragment: the four men, one married, on a cycling tour; the joke involving the lighter; their amusement with each other; their interest in geography; the skylarks; and their shyness in approaching the tavern. But the story that Pritchett fashioned from these details owes far more to his elaborate, artful transmutation than his initial idea.

"The Satisfactory," a farcical wartime story, also derives from a situation Pritchett observed. In early 1941, against the background of air raids and food shortages, he expressed an interest in writing stories "about feasts, gluttony & huge feeds, of how a man sacrificed a beautiful girl for a chop, or seduced another by promises of unlimited salmon."[107] The relationship between gluttonous Mr. Plymbell and his thin secretary, Miss Tell, is based on a situation he observed in his daily visit to a restaurant where a woman was feeding a man: "There was a certain trade in food coupons during the war. [. . .] It seemed comical and yet passionate to me—a trouvail [sic]."[108] In "The Satisfactory," the unlikely couple is bound by their wartime exchange—her supplementary rations for his love and sex.

A couple Pritchett observed in his neighborhood inspired three stories—"The Key to My Heart," "Noisy Flushes the Birds," and "Noisy in the Doghouse"—first published separately in the *New Yorker* and later in book form as *The Key to My Heart*. He spoke of his find at length in correspondence with Brenan:

> My only pick-up is the local test-pilot, a nervous wreck & hard drinker and child, who has a "den", with practical jokes fitted up in it and small mechanical delights. At a party, he bows like a monkey man [?] [?] to the ladies & offers them a huge rusty door key saying "The Key to my heart." He was educated by the Jesuits who gave him a fixation about lavatories. He is always asking if one wants to pee, because the fathers stopped him at school! He lives

sinfully with a strong-minded divorced lady who bosses him. Unhappily they are heavy drinkers and pub-crawlers and that makes them too gregarious for our tastes....[109]

* * * *

The neighbours in this part of the world gradually reveal themselves. The Test Pilot next door [. . .] turns out to be rather much married, and to be full of awful little tricks. He arrives at a party holding a large door key with a label on it reading "The Key to My Heart", and a chain on his ankle when his mistress is taking it out of him. They are alcoholics. This lunatic is a bore and as you have always said, bores are invaluable material.[110]

Pritchett wrote this trilogy involving the pilot in homage to Chekhov, whom he admired for his ability and willingness to write any kind of story—including farce, the subgenre Pritchett believed "is very often tragedy out of uniform."[111] He thought that his keen visual and aural senses had a tendency to overpower other faculties—including the constructive one—often making observed things stand still. Therefore he was particularly pleased with this successful, fast-moving "series of farces" because they proved he could overcome this perceived shortcoming and make things move.[112] Although the stories were inspired by Pritchett's encounter with the test pilot and his mistress, they too are products of his imagination that involve much more than their actual counterparts.

The genesis of "On the Edge of the Cliff" seems to have been a composite of several experiences and observations. Once in Cornwall, Pritchett found himself sitting on the edge of the cliff admiring the view when he discovered the story's focus:

> I was thinking about just looking at the sea [. . .] and I would see the waves break over a small scroll then suddenly disappear. And I immediately thought, well everything's on the edge of something else here, at the moment. Even I am on the edge of something else. I'm inside myself, not to mention the cliff. I wasn't going to write a story about falling out of a cliff. But I wanted to therefore write a story about people on the edge of a change in their lives. [. . .] Landscapes mean a lot to me.[113]

And on another occasion he spoke of a large hole in the cliff being the first idea, and the second an ugly fair he passed while driving through Cornwall that suggested the story's counterpart. In his late seventies himself at the time of the story's composition, Pritchett believed that after collecting and studying them, he understood a great deal about old men that he could not have earlier in his life.[114] He used this experience to write sensitively and intimately about George in "On the Edge of the Cliff." Trevor, on the other hand, wrote many of his convincing portraits of the elderly when he was a relatively young man. Curiously enough, while praising Pritchett's collection of the same title in a discussion about the art of the short story with Pritchett, John Updike, Susan Hill, and host Robert Robinson, Trevor chose to talk about the title story "for a purely personal reason," even though he liked "Tea with Mrs. Bittell" and "The Fig Tree" best. He confessed that he himself had wanted to write something about the relationship between a very old man and a young girl. The idea had been "literally [. . .] knocking about at the back of [his] mind" for about seven years, but Pritchett's treatment freed him from this plan and he was grateful to him for writing it.[115] One of the most striking images in the story seems to have come from Pritchett's travels in Ireland. It was at Sea Point by the Martello Tower on sunny mornings in the winter that he saw "ones and twos of men in their sixties drive up, undress in a hut on the rocks below and dive into the famous Forty Foot."[116] The "inured cold-water swimmers" used to swimming naked at Sea Point probably inspired George's similar age-defying exploit in front of young Rowena. Finally, in describing the month-long visit in Malaga of Joanna Carrington, an "exquisite sylph of 23," when he himself was in his late sixties, Gerald Brenan mentioned "the sense of the incompatibility of young and old bodies"[117] that may have influenced Pritchett's treatment of this in the story. Short stories are often composites of several initially unrelated elements.

* * *

Surprisingly, Pritchett was already in his late forties when he first read Henry James's "The Real Thing" in a collection of the American's stories: "But one wonderful story—<u>The Real Thing</u>. I suppose you know it. I'd never read it before."[118] His appreciation of this story, and admiration for James's short fiction in general from this point on, signals his willingness to distance himself further from autobiographically based fiction: "I don't want to write like Hy James, I don't even [want?] to pinch his plots, and I certainly don't want his interests, but I do wish I could construct, think out, complicate and form things with the infinite convenience of the old monster."[119] The finest stories of his later years, including "When My Girl Comes Home," "The Camberwell Beauty," and "Blind Love," are more complex in their design and closer to James's in their genesis.

In a 1948 letter, Pritchett presented to Gerald Brenan the first of three prospective ideas for short stories drawn from his neighborhood. It became the basis for "When My Girl Comes Home":

> Still, by not writing, one notices the wreckage that is flowing by on the dirty stream of life. Really the people in this neighbourhood are fantastic.

> Our char's poor and disreputable sister-in-law, a woman of 70, slaves to the bone to welcome home her daughter of 25 years absent in Japan where she has borne a child by a Hindu and one by a Japanese. She arrived home today a woman of blinding, voluptuous beauty, educated, sensitive with excellent manners speaking three languages well; quite fitted to appear in the best society, after a childhood on the streets of London Town.[120]

Published twelve years later, it became Pritchett's favorite and most accomplished story, a tour de force of indirection and point of view that achieves novelistic scope in twenty thousand words. He used the details of the actual neighborhood situation as they were expressed in the letter and built the story on that foundation. But the story is in the telling. The reader experiences the story through the eyes and ears of a naïve young narrator who filters the dialogue and action of over twenty characters through his limited consciousness. Instead of imposing an elaborate plot, Pritchett used his strength, dialogue, to create an atmosphere full of rumor and innuendo. Like "Many Are Disappointed," this story is about expectations unfulfilled. The girl who comes home a woman, Hilda, comes from the streets of London, and, like Pritchett, grows beyond them, transcending her working-class world. But this story is not without precedent, even within Pritchett's oeuvre. "The Scapegoat," written many years earlier, also captures a sense of community or neighborhood feeling by incorporating a large cast of characters. Chekhov's "The Peasants," a famous story much admired by Pritchett, was undoubtedly an influence with its unusually large cast. Pritchett admired the way "Chekhov paid great attention to the peasants and local people"[121] and did the same with common English people.

According to Pritchett, the kernel for the title story in *The Camberwell Beauty*, Eudora Welty's personal favorite, came from a paragraph he read in a Wiltshire newspaper "about an antique dealer who got into serious trouble for keeping his young wife locked up in a shop."[122] For lack of anything else to write about, he used the newspaper story, supposedly basing the wife on a girl he knew in his late teens. (He believed that he was most successful when he went "back to some forgotten scene, incident or character, and join[ed] it to an idea or situation, however hazy, of to-day."[123]) From that point on, however, he "simply invented," confident in his knowledge of the antique trade he had acquired through observation of the shops: "you do know about life from looking at it."[124] He had demonstrated a more than passing interest in the trade many years before writing the story that helped him to capture the "collection of tricky eccentrics, watching one another like spies":[125]

> To go to Portobello Road on the off days is to be treated with suspicion: Are you in the trade? Their last Queen Anne mirror went on Thursday. [...] You

understand their attitude: Are you snooping around for someone? Who are you in with? They've never seen your face before. "Are you" —that inevitable stand-offish look says to you in a variety of accents from Joyce Grenfell's to Sairey Gamp's or from upper-class Cockney to van drivers' rhyming slang— "are you a 'member'?"[126]

Once again, it is through the story's point of view that Pritchett transforms a simple situation into a complex fiction. In fact, the self-deceived narrator, a failed antique dealer who returns to the district, obsessed by the girl who was the object of several dealers' desires, is the true focus. Not surprisingly, especially with a writer as widely read as Pritchett, some aspects of the story seem to have been influenced by literature itself. The older man's imprisonment of young Isabel recalls John Fowles' *The Collector*, her bugle blowing recalls Oscar's drum beating in Gunter Grass's *The Tin Drum*, and the absurd encounter at story's end between the narrator and Pliny is reminiscent of Humbert Humbert's showdown with the impotent Quilty in Nabokov's *Lolita*. With its wide range of characters and eerie portrayal of the antique trade, this richly imagined story proves again that Pritchett could write convincing fiction without relying on an autobiographical foundation.

The blocks out of which he created his fiction, however, were not always real. He was also capable of crafting stories that were purely products of his imagination. Although he often relied on his visual and aural acuity as a writer, he believed that the imagination could accomplish what the senses could not. During a 1941 BBC radio discussion, "Can Imagination Help?", he was already thinking about the perception of the blind:

> It's like our blind people, who, because they can't see, are in a position to know much more, where chairs and tables in a room exactly are. The blind man has to know more about them. He can't just open his eyes and content himself with our quick impression of a chair on his left and a table on his right, because he can't come by these quick impressions—he must know that the table is exactly ten feet from the wall and that the chair is six feet from the table.[127]

He speculated about what goes on in blind people's minds, and, in addition to trying to work it out intellectually, met two blind writers, one of whom, Borges, "did suggest certain things" over lunch together in Boston.[128] At some point, Pritchett heard that though people idealize them, "the blind are absolutely consumed with jealousy [. . .] to a degree [. . .] uncommon in ordinary life." He himself never perceived this, but he adopted the conclusion.[129] When he decided to write a story about a blind man, he was confident, as he was in writing "The Camberwell Beauty," that he knew a lot about the subject. As preparation for writing it, he simply closed his eyes and tried to live as though blind in order to experience how it felt: "So I used to try and go about like this [closes his eyes] and say where am I? What am I doing? And what would my reaction be? And so on."[130] There is no reason to doubt his claim that the story "Blind Love" is—whatever it may owe to Hawthorne's "The Birthmark" or Lawrence's "The Blind Man"—"totally outside [his] experience," nor that it was inspired by a story he heard about a blind man who went to a faith healer.[131] Like Henry James, Pritchett mastered the art of writing well outside his own experience, and, like William Trevor, proved that the imagination responsible for such rich transmutations of his personal experiences could synthesize powerful, realistic fiction all by itself.

The following chapter turns to important differences in the final published versions of Pritchett and Trevor stories dealing with similar themes. Despite their similarities, these texts are most remarkable for their differences. They reveal much about the essential individuality of Pritchett and Trevor, one a predominantly comic, the other a predominantly elegiac, even tragic, writer.

Chapter 7

The Roads Taken Make All the Difference: Comic Spirit and Tragic Comedian

Experience often tells us that the comic and the dire are often opposite sides of each other, yet somehow united. We laugh and cry at the same time.[1]

Although not one of Pritchett's most famous stories, "Our Wife" is nevertheless quintessentially Pritchettian. Like many others, it involves the conventional love triangle composed of two men and one woman, their relationships portrayed in comic rather than dramatic terms. The clever title anticipates the story's playfulness, conceived as a two-word summary, a provocative, titillating allusion to the central idea. In justifying its appropriateness, Pritchett claimed "the story was an explanation of the title and not a surprise; indeed the title was, in this sense, part of the story."[2]

Unlike Pritchett's other triangles, this isosceles regenerates during the narrative—a feature that determines the story's very structure. Instead of beginning in the past, the narrator, Tom, abandons strict chronology. He begins in the present, and in the present tense, choosing to tell the story out of sequence through a collage of character-revealing scenes. Chronologically speaking, the initial ménage à trois is formed when Tom, a bachelor, and narrator of the story, meets the married couple, Molly and Jack, while helping Jack remove a fallen tree from the couple's property in Southampton. Tom becomes the couple's repairman and friend and completes the initial trio. When Jack dies, Tom helps Molly sell Jack's collection of antique furniture, marries her, sells his boat, and is transferred to London, only to be returned to Southampton three months later where he meets Trevor, a man who must sell his own boat. The two sailors make a mutually beneficial, comical arrangement. Unbeknownst to Molly, whose acceptance of Tom's marriage proposal was contingent upon the sale of his boat, Tom appropriates Trevor's, docks it at a secret location, and, in exchange, Trevor assumes Tom's old role as the couple's handyman and third party, in effect completing a new ménage à trois. Trevor's motoring excursions with Molly in his Aston-Martin free Tom for sailing. The comedy results from the characters' unconventional responses to an ordinarily unsettling situation and the upheaval of marriage, death, widowhood, and remarriage. As in most of Pritchett's stories, the action is generated by, not separate from, the characters' reactions to their situation. Pritchett's emphasis on constantly evolving relationships and emotions takes precedence over a more conventional, elementary focus on plot.

The opening paragraph forecasts a story revolving around Molly, the wife. Consistent with his practice of defining characters through their behavioral idiosyncrasies rather than their appearances, Pritchett immediately captures Molly's contentious essence through a description of her eyes and her voice: "Even her little eyes long for trouble."[3] In the story's economical first sixteen lines, blending colloquial narration with dialogue, he fashions a small portrait of her, establishes her magnetic presence, and introduces all of the characters. A beguiling *provocatrice,* she commands male attention, not through her appearances, but through piquant, incessant verbal repartee. Her early disapproval of the Southampton sailors proves indicative of her indiscriminate criticism of all men, yet is another attention-getting strategy.

Invoking his penchant for comic figurative language and unusual, contextually poetic similes, Pritchett has Tom describe Molly as "noisy as a guttersnipe,"[4] an animated conversationalist with "a mouth that went sputtering gaily away like a motorbike,"[5] and recalls her first husband Jack's own comparison: "'As noisy as a blowlamp, but pretty.'"[6] Tom reveals that "when she laughed her eyebrows were like a pair of wings."[7] Furthermore, Molly's behavior and appearance, though adorable and terrier-like, are not particularly feminine. She constantly barks at men, gives "herself a little shake like a dog,"[8] and captivates them with her "little dog-like sniff"[9] and "small eyes."[10] Even her coiffure and mannerism are canine: "She wore her hair short and had the habit of giving a nervous sniff in the middle of her sentences—an original and wistful sound in the general clatter which attracted me."[11] Dispensing with traditional physical description enables Pritchett to focus on singular, comic terms of endearment that better communicate Jack's and Tom's attraction to their wife. The physical is subordinated to the emotional and behavioral in Pritchett's world. The two husbands and the reserved Trevor are united in their attraction to Molly's outspoken nature: "The noise is what has attracted us all to her. We have loved it. She has opinions about everything. She loves an argument. Anything will do."[12] Only Jack's death changes her. Usually exceptionally noisy, she becomes "a soundless person,"[13] temporarily muted while grieving for him. Compelled to create friction, Molly cannot accept that Tom and Jack are of identical height, for instance, and even after verifying the measurement, refuses to acknowledge the accuracy of the result. Under five feet tall, she is drawn to men over six feet.

The genesis of her contentious nature is explained by her childhood circumstances. She is a Captain's daughter[14] who "hated sailing more than anything,"[15] full of childhood resentment of her father's strict rules about boat behavior, undoubtedly jealous of his extra-familial passion. Paradoxically, Molly actively, if unconsciously, seeks men whose passion mirrors her father's. Her constant need to captivate two men at the same time is evident throughout the story, exemplified by a scene in a Kent coast pub witnessed by both Jack and Tom. While sitting between yet another pair of men at the bar, arguing about sailing, undoubtedly provoking their interest in her, the feisty Molly exclaims, "You want cooling down,"[16] and reaches unsuccessfully for a bucket of ice to pour on their heads.

She is simply too much for one man. Said "with a little malice," Jack's observation at the end of his life that "Molly is a girl who needs two husbands at a time" is something Tom "had never noticed," and leads him to conclude that Jack is either warning or nominating him, "—or even arranging for the succession."[17] Later in the story, when Jack has died, Tom, having taken his place as Molly's husband, concurs, interrupting their lovemaking to joke about Jack haunting the armoire: "Perhaps it was a sign that I was beginning to want help, as Jack had done. Hadn't he said she was a woman who needed two husbands?"[18] Indeed, throughout the story, Molly is always with men in tandem—initially Jack and Tom, then Tom and Trevor, the husband always requiring and receiving assistance from another man in order to satisfy Molly's insatiable appetite for talk and attention, not sex. This teamwork is demonstrated from the story's beginning. While married to Jack, she enlists Tom's help to remove a tree blown down in their garden. Recognizing that Jack "was not strong enough" as he hacked at the fallen tree "with a weak man's fury," Tom rescues the "exhausted" husband and completes the task while the couple observes. He further explains that he "was captured"[19] after coming to their aid, enlisted as a fix-it man, refurbishing their old house and repairing their car.

The first of Jack's furniture purchases, the wardrobe or armoire, as Molly insists on calling it, serves as Jack's legacy, surveying the bedroom after his death and, like Molly, eventually receives the attentions of the three men in succession: Jack, Tom, and Trevor. After having a "monumental row" about it with Jack, she threatened to send it back to the shop but Jack "saved it," making it "sacred in her eyes"[20] by writing a poem about it. Molly later dignifies this symbol of conflict with Jack, swearing it was brought over by the Huguenots in the seventeenth century. (The wardrobe is not the only inanimate object that commemorates enduring marital conflict. Tom paints a door bright blue after Molly and Jack quarrel about the colors.) After moving back to Southampton, Tom designates the ground floor for the armoire, but she insists that it be lifted into their bedroom, even though the move requires two days and three men. During Molly's marriage to Jack, Tom attempts to tame the wardrobe, repair the lock, and keep the doors from opening by themselves. Later, during his own marriage to Molly, he succeeds in repairing the temperamental lock. One night, however, "the door came groaning open like a hound."[21] The ensuing theatrical speculation about the "haunted" armoire, Jack's ghost, and the invading Huguenots makes comedy out of what would be a potentially disturbing issue in a more dramatic story: the first husband never ceasing to exist. Instead, the sexually uninterested Molly abandons their lovemaking to speculate, playing along to get more attention: "'It's weird,' she said. 'It *could* be haunted. Jack always said nothing is forgotten.' [. . .] She said that all things were permeated by the people who had touched them."[22] Consistent with the story's insistence on transference, Trevor is in turn summoned by Molly to assume the role of locksmith. Similarly, Tom, in speaking to Trevor of his wife, appropriates and reiterates Jack's description of her—"She's an old character"[23]—that Jack used when she was his wife.

Molly's need of male attention dictates her behavior. Especially volatile around "the stinking yachtsmen,"[24] she chastises them publicly, criticizing their maneuvers at the docks, yelling out "Stupid yachting people! [. . .] They can't even sail."[25] She constantly provokes men, claims they "are always up to something,"[26] and utters whatever will sustain a conversation and prolong their interest in her. In addition, Molly charges her men with guilt and conspiracy in order to fantasize about the prospect of their betrayal, first with Jack and Tom: "Look at Jack. Look at you. It's guilt."[27] And then with Tom and Trevor: "Guilt, that is what it is! There is something going on between you two. Men!"[28]

> I don't know what she meant by "guilt" and I don't think Jack did either, but it made us feel more interesting. She'd get on to "guilt" and say Jack was

oversexed, or turn about and say he was undersexed. Or that he threw money away. Or never spent a penny. Or was shut up in himself. Or perpetually running after other women.[29]

Later in the story, Molly contradicts herself in assessing Tom, preventing him from sleeping while indulging in a late-night conversation, initially exclaiming "I didn't know you were a jealous man,"[30] and, several hours later reversing herself, pleased that he is "not a jealous man."[31]

"Our Wife" questions assumptions about human relationships and offers a comic glimpse of an alternative ménage à trois free of male jealousy. When Jack dies, for instance, Tom mourns not only his passing, but his own unique relationship with both husband and wife: "I loved Jack. I loved her. I had, I felt, been married to both of them."[32] This is *Jules et Jim* in miniature without nostalgia, poignancy, anguish, or sexual passion. Although they find Molly's childlike self-absorption, provocation, and capriciousness fascinating, the men in "Our Wife" are only too pleased to share her burdensome maintenance. Instead of demanding exclusivity, dueling each other to win her love, they conspire to work together to achieve relationships of convenience. Physically, the men are seemingly interchangeable, all meeting Molly's height requirement. Jack and Tom are bound symbolically, measuring an identical six foot one and a half inches, and Tom and Trevor, Tom's inheritor, share a passion for sailing, Molly, and, eventually, Trevor's boat. When they first meet at the docks and admire Trevor's sloop, their echo-like dialogue anticipates their symbiosis:

> "She's *lovely*," I said.
> "*Lovely*," he said
> "*Cigarette?*" I said.
> "*Cigarette?* Thanks," he said. I am *selling* her."
> "*Selling her?*" I said.
> He nodded, I nodded.[33]
> (my italics)

Having recently purchased an Aston-Martin, Trevor cannot afford to keep his boat. Tom sympathizes with what he perceives to be Trevor's parallel dilemma, having been forced to sell his own boat in order to marry Molly: "he was a man like myself, a man giving up one thing for another. I sighed at our singular unity."[34] Of course the observation is comic. While both men are obliged to sell boats, Tom does so for his wife while Trevor, a bachelor, makes the sacrifice for a sports car.

In a comical reversal, boats, not women, fill Tom with desire. Upon regaining Southampton with Molly, he communicates their antipodal response to sailing: "There was the sea again. There were those *detested, lovely* white tents dotted over the water" (my italics).[35] Described as if they are attractive women, the boats seem to be a sex "substitute" for Tom, who yearns for them from his office window and dreams of Trevor's sloop as if she were a potential mistress, his boat-watching akin to girl-watching, the "fitful"[36] lovemaking with Molly giving him motivation for his eventual nautical dalliance:

> As I have said, there was always a sail or two in sight, and on week-ends there were scores of them. I had sometimes to go to the boatyards and there I would look with longing at some craft with beautiful lines on the stocks outside the sheds. [. . .] [I]t was while I was gazing in this weak mood at a beautiful, dark-blue thirty-foot sloop one afternoon that a man climbed out of her.[37]

Molly needs men to sacrifice their interests for her, clearly excited by the knowledge that they have relinquished something of importance to them in order to share her. She succeeds in exacting a promise from Tom before marrying him and, upon meeting Trevor, believes, erroneously, that he, like her husband, has renounced sailing and sold his boat as well:

> One more victory was in my wife's small eyes. And when Trevor arrived [. . .] she looked from one to the other of us to see who was the taller. I saw her immediate interest. Without realising it, I was at the beginning of a masterstroke. I had brought to the house a tall man who had given up boats. She was excited by the arrival of an ally.[38]

Ironically, Trevor is Tom's ally, not Molly's, and Tom welcomes another man to occupy his wife instead of finding him threatening.

"Our Wife" is full of comic irony and deception. Tom reveals that discord, not concord, is the secret of their compatibility. Molly's attacks on sailors were attacks on him, but, ironically, instead of creating irreconcilable friction, her criticism "was one of the bonds between us—her hatred of my boat."[39] Instead of being repelled by their conflict, "Trevor listened to [them] with appreciation as [they] wrangled. He lived alone, and he looked with pleasure at the excitements of home life."[40] Unable to control his passion for expensive antiques, Jack becomes a "secret furniture buyer,"[41] hides his acquisitions, and even enlists Tom in his clandestine operation. Despite "admiring [their] shadiness,"[42] upon discovering the secret holdings and uncovering the men's conspiracy, Molly sells all of the furniture except the wardrobe. Instead of being jealous of other women, she is jealous of objects that compete for male attention such as sailboats and furniture. Her obvious emotional insecurity inhibits her from making any direct expression of affection. She is a study in contradiction. At one point, Pritchett enables the reader to discern Molly's true emotions by having her express the opposite of what she feels. Obviously disturbed about Tom's transfer to London after Jack's death, for instance, she forces herself to endorse his departure enthusiastically with the pretext that it will separate him from the boat: "'It's a good thing!' she said. 'It will get you away from that idiotic boat.'"[43] Ironically, though "a victory for her opinion,"[44] it necessitates losing the man as well as the boat. Furthermore, Molly's condition for marriage is the sale of Tom's boat, but it is during her frightening ride on it that she consents to marry him, with the stipulation that he must sell it. The ride itself involves a comical reversal. Timid himself, Tom is emboldened by sailing, able to find the courage during their lone outing to express what he could not on land, while Molly, unusually outspoken and uninhibited, is frightened into silence, intimidated by the outing.

Although Molly openly mistrusts her men, accusing them of being deceitful, claiming "All yachtsmen are liars,"[45] she herself is dishonest and distorts the truth more than once to flatter herself. She intentionally misquotes Tom, for instance, claiming he has said his first wife haunted them, when in reality Tom had joked that the armoire was "haunted"[46] by the ghost of Molly's first husband, Jack. Similarly, in order to engage Trevor, she claims Tom was poor at handywork when he attended to all of their household problems while Jack was her husband. She even orders Tom to tell Trevor about his first wife's "iron boot,"[47] an obvious subterfuge too preposterous for even her to sustain. Her insistence that Tom allow Jack to depart to write poetry in peace is not out of concern for her husband's solitude, but fear of her own, a way of securing Tom's attention in place of her husband's.

* * *

There are a number of similarities between "Our Wife" and William Trevor's "The Piano Tuner's Wives," originally published in the *New Yorker*[48] twenty-six years later and collected in *After Rain* (1996). Like Pritchett's story, Trevor's has a small cast of characters and concerns their reactions to marriage, widowhood, remarriage, and third parties. In an inversion, the widow's remarriage in "Our Wife" is to a man she and her husband knew for many years, while the widower's remarriage in "The Piano Tuner's Wives" is to a woman he and his wife have known since they married. The men willingly share a wife in "Our Wife," even if she is legally bound to one man at a time, while two wives share the same husband in "The Piano Tuner's Wives," albeit at different stages of their lives. Whereas Trevor's women defer to the piano tuner, Pritchett's men defer to Molly. Both stories explore the meaning of fidelity, the relationship between love and jealousy, the human need for companionship, as well as exclusivity, deception, betrayal, and guilt. And, like Pritchett, Trevor accomplishes this through colloquial language.

Despite being bound by these elements, however, the two stories are most interesting for their contrasting treatment of similar material—treatment that contributes to defining Pritchett's and Trevor's different approaches to the short story, comic and near tragic. "The Piano Tuner's Wives" could never be retitled "Our Husband." Even the authors' ways of telling the stories betray their respective preferences for point of view: Pritchett's frequent use of the first-person singular and Trevor's predilection for omniscience; "Our Wife" is narrated by a character within while "The Piano Tuner's Wives" is told from without. Consistent with Pritchett's insistence on dramatization, "Our Wife" has more dialogue than "The Piano Tuner's Wives," giving the reader a more substantial interpretive role, while Trevor's more dominant exposition is reminiscent of the Irish oral storytelling tradition adapted for the printed page by Frank O'Connor, Liam O'Flaherty, and Sean O'Faolain. The narrative voice, a conscious written approximation of oral storytelling, is modeled after the colloquial influence of the *seanchai*—the old hearthside storyteller. One might meet such a storyteller on a County Mayo country road.[49] In reading the story with unmistakably Irish intonation to an audience in New York,[50] Trevor made a few alterations, stripping away a handful of words and phrases that would be less authentically colloquial when spoken aloud.

Instead of being set in a large English city, Trevor's story takes place in a small Irish village. "The Piano Tuner's Wives" is about Owen Francis Dromgould, a blind piano tuner living in rural Ireland, whose first marriage to Violet relegates her rival, Belle, to the role of spinster. When Violet dies, Belle, who has spent a lifetime yearning for Owen, finally becomes his wife. In contrast to Pritchett's employment of a regenerative ménage à trois, Trevor emphasizes the complete separation of two women living in the same village who, bound by their marriages to the same man, are forever conscious of each other's existence, though they never appear together with Owen. While there is little reverence for it in "Our Wife," the act of marriage in Trevor's story delineates strict and separate relationships.

Although admittedly not as provocative as Pritchett's, Trevor's title itself is, like the Englishman's, its story's summary—the narrative is an explanation of the title. In fact, imitative of the oral tradition, Trevor's teller opens with an eighteen-word synopsis: "Violet married the piano tuner when he was a young man. Belle married him when he was old."[51] Despite confining his narrative to the lives of three people, Trevor establishes a sense of community that pervades much of his fiction, particularly his Irish stories. The reader, therefore, is not the only observer. Interspersed as they are throughout the story, remarks and impressions of neighbors, parishioners, and community members alike create a collective consciousness, a chorus absent from Pritchett's story that gives the Trevor tale folkloric, historical breadth:

> There was a little more to it than that, because in choosing Violet to be his wife the piano tuner had rejected Belle, which was something everyone remembered when the second wedding was announced. "Well, she got the ruins of him anyway," a farmer of the neighbourhood remarked [. . .]. Others saw it similarly, though most of them would have put the matter differently.[52]

* * * *

> A decent interval had elapsed; no one in the church considered that the memory of Violet had not been honoured, that her passing had not been distressfully mourned.[53]

* * * *

> Some time later, when the new marriage had settled into a routine, people wondered if the piano tuner would begin to think about retiring. [. . .] But when, occasionally, this was put to him by the loquacious or the inquisitive he denied that anything of the kind was in his thoughts [. . .].[54]

* * * *

> They both knew, as they moved among the graves, that the parishioners who'd gone home were very much aware of the two who had been left behind.[55]

"The Piano Tuner's Wives" is quintessential Trevor in its Hardyesque poetry of loss. Owen's initial choice of Violet sentences Belle to forty years of quiet desperation. And although Belle finally wins his hand in old age, the ceremony itself cannot reclaim the past for her—her lost youth, her beauty, and the lifelong relationship with Owen she believes should have been hers. In place of the young Owen are "'the ruins of him,'"[56] and Belle must accept the consolation prize for having simply outlived her rival.

Yet the omniscient voice makes the reader painfully aware of Belle's own sense of loss. Instead of embarking on a new life, she is condemned to follow, literally and figuratively, in Violet's footsteps, her dearly achieved life with Owen haunted by Violet's ghost. The first wife is finally out of sight, but certainly not out of mind. During the church service, Belle and the parishioners are conscious of her occupying the same place and speaking the same words as Violet did forty years earlier. Though she found it too painful to attend Owen's first marriage, she remembers taking refuge in white-washing her chicken shed during it, crying, knowing that she was more beautiful and five years younger than the bride. Desperate to celebrate her Pyrrhic victory in old age, Belle implores the guests to stay after her ceremony because "she was determined to have a party."[57] But she is pitiful in her powerlessness. Time present has been usurped by time past.

While the absence of passion precludes jealousy in "Our Wife," Belle's passionate love for Owen in "The Piano Tuner's Wives" ensures her lifelong jealousy of Violet's long life with him. In fact, so devoted is she to the blind piano tuner that "there was no man in the town who lived up to the one who had been taken from her."[58] Tragically, Belle lives most of her solitary life sequestered at her brother's, minding the chickens instead of Owen, in mourning for the loss of a man who is very much alive but cannot see her. Violet freed Owen from his mother in a way that he, had he married Belle, would have freed her from her brother. Furthermore, relegated to the role of distant observer, Belle is envious of Violet's entirely successful management of Owen's career. He owes his life to Violet, who transforms him from a "charity"[59] into a respected member of the community. She finds pianos for him to tune, drives long distances, fixes rates, books subsequent tunings, and, a good businesswoman "keen on the profit,"[60] even exploits his violin playing, exacting payment for gigs that Owen formerly played for free. In stark contrast to the facile relationships of convenience in "Our Wife," Owen and Violet's is extraordinary for its fidelity and essential mutual dependence. More importantly, in describing his surroundings, Violet has created Owen's world for him. Even his memory is Violet's creation. After her death and his marriage to Belle, he witnesses everything through her eyes, making it impossible for Belle to wrest him away:

> He saw, through Violet's eyes, the gaunt façade of the McKirdys' house [. . .]. He saw the pallid face of the stationer in Kiliath. He saw his mother's eyes closed in death, her hands crossed on her breast. He saw the mountains, blue on some days, misted away to grey on others.[61]

While most spouses see things differently, Violet and Owen are unified in what Violet perceives for both of them.

In contrast to the playful, comic, and open speculation about the armoire being haunted by Jack in "Our Wife," Belle, although she hides her misery from Owen, is in torment, continually haunted by Violet. She cannot escape her, even after Violet's death, because Owen's first wife was, and remains, an inextricable part of his life: "He had become set in ways that had been hallowed in a marriage of nearly forty years: that was what was always there."[62] Belle "felt herself a follower"[63] from morning to night. Desperate to distance herself, she changes some of Violet's kitchen utensils, repaints banister rails and the inside of the front door, and replaces the kitchen floor vinyl. Even her food preparation is influenced by her predecessor, her dicing a reply to what she assumes was Violet's slicing. Achieving some kind of equilibrium is burdensome, vanquishing the ghost, futile:

> There was always this dichotomy: what to keep up, what to change. Was she giving in to Violet when she tended her flowerbeds? Was she giving in to pettiness when she threw away a frying-pan and three wooden spoons? Whatever Belle did she afterwards doubted herself. The dumpy figure of Violet, grey-haired as she had been in the end, her eyes gone small in the plumpness of her face, seemed irritatingly to command. And the unseeing husband they shared [...] did not know that his first wife had dressed badly, did not know she had thickened and become sloppy, did not know she had been an unclean cook.[64]

Ironically, Owen cannot appreciate any of the physical changes Belle imposes in the house. He is blind to them all. Nor can he appreciate Belle's beauty—a beauty that had always been excluded from Violet's usually exacting descriptions, she herself having been jealous of Belle's appearance, incapable of acknowledging it, purposely misrepresenting it whenever Owen enquired.

Needing to claim Owen for herself, Belle resorts to desperate measures in an attempt to replace Violet by replacing the images in Violet's descriptions. In her reports to Owen, she alters Violet's earlier accounts. The holy pictures in Mrs. Grehaghan's piano room are taken down, the somber wall paper replaced with striped; the Esso sign at Doocey's garage is changed to Texaco; the once silvery peacock at Barnagorm House is brass; the photograph of Owen's father shows a "sturdy," not a "lean," face; a schoolteacher has "false" not "gusty" teeth;[65] sofas have new covers with different patterns; the bright white of the McKirdys' façade is grey; the mountain blue, once a subtle blue of smoke, is suddenly, and ironically, forget-me-not blue. Finally, Belle removes Violet's plants from the flowerbeds and grasses them over, bold enough to attempt this metaphorical erasure of her memory. She seeks literally to change the landscape, however futile, unable to obliterate the longstanding images Violet embedded in Owen's mind's eye.

The final paragraphs shift to Owen's consciousness. He is blind, but his Miltonic vision enables him to see and accept his second wife's transformation of their physical world in order to claim Owen for herself. He understands that "It was hard on a new wife to be haunted by happiness."[66] Discreet and compassionate, Owen acquiesces, accepting that Belle "would win in the end because the living always do. And that seemed fair also, because Violet had won in the beginning and had had the better years."[67] Unlike Pritchett's comic muse that almost requires the unsaid, Trevor's empathic pathos is achieved through explicitness and his profound desire to convey his meaning. It is this crucial difference in tone that dictates their divergent technical approaches.

* * *

There are enough similarities between Pritchett's "Tea with Mrs. Bittell"[68] and Trevor's "Broken Homes"[69] to suggest that by the late 1970s, with its author now recognized as one of the most accomplished and prolific writers working in the genre, Trevor's work may have begun to impinge on Pritchett's. His avowed admiration for Pritchett's mastery of the genre was by this time reciprocated in Pritchett's unstinting praise for Trevor's own considerable achievements. In Pritchett's "Tea with Mrs. Bittell," the elderly widow of the title, out of step with modern England, befriends an awkward young homosexual who works at the tea counter of Murgatroyd and Foot's, a famous London shop that she frequents, and invites him regularly to tea on Wednesdays. In Trevor's "Broken Homes," Mrs. Malby, an elderly widow, also distanced from society, reluctantly participates in a community project, allowing a group of students from a local comprehensive school to repaint the interior of her home. Both stories involve the isolation of old women whose well-preserved old-world residences are ultimately violated by young strangers and may be viewed as tragicomic and comic-tragic allegories of modern England. Their authors capture rudderless early- to-mid-1970s England with its old norms and old forms of social deference disappearing, with the country questioning whether old political and social hierarchies remain functional.

The protagonists' families have been involved in the military: Mrs. Bittell's "had been Army people"[70] while Mrs. Malby's sons fought in the Second World War. They are representatives of a bygone England and proud curators of an antiquated way of life. Both women preserve history within their walls: the affluent Mrs. Bittell exhibits relics, heirlooms, and ancestral portraits in her apartment, while the more modest Mrs. Malby preserves interiors that have not changed for more than thirty years—since she read the two telegrams announcing the deaths of her sons on the same June day in 1945. Although largely out of circulation, they are conscious of the outside world encroaching on their sanctuaries, restricting their movement, and influencing their behavior. In "Tea with Mrs. Bittell," for instance, the tenants' complaints draw attention to "Clause 15" limiting Mrs. Bittell's piano playing to the hours between two and four o'clock in the afternoon despite her desperate appeal to play the piano anytime. She believes the doorman conspires to misinform visitors about her whereabouts, while in "Broken Homes" Mrs. Malby worries incessantly about the impression she makes on others, constantly fearing that any misunderstanding may result in accusations of senility that would condemn her to a rest home. Inevitably, both family names will be extinguished because Mrs. Malby's sons—her only children—were killed in the war, while the Bittell surname—a surname whose etymology is broached by an infrequent visitor ("Bataille," "Battle," "Bittell"[71])—cannot be passed on by her two married daughters. Once again, Mrs. Malby's physical decline suggests a fragile 1970s England: "She was a woman who had been tall but had shrunk a little with age and had become slightly bent. Scant white hair crowned a face that was touched with elderly freckling. Large brown eyes [. . .] were quieter than they had been, tired behind spectacles now."[72] Similarly, Pritchett's description of Mrs. Bittell conjures up an exhausted, ignorant England stagnating in tradition, out of fashion, resistant to change: "She was a *puddingy* woman, *reposing on a big sleepy belly;* her hair was white and she had *innocent blue eyes.* She wore, *as usual,* a loosely knitted pink jersey, low in the neck, a heather-mixture skirt, flat-heeled shoes, and *was very short*" (my italics).[73] Although the circumstances are different at the end of the stories, their respective crises render both women mute at that point. Similarly, the foreshadowing elements that intensify the inexorability of the old women's fates maintain both stories' suspense.

Once again, despite being bound by these similarities, the two stories, like the previous pair, are most interesting for their authors' contrasting treatment of similar material that further illustrates their divergent approaches to the short story. The very conception of the principal characters and their authors' accentuation of particular, stereotypically British attitudes determine the stories' markedly different tones. Mrs. Bittell is dim, gregarious, class-conscious, and condescending—a comical representative of British upper-middle-class pomposity. Mrs. Malby, on the other hand, is intelligent, circumspect, fiercely independent, and dignified—a somber embodiment of British discretion, integrity, and honor. Like many octogenarians living alone, Mrs. Malby has regular visitors who are not friends: two women from Meals on Wheels, a social worker, Reverend Bush, and the men who read the meters. Even her Jewish neighbors, the Kings, who have taken over her late husband's greengrocers, monitor her to see if she is alive.

The elderly women are both manipulated by their respective guests. Mrs. Malby's trouble begins inauspiciously with the arrival at her home of a nameless teacher from a local school, Tite Comprehensive. Trevor's limited third-person point of view immediately puts the reader in the old woman's consciousness. Like some mock Grim Reaper, everything about the man is poorly defined. Remarkably ordinary, he is small and "plump," with a featureless "plump face," grey stubble, and "grey hair falling into a fringe on his forehead"[74] that obscures his dark eyes. Mrs. Malby is struck by his noticeably slovenly, utilitarian appearance that seems incongruous with his position but is indicative of 1970s' waning social respect:

> He was untidily dressed, a turtlenecked red jersey beneath a jacket that had a ballpoint pen and a pencil sticking out of the breast pocket. When he stood up his black corduroy trousers developed concertina creases. Nowadays you saw a lot of men like this, Mrs. Malby said to herself.[75]

Armed with a hackneyed appeal to Mrs. Malby's sense of community, the teacher takes advantage of her polite reception, and, despite her protestations, through sheer insistence, arranges for a group of the school's students to repaint the interior of her house. Ironically, Mrs. Malby, fearful of misunderstanding his discourse "due to her slight deafness,"[76] hears his every word, while the schoolteacher, espousing the importance of communication, willingly ignores her plea to leave her home alone. Moreover, the nameless teacher, not the eighty-seven-year-old, senility-fearing Mrs. Malby, constantly repeats himself: "to her horror, he began all over again, as if she hadn't heard a thing he'd been saying."[77] Rife with hypocrisy, he patronizes Mrs. Malby, complimenting her as "'marvellous'" and "'splendid for eighty-seven'"[78] while attempting to enlist her sympathy and convince her of the project's mutual benefits: "'We're trying to help them,' he said, 'and of course we're trying to help you. The policy is to foster a deeper understanding.' He smiled, displaying small, evenly arranged teeth. 'Between generations,' he added."[79] Ironically, his condescending, aggressive recruitment of the reluctant Mrs. Malby blinds him to his violation of the policy. So intent is he on accomplishing his mission—obtaining her consent for students from broken homes to repaint her house free of charge—he argues for the principle of the "experiment in community relations"[80] above its practicality. After all, as the rational Mrs. Malby observes, "'it's just that my kitchen isn't really in need of decoration. [. . .] It's just that my kitchen is really quite nice.'"[81] In a portentous foreshadowing, his appearance reminds her of a history book picture of a Roundhead with its attendant associations of English Civil War unrest and revolution presaging the chaos his troops will bring to her own home. She does not understand how painting a home unnecessarily will benefit schoolchildren from broken homes the teacher promises to send the following Tuesday and is understandably fearful of the appointment, having passed the ugly modern school site and heard the unruly children shouting obscenities.

While Mrs. Malby avoids interacting with young people, the more sociable Mrs. Bittell actively seeks their company and unwittingly invites trouble into her home. Her charity, however, is self-serving, her unbecoming, pretentious, class-conscious posturing evident from the story's opening sentence:

> She liked to say it was "inconvenient," on the general ground that a lady should appear to complain beautifully when doing a kindness to someone outside her own class; lately she had been keeping an afternoon for a rather "quaint" person, a young man called Sidney, one of a red-jacketed ballet who hopped about at the busy tea counter in Murgatroyd and Foot's.[82]

Pritchett's use of limited third person facilitates the immediate exposure of Mrs. Bittell's ignorance and self-delusion. Her presumption of superiority is borne of ignorance rather than arrogance, however, making her sympathetic while forecasting her eventual comeuppance. In contrast to the perspicacious Mrs. Malby, who attempts to keep the wayward children from gaining access to her home, Mrs. Bittell feels it is her responsibility to enlighten troubled youths, especially those of an inferior class, despite being a poor judge of their character. She enjoys inviting "'quaint'" people such as Sidney and his friend Rupert to tea, but, reminiscent of Flannery O'Connor's naïve, casually religious characters, is blind to their amoral, sinister designs, their complete rejection of morality and religion.

Pritchett's comedy in "Tea with Mrs. Bittell" comes from situational and verbal irony—the obvious disparity between Mrs. Bittell's unreliable perceptions and reality. Initially, because the melodramatic circumstances of Sidney's "sad situation" are relayed through her consciousness, they cannot be verified: he is the lonely son of a coal-mining father languishing in hospital for years with "that dreadful thing miners get."[83] Yet in a subsequent conversation, Sidney corrects her: slate, not coal, is killing his father. While there was great sympathy for coal miners in the early 1970s, the reader can see Sidney exaggerating the hazards of slate mining in order to cultivate Mrs. Bittell's sympathy. Comically, removed as she is, the closest she can come to identifying the cold of the slate mines is to compare it to her sister

Dolly's identical impression while descending the catacombs outside Rome, "even though wearing a coat."[84] Mrs. Bittell's naïveté makes her laughably gullible. She is easy prey for Sidney and Rupert, oblivious as she is to their deception. Filtered through her consciousness, Sidney's description of the slate mines and Rupert's description of his vacation in the Bahamas reveal to the reader that they have not been to either place. Sidney describes mines in terms of Mrs. Bittell's block of flats and "like a buried church [. . .] in darkness,"[85] while Rupert's Bahamas have Victorians, English antiques, and fox-hunting pictures instead of beaches and palm trees. She tells her sister "The younger generation are hungry for Faith,"[86] heartened to see Sidney attend church with a friend, in a sign of Christian fellowship. Yet, Mrs. Bittell misjudges the young once again. Easily sated, the friend, Rupert, stops coming shortly thereafter.

Trevor and Pritchett invest their stories with a sense of place and history. Mrs. Malby's exact age and the story's internal dating make 1890 her year of birth and 1976 the year of the story's action. Trevor's economical, precise use of details indicates that she is decidedly lower-middle class. She lives on London's Catherine Street where her late husband was a greengrocer, owns budgerigars, and has geraniums on her window-sill. The bird was a popular pet for elderly people living alone in apartments, and the hearty geraniums were common in the 1970s, both species ideal for the elderly because they require minimal maintenance. But the story is not limited to the recent past and the adept use of types. The nameless teacher's resemblance to the Roundhead picture Mrs. Malby saw in grade school suggests a comical parallel—the teacher as Roundhead leading his Parliamentary charges (the students) against the Royalists (the establishment). Mrs. Malby, representing the establishment, and supported by Mr. King, survives, but sustains casualties from the rebellion.

In contrast to Mrs. Malby's modest residence above the greengrocers, Mrs. Bittell's is an expansive, lavishly furnished apartment opposite a fashionable Anglican Church in an affluent neighborhood—likely Belgravia—overlooking the embassies. Her large drawing-room "owned a large part of the London sky where the clouds prospered" and she looks down literally and figuratively at the lower classes. There are no budgerigars and geraniums here, only impressive distances between sofas, "satiny chairs and other fine things."[87] Upon arriving for tea, Sidney is immediately drawn to one of the large windows from which he spies the high-rise building "where he and his family distantly lived." He shares the experience of looking down on the lower class to which he belongs: "It was a high-rise block, a mile away, howling like cats, he told her, with the tenants' radios and television sets and children."[88] Though fifteen years older than the children in "Broken Homes," Sidney appears to be a product of a similar environment.

Sidney and Rupert represent many people of their generation bereft of morality, preying on their principled elders. Rupert's appearance makes him a mock satanic character, the Prince of Darkness incognito. His eyes are hidden by dark glasses, "as if, as yet, shy of the spiritual life."[89] And when he takes them off, he must squint in the light. Returning after his absence he "still looked unlike a real man but more like some photograph of a man."[90] Sidney's mention of the supposedly disturbing "undercurrents"[91] at Murgatroyd and Foot's subtly reinforces the reader's sense of Rupert's deviousness and his link to the underworld.

Mrs. Bittell's casual involvement with the Anglican Church contrasts with Mrs. Malby's sincere devotion to a strict moral code. She is sentimentally religious, not a devout believer, her Sunday service offering a pleasant ritual during which she can "snooze."[92] She speaks of "'The Kingdom of Heaven,'"[93] and is constantly proselytizing, only briefly aware of her hypocrisy: "'We must turn to God,' she said, though she knew that years ago [when her husband deserted her,] she had done nothing of the sort, that outrage had possessed her."[94] She does not practice what she preaches. Of course, this attitude makes her adoption and encouragement of Sidney all the more absurd and comical, especially her consoling him for his loss of Rupert. In contrast to Mrs. Bittell's unquestioned, sentimentalized Christianity is Mrs. Malby's religious skepticism. Yet she is morally devout without religion. Her speculation about death reveals her allegiance to the "human conscience" as a moral guide, instead of to a "loving omnipotent God."[95]

Anticipation of the cruel, undeserving punishment from which she cannot escape makes Mrs. Malby's plight all the more heartbreaking. Although she has successfully escaped until this point, she finally falls prey to the suggested disintegration of British society through her contact with its youths. Things have fallen apart. The troop of Tite Comprehensive's inarticulate, illiterate students from broken homes inadvertently violates the sanctity of her own. In a further grim irony, the students' impoverished language ensures a lack of communication "Between the generations," not a "deeper understanding," putting civilization itself in question. Instead of greeting her with respect, they employ informal language more appropriate for their adolescent peers. Victims themselves, they have adopted their generation's meaningless, all-purpose, colloquial expressions such as "no problem." They are frightening in their anonymity. Except for their different hair colors, they have identical uniforms: blue jeans with patches and sport badges advertising ephemeral mid-1970s mass culture: *Hot Jam-roll, Jaws*[96] and *Bay City Rollers*."[97] The lone girl even sports an irreverent T-shirt emblazoned with "I Lay Down with Jesus." American television culture infiltrating England marks the children as well. One of the boys responds to his friend using a famous actor's trademark line, "Who loves ya, baby?", from a popular American series.[98] When they arrive at her doorstep, their faulty grammar and unconscious disrespect offer a sharp contrast to Mrs. Malby's speech and demeanor:

> "We come to do your kitchen out," the blond boy said.
> "You Mrs. Wheeler then?"
> "No, no. I'm Mrs. Malby."[. . .]
> "I thought he says Wheeler."
> "Wheeler's the geyser in the paint shop," the fuzzy-haired boy said.[99]

* * * *

> "We come to paint out the old ma's kitchen," the boy called Billo explained. "We was carrying out instruction, mister."[100]

Upon discovering the children painting her kitchen instead of merely washing the walls, as she had requested when they arrived, Mrs. Malby turns off their portable radio blaring with "a voice inexpertly singing, a tuneless twanging." One of the boys exclaims "Hey, sod it, missus."[101] They are supposed to improve her home, but instead they defile it, as well as the memories associated with her "quiet shell-pink" kitchen walls with white trim, and leave a gaudy, indelible souvenir of their disturbing visit in its place—the "hideous yellow"[102] and blue enamel scheme that she will never have the means to redo in her lifetime. During their anarchic visit, sanctioned by the nameless teacher, they traumatize her with raucous music, have sex in her bed, release her budgerigars, stain the carpet with paint, address her impolitely, and even forget her name. Disenchanted, irresponsible, and detached, the children from broken homes are the casualties of an unhealthy society. Their unkempt appearance, crude, disrespectful language, and poor manners force Mrs. Malby to confront the erosion of the world as she knows it. In a striking parallel, for Pritchett's Mrs. Bittell the revelation of foul play at Murgatroyd and Foot's and Sidney's three-week absence from church signals nothing short of the fall of the British Empire. Her Old England has disappeared, leaving her in a foreign city:

> But now she saw that the city had become a swarming bazaar: swarms of foreigners of all colours—Arabs, Indians, Chinese, Japanese, and all people

jabbering languages she had never heard—came in phalanges down the pavements, their eyes avid for loot. If she paused because she heard an English voice, she was pushed and trodden on, more than once laughed at.[103]

As Trevor does in many of his English stories, such as "The Penthouse Apartment,"—also involving an old, fragile widow victimized by circumstances beyond her control—he incorporates seemingly inconsequential details upon which his characters' fates turn. Mrs. Malby knows she is ultimately responsible for her predicament. Her tacit acceptance of the schoolteacher's appointment introduces a potentially disastrous situation over which she has little control. Paralyzed by her fear of seeming senile, and anxious to please the community, she refrains from rejecting him outright. Crucial omissions bring about her inevitable victimization. Although a youthful eighty-six, she lacks the energy required to defend her interests, powerless to change the unalterable course of events once they have been set in motion. Flustered as she is during her meeting with the teacher, she neglects to ask his name—information that would have given her recourse to cancel her precipitous rendezvous. When the children do arrive with their paints, she asks them to wash the walls instead of painting them, but, against her better judgment, leaves them unsupervised while she shops, deceiving herself into believing they are carrying out her orders in her absence. Mrs. Malby's constant analysis shows her to be a shrewd, rational woman, hypersensitive to the reactions others have to her behavior. Yet she fails to follow her intuition. While shopping, she reassures herself that the children are not painting merely because she did not discuss colors with the teacher. Later, when her kitchen is irrevocably altered, she refrains from complaining further to her neighbors, the Kings, fearing they would consider her a nuisance for agreeing to let children into her kitchen to paint and then making a fuss.

Trevor's singular blending of painful, elegiac irony with absurd comedy, however, makes what would be insupportably dour situations tolerable—simultaneously disturbing and comic. When she seeks refuge in her bedroom, for instance, Mrs. Malby finds the girl and one of the boys having casual sex, defiling the bed she shared with her husband in which she conceived her two boys. Even her only companions, her pathetic, inadequate, inhuman substitute for the boys—the two budgies—have been displaced. In several lines, Trevor manages to capture the disturbance of the trespassing as well as its absurd comedy:

> They were in her bed. Their clothes were all over the floor. Her two budgerigars were flying about the room. Protruding from sheets and blankets

she could see the boy's naked shoulders and the back of his head. The girl poked her face up from under him. She gazed at Mrs. Malby. "It's not them," she whispered to the boy. "It's the woman."

"Hi there, missus." The boy twisted his head round. [. . .]

"Sorry," the girl said.

"Why are they up here? Why have you let my birds out? You've no right to behave like this."

"We needed sex," the girl explained.

The budgerigars were perched on the looking-glass on the dressing table, beadily surveying the scene.

"They're great, them budgies," the boy said.[104]

On the other hand, comic situational and dramatic irony resulting from the old woman's ignorance pervades "Tea with Mrs Bittell." This is a woman, after all, whose "mind moved as slowly as her feet":[105] "Questions took a long time sinking into Mrs. Bittell's head, which was clouded by kindness and manners and a pride in her relics."[106] The commentary she gives Sidney on her ancestral portraits reveals that she "had her own pride in her family's crimes."[107] A judge from her mother's family purportedly sentenced his own son to death. Her brief, subjective encapsulation of British history includes her self-portrayal as "the victim of history" that, unbeknownst to her, she will prove to be at the end of the story:

> She had known the family pictures all her life as furniture: they represented the boredom of centuries, of now meaningless anger. When her husband left her she had seen herself as a woman ruined by generations of reckless plunderers of land, putting down rebellions, fighting wars, gambling and drinking away their money, building big houses, losing their land to lawyers and farmers, grabbing the money of their wives and quarrelling with their children. She saw herself with unassuming pride as the victim of history. Even in the Mansions—her rising anger told her—her own class had betrayed her.[108]

While she gives Sidney the tour, he is mostly interested in the value of her antiques. She misinterprets his question about the Duke of Wellington's sincerity, sees him "struggling with a moral question," and wonders if he, like her, feels "that sincerity, honesty, consideration, were wearing thin in modern life."[109] Deluded and self-deceived, she compares Sidney with her ancestors, "and even with the Duke of Wellington," unaware of his ulterior designs: "Sidney was reaching towards the light; she could not say her forebears had ever done so."[110] Her encouragement of Sidney is comical, especially her consolation for his loss of Rupert, oblivious as she is to their homosexuality even while Sidney is sobbing with his head on her bosom, his howl "like a dog's howling at the moon."[111] Despite his open proclamation amidst tears—"I loved him"—Mrs. Bittell is blind to the nature of Sidney's involvement with Rupert. She merely continues her relentless evangelical proselytizing: "Love is never lost. In the Kingdom of Heaven, love is never lost, Sidney dear." Intensifying the irony is her claim of empathy because she has "been through it too."[112] Sidney's look of disbelief in reaction to this statement makes her uncomfortable enough to provoke further irony. Not only is she unaware of Sidney's sexual identity, she was oblivious to her husband's:

> And even while she felt compassion, she felt disturbed. Why had it never occurred to her, in her miserable troubles with her husband, long ago over, but for which her daughters blamed her, that there had been no "other woman"?[113]

Mrs. Bittell declares "There is no separation for the children of God"[114]—unaware of Sidney's lack of belief during his complete separation from Rupert. When Sidney leaves, she promises to pray for him and Rupert, doing so later while falling asleep: "Sidney and Rupert are children of God made in His image and likeness."[115] Of course, nothing is further from the truth. A simple, sentimental woman, she takes solace in clichés. Enraged by reports of random violence, she remembers one from the vicar's sermon: "'The darkest hour precedes the dawn.' This was a dark hour for the world and for Sidney." She tells Sidney that when "everything is dark […] we must pour in more love. We must open the floodgates."[116] Her prayers are answered when she sees Rupert and Sidney standing together in church: "The miracle had occurred. Rupert had returned. […] All the old prayers of her life that had never been answered became like rubbish. A real miracle had been granted her."[117] The deluded Mrs. Bittell continues to believe this, remarking how "delightful" it is "to see a miracle running" when the men—Rupert in particular—run for their bus, and later, when the two come to tea, expressing disappointment—upon learning that Rupert has been ill—"not to see the miracle in perfect health."[118]

The unsaid element is far more pronounced in "Tea with Mrs. Bittell" than in "Broken Homes." In a number of instances, the reader is entrusted to make inferences from indeterminate elements in the text. The convincing interpretation of the unsaid depends on the reader's ability to find plausible explanations that are consistent with the interpretation of the story as a whole. According to Sidney, he resigned from Murgatroyd and Foot's to protest the store's poor handling of staff theft and assumes that Rupert left the store for the same reason. A variety of goods were supposedly "'wheeled off to delivery and loaded onto vans'"[119] while the management looked the other way. Although Sidney's naïveté throughout the story seems as sincere as Mrs. Bittell's, the reader cannot be absolutely certain about the extent of Sidney's or Rupert's involvement in or knowledge of the situation. While Sidney might be telling the truth, Rupert may, nevertheless, have deceived him. On the other hand, there is reason to believe that Sidney has become Rupert's accomplice, perhaps willing to help him in exchange for a relationship. As the "excited familiar of the place," Sidney's eagerness to show Rupert "'Lily'"[120] during their tea at Mrs. Bittell's proves that Sidney had informed Rupert about the portrait of Psyche—possibly a Lely copy[121]— prior to tea. And Rupert's all too obvious evaluation of Mrs. Bittell's expensive antiques and paintings—even her teacups—indicates that he is indeed a thief, not merely an antiquarian. His mysterious comings and goings, subsequent two-month absence, obvious loss of weight, gaunt face, and pallor upon his return suggest that instead of spending his time sunning himself on vacation in the Bahamas as he explained, Rupert had most likely been incarcerated. The reader suspects that he was responsible for the disappearance of the six Persian rugs at Murgatroyd and Foot's and served time for taking them. While Sidney's sob story about his ill father may be true, it may simply be a way of winning Mrs. Bittell's sympathy. Rupert's and Sidney's class origins remain dubious because one cannot be certain of their identities. The coincidence that both her grandson and Sidney's friend share the name Rupert, as well as Rupert's climactic appearance in her apartment at the end of the story, remain unexplained.

* * *

Trevor distills the essence of his story's grim irony in the title itself: "Broken Homes." Used several times by the nameless teacher to excuse the schoolchildren's reckless, amoral behavior, the term is applicable to the Malby household in an entirely different way. Although she believes that the tragedy in her life "was no longer a nightmare," Mrs. Malby remains haunted by the loss of her sons, even though she has "come to terms with being on her own."[122] She loves her house, Catherine Street, and her daily routine. Yet strong feelings, deeply repressed, emerge during her unsettling battle with the children. Exhaustion from rubbing the paint stains out of her carpet gives way to disorientation: "Everything that had happened in the last few hours felt like a dream; it also had the feeling of plays she had seen on television; the one thing it wasn't like was reality."[123] In limbo between the real and the imagined, Mrs. Malby escapes from the all too nightmarish reality of both her present and her past into the wishful daydream world of possibility, expressed through Trevor's trademark use of the conditional tense:

> In a dream anything *could* happen next: she *might* suddenly find herself forty years younger, Derek and Roy *might* be alive. She *might* be even younger; Dr Ramsey *might* be telling her she was pregnant. In a television play it *would* be different: the children who had come to her house *might* kill her. What she hoped for from reality was that order *would* be restored in her kitchen, that all the paint *would* be washed away from her walls as she had wiped it from her carpets, that the misunderstanding *would* be over.[124] (my italics)

Later, the obliteration of the neat straight lines in her kitchen where the shell-pink met the white of the woodwork makes her recall a particularly vivid dream she had the previous week. In it, the Prime Minister had stated on television that the Germans had been invited to invade England since England could not manage to look after herself. So certain was Mrs. Malby of having seen the Prime Minister saying that he and the Leader of the Opposition had agreed invasion was the best for England that she consulted the newspapers for verification the following day. An obvious distortion of Second World War British resolve, and an extension of Chamberlain's fateful consent to the Munich Pact, Mrs. Malby's dream—her rewriting of history—expresses regret, her desire to alter the past, to retrieve the period preceding her boys' deaths. Inexplicably, the teacher's departure makes her think of her sons, Derek and Roy. Suddenly, she wants to tell him about them, but her desire to speak evokes an apocalyptic vision: "she imagined their bodies, as she used to in the past, soon after they'd been killed. They lay on desert sand, desert birds swooped down on them. Their four eyes were gone."[125] Clearly, despite her denial, "the awful double wound" remains in her consciousness. The society that her boys died fighting for is disintegrating. In a further twist, her boys died to save the free world and end the persecution of the Jews, who, represented by the Jewish couple, Mr. and Mrs. King, have taken her sons' places in the greengrocers.

* * *

Unlike Trevor's wholly realistic story, Pritchett's incorporates symbolism, albeit of a comic nature. The working title for "Tea with Mrs. Bittell," "Psyche," emphasizes the central symbol, the portrait of Psyche and Cupid on display in the old woman's drawing room, a supposed Lely copy Mr. Bittell wished to sell to Christie's. Pritchett suggests parallels between the allegorical centerpiece in Apuleius's *Golden Ass,* "Cupid and Psyche," and his short story. A comparison of the similar plots reveals comic disparities. Pritchett's fractured version is a mock literary, homosexual parody, with Rupert as Cupid, Sidney as Psyche, and Mrs. Bittell as Jupiter, reuniting Sidney with Rupert through prayer. Like Cupid's abandonment of Psyche, Mr. Bittell abandons Mrs. Bittell, and Rupert abandons Sidney, who wanders in search of his lover until Mrs. Bittell takes pity on him and prays for him. She thinks, foolishly and ironically, that her prayers are instrumental in reuniting him with Rupert. Her ignorance extends to the artist's rendering. For her, "Psyche was part of the furniture."[126] She believes Cupid was blind and that Psyche did not have legs. Her personalized, sentimental interpretation of the portrait contributes to the unexpected pathos at the end of the story when the painting is stolen from under her unsuspecting eyes, her soul (Psyche) taken by Rupert whose desire is purely material: "Of course—Psyche was the soul, a 'thee,' the thee of her dead baby, herself as a young girl before she married, a loss, a sadness. And Sidney too had a 'thee.'"[127]

The endings are consistent with their stories' respective approaches to their subjects. Pritchett's is humorous, if disturbing, while Trevor's sublimation of Mrs. Malby, with tragicomic touches, evokes heartbreaking pathos. In "Broken Homes," summoned by Mr. King when the unsupervised children have gone out of control, the schoolteacher defends their sloppy work and irresponsible behavior with his mantra-like excuse: "'These kids come from broken homes.'"[128] At the height of the confrontation, once the damage has been done, he begrudgingly offers to clean the carpet stains. At this point, Mrs. Malby makes her final stand in front of both Mr. King and the schoolteacher, yet however justified her complaint, her enfeebled voice betrays her, just as it had when she confronted the children in her bedroom:

> "But what about my kitchen?" she whispered. She cleared her throat because her whispering could hardly be heard.
> "My kitchen?" she whispered again.
> "What about it, Mrs. Malby?"
> "I didn't want it painted."
> "Oh, don't be silly now."[129]

The entire venture is farcically hypocritical, notable for both the pronounced absence of communication between generations and its lack of benefit to the old widow. The nameless teacher continues to pay lip service to a public relations scam, the children have learned nothing, and Mrs. Malby has been traumatized. At the end of the story, Trevor reveals her feelings through an unusually intimate limited third-person point of view that reads as if it has been converted from the first-person singular. His remarkable ability to empathize with beleaguered characters enables readers to enter their consciousness. Fear silences her in the end, forcing her to hold her tongue:

> She knew she mustn't speak. She'd known she mustn't when the Kings had been there; she knew she mustn't now. [. . .] She might have complained to the man as he rubbed at her carpets that the carpets would never be the same again. She watched him, not saying anything, not wishing to be regarded as a nuisance. [. . .] If she became a nuisance the teacher and the Kings would drift on to the same side, and the Reverend Bush would somehow be on that side also, and Miss Tingle, and even Mrs. Grove and Mrs. Halbert. They would agree among themselves that what had happened had to do with her elderliness, with her not understanding that children who brought paint into a kitchen were naturally going to use it.[130]

In the absence of someone with whom she can safely share her profound loss, the catastrophe that "smashed everything to pieces," she has an impulse to describe her happy pre-War family to the schoolteacher and explain the tragic circumstances that resulted in her own broken home. Yet she is once again inhibited "because it would have been difficult to begin, because in the effort there'd be the danger of seeming senile."[131] Ultimately, she claims responsibility for the breakdown in communication between herself and the children. She is surprisingly stoical about the episode as are many of Trevor's characters, who learn that circumstances, not people, are at the root of most suffering. The children are not malicious, merely misguided, victims themselves of a world increasingly bereft of morality.

In contrast to the protracted, psychologically taxing occupation of Mrs. Malby's flat, the invasion of Mrs. Bittell's, although perhaps stealthily conceived, is sudden, dramatic, and violent; yet it is described in comic terms that all but obscure its mock gothic horror. Pritchett's ending brings together all the story's elements—Mrs. Bittell's naïveté, her pitiful charity, her proselytizing, Psyche, her miscalculation of Rupert, "Clause 15," and her relationship with Sidney. Unlike Mrs. Malby, she is oblivious to her victim's role until the very end. She returns late one Sunday afternoon to her apartment expecting her grandson, Rupert. His suitcase and shoes appear to be in the hall and the door is open. But instead of her Rupert, she finds Sidney's Rupert in stockinged feet in her bedroom, rifling through her possessions. He stands up smiling ghoulishly with a bracelet in his hand whereupon Mrs. Bittell calls out calmly, as if to her grandson, that there is a man in her bedroom while she shuts and locks its door. Suddenly, the scene becomes mock Hitchcockian as she hears the door handle being wrenched by the satanic character she once believed angelic. Like Mrs. Malby, she is momentarily silenced by her circumstances:

> But now Mrs. Bittell had exhausted the words she could speak. She opened her mouth to scream, but no sound came. Lead seemed to fill her legs, her heart thundered in her ears; she saw through the doorway of the drawing-room (miles away, it seemed) the telephone. She began a slow trudge that seemed to take hours, as in a dream, while the man returned to hammering at the door, shouting, "I'll break your bloody neck, you silly old bitch."[132]

Upon arriving in the hall, she is stunned at what she sees. Psyche is missing, her frame empty—perhaps having walked away on the legs the old woman believed the mythological character did not have. She bangs the piano keys, "defying the whole block of flats,"[133] desperately hoping her intentional violation of "Clause 15" will provoke her neighbors into action, as Rupert simultaneously bangs on the closed bedroom door. The telephone rings repeatedly but Mrs. Bittell continues to bang on the keys while Rupert breaks through the door and makes his way toward her. But he slips on the parquet and falls on his back. Although she "had always planned to speak gently" if someone attacked her, and "ask them why they were so unhappy and had they forgotten they were children of God," Mrs. Bittell changes her mind when she wets herself, "like a child, all down her legs."[134] Visibly humiliated, she trips him by tipping over the piano stool. Instead of succumbing to the attack, she "became as strong as History," picks up the brass table lamp—the same object with which her husband had once hit her and with which she imagined she would defend herself earlier in the story if Sidney attacked her—and executes her daydream plan triumphantly, bashing Rupert several times on the neck and head before fainting.[135] Her neighbors and the doorman find her as the wounded burglar attempts to put on his shoes in the hallway and escape.

Yet consistent with a number of Pritchett endings, that of "Tea with Mrs. Bittell" resists closure, inviting the reader's speculation. "Tell Sidney to come," murmurs the old woman while the telephone continues to ring. The final lines are reminiscent of many Chekhov endings, arresting in their indubitable indeterminacy:

> "A man called Sidney," said the doorman, answering it. "He's asking for her."
> He turned to the crowd. "He says it's urgent."
> No one replied.
> With pomp the doorman returned to the telephone and said, "Mrs. Bittell is indisposed."[136]

Was Sidney aware of Rupert's scheme? Had they planned the robbery together? Is his call urgent because he wishes to warn Mrs. Bittell? Has her relationship with him helped reform him? Did he benefit from her cliché-ridden proselytizing? Does he miss their Wednesday afternoons?

* * *

Fifteen years after the publication of Pritchett's "Tea with Mrs. Bittell" in the *Times,* Trevor's "Timothy's Birthday," one of his darkest, most disturbing stories, was published in the *New Yorker.*[137] Once again, although markedly different stories—the first farcically comic, and the latter sinisterly tragic—their central relationships offer striking similarities. Both involve homosexuals in their thirties distanced from their families, with bleak futures and heartless, thieving homosexual lovers living on the fringe of society. In the Trevor story, Timothy, the homosexual son of aging parents, living in the house he inherited from a recently deceased older homosexual, boycotts his own birthday party at his parents' home, sending the bisexual Eddie instead, a devious young freeloader who serves as Timothy's kept man. The sinister counterpart to Pritchett's Rupert, Eddie eats lunch with the couple, drinks the entire bottle of gin they purchased for Timothy, and steals a small art object—two entwined silver fish—with sentimental value that symbolizes the parents' enduring love for each other—love that had apparently bred jealousy in their son Timothy. "Timothy's Birthday" is "Tea with Mrs. Bittell" in a minor key. In addition to pocketing the couple's artifact, Eddie, instead of returning, steals Timothy's car after lunch, coldly calculates where he will abandon it, and sells the artifact at a pawnshop en route. In contrast to Pritchett's essentially comic conception, Trevor's bleak variation, despite offering a small measure of hope in the parents' enduring love for each other, is essentially tragic, again making all the difference.

In the next, concluding chapter, we take a final view of our two writers, of their absolute individuality, and their haunting, beguiling relatedness.

Chapter 8

English Fantasy and Irish Entrapment

The element of fantasy is permanent in English life. If you look at an Englishman long enough you find this fantasy life which is part of his character.[1]

I write about people who are trapped in one way or another, just simply by circumstances. [. . .] That is really my particular obsession [. . .].[2]

Pritchett believed the English to be a "very romantic and fantasy-making"[3] people who "live for projecting the fantasies of their inner, imaginative life,"[4] and many of his stories include characters that indulge in the act of "self-imagination"[5] that he believed to be quintessentially English:

> My stories are mostly comedies, even sometimes farces; but I have been mostly interested in the fantasies by which people live. There is their real life, often extraordinary and very close to observed fact, and to current speech [. . .]—and their projection of themselves, that is to say their poetry. I look at people from the outside and listen for the words or await the acts, that betray them. My characters have often been called eccentric or unusual; but I do not think they are. I see [. . .] into the dream that they carry about with them, as they walk along.[6]

He recognized other English writers' portrayals of English identity that anticipate his concept of "self-imagination," including Meredith's: "No doubt he over-subtilises, but his people live in their imagination; it gives an ambience to their lives. They dwell in states of mind and heart, personal to them."[7]

Although he agrees that Dickens began as a caricaturist in the *Sketches of Boz*, taking a couple of dominant traits per character and exaggerating them, he also believes Dickens's world accurately reflects "the London mind [that] runs easily to fantasy and self-caricature."[8] An actor himself, Dickens perceived men "conscious of living in a personal drama and of acting a private role." While "all the straight characters head for some moral climax which will be melodramatic," all Dickens's comic characters "inflate themselves."[9] Pritchett's characters defy comparison with Dickens's more theatrical creations, but his concept of "self-imagination," though more subtle than his predecessor's, owes a debt to Dickens. That Pritchett's sense of duality is not confined to the English suggests it may also be a projection of his own pronounced schism. Just as he claims to see "the ape in everyone," he also sees their divided selves. In Ireland, he witnessed a physical manifestation of this split:

> The human faces in the mass are commonplace and there are a lot of big faces with shrunken or small faces set in the middle of them —the double face, one containing the outer, the other the inner life, is very general [. . .]. But all the faces are double, either because of that little face, as nervous as a watch; or (more often) because Irish faces are masked, the moment the man or woman speaks.[10]

There is an important distinction, however, between English and Irish masks. The English mask "is the public persona," learned and worn for the importance given to society's influence and demands; the Irish face "is masked by the policy of instant pleasing" consistent with a people Pritchett felt made little of the obligations of society.[11] Dickensian comedy "rises from the ludicrous condition of a man in the full pomp of public persona, who cannot restrain foolish items of his private, inner life from bursting out."[12]

Pritchett himself was as divided as any of his characters. The previously documented intrafamily dichotomies he experienced while growing up undoubtedly contributed to his divided self, interest in duality, and fixation on irreconcilable differences. Throughout his life, like many of his characters, he sought refuge in fantasy, eventually inventing an alter ego. Early in his correspondence with Brenan, he expressed appreciation of contrasting but complementary elements, unable, like Brenan, to conceive happiness without unhappiness any more than he could imagine good without evil or the soul without the body.[13] Yet despite this common ground, Pritchett did not share his friend's ultimate resolve: "But you've made up your mind about yourself & the world. I haven't. I stand, perforce, with one foot in the [?]—Freud territory and the other in a sort of spiritual

Selfridges [. . .]."[14] He was in constant conflict about his identity as a writer as well, split between literary journalism and fiction: "I get a cursed kick out of earning my living; and the artist in me is in perpetual harangue with the tradesman."[15] (In that respect, he was like his divided father, a frustrated artist and man of imagination in conflict with the—in Walter's case—impractical man of affairs.) In an enthusiastic carpe diem letter written from Stokke in the 1950s, he expressed a simultaneously puritanical and epicurean wish to split himself up into "communicating Departments," part of him traveling and part of him enjoying "strange new emotions" while he went on working simultaneously. He believed his plan to send these separate selves out daily and have them report at day's end showed his "marked sense of responsibility."[16] During the war he had ample opportunity to "get a curious masochistic and non conformist pleasure out of excessive work and specially work of the wrong kind."[17] His wartime "double life" as "Dr. (New Statesman) Jekyll in the country and Mr. (Ministry of Transport) Hyde in London" kept him from fiction.[18] Yet while writing a pamphlet titled "Transport in War Time," he took consolation in comparing himself to Svevo, "only not as prosperous, one moment the familiar of publicity managers, railway nobs, transport chiefs, the next a wailing litterateur 'and with no language but a cry.'"[19] By the end of the war, however, with his youth behind him, he was conscious of losing his "valet"—Pritchett's term for the young person who "does the living" for the writer—and along with it, his fragile duality: "In middle age one loses ones' shadow, that fantastic, scurrying, curious, inventive, excitable fellow who shoots out of your boots & invades the world. No doubt if I took more metatone or the sun shone I would feel less scrufy and bald & my shadow would reappear."[20] This is yet another example of duality that parallels the coupling of characters as ego and alter ego or two sides of one person in many Pritchett stories. Writing fiction was a "slow process," especially when "the great Boss Anxiety" paralyzed him with the reproach that he was not earning his living.[21] During his fallow period in the 1950s, at a time when contending with Dorothy's alcoholism limited him to literary journalism and travel writing, Pritchett was all too conscious of his imprisoned alter ego struggling for self-expression:

> [T]o be Prichnick has become my ideal, Prichnick is my lost self, the one time artist, a Chekovian figure of late forties, the stories written in the back room, the continuous change of address, the concern with only one thing — art. But Prichnick was swallowed alive by the worried figure of Pritchett. He still agitates my nerves at night, sends electric shocks through me and will be in at the death, but he works slowly, whereas Pritchett works so fast and is

never idle. I'd sooner be Prichnik, the direct descendent of Pricksnout—my name at school sometimes, prophetically shortened to Prick.[22]

* * *

Pritchett's most pronounced demonstration of "self-imagination" is his story-length illustration, "The Fall," based on an incident he witnessed at the end of a grand dinner party given for Compton Mackenzie:

> A grotesque incident took place afterwards. A haunted looking middle aged film producer, quite sober, threw himself down on the floor and then got up. Again, he threw himself down. He was demonstrating a stage fall to anyone who happened to be interested. He did it almost a dozen times which exhausted the interest of the guests; and afterwards I found him doing it, alone, for his own pleasure, in another room.[23]

As he did with the kernel for "When My Girl Comes Home," he preserved this situation and enhanced it, working from the outside in, investing it in this instance with his dominant English theme. One can consider it a mock comical reply to a parable like Kafka's "The Hunger Artist." Although a man making pratfalls seems gossamer material on which to base a short story, Pritchett's ingenious transmutation justifies its use. The subsequent notebook kernel for the story is small—as it is for many of his most successful efforts—but at this stage he has already begun transforming fact into fiction by altering setting, character, and situation. The Mackenzie party becomes a hotel managers' dinner; the film producer becomes a "man who wishes he had been an actor"; and the incident itself becomes the story of a moral or psychological fall:

> The Fall chac.; brother Si Possibly an hotel managers' dinner.
> At a birthday dinner, a film director or man who
> wishes he had been an actor, shows friends
> how you fall down. It's quite easy. He falls.
> And then to interested groups, and then alone.
> Could this go into the Hollins-clerk story? Or
> its the story of a moral, psychological etc "fall"?[24]

In the published version of "The Fall," a thirty-eight-year-old accountant, Charles Peacock, returns to the Midland city of his birth for the accountants' annual black-tie dinner. From the outset of the story, while dressing in front of his hotel room's wardrobe mirror, he is clearly imprisoned by his self-consciousness. Once "relieved of nakedness," he visits other mirrors—the one in the bedroom, the two in the bathroom—"assembling the scattered aspects of the unsettled being called Peacock 'doing'—as he was apt to say —'no so badly' in this city [. . .]."[25] His obsession with his reflection continues in the hotel lift, the foyer, and outside in "favourable and assuring shop windows" before the "love affair" with the mirror resumes by the mirrors of the Assembly Rooms' tiled corridors leading to the two-hundred chartered accountants drinking beneath the "chandeliers that seemed to weep above their heads."[26] The mildly agoraphobic Peacock is frightened by crowds and "occasions": "They engaged him [. . .] in the fundamental battle of his life: the struggle against nakedness, the panic of grabbing clothes and becoming someone."[27] Although he finds some assurance in his fully clothed mirror image, once in front of his colleagues, the chameleonic Peacock dresses further still, using incessant mimicry and an array of national and regional accents and vernaculars to mirror them and obscure his own persona. Superficially, he appears to integrate with ease, but none of his immediate office and boardroom colleagues is aware of the exhaustive preparations he must make to be dressed for his part. And like a performer, he is "whole at last among their shouts of laughter."[28] After speaking to several people, however, "the fragments called Peacock closed up." Ill at ease, he begins to drink. In the event that he panics, he can drop "into music hall Negro," [29] acting yet another role. He uses the "old reliable Negro voice"[30] for the first time when asked about his brother, Shelmerdine Peacock, a famous stage and film actor.

Peacock's crippling insecurity is a result of his brother's fame. Living beneath Shelmerdine's shadow, he has become one himself. Wherever he goes, his brother's reputation precedes him. Without any identity of his own, Peacock makes the most of his brother's, usurping the attention intended for him in his absence: "Shel often cropped up in Peacock' life, especially in clubs and at dinners. It was pleasing. There was always praise; there were always questions." Pathetic Peacock simply lives "for one more glance of vicarious fame," "enjoying one of those pauses of self-possession in which, for a few seconds, he could feel the sensations Shel must feel when he stepped before the curtain to receive the applause of some great audience in London or New York." [31] Yet while living vicariously through his brother's accomplishments, Peacock is obviously jealous, and resents him for mentioning their family's "*Bankrupt* Fried Fish Shop," a humiliating revelation: "Why, after they were all doing well, bring ridicule upon the family?"

Metaphorically, Peacock plays a minor role after dinner, as he does in life, an anonymous accountant craving attention. Full of drink, having lost his dinner companions' interest, and unable to engage others in conversation, the lonely man sees his prospective audience departing. Instead of performing before spectators in a theater as Shelmerdine does, however, he draws attention to himself by performing stage falls for the remaining accountants in the hotel dining room, and, desperate for their interest, chases after his audience, repeatedly demonstrating "the stage fall" he claims is "'an art.'" Pathetically, identifying with and posturing as the egotistical actor his brother must be, he voices contempt for his spectators while prostrated on the hotel carpet, literally groveling for attention:

> He grinned at their absurdity. He saw that he held them. They were obliged to look at him. Shel must always have had this sensation of hundreds of eyes watching him lie, waiting for him to move. [. . .] He never felt more completely himself. Even the air was better at carpet level [. . .].[32]

All by himself in the end, he continues to perform his "art" for an imaginary audience in the empty anteroom with Queen Victoria watching from her portrait. In the "wholeness" of his fantasy, self-realized in his imagination, he has no need of mirrors. In his inebriated state the Royal Box fills with "two or three other queens" joining her Highness, the noise of traffic becomes an orchestra, and the velvet window curtains are drawn up before the "dense applause" of a full house. As expert as he is at the stage fall, he literally falls flat on his face when he attempts to bow before the portrait of the Queen because "Shel had never taught him."[33] "The Fall" is Pritchett's paragon of "self-imagination," but there are other, subtler manifestations of this perspective throughout his oeuvre.

"Handsome is as Handsome Does" reveals the fantasies an English wife has while she is on holiday with her husband at a beach-front pension in France. Julia and Tom Coram, a childless English couple in their forties, are "an ugly pair"[34] in perpetual conflict. Yet they are united in their ugliness: "He was ugly in life, she was ugly in body; two ugly people cut off from all others, living in their desert island."[35] She is short and thin with graying hair, a clay-colored face, and a big, long nose and looks "rat-like" in her beach suit "with that peculiar busyness, inquisitiveness, intelligence and even charm of rats."[36] He is thickset, surly, blunt speaking, awkward, and inarticulate, his thoughts "tied up in knots like snakes, squeezing and suffocating him."[37] Except for their mutual unattractiveness, however, they are different in every way. He is from the working class; she from country gentry. Although he has transcended his modest beginnings through education and ambition, he is a social outcast, unable to join her class or the class of his colleagues. At first she admired his rise from meager beginnings, but she has become contemptuous of his natural meanness and gracelessness.

While pleasure "had been natural to her family for generations," "for him it was unnatural."[38] In turn, he cannot forgive his wife for coming from a rich family. Until their holiday, he had never been out of England while she had spent half her youth in foreign countries.

As poorly matched as they are, they are bound by their needs. Her guilt about not having children and his social difficulties make them mutually dependent, effecting an unlikely symbiosis: "She had sown her disappointment in him, he had sown his frustration in her." Mrs. Coram "was fascinated by his hulking incapacity" from the beginning.[39] She soothes the struggle within her boorish husband, who behaves like a child "without subtlety or wit." Despite enjoying the foppish sixty-year-old pension proprietor, Monsieur Pierre, she pretends to dislike him for her husband's sake after hearing him call the Frenchman a fraud. The reader learns that her life is full of such "pretences, small lies and exaggerations which she contrived for her husband's sake." Instead of being repelled by them, she seems to be drawn to his flaws, pitying and protecting him, as if justifying a marriage of which her family disapproved. Instead of attempting to enhance her looks, she cultivates a "shabbiness" in keeping with his unpleasant demeanor.

But their strange equilibrium is disrupted with the arrival of Alex, a tall, dark, handsome European Jew in his early twenties, educated in England, who speaks perfect French, German, and English. In addition to contrasting physically with the blue-eyed, white-skinned, golden-haired, pink-necked Mr. Coram, Alex, who to Mrs. Coram seems "like some fine statue centuries old," is astonishingly articulate and eloquent. Mr. Coram swims with clenched fists, not knowing where he is going, while Alex is an excellent swimmer who dares to go out beyond the waves.

The Corams' friendship with Alex arouses their paternal and maternal instincts because he is old enough to be the son they never had. As they go to sleep one evening, Mrs. Coram speculates about him, self-conscious about his impression of her, her husband, and their relationship. More disconcertingly, Alex's youth makes her increasingly conscious of her lost youth and her aging body full of unrequited desire. She believes life with her inarticulate husband has "injured her own full capacity to speak." She fantasizes about drawing "some of the magic exposition" from Alex in a kiss that would rejuvenate her as well: "And then his young face and his dark hair would take the lines from her face and would darken her grayness with the dark, fresh, gleaming stain of youth." While in the young man's presence, lost in her imagination, she dreams of her life in England twenty years earlier. Instead of protecting her husband and covering for his boorish behaviour, she is increasingly embarrassed, angry with him for exposing his stupidity before Alex. She berates her husband openly, as if such criticism will raise

Alex's esteem for her. Unsettled by her uncontrollable attraction to the young man, she even threatens to have a child with someone else.

Mrs. Coram's initial fantasy intensifies as she dreams of winning Alex by making him as inarticulate as her husband. While imagining his palms on her body, she promises herself she will seduce him with her own words, vowing to "break through this perfection of impersonal speech" by talking herself, making him halt and stammer, know her, bring herself close to him with words, and then touch. The story's most dramatic event, however, complicates her fantasy while giving another character one of his own. When Monsieur Pierre is seen drowning in the waves, Mr. Coram refuses to help and Mrs. Coram, humiliated by her husband's cowardice, summons Alex, who gallantly and heroically rescues the Frenchman. Once he catches his breath, however, the hotel proprietor, who has apparently put his life in danger before, ignores his savior, preferring to see himself as a hero who "once already had looked death in the face."

Pritchett's ending reveals Mrs. Coram's complex desires and emotions while bringing her fantasy to an end. After the lifesaving incident, she attempts to seduce Alex in his room. Yet she senses, as does the reader, that her advances will be rebuffed. Her half-hearted but obvious play for Alex exposes her uncertainty, her awkwardness, Alex's evident lack of interest in her, and her own sudden lack of desire. With little hope of seducing the young man, she abases and humiliates herself, destroying her fantasy in front of the perfect, godlike youth that was its end. She even hopes to be humiliated further by being seen leaving his room half-naked, but there is no one on the stairs. Although the reader cannot be certain of the truth, in analyzing her puzzling emotions and motives herself, she believes her desire for Alex disappeared upon hearing her husband's refusal to rescue Monsieur Pierre and seeing "the fear and helplessness in his eyes, the muddle in his heart." At that point, she believes her sublimated desire had not gone after the rescuer, but "angry, hurt, astounded and shocked towards her husband." Ironically, although she has destroyed her earlier fantasy, Mrs. Coram may have simply replaced it with another to protect her injured pride. According to her, she is ultimately drawn to her imperfect, shamed husband, for whom she willingly degrades herself in the hero's eyes in order "to abase herself to the depths of her husband's abasement." To prove her loyalty to her husband at the story's end, she gives a fictional account of the afternoon's dramatic rescue in front of all the guests, claiming that Tom, not Alex, saved Monsieur Pierre. Praised by some of the guests for her renowned storytelling skill, this embellishment calls the very legitimacy of her earlier self-analysis into question, while concluding the story itself with a fantasy she creates to protect her husband.

"Page and Monarch" [40] concerns the life of Lippott, the assistant to a retail tycoon who travels the world with his entourage in tow. The story is about how the overshadowed "Page" lives vicariously through the exploits and adventures of his "Monarch," Schneider, who, like the domineering character in "The Fall," never actually appears in the story, though he has effectively usurped the protagonist's life in his absence. Like Tom Coram, Lippott takes pride in being a self-made man who has risen from the working class, but in reality he owes his final, dramatic ascension to Schneider. Although the tycoon's personal secretary manages the empire's daily operations during Schneider's lengthy absences, Lippott exaggerates his significance in the tycoon's whirlwind life, believing he is "as vital to him as the braces which held up his trousers." And in order to strengthen his sense of identity, Lippott deludes himself further, imagining he is closer to Schneider than anyone else, even though he rarely sees him. Ironically, though he seems to have sprung from Schneider's conception and considers himself "Schneider's shadow," in his own mind "Schneider was a dream, a fantasy like an enormous electric sign on the front of a building" and he, in "restrained expensive clothes [. . .] was the reality." In fact, so consumed is he with the tycoon—"filled with Schneider"—that he cannot work on departure days. Long after his exit, Schneider continues to occupy Lippott's mind's eye, making his way on his boat, in his cabin, in Calais, and in Paris, putting Lippott in a state of intoxication, "like being filled with Schneider's champagne." Lippott's thoughts are dominated by Schneider's habits, his preferences, his restaurants, and favorite shops. The recipient of numerous gifts from Schneider, including a Daimler and a house, Lippott plays the stock market, following Schneider's millions with "occasional hundreds, a mouse nibbling where a rat had gnawed." Lippott even uses Schneider's old tailor and is flattered to be offered his old mistress. While Schneider is a self-made millionaire, a modern-day monarch, Lippott is simply his page. In his desperation to emulate the tycoon, he forfeits his own life, working for ten years without a holiday.

Ultimately, Lippott has a chance to revel in the power he borrows from absent Schneider, unaware of the consequences of his actions. In contrast to Charles Peacock, who lives reluctantly through his brother, Lippott willingly impersonates his master; but consumed by the idea that "Schneider must be paid for," and eager to prove that the firm is not "'a milch cow,'" he has no compassion for his men. Ironically, instead of embracing the role of the "page" with whom he identifies so strongly in the Christmas carol "Good King Wenceslas," Lippott resembles Dickens's Scrooge instead. After passing five seemingly idle employees at the entrance to Schneider's company, he immediately orders a manager to fire several of them on the spot, just ten days before Christmas.

In "A Trip to the Seaside," Pritchett chronicles the egotistical, self-flattering fantasy of Alfred Morton Andrews, a retired former carpet salesman and lonely recent widower looking for another wife.[41] Put off by the daunting prospect of finding one among the "general chorus of women he had seen in the streets," "taunting him with their indifference," Andrews decides to pursue Louisa Browder, his former secretary with whom he worked for years and seemingly the only available woman he knows, confident that she will welcome his interest even though he has not seen her for five years. She is an unthreatening alternative to the women who "might slap your face if you stopped them and explained your situation," though in his arrogance he considers her merely "a *faute de mieux*." At least they knew each other, and "In a funny sort of way they had had years of marriage in the office." Andrews the revisionist sees Louisa as "a friend," more intelligent than his wife.

So confident is he of success that he takes the train to her seaside address, arriving unannounced, believing "surprise was essential" in dealing with women. He carries her condolence note with him on the journey, desperate to fabricate tangible evidence of her enduring interest in him. Even though he knows the curt, perfunctory note was solicited—and could "be called a riposte"—he transforms it into a kind letter, speaking of it upon his arrival to justify his visit. Before reaching her residence, he looks at one or two seaside properties, fantasizing about buying one in which he will live with Louisa, until the high prices kill his dream. All has changed when he reaches her door and reality impinges further on the presumptuous man's fantasies. Instead of being welcomed by his wife to be, Andrews is almost spurned by her jealous sister, whose lie about Louisa's absence becomes apparent when Andrews hears her voice on the floor above.

Not surprisingly, Louisa has changed dramatically and no longer conforms to his five-year-old image. In place of the spinsterish, slender, mannish woman he expected, and to whom he felt superior, he finds an attractive, relaxed woman at ease with herself. Liberated from her London grind, free of him and her office duties, "her face was on holiday and open." He welcomes her metamorphosis, ironically oblivious to its exclusion of him. During their increasingly awkward reunion, he suddenly shouts out to Daisy, his late wife, to "the town," and to "the world" that he must get rid of his cleaning girl, before Louisa comes back into focus as one fantasy or delusion invades another. Instead of hoping for a relationship with Andrews, as she had in the past, Louisa discourages him from moving to the seaside, advising him that he would be better off staying near his children.

"One thing I've learned is that you can't live in the past," says Andrews, but that is precisely what he does in his quest to win Louisa. With his fantasy seemingly slipping away, he struggles to find common ground on which to reestablish a common bond. The very fact that she is "at the hotel" encourages him because, as a salesman who spent much of his life on the road, hotels made him feel at home. For Andrews they are "palaces of pleasure and money. Their very upholstery sent messages of erotic sensation when one touched it." The hotel staff and guests "were like figures in a dream as they walked silently from room to room.[...] One became a dream oneself."

Reality, however, does not accommodate Andrews' fantasy. He is stunned to learn that Louisa is a stepmother, not the frustrated, eligible spinster he imagined. In fact, he is so disturbed that he imagines the fit his late wife will have when he tells her the news. Pompous and arrogant in the face of his deflated hopes, he rages at the injustice of it all: "A rival widower had stolen a march on him! There was also the affront that, as a former employee and office possession, she had not consulted him first." Pathetically, he sees her letter of condolence "as a kind of invoice," but she will never make good on the payment. At the end of the story, the reader learns through his consciousness that he had rejected her sexual advances during their hotel stay at a trade exhibition in Brighton years earlier. Ironically, she has married the man with whom she slept the night after Andrews had spurned her.

In contrast to Andrews' protracted and humiliating fantasy about Louisa Browder, the young protagonist's fantasy in "The Diver" is spontaneous and successful. In this largely autobiographical story, the puritanical, aspiring young author is initially proud of his sexual innocence, despite suffering the constant taunting of his colleagues and Madame Chanson, a sensual forty-year-old married woman with a dry-cleaning service who works for the firm. When the narrator accidentally falls into the Seine, she takes him to her apartment for a change of clothes. He has an erection while dressing in her presence. She pretends to be insulted, but when next he sees her in the adjoining room, she is naked on her bed. In order to contradict her correct observation that he has never seen a nude woman, he tells a lurid story about finding one strangled to death on a bed when he was only twelve. His improvised fantasy simultaneously releases both his sexual and creative powers, transforming humiliation into conquest, enabling him to overcome his dual impotence. The formerly intimidating woman is both shocked and titillated, excited by the possibility that her young lover may indeed have been the murderer. She is dominated by the force of his imagination and sexual passion as he triumphs in his initiation as both lover and writer.

* * *

After emulating Pritchett's English social comedy early in his career, Trevor migrated, making Ireland his primary focus and Irish history his backdrop.

He portrays the remote rural and small-town Ireland of his youth in many of his stories. Taken for granted in his childhood, the town "became [his] writer's model, a microcosm to work with, to transform into an institution or a congregation, a family, a household, a temporary gathering of strangers. [. . .] I'm a provincial still. Small towns in Ireland are what I know best, and turn to first to find my bearings."[42] While Trevor lived in such towns, he was also made aware of the rural world immediately outside them. He first explored this territory in "The Ballroom of Romance" and subsequently in "Kathleen's Field," "The Potato Dealer," and "The Hill Bachelors." Although the stories are different, they share similar settings, characters, and traps, their characters' central preoccupation being the sacrilege of relinquishing farmland so dearly achieved. Trevor champions their pride, dignity, and stoic resolve to endure in a bleak environment. As an "experimentalist," he often revisits themes several times to create variations, likening the process to that of a Renaissance painter's multiple renderings of the Virgin and Child or the Nativity.[43] Published twenty-eight years apart, "The Ballroom of Romance" and "The Hill Bachelors" are obvious companion pieces, sister and brother stories, respectively. In "Ballroom," the central victim of circumstance is a young woman, and in "The Hill Bachelors" it is a young man.

In one way or another, all of the characters in "Ballroom" are trapped by circumstance.[44] The central character, thirty-six-year-old Bridie, lives with her one-legged widower father, isolated on a hill farm eleven miles from the nearest town, a spinster on the periphery of society, a prisoner of her father's farm. Unlike Mr. Hagerty in "Kathleen's Field," however, Bridie's nameless father feels compassion for his daughter's plight because "the weight of circumstances had so harshly interfered with her life," yet he is powerless to help her. As Bridie's male counterpart, one of the hill bachelors, says, himself with a widowed mother to care for, "you couldn't leave them to rot, you had to honour your mother and father." Every Saturday night, she bicycles seven miles to and from Justin Dwyer's roadside dance hall, *The Ballroom of Romance*, as she has done for twenty years. Isolated itself, prophetically "miles from anywhere," the ballroom has its complement of aging spinsters like Madge Dowding and Cat Bolger, desperate for what may be their last chance to find a husband, as well as middle-aged bachelors who "came down from the hills like mountain goats, released from their mammies and from the smell of animals and soil." They too are destined to lead solitary lives, punctuated by the occasional thrill of a woman's embrace in a field near the ballroom. While some of the participants are trapped by their familial duties, others more available have simply not been chosen. Even some of Bridie's former classmates from Presentation Nuns, who have supposedly escaped and are married and living in town, see themselves as "stuck in a hole," burdened with frequent pregnancies and the strain of controlling their large families.

The new generation mixes with the old on the dance floor, the awkwardness of the younger men and women initiated into courtship and romance contrasted with the desperation of the spinsters and bachelors whose time has already come and gone. While many will cease to attend, some of the newest participants will end up as spouseless regulars like Madge, Dano, and Bridie—members of dying generations excluded from having families of their own. The young man with whom Bridie first dances at the beginning of the evening vows to escape this trap. He lives up in the hills with an uncle, laboring fourteen hours a day for the hill farmer, whose stony acres are one farm removed from her father's. Like many young men of his time, he is determined to emigrate and she has no doubt he will. The youths who danced with her during her twenty years of Saturday nights at the ballroom all left for other places, near and far: town, Dublin, or Britain, "leaving behind them those who became middle-aged bachelors of the hills."

Left behind as well, Bridie escapes into fantasy past and present. She romanticizes her relationship with Patrick Grady, a boy with whom she danced briefly in her youth, and about whom she constantly dreamed, investing him with love for her he clearly never expressed, believing then that he would lead her from the dim ballroom to the town church altar. Her admission that another woman "scooped up Patrick Grady when he didn't have a chance" reveals her self-protective delusions. In turn, her wishful projections about Dano Ryan, the County Council road-mender, and drummer of the ballroom's amateur three-piece "Romantic Jazz Band," are just as self-deluded. Unlike the other bachelors, Dano has never even kissed her, although she once gave him a perfect opportunity while he inspected her bicycle. Nevertheless, she imagines him sitting with herself and her father in the farmhouse kitchen, eating a meal she has prepared, and working harmoniously with her father in the fields. The passage of time has diminished her expectations. She now hopes middle-aged Dano will eventually make her a bride, rescuing her from spinsterhood. As she listens to him sing "I think of you only, Only wishing you were by my side," she feels "Dano Ryan would have done." After all, "If you couldn't have love, the next best thing was surely a decent man." Yet as a sixteen-year-old, she considered him merely "part of the ballroom's scenery, like the trestle table and the lemonade bottles [. . .]." As soon as she has made equally self-protective, self-deluded excuses for Dano's inability to commit himself to her, Bridie resuscitates her memory of Patrick Grady, indulging in more conditional utopia, fantasizing about and regretting what might have been. She sees his youthful face in her mind's eye, imagines herself the mother of his many children, living in Wolverhampton where he was said to have escaped with his wife, going to the cinema in the evenings instead of caring for her handicapped father. And she promises herself that "If the weight of circumstances hadn't intervened she wouldn't be standing in a wayside ballroom, mourning the marriage of a road-mender she didn't love." More pathetically still, she dreams of waking in a bed with him and pretending for a moment that he is Patrick Grady. Even her vow never again to dance at the ballroom for fear of being "a figure of fun [. . .] dancing on beyond her time" seems self-deluded. As if to reaffirm her indomitable spirit, she bicycles home speculating about an eventual marriage to the more accessible Bowser Egan once their respective parents have died, although the eventuality of such a union is far from certain. As it is for many of Pritchett's characters, fantasy is Bridie's balm, the only consolation in her lonesome world.

"The Hill Bachelors"[45] is even more desolate than its sister story. A hill farmer's death brings his five children back to their widowed mother's farmhouse in the bogs for the funeral. Four of them depart immediately after the service, leaving the bachelor of the family to look after their mother. Having left the hills eleven years earlier, twenty-nine-year-old Paulie returns permanently from his life in the midlands a month after the funeral to literally step into his father's boots, knowing his mother cannot manage on her own. Even before relocating he loses his girlfriend, who has no interest in marrying and living on a farm. Without a wife and family, the hills will be even more desolate for him than they were for his father. Like Bridie's father, Paulie's mother contends with the guilt of depriving a child of a family of its own. Her receptivity to "taking a back seat" to his choice of wife, however, will not be tested. The bachelors of the hills find it increasingly difficult to attract a wife to the modest farms they inherit, and Paulie is no exception. Like Bridie, he lowers his expectations, but he is equally unsuccessful. Aileen Caslin, one of his only prospects, leaves for Tralee to join her older sister, and, after several dates with Paulie, Annie, the last of the Caslin girls, escapes to Drunberg to work in the fertilizer factory, repelled by the idea of farm life. Ironically, of all the children, he was his father's least favorite, and his mother realizes he "had been lost to her in the family, his shadowy place in it" influenced by her husband's attitude. It is therefore all the more extraordinary "that a twist of fate has made him his father's inheritor." Almost immediately, he takes over his father's role, quietly assuming all his responsibilities. The sheepdogs obey him as faithfully as they did his father, he inherits his father's pride in the big field, and executes his father's plans to improve it.

The land that takes possession of him transforms Paulie into his father. And his relationship with the sinister, land-hungry Mr. Hartigan, a middle-aged hill bachelor, merely strengthens his determination to cultivate his harsh yet coveted terrain. Hartigan has designs on the big field and attempts to weaken Paulie's resolve to stay with his mother by asking the same question that the young nephew of a hill farmer asked Bridie before emigrating: "Is it a life at all for a young fellow?" For Paulie as for Hartigan, maintaining the family land becomes a matter of honor and pride that pathetically robs them of their own lives. Paulie's mother fears her agreeable, good-hearted son will in time "become hard, as his father had been, and as grasping as Hartigan." The hill bachelors are married to their land, but absurdly will leave no progeny to inherit it. And though they continue heroically honoring the tradition of their forefathers, their ways will die with them. Initially, Paulie returns to the hill farm for his mother, but he remains for other reasons as well—and clearly will stay when she dies, the last born and the last to go. Although trapped, he is heroic precisely because he perseveres despite fighting a losing battle with an indomitable force, a warrior staving off the inevitable: "Enduring, unchanging, the hills had waited for him, claiming one of their own."

In "The Potato Dealer,"[46] a modern variation of the Nativity, Ellie and her mother are Mr. Larrissey's prisoners. Since the death of Ellie's father, they have lived with him on the farm "on sufferance," despite their substantial daily contributions, and Ellie's mother knows her brother considers her beholden to him. In taking them in, the uncle had hoped his niece's eventual husband would work on the farm, easing his own burden in the fields, finally paying the debt of taking in his sister and niece. Instead, Ellie's illicit affair and consequent pregnancy not only eliminate his chance to secure a "suitable young fellow" for the farm, but threaten to compromise the family's respectable reputation in the community as a religious family with mores. Ironically, it is a summer priest of their own church who impregnates Ellie in what later becomes a potato field. A "lifelong bachelor" with a burdensome farm, like those in the stories previously mentioned, Mr. Larissey makes his niece choose between going across the water and aborting the child, or, if he can arrange it, marrying Mulreavy, an unattractive middle-aged potato farmer and the only alternative given the desperate situation. In exchange for masquerading as father and husband, but without conjugal rights, Mulreavy is given a separate room in the house, storage space in the barn, and a dowry. Mr. Larrissey profits from the deal himself, using Ellie's trap to improve his own situation. He forces his sister to pay the dowry with savings from her late husband's insurance policy while he benefits from Mulreavy's contribution to the farm work. To enhance the offer, Mr. Larrissey allows "his own demise to dangle in the distance," promising Mulreavy that he will inherit their land. Ten years later, however, unable to live with the lie—"a deception of such magnitude perpetrated by her elders"—Ellie tells the child the identity of its natural father, exposing the once-confidential arrangement. Mulreavy, the one who profited most from the arrangement, loses most by its disclosure. An immediate laughing-stock and social outcast in the community, he plans to find lodgings in Moyleglass so that he can escape the unbearable atmosphere in the farmhouse, ironically and hypocritically claiming the elders had deceived him. Yet despite these unpleasant revelations, Mulreavy and the child continue to enjoy their father-daughter relationship just as before, proving that what is most precious between people can endure as well. And though he and his wife have never even embraced, his unexpected enquiry in the field about the identity of the child's father demonstrates his surprising recognition and understanding of this long-suppressed truth.

As pervasive as the essentially rural variety is, Trevor offers many other forms of entrapment in his Irish short stories. Not surprisingly, as a prisoner of his parents' tortured relationship, marriage is perhaps Trevor's most prevalent trap. In "Teresa's Wedding," it is perceived by several women in attendance as the only alternative to stultifying town life and spinsterhood. Although they once dreamt of the romantic ideal, they are ultimately trapped in loveless unions. Jaded Teresa marries out of necessity. A month and a half pregnant, she needs a father for her unborn child, even if he is not necessarily the one with whom it was conceived. One of her sisters marries a man simply because he is employed in Cork and can take her away from the town, and the other returns to her parents shortly after her wedding, repelled by the idea of sexual intercourse. Pathetically, Teresa takes comfort in her loveless trap, knowing there is no magic to destroy. "A Husband's Return" portrays a woman who ends her marriage against her will, refusing to accept her husband's repentance after he has been seduced by her sister only because her family disapproves of the shameful reunion. In "Honeymoon in Tramore," a precursor to "The Potato Dealer," Kitty, the patron's daughter, is forced to marry a lowly farm hand whom she does not love after the priest's cousin makes her pregnant. She will be forever trapped in an inappropriate marriage while he is grateful that another man's sexual conquest has given him the wife of his dreams. Isolated in a remote location like Bridie, and further handicapped in her search for a man by her severely shriveled leg, Dolores in "The Property of Colette Nervi" allows herself to be trapped by an undesirable, opportunistic bachelor twice her age, despite knowing he is a thief. So desperate is she to avoid spinsterhood and pretend to enjoy "the world of love and passion" represented in her father's sentimentalized novels that she allows him to marry her and exploit her in every way.

Trevor offers a completely different perspective on marital entrapment in "The Third Party." Fergus Boland, believing that a marriage as miserable as his own should "wither away," rather than being "swiftly cut out," meets in Dublin with his wife's lover, Lairdman, to discuss Lairdman and his wife's plans for her immediate departure and eventual divorce. Instead of acquiescing to the plan, however, Boland traps his wife permanently by disclosing a painful truth about their marriage that she obviously hid from Lairdman, "the mischance within her" that seems to have been responsible for their poisoned relationship. Knowing Lairdman envisions having a large family with Annabella, Boland reveals that she cannot have children, a fact he knows will chase the lover away. Yet in the end, he cannot fathom why he was unable to let her lover take her away and free him from his own imprisonment.

Trevor's treatment of entrapment is as wide-ranging outside the context of marriage as it is within. In several stories, for instance, the central characters' visions or apparitions control their lives, dictating their behavior. The first variation on this theme in Trevor's Irish stories, "The Raising of Elvira Tremlett" is one of his most disturbing psychological portraits of a young boy. Conceived in an adulterous affair between his mother and her husband's brother, the boy is merely a reminder of their sin, an outcast in both his family and his community. While visiting a Protestant church, he discovers a memorial tablet for an eighteen-year-old English girl, Elvira Tremlett, who died in 1873, fashions an identity for her, and makes her his imaginary friend. So powerful is her voice within him, however, that he is eventually unable to suppress it, trapped by his fantasy. Although he knows she is merely a figment of his imagination, he cannot control her voice and his family, fearing his evident insanity will endanger their business and reputation, institutionalizes him. Ironically, once confined within its walls, he claims to be free of this delusion. In "Lost Ground," the second variation on the theme, Milton Leeson, a Protestant boy living in Northern Ireland during the Troubles, starts seeing visions of a Catholic saint—St. Rosa of Viterbo—in the family's orchard, becoming increasingly obsessed with her apparition until he is compelled to share his experience with Reverend Cutcheon, Father Mulhall, and finally, his family. Like his counterpart in the previous story, he is trapped by his fantasy. After embarrassing his Protestant family by preaching about his experience in neighboring towns, he is imprisoned in his room. Finally, to silence his message of peace and reconciliation and exorcise the family shame, Milton's terrorist brother Garfield murders him with the cooperation of the family, simultaneously restoring his once-threatened "hard-man" reputation. In a recent treatment of this theme in *The Hill Bachelors,* "The Virgin's Gift," three visions of the Virgin Mary determine the entire course of a religious mystic's life.

There are of course several Irish stories involving entrapment that exist outside the previous groups. "The Distant Past," Trevor's first involving the

Troubles, is about the relationship between an elderly Anglo-Irish Protestant brother and sister living on the periphery of a provincial town and the local townspeople who are nationalistic Catholics. They remain on their run-down estate inherited from their father—who squandered his fortune on an affair with a Catholic Dublin woman—"instinctively" feeling that leaving it would have been cowardly, yet occasionally wondering why they had not simply sold it upon inheriting it. They accept their strange lives, aware that without children of their own, their deaths will signify the end of an outmoded, antiquated way of life. The outbreak of violence in Ulster, however, destroys their relationship with the Catholic community, and in their old age they are shunned by the townspeople. History cannot be forgotten. It catches up with the present, destroying relationships of fifty years and imprisoning them in their dilapidated, silent home: "Because of the distant past they would die friendless. It was worse than being murdered in their beds." And in "Three People," Trevor explores entrapment within an unlikely trio consisting of an elderly father, his spinster daughter, Vera, and their celibate handyman, Sidney. To escape the burden of being trapped in her home with her handicapped sister, Vera apparently murdered her in her youth; but Sidney, then a stranger, inexplicably perjured himself to save her from a trial. As long as her father is alive, Vera and Sidney must deceive him. Ultimately, desperate to free herself from one trap, Vera has simply exchanged it for another, imprisoned by deception.[47]

Although Pritchett's and Trevor's respective themes appear unrelated, they are actually of the same family, merely separated by their authors' tone. While Pritchett's English fantasize a second self, Trevor's Irish endure oppression through fantasy. In both cases, self-delusion sustains them.

*　*　*

V. S. Pritchett and William Trevor always expressed admiration, even reverence, for each other. Pritchett's short stories are among a handful of works by a small group of writers Trevor rereads.[48] Not surprisingly, much of what he admires in Pritchett's work can be seen in his own. In reviewing the *Collected Stories*, for instance, Trevor applauds the Englishman's brilliance in the genre that he himself believed "was the one to master," praises his ability to capture "the explosion of truth as in an Impressionist painting," employ an "Invisible technique" that "insistently gets everything right," and deftly communicate the subtleties of the British class system. Most importantly, he recognizes Pritchett's achievement in making the "parochial and domestic" universal, as he himself has done for provincial Ireland.[49] When *The Complete Collected Stories* was published, Trevor sang Pritchett's praises once again, this time as a constant experimentalist with a knack for fashioning variations on a theme.[50]

And Pritchett's praise for Trevor has been equally lavish. In discussing accomplished short-story practitioners in an article on the genre, he singled out Trevor as "outstanding, particularly in a terrifying Irish story like 'Attracta'—in which we see the effects of the memory of old violence. He moves to a subtle or to an arresting moral change in his people."[51] Reviewing Trevor's fourth collection of stories, he recognized a rare quality in him—that Pritchett happens to possess himself—while comparing the younger writer with his own idol: "As his master Chekhov did, William Trevor simply, patiently, truthfully allows life to present itself, without preaching."[52]

Like Pritchett, Trevor is devoted to the portrayal of the common man. For him there "are no ordinary people and there are no villains or heroes."[53] He too effaces himself in order to enable his characters to speak for themselves. And like Pritchett, who managed to avoid Bloomsbury even though he was living there, he has never belonged to a literary group, preferring to interact with people from his local town,[54] much in the way that Pritchett did while living in Maidencourt during the Second World War. Despite their common ground, however, Trevor is admittedly different—a poet of what is past or passing, a chronicler of lost opportunities and things about to disappear, like Hardy.[55] Praising Pritchett's biography of Turgenev, he too identified with the Russian writer's true subject matter, a world out of love and out of season. While pathos permeates his oeuvre, it seems almost absent in Pritchett's work. Yet just as many of Trevor's early "English" stories come close to Pritchett's, some of Pritchett's early work is surprisingly close to Trevor's Irish stories. Set on the Irish coast, "The Two Brothers," a disturbing, powerful, tragic story about a tortured fraternal relationship during the Troubles proves that Pritchett was capable of working Trevor's ground. And it is clear from a diary entry during the war that the Englishman's and Irishman's sensibilities were closer than one would imagine. Pritchett's sense of inevitable loss about Maidencourt, where he could not continue the disappearing farming tradition, parallels Trevor's Big House theme and the fading of the old order in such stories as "The Distant Past":

> This house, Maidencourt, has no right to exist. Its day is done. [. . .] Sitting here, in lovely fragments during the hours of the day, we have [. . .] a good way of living. [. . .] We alas a condemned generation are conscious of it [. . .]. The guilt and the regret are for enjoying a good thing in a time of catastrophe; in seeing a beautiful thing and knowing that society in oneself has condemned it to death; in knowing, like an accomplice, that such a moment of pleasure and admiration as I ~~hav~~ just had ~~when to~~ before I drew the shutters, had no future. That one was obliged to treat it as a dream, to wake up and dismiss all credence of it.[56]

Pritchett came to see that "the comic and the dire are often opposite sides of each other, yet somehow united. We laugh and cry at the same time."[57] Instead of emphasizing the pathos and loss in his own life, he made a conscious decision early in his career to transform them in his stories, a choice that ultimately made him a great comic artist. Trevor, on the other hand, despite his own real capacity for comedy, has chosen to embrace the pathos and yearning of the human heart as the focus of his fiction—a choice that has made him an equally great elegiac and lyrical artist.

Appendix

You Make Your Own Life
V.S. Pritchett
(Please note that this appendix begins with page two of the corrected typescript)

1   The shave had finished now, the barber was cutting

       the man's hair. It was glossy black hair and small
                                            custo   man
       curls of it fell on the floor. I could see the ~~man~~ in

       the mirror. He was ~~a well-made man~~ in his thirties
                                    brilliant
5   with a swarthy skin and ~~bright~~ long black eyes ~~like a~~

       ~~gypsy's~~. The lashes were long and the lids when he
                                There was just that suggestion of weakness.
       blinked were pale.∧ Now he was shaved there was a

sallow glister to his skin like a Hindu's and as the ~~young~~ barber

       clipped away and grunted his breaths, the dark man sat

10   engrossed in his reflection, half smiling at himself and

       very deeply pleased. ~~He was wearing bright violet socks~~.
                                        was a careful and responsible
       ~~He was a careful man~~, the barber, ~~slow and studious~~
                                                    in his 30s too
                    but nonchalant and   *He was*∧ *a young man with fair, receding hair*
       in his movements and∧ detached. ∧ ~~Sometimes he stepped~~
       brushed up from his forehead. He did not speak to his customer. His customer didnt speak to him.
Sometimes he stepped ~~back and looked at his customer in the mirror as a painter~~

15   ~~might look at a picture in a frame~~. And ~~h~~e went on from
                                        rattling his brush in the jar, wiping his razor,
       one job to the next silently. Now he was∧ pushing the

       chair forward to the basin. ∧now he gently pushed the man's
                                           amused
       head down, now he ran the taps and ~~was~~ soaping the
                        A peculiar look of ~~distant~~ *affection was on his face as he looked*
       head and rubbing it. ~~He looked~~∧ down at the soaped head.

20   ~~as if it were a piece of putty in which he was rather~~
                                The look which and
       ~~interested~~. Then∧ he had the man back, turbanned in a
                        He was all he cared for this man..
       ~~towel~~.

           "How long are you going to be?" I said. "I've

got a train".

25   He looked at the clock.   He knew the trains.

"Couple of minutes", he said.

~~He walked away and~~ He wheeled ~~an extraordinary~~ a machine

on a tripod to the back of the man.   A curved black thing

like a helme/t enclosed the head.   The machine was plugged

30   to the wall.   There were phials with coloured liquids

on it and soon steam was rushing out under the helmet.

It looked like a machine you see in a Fun Fair.   I don't

know what happened to the man or what the barber did. Shave,

hot towel, haircut, shampoo, this machine and then yellow

35   liquid like treacle out of a bottle – that customer had

everything.

I wondered how much he would have to pay.

~~And then, after many powderings, wipings, squirtings~~

~~of scent over that swarthy face, whose eyes closed into~~

40   ~~long slits with satisfaction like a cat's, and the final~~

Then the

~~offering of a clean towel from a drawer, the~~ job was over.

The clippers had been over the back of his neck and he looked like a guardsman

The dark man got up.   ∧   He was dressed in a square

shouldered grey suit, very dandyish for this town and he

had a silk handkerchief sticking out of his breast pocket.

45   He wore a violet and silver tie.   He patted it as the

He was delighted with himself.

barber brushed his coat, He ~~smiled slightly at himself~~

with a pleased

~~in the mirror and then, with the idle luxurious~~ step ~~of~~

APPENDIX 201

~~a cat, he went to the door~~.
    Fred *smiled faintly.* *The look of dandified derision*
"So long", he ~~said with a wide smile~~. *was unmistakable*
  Cheero *~~Alf~~ Albert*   *uprigh t*
50 "~~So long~~", said the^ barber and his lips closed to
                ironically *the barber*
a small, hardly perceptible smile too. Thoughtfully ~~he~~
       his handiwork
watched ~~him~~ go ~~out of the door and go down the stairs~~,

~~until he was out of sight~~. *The man hadn't paid.*

 ~~They were youngish men, both of them, the fair and~~
55 ~~the dark, much the same age~~.

 I sat in the chair. It was warm, too warm, where
the man had sat. The barber put the sheet round me.
The barber was smiling to himself like a man remembering a
tune. He was not thinking about me. ~~The small sardonic~~
60 ~~smile like the abstracted smile of a man who remembers~~
~~a story he has been told and is getting another unsuspected~~
~~flavour from it.~~

  ~~"What's that machine for?" I asked.~~ *I had to repeat the*
~~question~~   *The barber* *that machine*
  ~~He told me.~~ ~~I think~~ ~~he~~ said ~~it~~^ made steam open

65 the pores. ~~Some people liked it, some people didn't~~.
He glanced at the *people want* *he said* *want*
door where the "Some^ ~~like~~ everything, ^"some ~~like~~ nothing." *You had to have a machine*
man had gone.   *impatiently*   *like that*
  ~~"He"~~, ~~said the barber dryly, nodding to the door~~,
       wants
~~"That customer - likes everything"~~.

 He tucked in the cotton wool. He got out the
70 comb and scissors. His fingers gently depressed my head.
I could see him in the mirror bending to the back of my
                 ~~but resolute~~
head. He was clipping away. He was a dull^ young man

dry — with pale blue eyes and a look of stubbornness in him. *The small smile was still like claw marks at the corners of his lips.* *ironical*

75 ~~Insignificant as he was he seemed to carry in his usual movements an ironical sense of reliability.~~ ~~I sank into drowsiness in the warmth of the chair, into a dreamy state.~~ ~~And it seemed to me that the barber was in that state too, as if he were still with that man who had just gone out of the door.~~

80 "~~It works out expensive?~~" ~~I said.~~
"Three bob", he said. *a time* ~~"He has it every week".~~
He spoke into the back of my neck. *and nodded to the door*
~~"Some wont have anything else".~~ *He* has it every week". ~~He nodded to the door.~~
"~~Every Friday~~", ~~he said.~~ "~~Every Friday, I suppose,~~ *5 years* ~~for six or seven years~~".

85 He clipped away.

"His hair's coming out. That's why he has it. *Going bald* ~~Going bald~~. You cant stop ~~it~~. *that* You can delay it but you cant stop it. ~~That's what I tell him.~~ ~~If you're going bald you're going bald.~~ ~~That's all there is to it~~.

90 ~~Nothing to be done~~. Can't always be young. ~~A.D.'s an item~~. He thinks you can" He smiled ~~with dry~~ affection. *drily but with*

"A.D.?"

"~~Anno Domini. You get old, your hair comes out~~".

"But he wasn't so old".

95 The barber stood up. The smile became ~~stronger and more~~ sardonic. *faint*
He mused to himself with growing satisfaction. He worked away
That man!
"~~Him?~~" he said. "~~He~~ ought ~~to be dead~~" *in long silence as if ~~turning~~ trying every possible flavour of my remark. The result* *By rights he*

APPENDIX

~~He spoke with a dry musing satisfaction. There~~
of this meditation was to make him change his scissors for a finer pair.
~~had been this look of satisfaction and yet detachment too when~~
"He ought to be dead", he said.   *As if to say from a*
100 ~~the swarthy man had been in the room.~~
moral point of view it was a scandal that the man was alive.
"T.B.", he said with a kind of quiet scorn.
~~"It didn't look like T.B."~~
He looked at me in the mirror.

"It's wonderful", he said.   As if to say it was

nothing of the sort.
                              doctors can
105   "It's wonderful what ~~the right treatment can~~ do",

I said.
                              said
     "I don't mean doctors", he ~~muttered drily~~.
                      Tuh!
     "Consumptives! ~~Cor!~~ They're wonderful".   ~~As if~~
As much to say a sick man can get away with anything but you try if you're healthy & see what happens!
       ~~to say Lord Potts who started life as an errand boy and~~ ∧ ~~got~~

110 ~~away with it. Wonderful? I don't think~~.

     He went on cutting. There was a glint in his pale
                              amusedly
belue eyes.   He snipped away ~~patiently~~ as if he were

attending to every individual hair at the back of my head,
                              may be wonderful but you   *everything*
~~the sort of fellow who knows you cant get away with anything~~
~~to you may be wonderful but you cant have everything.~~   *everything*.
115 ~~you try and see~~.

     "You see his throat?" he said. *suddenly.*
     "What about his throat?" I asked.
          "~~Well", he said~~, "Did'/you notice anything? Didn't
                              He stood up & looked at me in the mirror.
see a mark, a bit at the side? ∧ "~~He cut his throat once",~~
"No", I said. He bent down to the back of my neck again. "He cut his throat once", he said quietly.
~~he said~~.   "Not satisfied with T.B." he said with a
It was a small firm ~~It was a~~ *friendly* grin. "So long, Fred. Cheero, Albert."
120 ~~quiet grin~~. "Had to commit suicide".

     "Wanted everything", I said.
     "That's it", he said.   ~~You may be wonderful but you cant have everything.~~
     "~~Yes, he did.   Five years ago that chap cut his own~~

~~throat with a razor~~. "That's why he comes in here~~.~~
Wont shave himself now. ~~/~~ Put the wind up him. ~~I~~ go over
to his house every day and shave him and he comes here on
Fridays~~/~~ Every day for five years. ~~No, six, seven years it is.~~ Afraid to shave himself"~~.~~

~~The barber was silent. He was leaving the story there.~~

"What happened" I asked~~.~~

~~"Usual story", said~~ the *young* barber. ~~did not answer~~

~~"Money?" I said. "Horses?"~~

~~"No", he said. "He had all the money and horses he wanted. Cor!~~ No, *the barber said.* ~~at last~~ a girl. ∧ "He fell in love with
~~a girl".~~ *a girl".*

He clipped away. *absently.*
"That's an item", said the barber ~~with a grim sort of pleasure.~~

He fell in love with *a*
"~~What happened? Did she jilt him?   No.~~ ∧ local
who *in bed*
girl. ∧ Took pity on him when he was ∧ ill. ~~when he was in bed.~~
Nursed him. Usual story. Took pity on him but wasn't
interested in him in that way.
"A very attractive girl", said the barber.
"~~But~~ *And* he got it badly?"

"They get it badly, consumptives. ~~Takes them worse than you and me~~".

"~~You can't blame her if he had T.B.".~~
stepping over for the
"Matter of fact", said the barber ~~thinning me out~~
clippers and shooting a hard sideways stare at me
~~on top.~~ "It was my wife".

~~His small pale eyes glared a little but the dry smile was still on his lips~~.

150 "Before she was my wife", he said.

"That's funny isn't it?" he said.   There was a touch of quiet ~~self importance~~ *amused resolution* in him.

~~Cor, he said,~~ H̶e'd known that chap since he was a
Used to be ~~Was~~ his best friend. Still was.
kid.   Went to school with him. ∧ Always a lad.   Regular

155 nut.   Had a milk business, was his own guv'nor till he got ill.   Doing well.   ~~"She knew him before she knew me. But she went away for a couple of years to look after a lady and when she got fed up she came back.   Then I took up with her".~~

160   "He knew I was courting her", he said ~~with something that was nearly a chuckle~~.   "That didn't stop him".
He nearly chuckled.   *There was a glint in his eye.*
~~"What did you do?"~~
"What did you do?" I asked.
"I lay low", he said.
                    had
She ~~got~~ a job in the shop opposite.   If you passed

165 that shop you couldn't help noticing her in the cash desk
"Its not for me to say – but she was
near the door.   ∧ "~~T~~he prettiest girl in th~~e~~*e* town", he said.

"Still is", he mused. *in after thought.*

"~~He used to slip across to talk to her~~", the barber
                amused
~~said in the~~ *same* ∧ ~~tone of amused scorn~~.   "~~I used to see

170 him.   I didn't mind.   She knew her mind and I knew mine.~~
           You came over it by the station
You've seen the river?" he said.   "Well he used to take her

I didn't mind. I knew my mind. She knew hers.

on the river when I was busy. ∧ ~~I was glad someone was looking after her~~. I knew it was all right", he said.

"I knew him", he grinned. "But I knew her.' ~~Take~~ Let him take you
175 ~~her~~∧ on the river ~~if you like~~', I said."
            the barber's
I saw ~~his~~ forehead and his dull blue eyes looking

up for a moment over my head in the mirror.
            he said reflectively.
"Damp river." ∧ "Damp mists, I mean, on the river.
                                    It started with him
Very flat, low lying, unhealthy", he said. "~~Didn't do him~~
180 ~~any good"~~. *taking her on the river"*

"Double pneumonia once", he said. "Sixty cigarettes

a day, burning the candle at both ends".

He grunted.
                                    Knocked him out"
~~"Going out with her on that river~~ made him ill", ~~he~~
        "He couldn't get away with it." he said. He was smiling at the past.
185 ~~said.~~
            When he got ill, the girl
~~She, that was, his girl~~, used to go and look after him
                                    in the afternoons.
~~the dark fellow who was ill~~. She used to go and read ~~to him~~.
            "Interesting man, really", he said. "Proper lad," he smiled   up
"~~Both of us used to go~~.   "I used to turn ~~in~~ in the
            too
evenings / when we'd closed".
            The barber
190 ~~He~~ came round to the front and took the brushes lazily.
                                    expecting to see
He glanced sardonically at the door as if∧ the man ~~were~~
                    Still that cocksure ⟨?⟩ irony
standing there. ~~There was something stubborn, incredulous~~,
                    that quiet amusement. seemed to warm up
~~ironical~~ in the barber~~, but there was no indignation~~.
as he did.   *he said sharply & suddenly and smiled*
"Know what he used to say to her?" ∧ 'Here Jenny', *when I*
                                                    was
195 he used to say, 'Tell Fred to go home and you pop into *startled.*
            The young barber
bed with me. I'm lonely' ". ~~He~~ gave a short laugh.

APPENDIX   207

~~The barber stared me hard in the face~~.
                                   ~~Of course~~ ~~Of course I've known him for years~~".
         "In front of me", he said.   ~~He grinned with quiet~~
~~assurance~~. *"What did you say?"*
              "I told him to keep quiet or he'd
200   ~~"Keep quiet", I said~~. ~~"Or you'll~~ be a corpse".

         ~~"And so he would if he didn't keep quiet", he said,~~
~~relaxing his stare~~.

         "Consumptives want it, they want it worse than others,
but it kills them", he said.

205   "I thought you meant <u>you'd</u> kill him", I said.

                 ~~The young barber gave a short, dry laugh~~. ~~He~~
chuckled
~~looked at me scornfully~~.
                           in astonishment,
         "Kill him?" he said.   "Me kill him?" He smiled. *scornfully*
I was an outsider in this.   *at me.*
         "He tried to kill <u>me</u>", he said. ~~with a chuckle~~.
                  ed
                                            almost with
210   He ~~seemed to~~ look / back on that episode ~~with~~ *particular*
artistic
~~a lazy~~ affection.   ~~"He wanted her. It takes them that way.~~
~~She wasn't his.~~ ~~Someone else had got her. See? He~~
~~He wanted everything"~~.

         ~~He went to the shelf and brought a long mirror~~.

215   "Back O.K.?" he said. *holding up a mirror*

         "Yeah", he said, ~~putting back the mirror and~~ wiping
his hands on a towel.   "Tried to poison me. Whisky.
It didn't work.   I dont drink".
                                      "I was his best friend
         "I went to his room", he said. ∧ "~~There~~ he was
220 lying on the bed. Thin! All bones and blue veins and
red patches as if he'd been scalded and eyes as bright as

that bottle of ~~those~~ bath salts
~~marbles~~.   Not like he is now.   There was a bottle of

whisky and a glass. *by the side of the bed. He wanted me to have a drop. He knew I didn't drink.*

225   ~~"Have a drop", he says.~~

~~"No thanks", I said.~~

~~"Go on, have one", he said.   "Do you good".~~

"I dont want one", I said.   "'Yes, you do', he said.
'You know I never touch it', I said.   'Well, touch it now',
he said.   'I tell you what', he said.   'You're afraid'.
230   'Afraid of what' I said.   'Afraid of catching what I've
got.   Touch your lips to it if you're not afraid.   ~~You~~ *Just have a sip to show."*
~~needn't drink it, just touch your lips to the glass'"~~. ~~'You're afraid', he said.~~

"I told him not to be a fool.   I took the bottle
from him.   He had no right to have whisky in his state.
235   ~~God~~, He was wild when I took it.   'It'll do some people
a bit of good', I said.   'but it's poison to you'".

'"It *is* poison", he said.'

"~~Of course I didn't take any notice.~~ I took the
bottle away.   I gave it to a chap in the town.   It nearly
240   finished him.   We found out it *was* poison.   He'd put
something in it".

~~"Singe?" said the barber.   "Seal up the ends?"~~
The barber
I said I'd have a singe.   ~~He~~ lit the taper.   I
"Seals up the ends" the barber said.
felt the flame warm against my head. ∧ He lifted up the
245   hair with the comb and ran the flame along ~~the ends~~. ~~His~~

~~lips were pursed in an interested~~ way.
"What did you do?"
"Nothing", he said.
"I rumbled him", ~~he said.~~ "~~See his idea.~~ ~~"I didn't~~
                                                the barber said
~~say anything~~. ∧ I just married my girl that week", ~~he~~ said.
              she
"When ~~we~~ told him we were going to get married he said,
                                    wont
250   'I'll give you something Fred ~~can't~~ give you'. We

wondered what it would be.   'Something big', he said.
'Best man's present' he said. He winked at her. ~~He was a lad.~~ "All I've got. I'm the best man."
'~~Dont spend too much~~', ~~I said.~~   '~~You want all you've got~~'.

~~He laughed.~~   '~~You wont get anything as big~~', ~~he said~~.
                                              bloody
'~~I'll spend everything~~'.   That night he cut his/throat".
"~~He was a lad~~". ~~The barber said~~
255   "~~How did they find him?~~" ~~in time~~"   The barber made a grimace
in the mirror, passed the scissors over his throat & gave a grin.
     "~~They didn't" said the barber~~. Then "He opened the
                                                        her
window and called out to a kid in the street to fetch ~~me~~.

~~I found him~~.   The kid came to me instead".
                      ~~That was his present~~
      The barber smiled. tolerantly. "~~Just as well~~", he said
                                      "Funny present"
260   "~~Got the wind up~~", he ~~said~~.   "Couldn't pull it off."
"He loved her then", I said. "Oh, he loved her all right", he said.
"What'll you have on?" he asked.   He combed,

he patted, he brushed. \/ He pulled the wool out of the

back of my neck. He went round it with the soft brush.

Coming round to the front he adroitly drew off the sheet.

265   I stood up.

       "He got over it", he said.   ~~They do, you know.~~
                                     ~~He's settled down.~~
Comes in every Friday, gets himself up. ∧ See him with a

(continued on the following page)

                                                              Comes round and
different one every week at the Pictures. ∧ ₽lays with my
                                                          now
kids on Sundays". *The only thing is he don't like shaving himself. I have*
           to go over every morning and do it for him."
270   "I never charge him", he said.

           He brushed my coat, he brought my hat. Business
                        He stood with his small grin, his steady eyes,
quiet? he asked. resolute *amused and resolute.*

      "Never has been much in this place", he said. "No

industry.   Just the town.   A quiet place", he said.

275 "You make your own life", he said.

                        - - - - - - - - - - - -

           It's a quiet *dead place, this, all right in the summer on*
                              just have to
           the river. You have to *make your own life."*

           He stood with his small grin, his steady eyes amused & resolute

     "He'll never settle down", he said.   *"They don't. They want*

everything".

     He brushed my coat, he brought my hat.

                              #

Notes

Chapter 1

1. V. S. Pritchett, "Book Talk" and "Recent Books," broadcast script, broadcast 8.5.44, BBC Home Service: London, Written Archives Centre. (Unless otherwise specified all radio programs are referred to by broadcast date and script.)
2. Pritchett, "Broadcasting About Literature," *BBC Quarterly*, vol. II, 4.47 to 1.48: 80.
3. Lloyd Williams to VSP 21.2.35, BBCTFI WAC.
4. Lloyd Williams to VSP 11.3.35, BBCTFI WAC.
5. Christopher Salmon to VSP 4.6.36, BBCTFI WAC.
6. C. S. M. Brereton to VSP 30.7.35 and Brereton to J. M. Rose-Troup 19.9.35, BBCTFI WAC.
7. VSP to Salmon 6.6.36, BBCTFI WAC.
8. Salmon to VSP 31.8.40, BBCTFI WAC.
9. Salmon to VSP 11.9.40, BBCTFI WAC.
10. VSP to Salmon 14.5.41, BBCTFI WAC.
11. Salmon to VSP 16.5.41, BBCTFII WAC.
12. Ibid.
13. Salmon to R.A. Rendall 16.5.41, BBCTFII WAC.
14. Salmon to VSP 12.8.41, BBCTFII WAC.
15. "Strength of Mind" was advertised as a "new series of broadcast discussions about thinking and the importance of thinking in human affairs." The first program, an introductory discussion between John Mabbott, Pritchett, and G. M. Young, was entitled "What is the point of arguing?" 3.10.41, BBC WAC.
16. Salmon to VSP 18.9.41, BBCTFII WAC.
17. "Strength of Mind" II: "Who Is Disposed to Think?" 10.10.41, BBC WAC.
18. Ibid.
19. Pritchett, BBC broadcast script, "Meeting at Ye Olde St. Martins," 7.42 B3F22 Berg.
20. Salmon to VSP 21.1.42, BBCTFIII WAC.
21. See scripts for "Living Opinion" 27.2.42, 24.3.42, 24.4.42, 22.5.42, 19.6.42, 17.7.42, 27.11.42, WAC.
22. Salmon to VSP 26.12.41, BBCTFII WAC.
23. VSP to Salmon 31.12.41, BBCTFII WAC.

24. Salmon to R. H. Boswell BBC Memo 16.1.42, BBCTFIII WAC.
25. Salmon to VSP 28.3.42, BBCTFIII WAC.
26. VSP to Salmon 29.8.46, BBC WAC.
27. *Build the Ships.* (The official story of the shipyards in wartime. Prepared by the Ministry of Information. Text by V. S. Pritchett.) London, 1946.
28. VSP to Dorothy Pritchett (p.m. 24.2.43) Newcastle-On-Tyne, B42F7PP.
29. Notebook #1 dated 1933 B40PP.
30. Notebook begun "June 1936," with some entries from the early 1940s. Pritchett Notebooks, F10PC.
31. See Orwell's "New Novels," *New Statesman and Nation (NS)*, vol. 21, no. 518, 25.1.41: 89–90; Pritchett's "The Short Story," *NS*, vol. 21, no. 519, 1.2.41: 111; Pritchett's "Books in General," *NS*, vol. 21, no. 521, 15.2.41: 162; and Orwell's "New Novels," *NS*, vol. 21, no. 522, 22.2.41: 190–192. The conclusion of this debate, however, came on the air in a discussion moderated by Desmond Hawkins titled "What's Wrong with the Modern Short Story?" #19 in the series "Turning over a New Leaf," broadcast 16.6.41 by the BBC Empire Service's Green Network. This script was thought to have been lost, but I found a copy of it in B3F27PP Berg.
32. "The Lively Arts," interview with VSP 16.6.67, BBC WAC.
33. VSP to GB 10.2.39, BCF1.
34. VSP to JL 22.12.40, JLP.
35. Pritchett, "Poor Gissing," *The Complete Essays of V. S. Pritchett* (London: Chatto & Windus, 1990), 529.
36. Pritchett, "Studies in English Letters":"Arnold Bennett," 16.7.46, BBC WAC.
37. Ibid.
38. Pritchett, "Literature in the West" (Second Series) 13: "Thomas Hardy," 14.7.46, BBC WAC.
39. Ibid.
40. Ibid.
41. Pritchett, *The Gentle Barbarian: The Life and Work of Turgenev* (London: Chatto & Windus, 1977), 58.
42. Ibid., 63.
43. GB to VSP 14.12.40, 19.2F5BC.
44. VSP to GB 19.12.40, F2 (1938–1952) PC.
45. VSP to GB 5.4.40, F2 (1938–1952) PC.
46. "Dialogue," p. 11, Lecture typescript, unpublished, B20F10PP.
47. "The Short Story," Lecture typescript, unpublished, B33F10PP. This lecture was most likely given in France.
48. Notebook #2, entry of 22.11.40, p. 20, B40PP.
49. "The Living Image," 4.12.41, Home Service BBC WAC. This was a discussion between Hugh Sykes-Davies, Elizabeth Bowen, H. L. Beales, and Pritchett.
50. Ibid.
51. "Dialogue," Lecture typescript, p. 12, B20F10PP.
52. "The Living Image," 4.12.41, BBC WAC.

53. Pritchett owned several of Eric Partridge's dictionaries and phrase books. See *Books from the Library of V. S. Pritchett,* Catalogue 292 (London: Bertram Rota Ltd., 2000).
54. "The Living Image," a discussion between Hugh Sykes-Davies, Elizabeth Bowen, H. L. Beales, and Pritchett, 4.12.41, BBC Home Service WAC.
55. "Strength of Mind" VI: "Our Selves and Our Surroundings," 7.11.41, BBC Home Service WAC.
56. "The World of Books," Pritchett interview with Walter Allen, 6.2.65, BBC WAC.
57. Pritchett, *Balzac* (London: Chatto & Windus, 1973), 47.
58. "London Dialogues" I, "How We Come to Form Opinions," 18.5.51, BBC London Calling Asia, WAC. Pritchett utters this remark while interviewing Margery Fry.
59. Walter Allen, "The Art of V. S. Pritchett," *The Penguin New Writing,* no. 34 (London: Penguin, 1948), 90.
60. "Manifesto," *New Writing,* no. 1, (Spring 1936): v.
61. Ibid.
62. VSP to JL 14.5.36, JLP.
63. VSP to JL 23.5.36, JLP.
64. V. S. Pritchett, interview with Ben Forkner and Philippe Séjourné, *Journal of the Short Story in English,* no. 6 (Spring 1986): 36.
65. VSP to JL 27.6.36, JLP.
66. Valentine Cunningham, *British Writers of the Thirties* (Oxford: Oxford University Press, 1988), 226.
67. VSP to JL n.d. [7.37], JLP.
68. JL to VSP 16.7.37, JLP.
69. JL to VSP 24.7.38, JLP.
70. VSP to JL 25.7.38, JLP.
71. Notebook #2, p. 38, entry 1.3.41, B40PP.
72. VSP to JL 22.12.40, JLP.
73. Published in *Folios of New Writing,* Autumn 1940, Vol. II (London: Hogarth Press, 1940), 54–70. The story was accepted by Lehmann on 22.8.40.
74. VSP to GB 19.12.40, F2 (1938–1952) PC.
75. VSP to JL 12.5.[38?], JLP.
76. VSP to JL 22.12.40, JLP.
77. VSP to JL 9.2.61, JLP.
78. Pritchett makes reference to "The Sailor," originally published in *New Writing,* no. 3, Christmas 1939.
79. VSP to JL 4.7.46, JLP.
80. Pritchett, "Documentary Writing" 15.8.44, Series: *New Writing* No. 5, BBC Eastern Service WAC.
81. Ibid.
82. Pritchett, "The Living Image" V: "Theatre" 19.2.42 BBC Home Service WAC.
83. GB to VSP 1.6.44, 19.2F5BC.

84. Pritchett, "Book Talk," "New and Recent Fiction," 23.4.45, BBC Home Service WAC.

CHAPTER 2

1. V. S. Pritchett, *MO*, 401.
2. Walter Allen, "V. S. Pritchett," *The Short Story in English* (New York: Oxford University Press, 1981), 268.
3. Paul Theroux, dust jacket, *The Complete Collected Stories* by V. S. Pritchett.
4. Valentine Cunningham, "Coping with the Bigger Words," review of *Collected Stories, Times Literary Supplement*, 25.6.82, 687.
5. Frank Kermode, dust jacket, *The Complete Collected Stories* by V. S. Pritchett.
6. William Trevor, "Pritchett Proclaimed," review of *Collected Stories, New Republic*, 2.8.82, 32.
7. Eudora Welty, "A Family of Emotions," review of *Selected Stories, New York Times Book Review*, 25.6.78, 1, 39–40.
8. Anon, "The Temptations of Technique," review of *When My Girl Comes Home, Times Literary Supplement*, 6.10.61, 657.
9. John J. Stinson, *V. S. Pritchett: A Study of the Short Fiction* (New York: Twayne Publishers, 1992), xi.
10. Susan Heath, review of *The Camberwell Beauty, Saturday Review/World*, 19.10.74, 28–29.
11. Douglas A. Hughes, "The Eclipsing of V. S. Pritchett and H. E. Bates: A Representative Case of Critical Myopia," *Studies in Short Fiction* 19 (Fall 1982): iii–iv.
12. Pritchett, preface, *The Collected Stories of V. S. Pritchett* (London: Chatto and Windus, 1982), ix.
13. Pritchett, interview with Ben Forkner and Philippe Séjourné, "An Interview with V. S. Pritchett," *Journal of the Short Story in English* 6 (Spring 1986): 24–25.
14. Pritchett, *MO*, 401.
15. Pritchett, interview with Forkner and Séjourné, *JSSE*, 23.
16. Oliver Pritchett, foreword, *The Pritchett Century: The Selected Writings of V. S. Pritchett* (London: Chatto and Windus, 1998), ix.
17. Ibid.
18. Gerald Brenan, *Personal Record, 1920–1972* (London: Cape, 1974), 338.
19. Stinson, *V. S. Pritchett: A Study of the Short Fiction*, 11.
20. The following discussion is based on the three successive drafts of "You Make Your Own Life" in the Pritchett Collection at the Harry Ransom Humanities Research Center, University of Texas at Austin: an autograph manuscript with autograph revisions (9 pp.), a composite autograph and typed manuscript with substantial autograph revisions (12 pp.), and a typed carbon copy manuscript with a few autograph emendations (11 pp.).
21. This autograph manuscript, the first known version of "You Make Your Own Life," is entitled "The Barber."

22. Autograph manuscript, first page of the heavily revised typescript of "You Make Your Own Life," PC. The transcription of the typescript continues from this point in the appendix.
23. Pritchett, "You Make Your Own Life," *The Complete Collected Stories* (New York: Random House, 1990), 150. (Hereafter, "*CCS*").
24. Ibid.
25. Ibid.
26. Ibid., 151.

Chapter 3

1. William Trevor in "The Shadows of William Trevor" by Stephen Schiff, *New Yorker*, 28.12.92/ 4.1.93, 161.
2. Trevor in "Guarded Celebrant of the Human Condition," Geordie Grieg, *Sunday Times*, 29.5.88, Section G, 8–9.
3. Schiff, "Shadows," 161.
4. Trevor, "Cocktails at Doney's," *New Yorker*, 8.4.85, 44, my italics.
5. Schiff, "Shadows," 161.
6. In his introduction to *The Oxford Book of Irish Stories* (Oxford: Oxford University Press, 1989), Trevor defines the short story as "the distillation of an essence."

Chapter 4

1. Roger Angell to Victor Pritchett 10.10.61, B788*NYR*. About reviews of *When My Girl Comes Home* (London: Chatto & Windus, 1961).
2. VSP to RA 20.10.61, B788*NYR*.
3. See Ronald Hingley, *A New Life of Anton Chekhov* (London: Oxford University Press, 1976); Donald Rayfield, *Chekhov, The Evolution of his Art* (London: Paul Elek, 1975).
4. Pritchett, "The Short Story," *London Magazine*, 9.66, 6.
5. Lobrano to Harold Matson 23.8.40, B341*NYR*.
6. Katharine White to VSP 22.7.46, B436*NYR*.
7. White to Matson 24.1.47, B450*NYR*.
8. White to VSP 22.7.46, B436*NYR*.
9. White to Matson 24.1.47, B450*NYR*.
10. White to Matson 23.1.48, B465*NYR*.
11. Ibid.
12. White to Don Congdon 12.2.48, B465*NYR*.
13. Robert Henderson to Congdon 19.7.48, B465*NYR*.
14. Lobrano to Congdon 12.8.48, B465*NYR*.
15. *New Yorker* bibliography for V. S. Pritchett, *New Yorker* Library, *New Yorker* Offices. This document was obtained in correspondence with the librarian.
16. White to Congdon 10.11.49, B479*NYR*.

17. Ibid.
18. Ibid.
19. Lobrano to Congdon 5.2.52, B713*NYR*.
20. "Two Roast Beefs" was republished as "The Satisfactory" in *More Collected Stories* (London: Chatto & Windus, 1983) and in *CCS*.
21. Angell, "Marching Life," an appreciation of V. S. Pritchett, *New Yorker*, 22/29.12.97, 126.
22. Ibid., 134.
23. Ibid.
24. Angell, "Marching Life," 126.
25. Roger Angell, interview with author, *New Yorker* offices, 18.4.2001.
26. Angell, "Marching Life," 134.
27. William Trevor, "Best to be young or dead?" *The Daily Telegraph*, 28 September 1993, p. 24. Trevor mentioned this as an example of one of the editorial queries. He appreciates the checking department, believing the magazine's renowned attention to detail "is what authors who like to get things right long for."
28. VSP to Lobrano 12.7.53, B526*NYR*.
29. RA to VSP 20.10.59, B771*NYR*.
30. Ibid.
31. RA to VSP 9.12.69, B49F4PP.
32. Ibid.
33. RA to VSP 8.5.64, B809*NYR*.
34. RA to Peter Matson 8.5.64, B809*NYR*.
35. RA to VSP 31.10.78, B49F4PP.
36. RA to VSP 17.1.80, B928*NYR*.
37. Angell, interview with author, *NY* offices, 18.4.2001.
38. RA to VSP 17.10.68, B838*NYR*.
39. RA to VSP 20.10.59, B771*NYR*.
40. RA to VSP 14.10.60, B780*NYR*.
41. RA to James Street of Harold Matson 14.10.60, B780*NYR*.
42. RA to VSP 13.4.62, B795*NYR*.
43. RA to VSP 11.2.60, B780*NYR*.
44. VSP to RA 20.2.60, B780*NYR*.
45. Ibid.
46. RA to VSP 23.7.73, B868*NYR*.
47. RA to Matson 19.1.77, B898*NYR*.
48. RA to Peter Matson 11.2.77, B898*NYR*.
49. Pritchett, Lecture "Dialogue," revised typescript, 14pp., B20F10PP.
50. RA to VSP 26.10.73, B49F4PP: "Did You Invite Me?"
51. RA to VSP 16.9.68, B838*NYR*: "The Cage Birds."
52. Angell, interview with author, *NY* offices, 25.4.2001.
53. Lobrano to Congdon 6.3.53, B721*NYR*.
54. Angell, interview with author, 18.4.2001.
55. RA to VSP 27.2.59, B771*NYR*.

56. RA to VSP 14.4.59, B771*NYR*.
57. RA to VSP 21.7.59, Western Union Cablegram, B771*NYR*.
58. RA to VSP 27.7.59, B771*NYR*.
59. RA to James Street (Harold Matson Co.) 21.7.59, B771*NYR*.
60. RA to VSP 10.4.62, B795*NYR*.
61. RA to VSP 17.10.62, B795*NYR*.
62. VSP to RA 22.10.62, RCA Communications Telegram B795*NYR*.
63. See Gregory LeStage's D.Phil. Thesis, "Forces in the Development of the British Short Story, 1930–1970: Some Writers, Editors, and Periodicals," University of Oxford, 1998, for a somewhat different view of this exchange.
64. VSP to RA 3.10.59, B771*NYR*.
65. VSP to RA 15.11.65, B816*NYR*.
66. Angell, "Marching Life," 126.
67. RA to VSP 23.8.62, B795*NYR*.
68. *CCS*, 790.
69. VSP to RA 10.2.68, B838*NYR*.
70. RA to VSP 8.7.69, B844*NYR*.
71. RA to VSP 8.7.69, B844*NYR*.
72. RA to VSP 12.9.69, B49F4*PP*.
73. VSP to RA 9.11.69, B844*NYR*.
74. Ibid.
75. VSP to RA 21.7.69, B844*NYR*
76. RA to VSP 2.12.69, B49F4*PP*.
77. VSP to RA 5.12.69, B844*NYR*.
78. "Our Wife," revised typescript (15pp.), p. 1, B26F1*PP*.
79. "The Captain's Daughter," *New Yorker*, 27.12.69, 28.
80. RA to VSP 2.12.69, B49F4*PP*.
81. "The Captain's Daughter," *New Yorker*, 27.12.69, 30.
82. RA to VSP 6.1.59, B771*NYR*.
83. VSP to RA 12.1.59, B771*NYR*.
84. Ibid.
85. The first of two identically titled stories the *New Yorker* published ten years apart: 28.5.60 and 20.6.70. The 1970 story was retitled "The Diver" in Pritchett's *The Camberwell Beauty* (London: Chatto & Windus, 1974), and in all subsequent publications.
86. RA to VSP 11.2.60, B789*NYR*.
87. RA to VSP 18.6.65, B816*NYR*.
88. RA to VSP 28.1.82, B49F4*PP*.
89. RA to VSP 17.3.[82], B49F4*PP*.
90. A. S. Byatt, introduction, *The Oxford Book of English Short Stories* (Oxford: Oxford University Press, 1998), xxiv.
91. RA to VSP 17.11.77, B49F4*PP*.
92. Ibid.
93. RA to VSP 17.11.77, B49F4.
94. VSP to Angell 24.11.77, B907*NYR*.

95. VSP to Angell 2.12.77, B898/NYR.
96. "On the Edge of the Cliff," final typescript carbon, 26 pp., PC, HRC.
97. VSP to RA 2.12.77, B898/NYR.
98. RA to VSP 9.12.77, B898/NYR.
99. RA to VSP 27.7.78, B49F4PP.
100. Ibid.
101. VSP to RA 8.9.78, B907/NYR.
102. RA to VSP 28.9.78, B49F4PP.
103. Ibid.
104. VSP to RA 11.10.78, B907/NYR.
105. RA to VSP 21.11.78, B49F4PP.
106. Angell, interview with author, NY offfices, 18.4.2001.
107. Angell, "Marching Life," 126.
108. RA to VSP 21.11.78, B49F4PP.
109. VSP to RA 25.11.78, B907/NYR.
110. RA to VSP 26.1.66, B823/NYR.
111. RA to VSP 19.1.78, B49F4PP.
112. "On the Edge of the Cliff," final typescript carbon, p. 20, PC.
113. RA to VSP 19.1.78, B49F4PP.
114. VSP to RA 30.1.78, B907/NYR.
115. VSP to RA 14.11.69, B851/NYR.
116. RA to VSP 11.11.69, B49F4PP.
117. Ibid.
118. VSP to RA 14.11.69, B851/NYR.
119. RA to VSP 2.2.59, B780/NYR.
120. RA to VSP 29.9.67, B831/NYR.
121. RA to VSP 26.1.73, B49F4PP.
122. Frances Kiernan, who was William Maxwell's secretary before becoming his colleague, recalled this in an interview with the author, 27.7.2001, New York.
123. RA to VSP 6.10.60, B780/NYR.
124. Ibid.
125. Ibid.
126. VSP to RA 16.10.[60], B780/NYR.
127. RA to VSP 14.10.60, B780/NYR.
128. RA to VSP 13.4.62, B795/NYR.
129. VSP to RA 3.5.62, B795/NYR.
130. RA to VSP 4.11.65, B816/NYR.
131. Ibid.
132. VSP to RA 15.11.65, B816/NYR.
133. Ibid.
134. RA to VSP 22.11.65, Western Union Cablegram, B816/NYR.
135. RA to VSP 23.11.65, B816/NYR.
136. RA to VSP 11.11.[69], B49F4PP.
137. Ibid.
138. Angell, interview with author, NY offices, 4.25.2001.

139. VSP to RA 31.12.73, B874*NYR*.
140. Katherine Anne Porter 15.12.60, B780*NYR*.
141. See D. T. Max, "Raymond Carver's Afterlife," *New York Times Magazine*, 9.8.98, section 6, 34–57, for a discussion of Lish's editorial contributions to Carver's stories while he was editing the writer at *Esquire* magazine. Max claims that Lish's papers at the Lilly Library, Indiana University show that Lish often played an important role in determining the "unsaid" in and modifying endings of some of Carver's most famous stories.
142. Trevor, "Best to be Young or Dead?" *The Daily Telegraph*, 28.9.93, 24.
143. Robert Hemenway to Claire Degener (Sterling Lord Agency) 7.12.66, B825 and Hemenway to Degener 15.7.70, B852*NYR*. Frances Kiernan suspects that Shawn was speaking through Hemenway in this instance because the judgment communicates his well-known squeamishness about violence. Telephone interview with author, 31.10.2002.
144. Derek Morgan to Annette Yager 9.11.71, B858*NYR*. In response to what must have been the agent's accusation, Morgan promised Yager "that racialism had nothing to do with our decision not to take it – 'Trevor' is, after all, a Welsh name."
145. Frances Kiernan, interview with author, 27.7.2001, NYC.
146. Ibid.
147. Kiernan, telephone interview with author, 27.10.2002.
148. Kiernan, interview with author, 27.7.2001.
149. Ibid.
150. Kiernan, telephone interview with author, 27.10.2002.
151. Charles McGrath, telephone interview with author, 18.11.2005.
152. "Torridge," *New Yorker*, 12.9.77.
153. Veronica Geng to Peter Matson 17.10.79, B919*NYR*.
154. Trevor's *New Yorker* bibliography supplied by *NY* library.

Chapter 5

1. William Trevor, *Excursions in the Real World* (London: Penguin, 1994), xii.
2. Marianne Moore, "Poetry," *Collected Poems* (London: Faber & Faber, 1951), 41.
3. Trevor, *Excursions*, xii–xiii.
4. Trevor, "Jigsaws," *The New Review*, vol. 4, nos. 45/46, 12.77/1.78: 25.
5. Mira Stout, "The Art of Fiction CVIII: Interview with William Trevor," *Paris Review* 110, 1989, 131. (Hereafter, "*PR*110.")
6. Jan Dalley, "The God Botherer Who Just Keeps on Winning," *Independent on Sunday*, 29.1.95, 6.
7. Stephen Schiff, "The Shadows of William Trevor," *New Yorker*, 28.12.92/4.1.93, 161.
8. Dalley, "The God Botherer," 6.
9. Hugh Montgomery-Massingberd, "An Unassuming Lapidary in words," *The Sunday Telegraph*, 21.1.90, 50.

10. Ibid.
11. Stout, *PR*110, 131.
12. Ibid., 132–133.
13. Stout, *PR*110, 130–131, and Montgomery-Massingberd, "An Unassuming Lapidary," 50.
14. Trevor, interview with Amanda Smith, *Publishers Weekly*, 28.10.83, 81.
15. Trevor, interview with Suzanne Paulson in *William Trevor: A Study of the Short Fiction* (Twayne: New York, 1993), 112–113.
16. Montgomery-Massingberd, "An Unassuming Lapidary," 50.
17. Ibid., 141.
18. Ibid., 140–141.
19. Trevor, interview with S. Paulson, 117.
20. Writing *outside* of experience instead of *from* experience naturally led Trevor to a combination of extremes, resulting in one critic's comment that he wrote mostly about little old ladies.
21. Trevor, interview with A. Smith, 81.
22. Schiff, "The Shadows," 161.
23. Trevor, interview with S. Paulson, 113–114.
24. Ibid., 117.
25. Trevor, interview with A. Smith, 81.
26. Trevor, *Excursions*, xii. See the opening paragraph of "Memories of Youghal" in *CST,* 46.
27. Trevor, *Excursions*, xii.
28. Trevor, "An Unfinished Life," review of *George Eliot: The Emergent Self,* by Rudy V. Redinger, *The Spectator* 13.3.76, 20.
29. Trevor, "The Bad and the Brilliant," review of *Somerset Maugham and his World* by Frederic Raphael, *The Spectator* 26.2.77, 18.
30. Trevor, "The Arts," "Independent Criticism of BBC Television," review of *Fragments of a Portrait*, a film on Francis Bacon, 29.9.66, *The Listener*, 477.
31. Trevor, *Excursions*, xi.
32. Ibid., xvi.
33. The *Excursions* version is dated 1971.
34. Trevor, "In County Cork," *Excursions*, 8–9. Trevor's impression of Miss Willoughby in "Jigsaws" is even more negative: "Miss Willoughby's school room was the least agreeable of the long series of schools my brother and I attended [. . .]. [. . .] [N]othing could be worse than Miss Willoughby's Methodist sarcasm. Nothing ever was [. . .]." See "Jigsaws," 27–28.
35. See "Miss Quirke," *Excursions*, 26–29.
36. Trevor, "Sounds of Dublin," *Guardian*, 25.10.79, 11.
37. Typescript of "Miss Smith," 3, Trevor Collection, B4F13, McFarlin Library Special Collections, University of Tulsa, Tulsa, Oklahoma. (Hereafter, "'Miss Smith' typescript.")
38. "Miss Smith" typescript, 1.
39. Trevor, *Excursions*, 8.
40. "Miss Smith" typescript, 3.
41. Trevor, *Excursions*, xii.

42. "Miss Smith" typescript, 2.
43. Ibid., 4.
44. Ibid., 5.
45. Trevor, "Miss Smith," *The Collected Stories of William Trevor* (London: Penguin, 1993), 135.
46. "Miss Smith" typescript, 5.
47. Ibid., 4.
48. Ibid.
49. *CST*, 135. In the typescript version James knows that if ever he forgets to speak to God about her, Miss Smith would be nastier than ever and say something that could drive him to suicide.
50. "Miss Smith" typescript, 5.
51. See "Miss Smith" typescript, 3, first paragraph. Unable to complete a weekend assignment requiring him to write six sentences about dogs, James solicits the help of a man hired to cut the grass who produces six flat statements on the subject. The grass cutter from this deleted paragraph plays a pivotal role in the final version.
52. *CST*, 136. See identical presentation in "Miss Smith" typescript, 5.
53. "Miss Smith" typescript, 3.
54. *CST*, 136–137, from typescript, "Insert B."
55. *CST*, 136. (Identical to the "Insert B" wording except for the deleted "probably" before "to intervene.")
56. *CST*, 137, taken verbatim from "Miss Smith" typescript, 6.
57. Trevor believes detective stories to be the major influence on his fiction: "I still read thrillers and mysteries, and I think I sense the form of the detective story as a pattern in my work. See Trevor, interview with S. Paulson, 118.
58. *CST*, 137, taken verbatim from "Miss Smith" typescript, 6.
59. *CST*, 137–138, taken verbatim from "Miss Smith" typescript, 6.
60. "Miss Smith" typescript, 7. Rephrased in published version: "Consciously or otherwise she was trying to kill their child" (*CST*, 139).
61. The approximately 1,200-word insert between pages 6 and 7 of the penultimate draft is written on two legal-sized white sheets that set it apart from the manuscript's standard-sized light-blue sheets. Three quarters of it was preserved while the last quarter, transferred verbatim from "Insert A" of an incomplete, independent four-page double-spaced segment, was abandoned.
62. *CST*, 138, verbatim from 1,200-word insert.
63. Except for the husband's more exaggerated feeling of receiving a physical blow to the face upon smelling the gas and being momentarily stunned and helpless—a description excised in the typescript—the published version is identical to the "Miss Smith" typescript, white legal paper insert, 1.
64. *CST*, 138–139, almost identical to "Miss Smith" typescript, white legal paper insert, 1.
65. *CST*, 139, from "Miss Smith" typescript, white legal paper insert, 1.
66. New material from this three-quarter-page typed insert replaced the crossed out first paragraph of the penultimate draft's seventh page. Both pages begin with "to release the catch himself" and end with Miss Smith's self-reproach.

67. *CST*, 140, verbatim from "Miss Smith," three-quarter-page typed insert.
68. *CST*, 140, verbatim from "Miss Smith," three-quarter-page typed insert except without "for" before "a miracle."
69. *CST*, 140, verbatim from "Miss Smith," three-quarter-page typed insert.
70. "Miss Smith" typescript, 7. Reprinted in *CST*, 140.
71. *CST*, 140–141.
72. *CST*, 141.
73. Ibid.
74. "Miss Smith" typescript, "Insert A."
75. *CST*, 141.
76. Ibid., 135.
77. Ibid., 141.
78. Ibid. Trevor's allusion to Conrad's *Heart of Darkness* is unmistakable.
79. William Trevor, "The Bad and the Brilliant," *The Spectator*, 26.2.77, 18.
80. See Trevor, *Excursions*, 15–19.
81. "Kathleen's Field was published in the *New Yorker*, 12.5.86, and in the short-story collection *Family Sins* (1990). See *CST*, 1245–1261.
82. Trevor, "Jigsaws," 27.
83. Ibid., 28.
84. A similar kind of sacrifice is made in "Good News," in which a fading soap opera actress living vicariously through her daughter, Bea, finds a role for her, unwittingly exposing her to the production's pedophile star. Like Kathleen, Bea keeps the unpleasant situation a secret, believing that the "good news" of her participation will reunite her parents. See *The Hill Bachelors*, 40–62.
85. "Alma Mater," *Excursions*, 65.
86. Trevor, "Kathleen's Field," *CST*, 1260.
87. The central land issue is also related to Trevor's past. His parents were of farming stock, his father from Co. Roscommon, his mother from Co. Armagh. The Co. Roscommon farm disappeared altogether, gambled away by Mr. Cox's older brother. See Trevor, "Jigsaws," 25.
88. Trevor, *Excursions*, 16.
89. Ibid., 109–115.
90. Trevor was intrigued from childhood by enigmatic women in tragic circumstances: "There was a famous love affair in Youghal: he was a married doctor, she was a stylish lady in a series of cloche hats, who'd lost her youth through waiting for him." See Trevor, "Jigsaws," 25.
91. Trevor, "Assia," *Excursions*, 113.
92. Ibid., 111–112.
93. Trevor, "The Table," *CST*, 57.
94. Trevor, interview with Melvin Bragg, *The South Bank Show*, ITV, broadcast 24.4.83, BFI.
95. Trevor, "Some Notes on Writing Stories," *London Magazine* 3.70/vol. 9, no. 12, 10–12.
96. Trevor, "Some Notes," 10.
97. Ibid., 12.

98. Trevor, interview with A. Smith, 81.
99. Trevor, *Not Quite Among Friends*, BBC Radio 3, Producer: Judith Bumpus, broadcast 30.9.81. (Hereafter, *NQAF*.)
100. *Woman's Hour*, BBC Radio 2, interview with William Trevor by Marjorie Anderson, broadcast 1.9.71. NSA, BL.
101. *NQAF*.
102. Ibid.
103. Ibid.
104. Trevor, *Writers and Places*, "A City to Plunder," written and narrated by William Trevor, BBC Television, 22.1.81.
105. *NQAF*.
106. Ibid.

Chapter 6

1. V. S. Pritchett in interview with Ben Forkner and Philippe Séjourné, *Journal of the Short Story in English*, no. 6 (Spring 1986): 33.
2. Pritchett, *A Cab at the Door and Midnight Oil* (London: Hogarth Press, 1991), 211.
3. *CD*, 26.
4. *CD*, 29.
5. VSP to GB 9.11.52, F5PC.
6. Interview with V. S. Pritchett, *The Lively Arts*, BBC 16.6.67, WAC. This excerpt is from an out-take that was not broadcast.
7. Pritchett, interview with Frank Delaney, *Bookshelf*, BBC Radio 4, produced by Brian Cook, broadcast 23.3.80, NSA, BL.
8. *CD*, 9.
9. Conversely, one couple in the neighborhood had such a harmonious marriage that Victor wanted to move his own parents out of the house and replace them with Mr. and Mrs. Norman.
10. *MO*, 422.
11. *MO*, 382.
12. *London Dialogues* I, "How We Come to Form Opinions," Miss Margery Fry, interview with V. S. Pritchett, BBC London Calling Asia, broadcast 18.5.51, WAC.
13. *CD*, 208.
14. Pritchett in interview with John Haffenden, *Novelists in Interview* (London: Methuen, 1985), 217.
15. *London Dialogues* I.
16. Pritchett, *The Gentle Barbarian* (London: Chatto & Windus, 1977), 146.
17. Pritchett, interview with Mavis Nicholson, *After Noon Plus*, ITV, 11.1.80, BFI.
18. Ibid.
19. VSP to GB 1.3.68, BC19.3.

20. Pritchett, *Gentle Barbarian*, 54.
21. VSP to GB 24.1.68, BC19.3.
22. *MO*, 329.
23. Pritchett, *The Lively Arts*, BBC broadcast 16.6.67, WAC.
24. Pritchett, interview with Mavis Nicholson, *A Plus 4*, Channel 4, 4.12.85, BFI.
25. In his discussion with Mavis Nicholson, Pritchett says he was ten or twelve at the time, but mention of the Battle of the Somme (1916) means he would have been nearly sixteen.
26. *Professional Portrait: Novelist* by V. S. Pritchett. Produced by Stephen Potter with James McKeohnie as "The Novelist." BBC Home Service broadcast 11.2.44, WAC.
27. Ibid.
28. Pritchett, interview with Edwin Mullins, *Kaleidoscope*, BBC R4, 9.5.78, NSA, BL. In his Preface to *Collected Stories*, x, Pritchett reiterates his belief that it is a writer's duty to justify people, but is more emphatic about the reason for the writers' crusade: "we all feel that for good or ill, we are exceptional and justified in being what we are." This recurring idea also appears in Haffenden, *Novelists in Interview*, 212.
29. Trevor argued that as a writer "one is going to be much more curious about women if one happens to be a man" and "if you're a woman [. . .] it's surely more interesting to write about men [. . .]. Trevor interviewed by Russell Harty, *All About Books*, BBC 1, 19.6.80, BFI.
30. Pritchett, interview with Maris Nicholson, *A Plus 4*.
31. VSP to Claire Larrière 13.4.70. Madame Larrière supplied the author with a photocopy of this letter with a covering letter of her own dated 10.2.2002. The original remains in her possession.
32. Pritchett, *Gentle Barbarian*, "Acknowledgements."
33. The train was Pritchett's favorite form of transportation. See Pritchett interviewed by Mavis Nicholson, 11.1.80. In a letter to Harold Raymond dated 18.11.50, Pritchett revealed the source of the novel's title: "The name Beluncle is taken from a small railway halt or siding I once saw fifteen years ago in some place on the Thames Estuary. It caught my fancy." See the Chatto & Windus archive, Special Collections, University of Reading Library. Its substitution for his father's name may be a discreet expression of the author's submerged, seldom expressed tender feelings amidst his largely unflattering portrait.
34. Pritchett, interview with Forkner and Séjourné, *JSSE*, 25.
35. VSP to GB 30.5.66, BC19.3.
36. VSP to GB 9.6.67, BC19.3.
37. "(I have described some of this in a scene in *Mr Beluncle*, for it oppressed my mind [. . .].)" *MO*, 387.
38. VSP to GB n.d. [First line: "How good to hear from you."], BC, 19.3.
39. *CD*, 30.
40. Christian Science is a Christian sect founded by Mary Baker Eddy in 1879. Members hold that only God and the mind have ultimate reality, and that sin and illness are illusions which can be overcome by prayer and faith.

41. *CD*, 140.
42. Ibid., 140–141.
43. Ibid., 141.
44. Ibid., 144.
45. Ibid., 145.
46. Ibid., 148.
47. Ibid., 186.
48. Ibid., 187.
49. Ibid., 150–151.
50. Ibid., 151.
51. Ibid., 143.
52. Ibid.
53. See autograph manuscript of "The Saint," PC, HRC.
54. *CCS*, 187.
55. *CD*, 145.
56. *CCS*, 188.
57. Ibid., 187.
58. Ibid.
59. Ibid., 187–188.
60. Ibid., 188.
61. VSP to GB 2.2.44, F2PC.
62. Pritchett to a Mr. Franceschetti 3.12.69, B42F1PP.
63. *CCS*, 188.
64. Ibid., 189.
65. Ibid.
66. Ibid.
67. Ibid.
68. Ibid.
69. Ibid., 191.
70. Ibid., 190.
71. *MO*, 422. The Christian Science Church refused to recognize Walter as a Christian Science Practitioner.
72. *CCS*, 189.
73. Ibid., 190.
74. Ibid.
75. Ibid.
76. Ibid.
77. Ibid., 191.
78. Ibid., 191–192.
79. Ibid., 192.
80. Ibid., 194.
81. Ibid., 195.
82. Ibid.
83. Ibid., 197.
84. Pritchett, "The Landscape of Castile," BBC Third Programme, broadcast 24.11.51, WAC.

85. *MO*, 332.
86. Pritchett saw the "Spanish paradox" in *Del sentimiento tragica de la vida*: "life intensely felt in the flesh and made whole by the contemplation of death." See *MO*, 346. Pritchett's interpretation of Unamuno suggests John Keats's "Death is Life's high mead" and Wallace Stevens's "Death is the mother of beauty."
87. *MO*, 380.
88. *CD*, 135.
89. VSP to GB, [c.1938], first line: "I am overwhelmed [. . .]." F1PC.
90. VSP to GB, [c.1938], first line: "I owe you [. . .]." F1PC.
91. Ibid.
92. *CCS*, 199.
93. See "The Saint" in *Horizon*, vol. I, no. 4, April 1940: 288.
94. See Tennyson's *In Memoriam*, poem CXVIII.
95. Preface to *Collected Stories*, ix–x.
96. See "The Oedipus Complex," *CCS*, 238–242.
97. "The Dentist," Notebook F10PC.
98. *CCS*, 241.
99. *CCS*, 241–242.
100. "'And I bet you're thinking why didn't Lord Pollfax let sleeping dogs lie [. . .].'"
101. *CCS*, 242.
102. For another instance of Pritchett's extraordinarily creative and moving transmutations of an autobiographical setting and episode, see VSP to GB 30.9.50, F5PC; and his short story "The Lion's Den," originally collected in *It May Never Happen* (1945) and republished most recently in *CCS*.
103. *CCS*, 261.
104. Ibid., 266.
105. Pritchett, interview with Douglas Hughes, *Studies in Short Fiction*, vol. 13, no. 4 (Fall 1976): 430–431.
106. Notebook B2F10PC.
107. VSP to GB 13.3.41, F2PC.
108. Pritchett, interview with Forkner and Séjourné, *JSSE*, 35–36.
109. VSP to GB 7.12.[54] p.m. 8.12.54, 19.3BC.
110. VSP to GB 26.5.[55] p.m. 28.5.55, 19.3BC.
111. Haffenden, *Novelists in Interview*, 225.
112. Pritchett interviewed by Walter Allen, "The World of Books," BBC broadcast 6.2.65, WAC.
113. Pritchett, *A Plus 4*, 4.12.85. When he was a young writer, Pritchett wrote extensively of landscape. Although he came to focus almost exclusively on people, natural settings inspired some of his best work.
114. Pritchett interviewed by Michael Oliver, "Kaleidoscope," BBC Radio 4, 27.2.80, NSA, BL.
115. *The Book Programme*, "Capturing the Moment," BBC 2, 8.6.80, BFI. Robert Robinson chaired a discussion of the "Art of the Short Story" with guests Susan Hill, V. S. Pritchett, William Trevor, and John Updike.
116. Pritchett, *Dublin: A Portrait* (London: Bodley Head, 1967), 39.

117. GB to VSP 7.4.57, 19.3F6BC.
118. VSP to GB n.d. "Wednesday" [1 March 1947 added in ink], F3PC.
119. VSP to GB 31.12.48, F3PC.
120. VSP to GB 23.1.48, F3PC.
121. Pritchett interviewed by Nigel Forde, *Bookshelf*, BBC Radio 4, 15.2.90, NSA, BL.
122. Haffenden, *Novelists in Interview*, 225.
123. VSP to GB 23.7.69, 19.3BC.
124. Haffenden, *Novelists in Interview*, 225.
125. Pritchett, *London Perceived* (London: Chatto & Windus, 1962), 26.
126. Ibid., 25.
127. *Strength of Mind*, 7. "Can Imagination Help?" W. G. Newton, Arthur Koestler, V. S. Pritchett, and John Mabbott. Broadcast 14.11.41, BBC Home Service, WAC.
128. Pritchett, however, never disclosed what those "certain things" were. The other writer was Ved Mehta.
129. Haffenden, *Novelists in Interview*, 225–226.
130. *A Plus 4*, 4.12.85.
131. Pritchett, interview with Douglas Hughes, 431.

Chapter 7

1. V. S. Pritchett, interview with Ben Forkner and Philippe Séjourné, *Journal of the Short Story in English*, no. 6, Spring 1986: 34.
2. VSP to Angell 9.11.69, B844*NYR*.
3. *CCS*, 928.
4. Ibid.
5. *CCS*, 930.
6. Ibid., 928.
7. Ibid., 936.
8. Ibid., 933.
9. Ibid., 937.
10. Ibid., 935.
11. Ibid., 930.
12. Ibid., 928.
13. Ibid., 931.
14. The *New Yorker* retitled the story, "The Captain's Daughter."
15. *CCS*, 929.
16. Ibid.
17. Ibid.
18. Ibid., 933.
19. Ibid., 929.
20. Ibid., 931.
21. Ibid., 933.
22. Ibid.

23. Ibid., 937.
24. Ibid.
25. Ibid., 928.
26. Ibid., 930.
27. Ibid.
28. Ibid., 937.
29. Ibid., 930.
30. Ibid., 933.
31. Ibid., 934.
32. Ibid., 931.
33. Ibid., 934.
34. Ibid. Tom's use of "singular" in this context has, paradoxically, a dual meaning—"remarkable" and "single"—that renders "singular unity" both thematically appropriate and oxymoronic.
35. *CCS*, 932.
36. Ibid., 933.
37. Ibid., 934. In the book of The Clark Lectures for 1969, *George Meredith and English Comedy* (New York: Random House, 1969), Pritchett observed that "Meredith liked comparing women to yachts" (109). Furthermore, he seems to have found the very title of the story in a passage he quotes from Meredith's *The Egoist*: "'[H]e was to learn the nature of that possession in the woman who is *our wife*'" (my italics, 118).
38. *CCS*, 935.
39. Ibid., 929.
40. Ibid., 935.
41. Ibid., 931.
42. Ibid.
43. Ibid., 932.
44. Ibid.
45. Ibid.
46. Ibid., 933.
47. Ibid., 935.
48. The *New Yorker,* 30.10.95: 94.
49. Trevor describes his encounter with a County Mayo police sergeant in his introduction to *The Oxford Book of Irish Short Stories* (Oxford: Oxford University Press, 1989), ix.
50. In an exceptional public appearance, Trevor read both "Teresa's Wedding" and "The Piano Tuner's Wives" at the 92nd Street YMCA 12.05.97. The story was recorded and can be heard by accessing the following website: www.nytimes.com/books/98/09/06/ specials/trevor.html.
51. Trevor, "The Piano Tuner's Wives," *After Rain* (New York: Viking, 1996), 1.
52. *AR*, 1.
53. Ibid.
54. Ibid., 3.
55. Ibid., 8.

56. Ibid., 1.
57. Ibid., 3.
58. Ibid., 7.
59. Ibid., 4.
60. Ibid.
61. Ibid., 5–6.
62. Ibid., 9.
63. Ibid., 8.
64. Ibid., 8–9.
65. Ibid., 14.
66. Ibid., 15.
67. Ibid.
68. Pritchett, "Tea with Mrs. Bittell," *The Times*, "Saturday Review," 26.1.80, 8–9. As one of the stories in *On the Edge of the Cliff*, published 28.2.80, this first appearance of "Tea with Mrs. Bittell" served to interest prospective readers in the collection that would appear five weeks later.
69. Trevor, "Broken Homes," *The New Review*, vol. 3, no. 31, 10.76: 19–24.
70. *CCS*, 1061–1062.
71. Ibid., 1074.
72. Trevor, "Broken Homes," *The Collected Stories of William Trevor* (London: Penguin, 1993), 524.
73. *CCS*, 1061.
74. *CST*, 522.
75. Ibid.
76. Ibid.
77. Ibid., 523.
78. Ibid., 522.
79. Ibid.
80. Ibid., 523.
81. Ibid.
82. *CCS*, 1061.
83. Ibid.
84. Ibid., 1062.
85. Ibid., 1063.
86. Ibid., 1061.
87. Ibid., 1062.
88. Ibid.
89. Ibid., 1077.
90. Ibid., 1076.
91. Ibid., 1073.
92. Ibid., 1061.
93. Ibid., 1070.
94. Ibid., 1069.
95. *CST*, 524.
96. *Jaws*, a disaster film, was a box-office hit in the summer of 1975.

97. Scottish rock group.
98. *Kojak*, starring Telly Savalas as a New York detective, was a popular syndicated series by the mid-1970s.
99. *CST*, 526.
100. Ibid., 532.
101. Ibid., 527.
102. Ibid.
103. *CCS*, 1075.
104. *CST*, 529.
105. *CCS*, 1071.
106. Ibid., 1070.
107. Ibid., 1066.
108. Ibid., 1067.
109. Ibid.
110. Ibid.
111. Ibid., 1069.
112. Ibid.
113. Ibid.
114. Ibid., 1070.
115. Ibid., 1072.
116. Ibid., 1073.
117. Ibid., 1076.
118. Ibid., 1077.
119. Ibid., 1073.
120. Ibid., 1078.
121. Sir Peter Lely (1618–1680), Dutch portrait painter, resident in England from 1641. He became principal court painter to Charles II.
122. *CST*, 524.
123. Ibid., 528.
124. Ibid., 529.
125. Ibid., 535.
126. *CCS*, 1071.
127. Ibid., 1072.
128. *CST*, 534.
129. Ibid.
130. Ibid., 534–535.
131. Ibid., 535.
132. *CCS*, 1080–1081.
133. Ibid., 1081.
134. Ibid.
135. Pritchett was no stranger to domestic violence. His wife, Dorothy Pritchett, once attacked him with a "telephone instrument," hitting him in the mouth. For several years during the 1950s he lived in fear of her violent alcoholic behavior, never sleeping a night without wondering whether she would attack him in his sleep. See letter from Kingsley Martin to Leonard Woolf, 18.11.57, Leonard Woolf Papers (SX MS 13) I.H.3d, V. S. Pritchett loan, University of Sussex

Library, Special Collections. There are instances of marital violence in other stories that reflect his own. In "When My Girl Comes Home," Mr. Fulmino, suffering from a "genuine black eye" sustained in a "family battle," explains that "Mrs. Fulmino's emotions were in her arms" (*CCS*, 478). In "A Careless Widow," Frazier learns that Mrs. Summers divorced her first husband, who once hit her over the head with a bottle (*CCS*, 1115). And in "Things as They Are," Jill vows never to be hit again, implying that she was her fourth husband's victim (*CCS*, 385).

136. *CCS*, 1081.
137. See the *New Yorker*, 22.2.93, 143.

CHAPTER 8

1. V. S. Pritchett, (notebook) c. 1966, 35, B3F19 PC.
2. William Trevor interviewed by Marjorie Anderson as "Guest of the Week," *Woman's Hour*, BBC R2, 1.9.71, NSA, BL.
3. VSP to Claire Larrière 13.4.70. The original is in Madame Larrière's possession.
4. Pritchett, Preface, *Collected Stories* (London: Chatto & Windus, 1982), x.
5. VSP to Claire Larrière 13.4.70.
6. VSP to a Mr. Franceschetti 3.12.69, B42F1PP.
7. Pritchett, *George Meredith and English Comedy* (New York: Random House, 1970), 121.
8. Pritchett, *London Perceived* (London: Chatto & Windus, 1962), 81.
9. Ibid.
10. Pritchett, *Dublin: A Portrait* (London: Bodley Head, 1967), 29. Pritchett uses this interplay between the inner and outer face in describing the Walter Pritchett surrogate's evolution in "The Fly in the Ointment." See *CCS*, 300.
11. Ibid.
12. Ibid., 29–30.
13. VSP to GB 26.3.38, 1938–1952F1PC.
14. Ibid.
15. VSP to GB 27.5.38, 1938–1952F1PC. Pritchett once pointed out that his first story, "Tragedy in a Greek Theatre," "has a theme that occasionally recurs: —the practical man of affairs v. the artist or man of imagination." See VSP to a Mr. Franceschetti 3.12.69, B42F1PP.
16. VSP to GB n.d. [c. 1952?] [last line: "Write to me quickly about your X-ray."] F1PC.
17. VSP to GB 27.5.38, 1938–1952F2PC.
18. In turning down the opportunity to lecture for six months at Melbourne University and write as a guest for a Melbourne newspaper, Pritchett once again expressed the secret wish for a "double life" in which he could "combine travelling with the advantages of staying put." See VSP to GB 31.12.48, 1938–1952F3PC.

19. VSP to GB 11.9.41, 1938–52F2PC. The line Pritchett quotes (without the initial capital letter) is from poem LIV of Tennyson's *In Memoriam*.
20. VSP to GB 2.2.44, 1938–1952F2PC.
21. VSP to GB 28.6.52, 1938–1952F5PC.
22. VSP to GB p.m. 20.7.53, F19.3BC.
23. VSP to GB 14.2.53, F19.3BC. The story based on this observation was published seven years later in the *New Yorker*.
24. Pritchett, notebook [c. 1958–1959], B2F15PC.
25. *CCS*, 429.
26. Ibid.
27. Ibid.
28. Ibid., 431.
29. Ibid., 430.
30. Ibid., 431.
31. Ibid.
32. Ibid., 438.
33. Ibid., 440.
34. Ibid., 38.
35. Ibid., 55.
36. Ibid., 38.
37. Ibid., 39.
38. Ibid., 40.
39. Ibid., 51.
40. Pritchett, "Page and Monarch," *CCS*, 131–141.
41. Pritchett, "A Trip to the Seaside," *CCS*, 1155–1167.
42. Trevor, *Hidden Ground*, BBC Northern Ireland 30.5.90.
43. Trevor, interview with S. Paulson, 116.
44. Trevor, "The Ballroom of Romance," *CST*, 189–204.
45. Trevor, "The Hill Bachelors," *Hill Bachelors* (London: Viking, 2000), 224–245.
46. Trevor, "The Potato Dealer," *AR*, 132–147.
47. Although entrapment is a central theme in Trevor's Irish stories, it appears throughout his oeuvre. See the following stories: "The General's Day"; "The Penthouse Apartment"; "The Grass Widows"; "Going Home"; "A Trinity"; "A Day"; and "Good News."
48. Trevor, *PR*110, 134.
49. Trevor, "Pritchett Proclaimed," review of *Collected Stories* by V. S. Pritchett, *The New Republic*, 2.9.82, 30–32.
50. Trevor, "Child of the Century." Review of *Complete Collected Stories* by V. S. Pritchett, *New York Review of Books*, 13.6.91, 9.
51. Pritchett, "The Writer's Tale," *Vogue*, 3.81, 362.
52. Pritchett, "Explosions of Conscience." Review of *Lovers of Their Time and Other Stories* by William Trevor, *New York Review of Books*, 19.4.79, 8.
53. Geordie Grieg, "Guarded Celebrant of the Human Condition," *Sunday Times*, 29.05.88, 8–9.

54. Stephen Schiff, "The Shadows of William Trevor," *New Yorker*, 28.12.92/04.01.93, 161.
55. Trevor once said that all his gloom came from Hardy. See "Gentle Gerontocrat," 7.
56. Pritchett, Second World War Journal 22.10.40, B40PP.
57. Pritchett, interview with Ben Forkner and Philippe Séjourné, *JSSE 6*, 34.

Bibliography

Primary Sources:

A. Unpublished

Angell, Roger. Interview with the author, 18.04.01.
———. Interview with the author, 25.04.01.
Bodley Head archive, University of Reading Library, Special Collections.
Brenan, Gerald, Collection. The Harry Ransom Humanities Research Center, Special Collections, University of Texas at Austin, Texas. Correspondence with V. S. Pritchett 1950–1978.
British Broadcasting Corporation Written Archives Centre, Caversham Park, Reading. Correspondence between the BBC and V. S. Pritchett from 1936 to1982 and between William Trevor and the BBC from 1965, as well as scripts for numerous broadcasts from 1941 onwards involving both Pritchett and Trevor.
British Film Institute, London. Television programs involving V. S. Pritchett and William Trevor.
Chatto and Windus archives, University of Reading Library, Special Collections.
Kiernan, Frances. Interview with the author, 27.07.01.
———. Telephone interview with the author, 27.10.02.
Lehmann, John, Papers. Harry Ransom Humanities Research Center, Special Collections. This collection includes a significant correspondence with V. S. Pritchett.
McGrath, Charles. Telephone interview with the author, 18.11.05.
National Sound Archive, The British Library, London. BBC Radio broadcasts involving V. S. Pritchett and William Trevor.
Porter, Katherine Anne. Correspondence with the *New Yorker*. The *New Yorker* Records, Manuscripts and Archives Division, New York Public Library.
Pritchett, V. S., Collection. Harry Ransom Humanities Research Center, Special Collections. University of Texas at Austin, Austin, Texas. Holdings include over 40 boxes of autograph manuscripts, corrected typescripts with author's revisions, and final typescripts for 65 short stories. There is a large collection of notebooks and extensive correspondence with other writers, including 185 autograph letters to Gerald Brenan from 1938–1978.

Pritchett, V. S. Correspondence with the *New Yorker*. The *New Yorker* Records, Manuscripts and Archives Division, New York Public Library.

Pritchett, V. S. Letter to Claire Larrière, 13.04.70. In Madame Larrière's possession.

Pritchett, V. S. Manuscript of "The Wheelbarrow." Add. Mss. 56351C. The British Library, Students' Reading Room, London.

Pritchett V. S., Papers. The Berg Collection, New York Public Library, New York. Comprises 51 boxes of manuscripts, notebooks, and correspondence from 1930–1990. There are over 400 manuscripts of stories, lectures, essays, and books as well as 18 manuscript notebooks. Correspondence includes over 500 letters from Pritchett to his wife Dorothy and over 1,500 letters to Pritchett from friends, authors, and editors.

Trevor, William, Collection. McFarlin Library Special Collections, University of Tulsa, Tulsa, Oklahoma. Contained in 15 boxes, this collection consists of autograph, typescript, and carbon copy typescript manuscripts as well as unbound proofs of short stories, novels, novellas, radio and television adaptations from published work, stage plays, essays, articles, and book reviews. The material dates from 1964 to 2000.

Trevor, William. Correspondence with the *New Yorker*. The *New Yorker* Records, Manuscripts and Archives Division, New York Public Library.

———. *Hidden Ground*. BBC Northern Ireland, 30.05.90. Written and narrated by Trevor. Copy of broadcast obtained from the BBC Commercial Unit, London.

———. *A City to Plunder*. BBC, 22.01.81. Written and narrated by Trevor. Copy of broadcast obtained from the BBC Commercial Unit, London.

Woolf, Leonard, Papers. University of Sussex Library, Special Collections.

B. Published

New Statesman and Nation. London: Statesman and Nation, 1931–1957.

New Writing. vols. 1–5 (Spring 1936–Spring 1938); New Series. vols. 1–3 (Autumn 1938–Christmas 1939). London: Hogarth Press, 1936–1939.

Folios of New Writing. (Spring 1940–Autumn 1941). London: Hogarth Press, 1940–1941.

New Writing and Daylight. London: Hogarth Press, 1942–1946.

Penguin New Writing, ed. John Lehmann. Harmondsworth, England: Allen Lane, Penguin Books, 1940–1950.

New Statesman. London: Statesman and Nation Publishing Co., 1957–1988.

Pritchett, V. S. *Marching Spain*. London: Benn, 1928.

———. *Clare Drummer*. London: Benn, 1929.

———. *The Spanish Virgin and Other Stories*. London: Benn, 1930.

———. *Shirley Sanz*. London: Gollancz, 1932.

———. *Nothing Like Leather*. London: Chatto & Windus, 1935.

———. *Dead Man Leading*. London: Chatto & Windus, 1937.

———. *You Make Your Own Life*. London: Chatto & Windus, 1938.

———. "The Saint." *Horizon Magazine,* vol. 1, no. 4. April 1940.
———. *Build the Ships.* (The official story of the shipyards in wartime. Prepared by the Ministry of Information. Text by Pritchett.) London, 1946.
———. "Broadcasting about Literature." *BBC Quarterly,* vol. 2, no. 2, July 1947: 77–82.
Pritchett, V. S., Elizabeth Bowen, and Graham Greene. *Why Do I Write?* London: Marshall, 1948.
Pritchett, V. S. *Mr. Beluncle.* London: Chatto & Windus, 1951.
———. *The Spanish Temper.* London: Chatto & Windus, 1954.
———. "Citizen." *New Yorker,* 9 May 1959.
———. "The Fall." *New Yorker,* 28 May 1960.
———. "The Wheelbarrow." *New Yorker,* 16 July 1960.
———. *When My Girl Comes Home.* London: Chatto & Windus, 1961.
———. *London Perceived.* London: Chatto & Windus, 1962.
———. *The Key to My Heart.* London: Chatto & Windus, 1963.
———. *Foreign Faces.* London: Chatto & Windus, 1964.
———. "The Short Story." *London Magazine,* September 1966, 6–9.
———. *Dublin: A Portrait.* London: Bodley Head, 1967.
———. *Blind Love and Other Stories.* London: Chatto & Windus, 1969.
———. "The Captain's Daughter." *New Yorker,* 27 December 1969.
———. *George Meredith and English Comedy.* New York: Random House, 1969.
———. "The Fall." *New Yorker,* 20 June 1970.
———. *Balzac.* London: Chatto & Windus, 1973.
———. *The Camberwell Beauty and Other Stories.* London: Chatto & Windus, 1974.
———. *The Gentle Barbarian: The Life and Work of Turgenev.* London: Chatto & Windus, 1977.
———. "On The Edge of the Cliff." *New Yorker,* 20 February 1978.
———. "Explosions of Conscience." Review of *Lovers of Their Time* by William Trevor. *New York Review of Books,* 19 April 1979, 8.
———. "Tea with Mrs. Bittell." "Saturday Review," *The Times,* 26 January 1980.
———. *On the Edge of the Cliff.* London: Chatto & Windus, 1980.
———. Introduction. *The Oxford Book of Short Stories.* New York: Oxford University Press, 1981.
———. "The Writer's Tale." *Vogue,* March 1981.
———. *The Collected Stories of V. S. Pritchett.* London: Chatto & Windus, 1982.
———. *More Collected Stories.* London: Chatto & Windus, 1983.
———. *Chekhov: A Spirit Set Free.* London: Hodder & Stoughton, 1988.
———. *A Careless Widow and Other Stories.* London: Chatto & Windus, 1989.
———. *The Complete Essays.* London: Chatto & Windus, 1990.
———. *The Complete Short Stories of V. S. Pritchett.* London: Chatto & Windus, 1990.
———. *The Complete Collected Stories* of V. S. Pritchett. New York: Random House, 1990.
———. *A Cab at the Door and Midnight Oil.* London: Hogarth Press, 1991.
Trevor, William. "Leaving School." *London Magazine,* vol. 4, no. 9, 1964: 36–42.
———. *The Old Boys.* London: Bodley Head, 1964.

———. "The Arts." Review of *Fragments of a Portrait*, a BBC film on Francis Bacon, *Listener*, 29 September 1966, 477.

———. *The Day We Got Drunk on Cake and Other Stories*. London: Bodley Head, 1967.

———. "Involvement: Writers Reply." *London Magazine*, vol. 8, no. 5, August 1968: 8–9.

———. "Some Notes on Writing Stories." *London Magazine*, vol. 9, no. 12, March 1970: 10–12.

———. *The Ballroom of Romance and Other Stories*. London: Bodley Head, 1972.

———. "A View of My Own." *Nova*, September 1974.

———. *Angels at the Ritz and Other Stories*. London: Bodley Head, 1975.

———. "An Unfinished Life." Review of *George Eliot: The Emergent Self*, by Ruby V. Redinger. *The Spectator*, 13 March 1976, 20.

———. "Broken Homes." *The New Review*, vol. 3, no. 31, October 1976.

———. *The Children of Dynmouth*. London: Bodley Head, 1976.

———. "The Bad and the Brilliant." Review of *Somerset Maugham and his World*, by Frederic Raphael. *The Spectator*, 26 February 1977, 18–19.

———. "Absolute Sadness." Review of *Gentle Barbarian: The Life and Work of Turgenev*, by V. S. Pritchett. *The Spectator*, 25 June 1977, 21–22.

———. "Torridge." *New Yorker*, 12 September 1977.

———. "Jigsaws." *The New Review*, vol. 4, nos. 45/46, December 1977/January 1978: 25–28.

———. *Lovers of Their Time and Other Stories*. London: Bodley Head, 1978.

———. "Sounds of Dublin." *Guardian*, 25 October 1979, 11.

———. *Beyond the Pale and Other Stories*. London: Bodley Head, 1981.

———. "Pritchett Proclaimed." Review of *Collected Stories*, by V. S. Pritchett. *New Republic*, 2 August 1982, 30–32.

———. *Fools of Fortune*. London: Bodley Head, 1983.

———. *The Stories of William Trevor*. Hammondsmith, UK: Penguin, 1983.

———. *A Writer's Ireland: Landscape in Literature*. London: Thames & Hudson, 1984.

———. "Cocktails at Doney's." *The New Yorker*, 8 April 1985.

———. "Kathleen's Field." *New Yorker*, 12 May 1986.

———. *The News from Ireland and Other Stories*. London: Bodley Head, 1986.

———. Introduction. *The Oxford Book of Irish Stories*. Oxford: Oxford University Press, 1989.

———. *Family Sins and Other Stories*. London: Bodley Head, 1990.

———. "Child of the Century." Review of *Collected Stories*, by V. S. Pritchett. *New York Review of Books*, 13 June 1991, 8–10.

———. "Best To Be Young or Dead?" *The Daily Telegraph*, 28 September 1993, 24.

———. *William Trevor: The Collected Stories*. London: Penguin, 1993.

———. *Excursions in the Real World*. London: Penguin, 1994.

———. *After Rain*. London: Viking, 1996.

———. *Cocktails at Doney's and Other Stories*. London: Bloomsbury, 1996.

———. *The Hill Bachelors*. London: Viking, 2000.

———. *A Bit on the Side*. London: Viking, 2004.

Secondary Sources

Allen, Walter. *The Short Story in English*. Oxford: Clarendon Press, 1981.
Amis, Martin. "In Praise of Pritchett." *The War Against Cliché: Essays and Reviews 1971–2000*. London: Cape, 2001, 65–71.
Angell, Roger. "Marching Life." *New Yorker,* 22 and 29 December 1997, 126–134.
Anon. "The Temptations of a Technique." Review of *When My Girl Comes Home,* by V. S. Pritchett. *Times Literary Supplement,* 6 October 1961, 657.
Aronson, Jacqueline Stahl. "William Trevor: An Interview." In *Writing Irish,* edited by James P. Myers Jr. Syracuse, NY: Syracuse University Press, 1999, 37–49.
Baldwin, Dean. "The Tardy Evolution of the British Short Story." *Studies in Short Fiction,* vol. 30, no. 1, Winter 1993.
———. *V. S. Pritchett*. Boston: Twayne Publishers, 1987.
———, ed. *British Short Fiction Writers, 1945–1980. Dictinary of Literary Biography.* London: Gale Research, 1994.
Banville, John. "Revelations." Review of *After Rain,* by William Trevor. *New York Review of Books,* 20 February 1997, 19.
Bates, H. E. *The Modern Short Story: A Critical Survey.* London: Michael Joseph, 1972.
———. *The Modern Short Story from 1809 to 1953*. London: Hale, 1988.
Bayley, John. *The Short Story: Henry James to Elizabeth Bowen*. Hemel Hempstead: Harvester Press, 1988.
Beachcroft, T. O. *The Modest Art: A Survey of the Short Story in English*. London: Oxford University Press, 1968.
Bloom, Jonathan. "Revision as Transformation: The Making and Re-Making of V. S. Pritchett's 'You Make Your Own Life.'" *Journal of the Short Story in English/ Les Cahiers de la nouvelle,* no. 45, Fall 2005.
———. "V. S. Pritchett's Ministering Angell." *Sewanee Review,* vol. 112, no. 2, Spring 2004: 212–239.
Books from the Library of V. S. Pritchett, Catalogue 292. London: Bertram Rota, 2000.
Bowen, Elizabeth, Graham Greene, and V. S. Pritchett. *Why Do I Write? An Exchange of views between Elizabeth Bowen, Graham Greene and V. S. Pritchett*. London: Percival Marshall, 1948.
Bragg, Melvin. "William Trevor—The Most English of Irishmen." *Good Housekeeping,* December 1984, 64–65.
Briggs, Asa. *The History of Broadcasting in the United Kingdom*. Oxford: Oxford University Press, 1995, vols. 1–5.
Brenan, Gerald. *Personal Record, 1920–1972*. London: Cape, 1974.
Buford, Bill. "The Seductions of Storytelling." *New Yorker,* 24 June 1996.
Byatt, A. S, ed. Introduction. *The Oxford Book of English Short Stories*. Oxford: Oxford University Press, 1998.
Callahan, James M. *The Irish Novel: A Critical History.* Dublin: Gill and Macmillan, 1988.
Casey, Kevin. "Trevor Country." *Hibernia,* 12 April 1979, 23.

Corcoran, Neil. *After Yeats and Joyce: Reading Modern Irish Literature.* Oxford: Oxford University Press, 1997.

Cunningham, Valentine. *British Writers of the '30s.* Oxford: Clarendon Press, 1988.

———. "Coping with the Bigger Words." Review of *Collected Stories*, by V. S. Pritchett. *Times Literary Supplement*, 25 June 1982, 687.

———. "The Flesh and Bone Merchant." Review of *Complete Short Stories*, by V. S. Pritchett. *Times Literary Supplement*, 23 November 1990, 1255–1256.

Dalley, Jan. "The God Botherer Who Just Keeps on Winning." *Independent on Sunday*, 29 January 1995, 6.

Deane, Seamus. *A Short History of Irish Literature.* London: Hutchinson, 1986.

Donoghue, Denis. "Reality Bites." Review of *Excursions in the Real World*, by William Trevor. *New Republic*, 14 March 1994, 38–40.

Epstein, Joseph. "The Enduring V. S. Pritchett." *The New Criterion*, vol. 2, no. 7, March 1993: 19–27.

Flora, Joseph, ed. *The English Short Story, 1880–1945.* Boston: Twayne Publishers, 1985.

Flower, Dean. "The Reticence of William Trevor." *The Hudson Review*, vol. 43, no. 4, Winter 1991: 686–690.

Forkner, Ben, and Philippe Séjourné. "An Interview with V. S. Pritchett." *Journal of The Short Story in English*, no. 6, Spring 1986: 9–38.

Forster, R. F. *Paddy and Mr. Punch: Connections in Irish and English History.* London: Allen Lane, 1993.

Gibbs, Wolcott. "Theory and Practice of Editing New Yorker Articles." *Genius in Disguise: Harold Ross of The New Yorker,* by Thomas Kunkel. New York: Random House, 1995.

Gill, Brendan. *Here at The New Yorker.* London: Heinemann, 1975.

Greig, Geordie. "Guarded Celebrant of the Human Condition." *Sunday Times,* 29 May 1988, G9.

Guppy, Shusha, and Anthony Weller. "The Art of Fiction CXXII: V. S. Pritchett." *Paris Review*, no. 117, Winter 1990: 182–207.

Haffenden, John. "V. S. Pritchett." *Novelists in Interview.* London: Methuen, 1985, 210–230.

Head, Dominic. *The Modernist Short Story.* Cambridge: Cambridge University Press, 1992.

Heath, Susan. Review of *The Camberwell Beauty. Saturday Review/World*, 19 October 1974, 28–29.

Hildebidle, John. *Five Irish Writers: The Errand of Keeping Alive.* Cambridge, MA: Harvard University Press, 1989.

Hingley, Ronald. *A New Life of Anton Chekhov.* London: Oxford University Press, 1976.

Hodgart, Matthew. Review of *The Camberwell Beauty. New York Review of Books,* 20 March 1975, 32.

Howe, Irving. "Tales of Weary England." Review of *The Sailor, Sense of Humour, and Other Stories. New Republic,* 17 September 1956, 19–20.

Hughes, Douglas A. "The Eclipsing of V. S. Pritchett and H. E. Bates: A Representative Case of Critical Myopia." *Studies in Short Fiction,* vol. 19, no. 4, Fall 1982: iii–iv.

———. Untitled article included in John Stinson's *V. S. Pritchett: A Study of the Short Fiction*. New York: Twayne Publishers, 1992: 108–121.

———. "V. S. Pritchett: An Interview." *Studies in Short Fiction*, vol. 13, no. 4, Fall 1976: 423–432.

Johnson, Robert Owen. *An Index to Literature in the New Yorker*. Vols. 1–15, 1925–1940; vols. 16–30, 1940–1955; vols. 31–45, 1955–1970; vols. 46–50, 1970–1975. Metuchen, NJ: Scarecrow Press, 1969.

Kakutani, Michiko. "Gentle Illuminations." Review of *More Collected Stories*, by V. S Pritchett. *New York Times Book Review*, 18 September 1983, 11, 37.

Kermode, Frank. "A Century of Stories." Review of *V. S. Pritchett: The Complete Collected Stories*. *New York Times Book Review*, 24 March 1991, 1, 28–29.

Kreilkamp, Vera. *The Anglo-Irish Novel and the Big House*. Syracuse, NY: Syracuse University Press, 1998.

Lee, Hermione. "Boasters on Their Dangerous Journeys." *Times Literary Supplement*, 4 November 1983, 1214.

LeStage, Gregory. "Forces in the Development of the British Short Story, 1930–1970: Some Writers, Editors, and Periodicals." DPhil thesis. University of Oxford, 1998. Unpublished.

Lodge, David, ed. Introduction. *The Best of Ring Lardner*. London: J. M. Dent, 1993, ix–xviii.

Lohafer, Susan. *Coming to Terms with the Short Story*. Baton Rouge: Louisiana State University Press, 1983.

Lohafer, Susan, and J. E. Clarey. *Short Story Theory at a Crossroads*. Baton Rouge: Louisiana State University Press, 1989.

MacKenna, Dolores. *William Trevor: The Writer and His Work*. Dublin: New Island Books, 1999.

Max, D. T. "Raymond Carver's Afterlife: The Carver Chronicles." *New York Times Magazine*, 9 August 1998, Section 6.

May, Charles E., ed. *New Short Story Theories*. Athens: Ohio University Press, 1994.

May, Derwent. "Pritchett's Triangle." *Times Literary Supplement*, 17 January 1992, 27.

McCormack, William John. *Ascendancy and Tradition in Anglo-Irish Literary History from 1789–1939*. Cork: Cork University Press, 1994.

Mellors, John. "V. S. Pritchett: Man on the Other Side of a Frontier." *London Magazine*, April 1975, 5–13.

Montgomery-Massingberd, Hugh. "An Unassuming Lapidary in Words." *Sunday Telegraph*, 21 January 1990, 50.

Moore, Marianne. "Poetry." *Collected Poems*. London: Faber & Faber, 1951.

Morrison, Kristin. *William Trevor*. New York: Twayne Publishers, 1993.

———. "William Trevor's 'System of Correspondences.'" *Massachusetts Review*, 28, Autumn 1987: 489–496.

Mortimer, Mark. "The Short Stories of William Trevor." *Etudes Irlandaises* 9, December 1984: 161–173.

Moynihan, Julian. *Anglo-Irish: The Literary Imagination in a Hyphenated Culture*. Princeton, NJ: Princeton University Press, 1995.

———. "Tales of Two Nations." Review of *The Silence in the Garden* by William Trevor. *New Republic*, 6 February 1989, 37–40.

Oates, Joyce Carol. "On Small Farms from Cork to Cavan." Review of *The Hill Bachelors*. *Times Literary Supplement*, 29 September 2000, 22–23.

O'Connor, Frank. *The Lonely Voice: A Study of the Short Story*. London: Macmillan, 1963.

O'Donoghue, Bernard. "The Plain People of Ireland." Review of *Collected Stories of William Trevor*. *Times Literary Supplement*, 13 November 1992, 19.

O'Faolain, Sean. *The Short Story*. London: Collins, 1948.

Paulson, Suzanne Morrow. *William Trevor: A Study of the Short Fiction*. New York: Twayne Publishers, 1993.

Peden, William. "Realism and Anti-Realism in the Modern Short Story." *The Teller and the Tale: Aspects of the Short Story*, edited by Wendell M. Aycock. Lubbock, Texas: Texas Tech Press, 1982.

Price, Reynolds. "A Lifetime of Tales from the Land of Broken Hearts." Review of *Collected Stories*, by William Trevor. *New York Times Book Review*, 28 February 1983, 1, 25–27.

Pritchett, Oliver, ed. Foreword. *The Pritchett Century. The Selected Writings of V. S. Pritchett*. London: Chatto & Windus, 1998.

Ralph-Bowman, Mark. Interview with William Trevor. *Transatlantic Review* (London), vols. 53–54, February 1976: 5–12.

Rayfield, Donald. *Chekhov, The Evolution of his Art*. London: Paul Elek, 1975.

Rhodes, Robert E. "'The Rest Is Silence': Secrets in Some William Trevor Stories." *New Irish Writing* III: *Essays in Memory of Raymond J. Porter*, edited by James D. Brophy and Eamon Grennan. Boston: G. K. Hall, 1989, 35–53.

———. "William Trevor's Stories of the Troubles." *Contemporary Irish Writing*, edited by James D. Brophy and Raymond J. Porter. Boston: Twayne, 1983: 95–114.

Scannell, Paddy, and David Cardiff. *A Social History of British Broadcasting, 1922–1939*. Oxford: Oxford University Press, 1991.

Schiff, Stephen. "The Shadows of William Trevor." *New Yorker*, 28 December 1992/4 January 1993, 158–163.

Schirmer, Gregory A. *William Trevor: A Study of His Fiction*. London and New York: Routledge, 1990.

Shaw, Valerie. *The Short Story: A Critical Introduction*. London: Longmans, 1983.

Smith, Amanda. "Publishers Weekly Interviews: William Trevor." *Publishers Weekly*, 28 October 1983, 80–81.

Special V. S. Pritchett Issue. *Journal of the Short Story in English* 6 (Spring 1986).

Stinson, John J. "Replicas, Foils, and Revelation in Some Irish Short Stories of William Trevor." *Canadian Journal of Irish Studies*, vol. 11, no. 2, December 1985: 17–26.

———. *V. S. Pritchett: A Study of the Short Fiction*. New York: Twayne Publishers, 1992.

Storey, Michael L. "William Trevor: *The Collected Stories*." *Studies in Short Fiction*, vol. 30, no. 4, Fall 1993: 603–604.

Stout, Mira. "The Art of Fiction CVIII: Interview with William Trevor." *Paris Review*, 110, 1989: 118–151.

Thomas, Michael W. "Usurping Spiv and Gentry: William Trevor's London." *Irish University Review*, Spring 2002: 376–385.

Towers, Robert. "Gleeful Misanthropy." Review of *The Stories of William Trevor*. *New York Times Book Review,* section 7, 2 October 1983: 1, 22–23.

Treglown, Jeremy. "The Logical Foreigner in Love: V. S. Pritchett's Spanish Travels." *Times Literary Supplement,* 12 July 2002, 13–15.

———. *V. S. Pritchett: A Working Life.* London: Chatto & Windus, 2004.

Vannatta, Dennis, ed. *The English Short Story, 1945–1980: A Critical History.* Boston: Twayne Publishers, 1985.

Webb, W. L. "Gentle Gerontocrat." *Manchester Guardian,* 1 May 1965, 7.

Welty, Eudora. "A Family of Emotions." Review of *Selected Stories* by V. S. Pritchett. *New York Times Book Review,* 25 June 1978: 1, 39–40.

Wood, James. "An English Chekhov: V. S. Pritchett and the Condescension of Posterity." *Times Literary Supplement,* 4 January 2002, 12–13.

———. "V. S. Pritchett and English Comedy." In *On Modern British Fiction,* edited by Zachary Leader. New York: Oxford University Press, 2002, 8–19.

Yagoda, Ben. *The New Yorker and the World It Made.* New York: Scribners, 2000.

Index

"Access to the Children" (WT), 89
"Accompanist, The" (VSP), 73
Adventures of Huckleberry Finn, The, 20
After Rain (WT), 36, 157
Agony in the Garden (Pietro Perugino), 55
Allen, Walter, 13, 19
Alleyn's School (Dulwich), 122
Angell, Roger, 65, 69–88
    career overview of, 69–70
    editorial queries and suggestions of, 74–88
    narrative indirection objectionable to, 75, 85
    negotiations with William Shawn, 83–84
    VSP's relationship with, 69–88
    rejection of VSP's submissions, 71–74
"Ape, The" (VSP), 14, 15, 129
"Aristocrat, The" (VSP), 2, 18, 67
"Attracta" (WT), 90, 117, 197
"August Saturday" (WT), 109
"Aunt Gertrude" (VSP), 15
"Autumn Sunshine" (WT), 90

Bacon, Francis, 97
"Ballroom of Romance, The" (WT), 89, 117, 190
    entrapment in, 190–192
    rural Ireland depicted in, 190
Balzac, Honoré de, 12–13
"Barber, The" (VSP), 21.
    See "You Make Your Own Life" (VSP)

Barthelme, Donald, 70, 90
"Beast in the Jungle, The" (Henry James), 62
Beattie, Ann, 70, 90
Beethoven, Ludwig van, 126
Bennett, Arnold, 6, 8
"Beyond the Pale" (WT), 90, 117
"Birthmark, The" (Nathaniel Hawthorne), 150
"Blind Love" (VSP), 11–12, 72, 87, 88, 147
    and genesis of, 149–150
"Blind Man, The" (D. H. Lawrence), 150
Bloomsbury, 7, 197
Borges, Jorge Luis, 149
Brandeis University, 70
Brenan, Gerald, 19, 136, 145, 147, 180
    praise for VSP, 16
    on VSP's choice of subjects, 9
    VSP's *Mr Beluncle* subsidized by, 68
    reader for VSP, 70
British Broadcasting Corporation (BBC)
    broadcast issues, 5
    change of policy; Second World War propaganda, 3
    class consciousness, 1, 2, 3, 4, 5
    English literature broadcasts, 1
    VSP's start with, 1
    VSP's broadcasting audition, 1–2
    VSP's microphone technique for, 2
    VSP as broadcaster for, 3, 4
    VSP as scriptwriter for, 3, 4–5

radio programs involving VSP:
  "Book Talk," 1 (n.1), 3, 16 (n. 84)
  "Literature in the West," 8 (n. 38)
  "Lively Arts, The" 7 (n. 32)
  "Living Image," 3, 4, 12 (n. 49) (n. 50) (n.52) (n. 54), 16 (n. 82)
  "Living Opinion," 3, 4–5
  "London Dialogues," 13 (n. 58)
  "New Writing," 16 (n. 80, n. 81)
  "Strength of Mind," 3–4, 12 (n. 55)
  "Studies in English Letters," 8 (n. 36, n. 37)
  "Turning Over a New Leaf" ("What's Wrong with the Modern Short Story?") Orwell, Hawkins, VSP, 7 (n. 31)
  "Writer and His Public, The" 2
British Writers of the Thirties (Valentine Cunningham), 14 (n. 66)
"Broadcasting About Literature" (VSP), 1 (n. 2)
"Broken Homes" (WT), 95
  compared to "Tea with Mrs. Bittell" (VSP), 162–164, 165, 166
  discussion of, 162–165, 166, 167–168, 169–170 172–173, 174–175
Browning, Robert, 138, 142
Build the Ships (VSP), 5
Byatt, A. S., 79

Cab at the Door, A (VSP), 119–122, 125–127, 136, 124
"Cage Birds, The" (VSP), 74
Camberwell Beauty, The (VSP), 148
"Camberwell Beauty, The" (VSP), 12, 87–88, 147
  genesis of, 148–149, 150
"Captain's Daughter, The" (VSP), 78
  See "Our Wife"
"Careless Widow, A" (VSP), 12
  marital violence in, 230–231 (n. 135)

Carrington, Joanna, 147
Carver, Raymond, 88
"Casabianca" (Felicia Hemens), 142
Cervantes, Miguel de, 136
"Chatty" (VSP), 77, 84
Cheever, John, 88
Chekhov, Anton, 8, 18, 20, 34, 65, 66, 143, 146, 148, 197
"Chestnut Tree, The" (VSP), 14, 15, 128
Christian Science, 125–127
  definition of, 224 (n. 40)
  VSP's experience with, 125–127
  satirized in "The Saint," 127–137
Christian Science Monitor, ix, 66
"Citizen" (VSP), 74, 75
"Cocktails at Doney's" (WT), 114
  composition and analysis of, 35–64
Collected Stories (VSP), 17, 17 (n.6), 137, 196
Collected Stories, The (WT), 37, 41, 99
Collector, The (John Fowles), 149
Columbia University, 70
"Commercial Traveller" (VSP), 13
  See "Sense of Humour" (VSP)
Complete Collected Stories (VSP), 17 (n. 5), 88, 123, 196
Congdon, Don, 67, 68
Conrad, Joseph, 51
County Cork, 94, 95, 96
County Roscommon, 94
Cox, James (WT's father), 94, 120
Cunningham, Valentine, 14, 17

Darwin, Charles, 127
"Day, A" (WT), 232 (n. 47)
Day We Got Drunk on Cake and Other Stories, The (WT), 98, 99
"Dead, The" (James Joyce), 7
"Death in Jerusalem" (WT), 90
Del sentimiento tragica de la vida (Miguel de Unamuno), 135, 226 (n. 86)
"Dialogue" (VSP, lecture typescript), 10 (n. 46)
Dickens, Charles, 61, 72, 180

"Did You Invite Me?" (VSP), 73
"Distant Past, The" (WT), 195–196, 197
"Diver, The" (VSP), 83–84, 189
   originally titled "The Fall" (*New Yorker*, 1970)
documentary writing, 15–16
Don Quixote (Cervantes), 136
"Double Divan" (VSP), 67
Dublin: A Portrait (VSP), 180 (n. 10), 231 (n. 10, n. 11, n. 12)

Eddy, Mary Baker (Christian Science's founder), 127
"Editor Regrets, The" (VSP), 72
"Educated Girl, The" (VSP), 72, 73
Egoist, The (George Meredith), 228 (n. 37)
Eliot, George, 97
Emma (Jane Austen), 99
Esquire (magazine), 88
Excursions in the Real World (WT), 93 (n. 1, n. 3), 96–97, 98 (n. 33, n. 34, n. 35), 100 (n. 39, n. 41), 114, 114 (n. 90), 115 (n. 91, n. 92)

"Fall, The" (1960, VSP), 78–79
   discussion of, 182–184
   genesis of, 182
"Fall, The" (1970, VSP), 83–84
   (retitled "The Diver" in book form)
"Family Man, A" (VSP), 12
"Fig Tree, The" (Katherine Anne Porter), 88
"Fig Tree, The" (VSP)
   revisions of, 81–83
   Trevor's appreciation of, 147
"Fly in the Ointment, The" (VSP), 12, 137, 180 (n. 10)
Folios of New Writing, 14 (n. 73)
Fortnightly Review, 14
Fowles, John, 149
Freud, Sigmund, 141, 180
Fry, Margery, 4, 120

Garbo, Greta, 8
Garland, Judy, 53
"General's Day, The" (WT), 95, 232 (n. 47)
Geng, Veronica, 89, 90
Gentle Barbarian, The (VSP), 121 (n. 16), 122 (n. 20), 124
George Meredith and English Comedy (VSP), 228 (n. 37)
"Gift Horse, The" (VSP), 66
Gissing, George, 6, 8
"Going Home" (WT), 116, 232 (n. 47)
Golden Ass, The (Lucius Apuleius), 173
"Good News" (WT), 111 (n. 84), 232 (n. 47)
Grass, Günter, 149
"Grass Widows" (WT), 232 (n. 47)
Grenfell, Joyce, 149

"Haircut, The" (Ring Lardner), 20
"Handsome Is As Handsome Does" (VSP), 12
   English fantasy in, 184–186
Hardy, Thomas, 8–9, 54, 197, 197 (n. 55)
Harper's (magazine), 66, 67
Harvard College, 69
Hawkins, Desmond, 2
Hawthorne, Nathaniel, 150
Heart of Darkness (Joseph Conrad), 109 (n. 78)
Heath, Susan, 18 (n. 10)
Hemans, Felicia, 142
Hemenway, Robert, 89 (n. 143)
Henderson, Robert, 67, 68, 89
Hidden Ground (WT), 190 (n. 42)
Hill Bachelors, The (WT), 192 (n. 45), 195
"Hill Bachelors, The" (WT)
   rural Ireland depicted in, 190
   entrapment in, 192–193
Hill, Susan, 147
Hingley, Ronald, 65 (n. 3)
Holiday (magazine), 69

"Honeymoon, The" (VSP), 72
"Honeymoon in Tramore" (WT), 194
Horizon (magazine), 137
Horizon Stories, 66
Hughes, Douglas, 18–19
Hughes, Ted, 114, 115
"Hunger Artist, The" (Franz Kafka), 182
"Husband's Return, A" (WT), 194
Huxley, Thomas Henry, 127

"Incident of the French Camp" (Robert Browning), 142
"In County Cork" (WT), 98
"In Isfahan" (WT), 114
"In Love with Ariadne" (WT), 109
In Memoriam (Tennyson), 137 (n. 94), 181 (n. 19)
It May Never Happen (VSP), 13, 66, 226 (n. 102)

James, Henry, 6, 10, 62, 116, 147, 150
James, William, 127
"Jigsaws" (WT; article), 94 (n. 4), 110, 220 (n. 34), 222 (n. 87)
John the Baptist, 133
Journal of the Short Story in English, 14 (n. 64), 19 (n. 13), 119 (n. 1), 124 (n. 34), 145 (n. 108), 151 (n. 1)
Joyce, James, ix, 7, 10, 16, 18
Jules et Jim (Henri-Pierre Roché), 155

Kafka, Franz, 182
"Kathleen's Field" (WT), 110–114
    autobiographical elements in, 110, 111–113,
    class schism in, 113
    rural Ireland depicted in, 190
Keats, John, 25, 226 (n. 86)
Kermode, Frank, 17
Key to My Heart, The (VSP), 145
"Key to My Heart, The" (VSP), 12, 78, 145
    genesis of, 145–146

Kiernan, Frances, 85, 89–90, 91
"Kitty" (WT), 110
Koestler, Arthur, 4
Kundera, Milan, 90

"Ladder, The" (VSP), 68
"Landlord, The" (VSP), 11, 67, 68
Lardner, Ring, 20
"Last Throw, The" (VSP), 73
Lawrence, D. H., x, 17, 150
Lehmann, John, 8, 13–15
LeStage, Gregory, 76 (n. 63)
"Lion's Den, The" (VSP), 226 (n. 102), 137
Lish, Gordon, 88
Lobrano, Gus, 66, 67, 69, 74
Lolita (Vladimir Nabokov), 149
London Magazine, 15, 66 (n. 4), 116
London Perceived (VSP), 148–149 (n. 126, n. 127), 180 (n. 8, n. 9)
"Lost Ground" (WT), 195
"Lovers of Their Time" (WT), 117–118

Mabbott, John, 4
Mackenzie, Compton, 182
MacKenzie, Rachel, 89
"Many Are Disappointed" (VSP), 14, 15
    genesis and discussion of, 143–145
    compared to "When My Girl Comes Home," 148
"Mark-2 Wife, The" (WT), 117
Marx Brothers, 88
"Matilda's England" (WT), 95
Matson, Harold, 66, 67, 73, 87
Maugham, W. Somerset, 80, 97, 109, 110
Maupassant, Guy de, 65, 66, 109
Max, D. T., 88 (n. 141)
Maxwell, William, 66, 85, 88, 89
Mayor of Casterbridge, The (Thomas Hardy), 8
McGrath, Charles, 89, 90

"Memories of Youghal" (WT), 96–97
Meredith, George, 121, 179
Midnight Oil (VSP), 17 (n. 1), 120, 122, 130, 135, 136
Ministry of Information, 5
Ministry of Transport, 5
"Miss Smith" (WT)
    autobiographical experience in, 99–100
    composition of, 98–118
    genesis of, 98–99
Mr Beluncle (VSP), 19, 68, 124, 127
    and source of title, 224 (n. 33)
"Mr. MacNamara" (WT), 109
Moore, Marianne, 93
Morgan, Derek, 89 (n. 144)
Muir, Edwin, 2
"Mulvihill's Memorial" (WT), 90, 118
"My Last Duchess" (Robert Browning), 138

Nabokov, Vladimir, 149
Nash's Annual, 68
"Necklace, The" (Guy de Maupassant), 109
"Neighbors" (VSP), 79
Neri di Bicci, 40, 52
"Nest Builder, The" (VSP), 79
News from Ireland, The (WT), 36, 41
New Statesman, 2, 7 (n. 31), 13, 19, 68
New Writing (magazine), 13–15, 16
New Yorker (magazine), 37, 38, 41, 56, 66, 67, 68, 145, 157, 177
    editorial policy of, 74
    editorial system of, 71
    Fiction Department of, 68, 71, 89
    First Reading Agreement at, 68–69, 86
    technique of indirection spurned by Fiction Department, 86
    VSP's and WT's relationship with, 65–91
    VSP's financial arrangement with, 68–69
    WT's early interest in, 88–89
    WT on Fact Checking Department at, 71 (n. 27)
"Noisy Flushes the Birds" (VSP), 145
"Noisy in the Doghouse" (VSP), 74–75, 145
Not Quite Among Friends (WT), 117 (n. 99, n. 101, n. 102, n. 103, n. 105)

O'Connor, Flannery, 165
O'Connor, Frank, 15, 91, 158
"Oedipus Complex, The" (VSP), 66
    composition and analysis of, 137–143
    Englishness in, 142
O'Faolain, Sean, 158
"O Fat White Woman" (WT), 117, 118
"Office Romances" (WT), 118
O'Flaherty, Liam, ix, 158
Old Boys, The (WT), 95
"On the Edge of the Cliff" (VSP),
    genesis of, 146–147
    revisions of, 79–81
    Trevor's appreciation of, 147
"On the Scent" (VSP), 85
ordinary people:
    VSP's commitment to them as subjects for fiction, 6, 7, 8, 9–10
    VSP's portrayal of, 6, 8, 9
Orwell, George, 7
"Our Wife" (VSP), 77–78
    compared to "The Piano Tuner's Wives" (WT), 157–159, 160, 161
    discussion of, 151–157
"Over the Rainbow" (song), 53
Oxford Book of English Short Stories (ed. A.S. Byatt), 79
Oxford Book of Irish Short Stories (ed. WT), 64 (n. 6), 158 (n. 49)
Oxford Book of Short Stories (ed. VSP), 116

"Page and Monarch" (VSP), 187
Parker, Dorothy, 89
"Passing the Ball" (VSP), 69
"Peasants, The" (Anton Chekhov), 148
Penal Times (Ireland), 94
"Penthouse Apartment, The" (WT), 89, 95, 232 (n. 47)
"Piano Tuner's Wives, The" (WT)
　discussion of, 157–162
　compared to "Our Wife" (VSP), 157–159, 160, 161
Plath, Sylvia, 115
Porter, Katherine Anne, 88
Portrait of a Lady, The (Henry James), 99
"Potato Dealer, The" (WT)
　entrapment in, 193–194
　rural Ireland depicted in, 190
Princeton University, 70
Pritchett, Beatrice (VSP's mother), 126, 130
Pritchett, Cyril (VSP's brother), 120, 121, 126
Pritchett, Dorothy (VSP's second wife), 19, 70
Pritchett, Gordon (VSP's brother), 120
Pritchett, Kathleen (VSP's sister), 120
Pritchett, Oliver (VSP's son), 19
Pritchett, V. S.
　aesthetic development of, 4, 5–7, 9–13, 121, 122–123
　RA's relationship with, 69–88
　becoming a foreigner, 121, 123
　becoming someone else, 123
　childhood and youth of, 119–121
　and Christian Science, 125–127
　class consciousness of, 4, 5, 6, 8, 9–12, 120
　colloquial language, use of, 10–12, 139–140,
　duality in, 180–182
　education of, 119
　English identity of, 122
　family background of, 120–121
　fantasy in short stories of, 179–189
　foreigner's perspective of England, 121
　identification with his subjects, 12
　marital violence in his short stories that reflects his own, 230–231 (n. 135)
　portrayal of working class, 5
　reputation of, 17–20
　self-image of, 180–182
　style of, 7
　WT compared to, ix–x, 8, 16, 34, 35, 36, 63, 93–94, 96, 119, 120, 121, 122, 123, 124, 136, 143, 150, 162, 196–198
　work ethic of, 7–8
　on working class values, 4, 5
Pritchett, Walter (VSP's father), 119, 120
　and religion, 124–125, 127, 130
　inner conflict, 181
Professional Portrait: Novelist (VSP), 123 (n. 26)
"Property of Colette Nervi, The" (WT), 194
Proust, Marcel, 10, 16

"Raising of Elvira Tremlett, The" (WT), 195
Rayfield, Donald, 65 (n. 3)
"Real Thing, The" (Henry James), 147
"Rescue, The" (VSP), 84
Robinson, Robert, 147
Ross, Harold, 67, 71

"Sailor, The" (VSP), 14, 15, 15 (n. 78), 136
"Saint, The" (VSP), 66, 67
　as comic satire of the Pritchetts' Christian Science experience, 127–137
St. John's College, Oxford, 4
Salmon, Christopher, 2, 3, 4, 5,
"Satisfactory, The" (VSP), 145

Savile Club, 9
Savonarola, Girolamo, 40
"Scapegoat, The" (VSP), 10–11, 148
"Sense of Humour" (VSP), 13, 14, 15
Shawn, William, 70, 72, 77, 80, 81, 83, 90, 219 (n. 143)
   censorship of passages in VSP's stories, 83–84
"Skeleton, The" (VSP), 86–87
Sketches of Boz (Dickens), 180
Smith College, 70
"Some Notes on Writing Stories" (WT), 116
"Speech, The" (VSP), 73, 86
Spender, Stephen, 1
Standard of Behavior, A (WT), 95
Stevens, Wallace, 93, 226 (n. 86)
Stinson, John J., 18 (n. 9), 20 (n. 19)
Stone Arbor and Other Stories, The (Roger Angell), 69
Suvorin, Alexei, 65
Svevo, Italo, 181

"Table, The" (WT), 89, 115
"Tea with Mrs. Bittell" (VSP), 72, 147
   compared to "Broken Homes" (WT), 162–164, 165, 166
   discussion of, 162–163, 165–167, 168–169, 170–172, 173–174, 175–177
"Teddy Bears' Picnic, The" (WT), 90
Tennyson, Alfred, 226 (n. 94)
"Teresa's Wedding" (WT), 194, 228 (n. 50)
Tess of the D'Urbervilles (Thomas Hardy), 8
Theroux, Paul, 17
"Things" (VSP), 72
"Things as They Are" (VSP)
   marital violence in, 230–231 (n. 135)
"Third Party, The" (WT), 194–195
"Three People" (WT), 196
Thurber, James, 88

"Timothy's Birthday" (WT), 177
Tin Drum, The (Günter Grass), 149
Tolstoy, Leo, 126
"Tombales, Les" (Guy de Maupassant), 109
"Torridge" (WT), 90
"Tragedy in a Greek Theatre" (VSP), 231 (n. 15)
"Transport in War Time" (VSP), 181
Treglown, Jeremy, 19
Trevor, William, 8, 16, 17, 34, 35, 93–118, 119
   approach to writing, 95–96, 190
   on becoming someone else, 96
   childhood in Ireland, 94
   class consciousness of, 113
   compositional process of, 36
   family background of, 94
   fantasy in short stories of, 189–196
   VSP compared to, ix–x, 8, 16, 34, 35, 36, 63, 93–94, 96, 119, 120, 121, 122, 123, 124, 136, 143, 150, 162, 196–198
   reputation of, 35
   sense of identity, 94–95
   submissions to the *New Yorker*, 89–91
"Trinity, A" (WT), 232 (n. 47)
"Trip to the Seaside, A" (VSP), 188–89
Trollope, Anthony, 72
Turgenev, Ivan, 8, 9, 121, 122, 123, 197
"Two Brothers, The" (VSP), 67, 197
"Two Roast Beefs" (VSP), 69 (and n. 20) (retitled "The Satisfactory")

Unamuno, Miguel de, 135
University of California at Berkeley, 70
Updike, John, 70, 88, 147

"Virgin's Gift, The" (WT), 195

Warner, Sylvia Townsend, 71
Wells, H. G., 6, 8
Welty, Eudora, 18

Wevill, Assia, 114–115
Wevill, David, 114–115
"Wheelbarrow, The" (VSP), 12, 74, 75
"When My Girl Comes Home" (VSP), 18, 73, 86, 182
    compared to "Many Are Disappointed," 148
    genesis of, 147–148
    marital violence in, 230–231 (n. 135)
White, Katharine, 66–67, 68
Wilde, Oscar, 10
Williams, Lloyd, 1
Woman's Hour (BBC), 117

Woolf, Virginia, 6, 10, 16
Woolsey, Gamel, 122
"Worshippers, The" (VSP), 73

Yeats, W. B., 138
You Make Your Own Life (VSP), 11, 13, 21, 66
"You Make Your Own Life" (VSP), 11, 12, 14, 17, 20, 36, 50, 63, 137, 138
    analysis of, 21–33
    transcription of corrected first typescript for (*see* appendix, 199–210)